continued . . .

Praise for the Crown Family Saga

Homeland

"First-rate . . . chock-full of fascinating period detail . . . brings to life the sounds, smells, and tastes of turn-of-the-century America in a manner comparable to Michener's *Hawaii* and Doctorow's *Ragtime*. An absolute must."
—*Publishers Weekly*

"This intelligently written novel, full of colorful characters, moves swiftly along, vividly resurrecting the America of the 1890's. Quite simply, *Homeland* is John Jakes's best work."
—*The Philadelphia Inquirer*

"A powerful tour de force, a rich, sweeping story of America as only Jakes can tell it . . . *Homeland*, interspersed with real characters such as Teddy Roosevelt, Black Jack Pershing, and Jane Addams, is a marvelous blend of fact and fiction, the stuff of great historical novels. Another winner from an old pro."
—*Nelson DeMille*

American Dreams

"Jakes has a grand old time spinning his yarns. . . . He mixes his fictional offspring with the likes of Charlie Chaplin and Mary Pickford, making us feel as if we too have brushed our shoulders with celebrity."
—*The Blade* (Toledo)

"Realistic detail and period color galore keep this swift-moving story grounded . . . as the automobile and WWI arrive to shake the republic out of its golden idyll."
—*Kirkus Reviews*

"Historical fiction at its finest, as only John Jakes can tell it."
—*Wheaton Gazette*

"A worthy successor to *Homeland*."   —*Columbia State* (SC)

Praise for the *North and South Trilogy*

North and South

"In the history of U.S. book publishing, there's never been a success story quite like that of John Jakes."
—*The New York Times*

"A panoramic, populous . . . lusty trek through the pages of American history . . . thick as a brick with period detail drawn from extensive research."
—*San Francisco Chronicle*

Love and War

"A feisty assortment of fictional heroes and heroines."
—*People*

"Massive, lusty, highly readable. . . . In delicious detail are the wicked and tawdry doings of a memorable cast of characters. . . . A graphic, fast-paced amalgam of good, evil, love, lust, war, violence, and Americana."
—*The Washington Post Book World*

Heaven and Hell

"Remarkably vivid."
—*Los Angeles Times*

"He shows you George Armstrong Custer, Andrew Johnson, Buffalo Bill Cody, and a vast array of historical figures whose contending ambitions control the events . . . but he also shows you what people wore, what they read, and what they drank and ate. . . . What you get is the feeling that this is life. That's art."
—*Chicago Sun-Times*

By John Jakes

*On Secret Service
*American Dreams
*Homeland
*California Gold

NORTH AND SOUTH TRILOGY

*North and South
*Love and War
*Heaven and Hell

KENT FAMILY CHRONICLES

The Bastard
The Rebels
The Seekers
The Furies
The Titans
The Warriors
The Lawless
The Americans

*Published by Signet

JOHN JAKES

ON SECRET SERVICE

A SIGNET BOOK

SIGNET
Published by New American Library, a division of
Penguin Putnam Inc., 375 Hudson Street,
New York, New York 10014, U.S.A.
Penguin Books Ltd, 27 Wrights Lane,
London W8 5TZ, England
Penguin Books Australia Ltd, Ringwood,
Victoria, Australia
Penguin Books Canada Ltd, 10 Alcorn Avenue,
Toronto, Ontario, Canada M4V 3B2
Penguin Books (N.Z.) Ltd, 182–190 Wairau Road,
Auckland 10, New Zealand

Penguin Books Ltd, Registered Offices:
Harmondsworth, Middlesex, England

Published by Signet, an imprint of New American Library,
a division of Penguin Putnam Inc.
Previously published in a Dutton edition.

First Signet Printing, April 2001
10 9 8 7 6

This is for
my friend and colleague
Evan Hunter

That war ... produced the nation's first mass armies, and a brutality that shocked the sensibilities of the day. It had aircraft, balloons, submarines, ironclad warships, automatic guns, trenches, a military draft—and the first organized espionage that the country ever knew.

> —Harnett T. Kane
> *Spies for the Blue
> and Gray*

Intelligence work requires people who are patriotic and sincere, and it is exactly these people who can accumulate the most emotional scars in pursuing it.

> —Tidwell, Hall, and Gaddy
> *Come Retribution, the Confederate
> Secret Service and the Assassination
> of Lincoln*

It is pardonable to be defeated, but not to be taken by surprise.

> —Frederick the Great

Indeed, our employment may be reckoned dishonest, because, like great statesmen, we encourage those who betray their friends.

> —John Gay
> *The Beggar's Opera*

secret service secret work for a
government, esp. espionage [1730–40]

—*Random House Dictionary
of the English Language*

Part One

DETECTIVES

1

January 1861

"We must be near Galena already," Lon said with a look at the closed door of the baggage car. "Nothing's happened."

"Wait," his partner said. Sledge sat on a crated shipment, legs stuck out, the payroll bag between his heels. His boots were dirty and scarred. Lon's were spotless except for a few streaks of slush. Around the office they called him Gentleman Lon because of his manners and neatness. He out-Englished the English operatives, of which there were several.

The Chicago & Galena express was traveling northwest, toward Dubuque across the Mississippi. Adams Express paid almost four hundred dollars a month to rent space in the line's baggage cars. Its competitor, American Express, had similar arrangements, necessary because trains were favorite targets of thieves, and their routes crossed the territories of a legion of sheriffs who were crooks, bunglers, or both. Lon Price's agency had contracts with both express companies and a group of six rail lines who together put up ten thousand dollars a year for protection for their real estate and rolling stock.

Lon and his partner were replacing a regular guard because of a robbery attempt on the same train at the same time last month. The attempt failed; the inept holdup men had blocked the track with a flimsy barrier of barn siding. The engineer had smashed the locomotive right through without stopping. The boss had tried to persuade the Chicago & Galena to ship its next Dubuque payroll by another train, at another time, but management lived by schedules and timetables. So here they were, rolling through the winter night, waiting.

Lon blew on his hands. The car was frigid even though he could see flames in the small stove. The flue pipe went out through the solid wall at the head of the car. Near the stove, the railway mail clerk sat on a stool with his elbows on the counter. All his mail was sorted in pigeonholes and he appeared to be dozing. The clerk struck Lon as suspiciously furtive. Careful observation was a habit the boss demanded.

From his left pocket Lon took a well-thumbed book. Sledge Greenglass, whose given name was Philo, worked his gold-plated toothpick in a crevice in his teeth. Where Lon was fair and broad-shouldered, but otherwise slight, Sledge was taller, heavier, with curly black hair and perhaps an Italian or Greek ancestor. He was ten to fifteen years older than Lon.

"What's that?" Sledge said with a nod at the book.

"The latest by Charles Dickens. The latest novel published here, I mean. There's a new serial running in England, *Great Expectations*. Dickens is my favorite writer after Edgar Poe." Lon showed the book's spine.

"*A Tale of Two Cities*. Invite him over, maybe he'll write *A Tale of Two Countries*."

Sledge's sarcasm was justified. The Union was collapsing. Five days before Christmas, South Carolina had passed its ordinance of secession, and other Southern states were following—Mississippi, Florida, and Alabama last week. The commander of the Army garrison in Charleston had shifted his men to Fort Sumter in the harbor, and *Star of the West*, lame-duck President Buck Buchanan's relief ship carrying reinforcements, had already been turned back by Charleston harbor defenses. The problem would confront the President-elect, whom Lon had met once in Chicago. He was a downstate lawyer who had for a while represented the Illinois Central. Lon wondered if such a peculiar, ugly man could do anything to save the country from war.

The locomotive whistled mournfully. The train creaked and rattled around a bend. Three oil lamps hanging from the ceiling swayed and smoked. The car reeked of old cigars. Lon read half a page, then read it twice more. He shut the book and made a face.

Sledge said, "Nervous?"

"Some. I've only been at this for a couple of years. Do you ever get used to the danger?"

They noticed the mail clerk watching. Sledge lowered his

voice. "Been a copper nearly thirteen years, since I joined the New York force." Sledge and the agency's senior operative, Tim Webster, a former police sergeant, had been assigned to guard the Crystal Palace exhibition in 1853. The boss had met them, liked them, and hired them away.

Sledge continued, "I been shot at, knifed, mauled in the line of duty maybe a dozen times. And no, I'm not used to it. But even if they hit us tonight, I wouldn't worry too much. Holdup men aren't only crooked, most of them are stupid. Look how they mucked up last time. The rule is, no matter how scared you are, no matter what your belly's telling you, keep it hid and always give back more than you take. That's how you stay alive. That's how you win."

Lon Price mostly liked his more experienced partner, but not this kind of talk. "We're supposed to be professional operatives, not roughneck detectives." In fact the boss forbade the use of the word detective in his presence.

"Oh, I forgot," Sledge said with his familiar mockery. "You grew up with a preacher in a preacher's house. All hymns, holiness, heaven, and hallelujah."

"Listen, Sledge. My father was a good man. He cut his life short trying to help Negroes escape to Canada. He was even shot once by slave-catchers. You can say anything you want about me but keep still about him."

"Sorry. Forgot my manners. Police work slaps 'em out of you pretty fast."

Lon was silent. Sledge changed the subject. "Think those Southron hotheads will start a war?"

"I hope not. They can't be allowed to destroy the Union. They can't go on enslaving an entire race and breaking up families for profit. The Negroes have got to be free."

"And then we'll all invite a few of them to our parlors for tea? Like they was white? I doubt it."

"Damn it, Sledge, that doesn't—"

Sledge shot his hand up for silence. He eyed the car ceiling. Lon heard faint thumps, moving toward the blind end of the car next to the tender. "Someone's up there."

Sledge turned back his coat and put a hand on the butt of the shiny new Remington .36-caliber stuck in his belt. Lon carried a smaller Colt, a .31-caliber pocket pistol, a city weapon; a gentleman's gun. "Bastards are already on the train," Sledge said. "Sons of bitches bought their own tickets."

He ran to the wide door and slid it open. Icy wind blew in and a few snowflakes. Outside, snow-covered fields flashed by, lit by the moon. Trees by the right-of-way slashed the side of the car like whips. Sledge hung on and leaned out, trying to see whoever was clambering down over the tender to force the engineer to stop the train. Someone else would uncouple the rest of the cars, and the engineer would pull the train a mile or so ahead, where the baggage car would be looted.

In the corner of his eye Lon saw the clerk open a drawer. "Sledge, watch out!" The Colt .31 snagged in the lining of Lon's pocket. The clerk pulled a revolver from the drawer and pointed it at Sledge's embroidered vest.

"You stand still. I mean it." The car was freezing, the wind moaning and tossing snowflakes in, yet the clerk's pale face ran with sweat. "Put your hands in the air."

Sledge obeyed. "They bought themselves a worm inside," he sneered. Lon freed the pocket Colt. He stood with his left side toward the clerk, who was so nervous he either missed the movement of Lon's right arm or didn't know what to do about it. Lon heard a noise to his right, the door at the rear of the car. He wheeled, gun in hand. A lanky man in a black floppy hat and long, fur-collared coat stepped inside with a drawn revolver.

"All over, boys. Get their pieces, Vernon."

The clerk stayed at arm's length as he pulled Sledge's Remington from his belt. Sledge looked mad enough to bite the clerk's arm off. Visibly trembling, the clerk turned around toward Lon. Sledge threw an arm around the clerk's neck and pulled him against his chest as the other man fired. In the next coach passengers screamed.

Sledge was a hair faster than the gunman, shoving the clerk forward and dropping to the floor. The gunman's round killed the clerk instantly. He fell on his side near the open door. The train curved into another bend, losing speed. The ceiling lanterns swayed, flinging shadows across the walls. Lon turned right to present a narrow target. He shot the older gunman a second before the gunman could fire.

Lon's round went low, catching the gunman in his middle

He fell face forward. His revolver spun away out of his hand. It landed a foot and a half from his spread fingers.

The cries and shouts from the day coach were louder. The drive wheels shrieked on the rails. Even if the man in the cab had the engineer and fireman at bay, he wouldn't know what the shots meant. The gunman on the floor made whimpering sounds. His hat had fallen off, revealing long, stringy, gray hair and a sizable bald spot. To Lon, recently turned twenty-three, he looked old and somehow pitiable.

Lon moved to pick up the man's revolver but turned around when Sledge snarled, "Goddam. Bet there's just two of them—two, and this slug." He shoved the clerk with his scuffed boot; the body dropped out the door. "You need four or five to pull a train robbery. I told you holdup men are stupid." Sledge peered past Lon. "For Christ's sake, shoot that one."

"Why? He's down." Sledge reached out with his revolver and fired past Lon, planting his bullet in the middle of the robber's forehead, a third eye. The dead man had grasped the butt of his gun before Sledge got him.

In his two years with the agency Lon had only been in one other shooting scrape, and he shook as much now as he had then. Sledge hung from the door of the car and shouted, "Hey, you, jackass! You up there in the cab. Both your pals are dead. They're *dead*, get that?"

The baggage car moved over a level crossing with a lamplit farmhouse nearby. The shouted reply was faint but clear because the locomotive had slowed down. "Who is that?"

"Operative Greenglass of the Pinkerton agency. You know, the Eye. There's two of us and one of you. The clerk and the old man are goners. You better get off and save yourself."

"We should take him into custody," Lon said.

"How? Time I climb up there, he's liable to kill the driver or the fireman. And I'll be a fine target in the moonlight."

"I'm willing to try it."

Sledge gave him a sharp look. "I think you would. You're a damn polite fellow, but you've got sand." He leaned out the door again. "Jackass? Listen here!"

The locomotive and train had stopped. Sledge's shout was followed by a heavy, slamming sound. A moment later they heard the engineer:

"Feeny brained him with his shovel. He's out."

Sledge stepped back in the car and laughed. "All accounted for, then." He picked up the canvas payroll bag. "The C-and-G boys around Dubuque will get their pay. I'd say it's a fine night's work."

"Two men are dead." Lon couldn't feel any of Sledge's pleasure.

Sledge shrugged. "Remember what the boss says. The end justifies the means if the end is justice."

"Mr. Pinkerton says a lot of things I admire, but that isn' one of them."

"Someday maybe you'll figure out that we're in a dirty line of work." Sledge walked over and clapped Lon on the shoul der. "In the meantime, we make a pretty good team."

2

January 1861

Back in Chicago, waiting for a new case, Lon thought over the secession crisis. When he reached a conclusion, he went to the agency's general superintendent, George Bangs, a tall, dandi fied man with the air of a banker who routinely said no. Bang was Pinkerton's gatekeeper and was shuffling employmen applications with visible annoyance.

"We can't find enough men for the Protective Patrol," h grumbled as though Lon were responsible. The Protective Pa trol was a separate group in the company, men who wore uni forms and guarded business properties. "Know anyone?"

Lon said he didn't. He asked for an appointment. Bang told him Pinkerton would be out with a potential client unti early afternoon. He inked Lon's name in the appointmen book for one o'clock.

At his desk in the large central office, Lon wrote his report o the Chicago & Galena affair. Himself a writer of voluminous re ports, Pinkerton demanded that his operatives write them too. Sledge said Lon had the education to write for both of them.

Lon finished about noon. He looked for his partner and found him in an adjoining room, experimenting with false mustaches from one of the agency's disguise kits. Sledge held a droopy mustache to his upper lip.

"What do you think?"

"What are you supposed to be, a Chinese mandarin?"

Sledge threw the mustache back in the box and chose another, shorter, neater. "I'm posing as a gent renting a fancy rig for an outing. Someone's stealing expensive horses from a big livery out in Rockford."

Lon nodded. "That one fits."

"What are you working on?"

"Nothing yet." Lon didn't tell Sledge he intended to resign.

Timothy Webster, the bearded and dignified senior operative, came in from the rogues' gallery to ask if Lon wanted to have lunch. The agency had pioneered in building a fact and picture file on known or suspected criminals. Tim Webster had the latest wet-plate print in hand. On the back, information was inscribed in a fine copperplate hand.

"Who's that?" Lon asked.

"Ralph McSwiney, otherwise known as James Smithfield and Samuel Smythe. Travels as an itinerant portrait photographer. His palaver and equipment get him into fine homes where he proceeds to cosh the owners and strip the place. Lunch?"

Lon made excuses; he needed time to rehearse his resignation speech. He left through the frosted-glass door with the big painted eye staring at visitors over the slogan THE EYE THAT NEVER SLEEPS.

A sudden thaw had turned the unpaved streets to brown sludge. The sunny day was fouled by coal smoke and the smell of manure piles on every other corner. A mild breeze off the lake added the stench of the lakefront slaughterhouses. Traffic was horrible, made worse by drovers herding their cattle, and pigs running everywhere, seemingly with no supervision. In the constant din, loudest of all were the throaty horns of the lake boats and the shriek and puff of the trains.

In spite of the squalor and disorder, Lon loved the sprawling city he'd fled to when he ran away from southern Ohio. A frontier trading post that had turned into a metropolis, Chicago was a booming grain, meat, and rail center; home to more than one hundred thousand people. Among the mobs of pedestrians, Lon cut a noticeable figure in his English-style, knee-length coat, which he'd bought from a pushcart peddler because of the stylish black velvet collar. The coat complemented a rakish black felt hat, shallow-crowned with a narrow red silk band and wide curled brim. Unlike most of his colleagues, Lon didn't wear a beard. Beards itched.

Unfortunately he chose the wrong saloon for a sandwich and some reflection. When he returned to the office at twelve forty-five, both cheeks were purpling. One of the hip-level pockets of his coat was ripped, hanging like a panting tongue. A slim and smartly dressed brunette in her late twenties came out the door before he could open it.

"Hello, Kate."

"My heavens, what happened to you?"

"I got into a discussion about Fort Sumter."

"A discussion?" she said with an eye on his bruises.

"Well, an altercation. Two of them, one of me. I didn't realize there were so many slaveocrats in Chicago."

"Everywhere," Kate Warne said. "Except in this office." Kate was in charge of the agency's several female operatives. She'd come to the boss as a young widow in 1856, intent on a career in police work. No city force would hire a woman, but Pinkerton saw the wisdom of having female investigators and hired her immediately.

"On a case?" Lon asked.

Kate batted her eyes. "Just a poor single woman off to consult a lawyer. Two of the lawyer's clients say that he defrauded them of a big settlement. We'll see." Waving, she went down the stairs.

On his way to Bangs's desk Lon met John Scully, an operative most of the others regarded as a Pinkerton mistake. The disheveled Scully said, " 'Lo," and stumbled by, trailing his usual cloud of whiskey fumes.

"He's returned," Bangs said before Lon could ask. "He's waiting."

The boss's corner office was large and almost overwhelmed

by books, files, and piles of correspondence and case reports. It was saved from chaos by Pinkerton's passion for organization. Each neat stack was identified by a sheet of foolscap with a notation. The one clear area was the long polished table behind Pinkerton's desk. There he kept a small American flag in a wooden stand, a photograph of himself with his wife, Joan, and their sons, a few books including a collection of the speeches of Frederick Douglass, and a leatherbound copy of the agency's "Statement of General Principles," which Lon had been required to read and agree to before Pinkerton would employ him. The document said the agency handled no divorces or "scandals." It accepted no contingency fees, gratuities, or "special rewards or incentives." Pinkerton had founded the business ten years ago. It was the first of its kind in the United States. He considered himself a professional and insisted on being treated, and paid, accordingly.

Allan Pinkerton's eyes fixed on his visitor. Gray-blue, they were a shade lighter than Lon's. "I have your report. I'll read it tonight. Excellent work, Alonzo." Pinkerton employed maximum formality with his employees. After six months, Lon had told the boss he despised his given name, but the boss couldn't be moved. He couldn't be moved on anything he believed strongly.

"Philo too, sir. He acted bravely."

"Philo too," Pinkerton agreed, though a flicker of his eyelids suggested he didn't altogether approve of Sledge or his methods. "Take a chair. Where did you get those bruises?"

"A small discussion of slavery where I ate lunch. I shouldn't have joined in, but I did." Pinkerton tilted his head, his equivalent of an approving nod. Lon was on safe ground; twice he'd been invited to Pinkerton's house on Adams Street to meet escaped slaves. Pinkerton was a foreman on the Underground Railroad. Foremen operated the stations, forwarding the packages or freight, the runaways, to the next station on the route to Canada.

Lon admired his boss in many ways. It would be hard to work for a man of his disposition if you didn't admire him. Pinkerton seldom smiled and he wasn't smiling now. He demanded absolute loyalty from his operatives, but he returned it. As Tim Webster said, "He'll storm the gates of hell for you but cross him and he'll leave you to burn there."

Pinkerton waited for Lon to begin. "Sir, I've come to offer my resignation." Pinkerton sat back and folded his hands. "I want you to know first that I have no dissatisfaction with my work. In fact I love it more every day."

"Then what prompts you?"

"I believe war's coming. I don't know where, or when, but all that I read and hear convinces me the South's controlled by a few fanatics who won't back down."

"All Southerners are fanatics," Pinkerton said. Lon distrusted Southerners because his preacher father had raised him to hate slavery. Pinkerton not only hated the institution, he hated those who practiced it, every last one. "I agree with your feeling about a war. But why should that make you resign?"

"Men will be needed for the Army. It's my duty to go. Of course I'll stay on the job until it's time to enlist."

"Your sentiments are admirable, Alonzo. But they lead to a misguided conclusion."

Puzzled, Lon said, "Sir?"

"I had a letter from the Captain last week. If war comes, the Captain expects to be called up, along with other West Point graduates. Some of the secesh from the Academy will turn traitor and go South. The lot of them will be fighting each other soon enough."

Pinkerton turned in his swivel chair—always well oiled, never a squeak. He gazed at a framed photograph on the wall above the credenza: Allan Pinkerton standing with the Captain, G. B. McClellan, in the Illinois Central yards on a sunlit day. The men were about the same height, five feet eight, two inches shorter than Lon. McClellan was youthful, in his early thirties; Pinkerton had turned forty a couple of years ago, with lines in his face to show it. McClellan's expression was pleasant, Pinkerton's typically dour. Pinkerton wore an undistinguished beard, McClellan a handsome mustache and small Napoleon-style imperial. The photo dated from McClellan's time as chief engineer of the railroad. He'd hired the agency to protect I.C. real estate and rolling stock. Recently he'd gone to Cincinnati as superintendent of the troubled Ohio &

Mississippi. His annual salary was rumored to be an incredible $10,000.

The close friendship between the two men puzzled everyone in the office. McClellan was urbane, well educated, widely traveled. Before resigning his Army commission, he'd campaigned in Mexico, risen slowly from lieutenant to captain, been honored with a posting overseas to observe the war in the Crimea. Pinkerton, with little schooling, had come out of the slums of Glasgow. Lon had dined with the Captain once; he knew McClellan relished fine food, wine, and cigars. Pinkerton didn't smoke, drink, or curse. It was an unlikely friendship but for one thing. Both men were driven by ambition and fierce devotion to hard work, long hours, the myriad details of business. Lon guessed that must be their bond.

"I'm sorry, sir, I don't see what Captain McClellan's future has to do with us."

"Intelligence. Military intelligence. The Army general staff has no department to provide it. Each general must shift for himself. The Captain is way ahead of the pack. He wrote to say that when he's called back, he will hire this agency for special duty."

Was it a trick of the sunlight through the spotless window, or did Pinkerton almost smile? Lon couldn't be sure. The word *spy* leaped to mind but he didn't utter it.

"Alonzo, as soon as war comes—and like you I believe it will, it must, to punish those vicious madmen down South— the Captain is sure to become a general, and he is already recruiting us. Any man can die in an infantry charge, but nowhere else in this country, or in the world so far as I know, will you find men who can do what we do. Men ready to be of service in a secret war. Don't leave the organization when you're needed most."

The blue-gray eyes held a tinge of fire. Lon pondered no more than five seconds. He withdrew his resignation and left the office, convinced he would soon enter a new, unmapped area of his profession. He was excited about it all day, and for days afterward.

3

January 1861

Fingal's Crab House overlooked the inner harbor from Pratt Street. The original shop was a waterman's shack filled with so many lobster pots and crab traps there was no space for tables. It had crept outward like moss, growing to its present state: a maze of connected rooms and sheds catering to a large and steady clientele. The furnishings were plain but the fare delicious. Margaret ate Baltimore crab cakes, her father fresh oysters.

"When do you plan to go back to Washington?" Calhoun Miller asked as he opened another shell with an oyster knife.

"Tomorrow afternoon, I think." Margaret dabbed the corner of her mouth with the square of butcher paper provided in lieu of a napkin. Candles in oddly assorted bottles and jars lit the scarred tables. Snowflakes flying against the windows glowed like fireflies before they melted.

"You've hardly been home three weeks."

"You bought the other town house so that we could enjoy the capital, Papa."

"I bought it primarily to help the paper. It keeps me close to the Congress."

"And I'm quite comfortable there."

"Living by yourself. No servants. Gadding about wherever and whenever you please. I'm old-fashioned, Margaret. don't consider it seemly for a girl your age to do that sort of thing."

Margaret reached across to squeeze her father's hand. She loved him for his concern, stifling though it was sometimes. "You know you can trust me to behave, and to be cautious. But cities don't frighten me. Men don't frighten me. I am twenty-two, after all."

"With no mother to guide you for the past nine years," Miller said with a sigh. He was a huge, dignified man, six foot four; Margaret had inherited her height from him. Thick silver hair always in need of trimming curled over his collar. He bought fine clothes, then stained every cuff and shirtfront with ink from his quill or the presses. The right sleeve of his tan frock coat was no exception.

"That's why I learned to fend for myself," she said.

"I still don't understand your need to rush away."

"The holidays are over, Donal's gone off on another tour of the company offices—"

"Where is he, by the way? Nassau? Savannah?"

"I've no idea. Donal's not one for writing letters. I don't want to miss the rest of the Washington season. Besides, I'm worn out with all the secession talk in this town."

Not merely talk, but displays of pro-Southern sentiment, everywhere. In the room nearest the street, the proprietor had tacked up a South Carolina flag and two engravings, one of Fort Sumter in Charleston harbor, the other of Baltimore's harbor, as if to suggest a connection.

"You won't escape it in Washington, my girl."

"Rose doesn't allow hotheads in her salon, just gentlemen and ladies."

"There's another thing. That Greenhow woman. I thought she was in mourning for one of her daughters."

"It's true. She isn't going out yet, but she still receives visitors."

"I grant you that she was generous to take you up, introduce you to people—"

"She likes me. She's from Maryland, and she supports the South as strongly as you."

Her father studied the golden inch of lager at the bottom of his glass. "She has a reputation for less than perfect morality."

"Oh, Papa, that's gossip. People resent women with forceful opinions. Rose is a respectable widow. Her youngest daughter, little Rose, lives right there in the same house. And the best of Washington comes to call. Senators, congressmen, Army officers—President Buchanan is one of her most faithful visitors."

"Old Buck," Miller said gloomily. "He dithers and prays and does nothing about the crisis."

"Frankly I wish it would all go away. If there's a war, I'll jus spit. So many things would be interrupted."

"No sane person wants armed confrontation. But it's m duty to write and publish what I believe. Maryland must se cede, and join her Southern sisters. We are more Dixie tha damn Yankee in this state."

Margaret took a last sip of the second-rate claret Fingal served. She never ordered more than one glass of wine an seldom drank more than half. "Do you really think Marylan can secede peacefully?" she asked.

"That is the position I've taken in the paper, that it can, an must." As owner and chief editorialist of the *Baltimor Independent*, successor to another *Independent* in wester Virginia where they'd lived before, Calhoun Miller defende his native state, South Carolina, and the entire South. He ar gued his case with a businessman's practicality. The North an England needed Southern cotton. Northern industry neede Southern markets. Until the South's peculiar labor syster withered naturally, as he believed it would, it should be le alone, in deference to profits, and to the principle of state rights, the passion of the great John Calhoun for whor Miller's parents had named him. In recent months, Margare had seen her father move from that position of accommoda tion to a belief that Northern hostility was now too grea forcing the South to declare its independence. He didn't go s far as the Richmond papers that called on Marylanders t seize the nation's capital, but he promoted secession.

Miller noted her empty plate. "May we go?"

"Of course. You must be tired after another long day."

From a wall peg Miller retrieved his daughter's cloak, fashionable dark green burnous with vertical white stripe She tied her small, round English porkpie hat under her chi green flirtation ribbons trailed down behind. Margaret was handsome, long-legged young woman, with an attractive fu bosom. Her long dark hair was done up in a stylish bun ne ted in black velvet. Her outfit featured a smart fitted skirt; sh thanked the Almighty for driving stiff, steel-hooped crinoline out of fashion. Because of her upbringing in the house of journalist and her education at Mount Washington Femal College, she was unusually sophisticated for her age.

She linked arms with her father. On the way out Miller consulted his pocket watch. "Simms should be here. I told him seven sharp. Ah, there he is." Their black houseman was bundled in a greatcoat on the driver's seat of Miller's splendid six-passenger rockaway. The roof extended forward above him but gave little protection from the spatters of snow. If he felt the damp and the chill, like a good servant he didn't show it.

"We'll go home, Simms," Miller said as he helped Margaret in.

"Yes, sir. Thank you, sir." Simms always took orders by thanking the giver. A freedman in his sixties, he wanted no truck with abolitionists. Margaret assumed the turmoil in the country baffled or frightened him; he never discussed it.

Miller closed the door and drew a lap robe over them. A ship's horn sounded distantly as they bumped down Pratt Street, leaving the harbor.

"Was your brother home earlier?" he asked.

"No."

"Where did he go?"

"I've no idea. Cicero tells me nothing about his odd comings and goings. Surely he doesn't have midnight meetings at the firm." After graduation from the University of Virginia at Charlottesville, Margaret's older brother had decided to read law with a prominent local attorney. He'd spent four years at it, with little progress, and no apparent desire to hurry. Margaret had long ago given up trying to understand him, except in the most basic physical terms—his injury.

"If Donal returns when you're in Washington, shall I tell him where to find you?"

"I suppose you must."

"Such rampant enthusiasm," Miller said with a laugh.

"Donal's a fine man, Papa, and I do intend to marry him, but I don't have to moon over him, do I?"

"Isn't that customary when one's in love?"

Margaret turned her face to the passing city lights, not answering. Rather than rushing eagerly, she had slipped and slid into her engagement to Donal. Donal's forebears had owned the firm of McKee, Withers, cotton brokers, for over a hundred years. The firm began in London but Donal ran it from its American headquarters in lower Manhattan. Donal's

mother was a belle, a Mercer of the Georgia Mercers; thus h
father had chosen to live in the States most of his life. Dona
preferred it too, though he kept his British citizenship. He sai
it facilitated travel and enabled him to get around certain an
noying import and export laws. When Margaret wondere
about these, Donal smiled and suggested she not trouble he
head about men's affairs.

Margaret was distressed whenever she consciously faced u
to her feelings about her fiancé. Lack of feelings, rather. Tha
lack generated guilt, something missing from her righteous an
noyance over a possible war. If war came, many in Rose Gree
how's circle predicted that it wouldn't last more than nine
days because of public indignation. Margaret took no comfor

Music drifted to them; a popular melody played on a mout
organ. Miller said, "What a topsy-turvy world we live in. Da
Emmett wrote 'Dixie' for his minstrels, the Lincoln Republ
cans marched to it last fall, and now it seems to be the Sout
ern anthem. Passing strange."

In ten minutes they reached the imposing red-brick tow
house north of the city center. Lamplight glowed in the fa
shaped window above the lacquered front door. Simms reine
the horse by the hitch post.

Calhoun Miller took off his beaver top hat and left the ca
riage on the street side. He spoke to Simms as Margar
stepped down on the curb side. The town-house door opene
A spill of light revealed her brother and an unfamiliar visito
an appallingly shabby plug-ugly wearing a green tweed cap.
small parcel wrapped in brown paper passed from the visit
to Cicero. The shape, a right triangle, suggested a revolv
with a long barrel.

The plug-ugly ran down the steps and sped away witho
looking at Margaret. Calhoun Miller patted the horse's mu
zle as he stepped around to the curb. "Feed him, wipe hi
down, and that's all for the evening, Simms."

"Yes, sir, thank you, sir." Simms shook the reins and t
horse started its plod around the block to the rear carria
house. Margaret was unsettled by the visitor. Why would t
plug-ugly slip her brother a weapon, if that's what it was?

Cicero waited for them in the entry hall. He was twent
nine, a frail, bookish man already bald except for a fringe

rust-colored hair. An accident with a pet pony when he was four had permanently crippled his left leg. He wore a special shoe with a two-inch sole. He listed on that side when he walked.

Miller tossed his outer coat onto a bench and strode into the parlor where an unseen hearth blazed. Margaret paused dutifully to kiss Cicero's pale cheek. She did her best to love her brother, but he was neither warm nor affectionate. She felt a certain guilt about his childhood accident, although she hadn't been born when it happened. Their father was the one who'd mishandled the pony.

"Have a pleasant supper?" Cicero asked.

"Yes, I'm sorry you couldn't come along."

He shrugged and hobbled after her. "Business."

"With that person who was just here? Surely he isn't a client."

"No, just a friend."

"Since when do you cultivate friends who look like bare-knuckle prizefighters?"

"He's a member of an organization I've joined."

"A lodge? You're not the sort, Cicero."

"It isn't a lodge, it's a patriotic society. I can't tell you more. Even the name is secret." He craned toward her in a way that reminded her of a turtle shooting its head from its shell. "No more questions, please." It was said lightly, but she heard the warning.

Cicero was much more of a political fire-eater than their father. In public he dared to refer to General Winfield Scott, the noble old Virginian who led the Army, as "that free-state pimp." Cicero blithely said that Abe the Ape might not live to be inaugurated "if we are fortunate." Margaret hated such talk. She hated the epidemic of secession fever sweeping Baltimore and infecting her own household. She couldn't wait to return to the small, safe universe of Rose Greenhow's salon.

4

January 1861

When he walked into the Senate gallery on Monday, the twenty-first, he felt like a man lost on a stormy moor with no lantern and no signposts. The U.S. government had educated him, in return asking only that he give service, which he was glad to do. The military life with its order and predictability suited him. Further, there was this unspoken truth: West Point men from the South controlled the Army. Faced with the influence of this cadre, capable officers from the North resigned and looked to civilian life for advancement. Now Southern officers were resigning for a different reason.

Word of the speech had spread quickly. Lines formed before dawn. By nine o'clock the gallery was nearly full. Varina Davis came in quietly, to a place reserved for her. The notorious socialite Mrs. Greenhow made an ostentatious entrance, obstructing the view of those behind her with the yellow ostrich plumes on her hat. Though asked, she would not remove it.

He saw a seat in the last row, claimed it, and gave it up five minutes later when there were no more places for women. He stood at the head of the aisle, by the door, a look of brooding concentration on his face. It wasn't a handsome face in the conventional sense, but an arresting one: carrot-colored hair, pale red brows, gray-green eyes, a large nose. Men under his command never argued when he gave orders. Or if they did, they only did it once.

Second Lieutenant Frederick Scott Dasher, West Point '57, wore civilian clothes today. Part of his special duty, which he disliked. A bachelor and a Virginian, he'd grown up on a horse farm near Front Royal, in the Shenandoah. He owned the farm but no longer had family there. His father was gone, a casualty of alcohol. His younger brother had died of scarlet fever at age eight. His older sister, Marie, lived in Tennessee with her husband. His poor mother was cared for by Marie in Knoxville, though she might as well have been on the moon, given her lack of recognition of her surroundings. Fred had always assumed he would find the right young woman, marry, and rebuild the Dasher line. He no longer assumed it. He wondered if anyone in America had a dependable future.

Time dragged as the Senate disposed of its morning business. Every seat was taken, the aisles and outer stairways clogged with standees. The first of the cotton-state senators rose to speak his farewell. Others followed. The spectators were polite but restless. They'd come to hear the senator from Mississippi, who had left his sickbed for the occasion. When he rose, the huge hall and gallery collectively held its breath.

Jefferson Davis's voice was faint from illness. He was a few years past fifty, but stress had added a decade to his wasted, craggy face. A West Point graduate, he had fought in Mexico with Lee, Sam Grant, Tom Jackson, George Pickett. He'd served President Pierce as secretary of war, then represented his state honorably in the Senate. Now, he said, he was going. He felt it was the only course left.

"Mr. Calhoun, a great man who now reposes with his fathers, advocated the doctrine of nullification as a remedy, but a peaceful one. Secession belongs to a different class of remedies, but it is justified on the basis that the states are sovereign. There was a time when none denied it." He paused, his tired, feverish eyes on the galleries. His wife, Varina, was like marble, whatever pain she felt suppressed, hidden.

"I feel no hostility to you, Senators from the North. I am sure there is not one of you, whatever sharp discussion there might have been between us, to whom I cannot now say, in the presence of God, I wish you well. That said, Mr. President and Senators, and having made the announcement which the occasion seemed to require, it only remains for me to bid you a fond farewell."

Davis's colleagues sat silent out of respect, and sorrow. Sobs resounded in the gallery, some of the loudest those of the widow Greenhow. She covered her face and rocked in her seat. Fred Dasher's chest was tight with tension. He was deeply moved. He charged out the door, too upset to apologize to those he jostled.

Outside the Capitol the day was foggy, saturated with dampness. Like a man in a maze, he turned this way and that through the disgraceful litter of Corinthian columns, marble slabs, and lumber. Civilian gawkers—tourist families, single women—mingled with slovenly workmen, who seemed to be making only snail's progress on construction of the Capitol dome. The cast-iron base was complete but wrapped in ugly scaffolding. The statue of Armed Freedom that would surmount the dome lay on its side in the mud.

Every step spattered mud on Fred's fawn trousers. His head was clearing after the wrenching speech. If someone as brilliant and important as Davis could stand up to the government's assault on liberty, so could he.

He failed to see the strolling whore until she barred his way, cooing at him with her rouged mouth. "Buy my muffin, dearie. Nice warm muffin."

Fred Dasher treated women politely, but not this time. He shoved her so hard she stumbled against a block of uncut marble. "Ow! Dirty bastard!" He settled his beaver hat more securely and strode into the miasmic fog lying on the Mall. He could already smell the canal where he was to rendezvous at twelve.

He walked rapidly over the rough ground, past the towers of the Smithsonian, poking up like strange red fingers, and onward, till he was south of President's Park, with the unfinished trunk of the monument to George Washington just visible in the distance. Subscriptions had dwindled; people said the monument would never be finished.

He threw a rock at some pigs rooting in the mud. The area was a disgrace and by night, dangerous. It was marsh and mudflat, with the old municipal canal cutting across. Once the canal had linked the Potomac and the East Branch. Now it was abandoned, clogged with garbage, night soil, the occasional horse or dog carcass rotting away. Though not a delicate person, Fred held a linen handkerchief over his nose and mouth as he approached an iron bridge spanning the canal. On the opposite side, among bare trees, a man in a dark gray caped overcoat and unmarked forage cap lurked like a foot pad. Fred was filled with disgust. Was this fit duty for a professional soldier?

"Colonel," he said as he approached the other man. He had been ordered not to salute where he might be observed.

"Lieutenant," the colonel said. "What have you discovered?"

"It's as you suspected, sir. The National Rifles are practically all secesh."

Colonel Charles Stone, West Point '45, was in charge of the defenses of the District. He was given the responsibility by the bloated egomaniac at the head of the Army, old Fuss and Feathers Scott. Fred Dasher was Stone's aide, forced to operate as a glorified detective. Until companies of the regular Army could be pulled from Kansas, upstate New York, and two Southern arsenals from which they'd been driven, four militia units including the National Rifles were the city's only protection. Fred had used the name Frederick Danner, and his credentials as a Virginian, to join and drill with the Rifles.

"What's your assessment of the militia commander?" Stone asked.

"Captain Schaeffer's hard to read, sir. He's careful to say nothing partisan or controversial. On the other hand, the men he's recruited constitute evidence against him. He must have picked every one of them for their secesh sympathies. The unit is well armed. Sabers, revolvers, two mountain howitzers."

"Good God."

Fred delivered the coup de grâce. "Everything's straight from the Army arsenal, I confirmed that."

"Fine work, Lieutenant. The weapons will be confiscated but we must keep watching. I suggest we meet again—"

"Sir."

"—Friday. We might manage someplace warmer."

"Sir, I can't make arrangements for Friday."

"Why not?"

"Do I have permission to speak candidly?"

"You do," Stone said, his tone less comradely than before.

"I don't care for this kind of work, sir. Skulking. Telling lies about my identity."

"Lieutenant, this city is ringed by enemies who could rise

up and attack at any time. Part of my duty is to ferret out weaknesses in our defense force. The work's necessary, and I have no one else to do it."

Fred felt an enormous, buoyant relief even before he spoke the words he'd rehearsed. "It's nothing personal, Colonel, and I am sorry to abandon you—"

"Christ in heaven. Not you too."

"Yes, sir. I will hand in my resignation from the Army effective today."

"Then damn you, sir. God damn you for a traitor."

Hurt and angry, Fred didn't know what to say. He had no animosity toward his commander. They shared a moment of helpless silence in the fog. Finally Stone said, "Where are you going, then?"

"South," Fred Dasher said. "Wherever they will have me."

5

January 1861

"As a young girl I lived for a time at the Old Capitol," Rose said to her captive, a pop-eyed young man new to the salon. Those nearby listened politely, though most had heard the story many times. Margaret had.

"It's a pity they've turned it into a jail, it has such a distinguished history. Congress met in the building after the British burned Washington in 1814. When Congress moved out, it became a fashionable boardinghouse. Mrs. H. V. Hill, the proprietor, was my aunt. Living there was an education for a young woman. I met Henry Clay, and Daniel Webster. I heard Chief Justice Marshall discourse on the law in the Supreme Court's room in the basement. Great men. Statesmen. Not the weasels infesting the town today. The greatest of them was John C. Calhoun. He loved my aunt's hospitality. I was privileged to sit at his bedside during his last days. Offer him sips of water or a cool cloth for his head. He had a profound influence on my thinking. Before he died, he predicted a fatal conflict with the North."

Rose O'Neal Greenhow was a strikingly attractive woman, with dark eyes like Margaret's, and a complexion of a deeper olive hue. No one knew her exact age. Somewhere in the forties, Margaret guessed. Her raven-black hair, center parted, showed only a few hints of gray. Her attire was somber: a short jacket of black wool grenadine over a black silk dress, and a rope of pearls on her lush bosom.

A dozen guests were gathered in the parlor of her manse at No. 398 Sixteenth Street, left to her by her late husband, Dr. Greenhow. It was the last Monday of the month. Rose received on Mondays, Fridays, and Sunday afternoons.

"Ah, but here's the person you must meet," she exclaimed to the pop-eyed visitor. Senator Seward, slender and rather stooped, entered arm in arm with the chairman of the Military Affairs Committee, Henry Wilson of Massachusetts. The plain and corpulent Wilson reminded Margaret of a farmer. He was a frequent guest. Infatuated with Rose, Margaret suspected. He never brought his wife.

"Governor," Rose said, sailing over to Seward with her visitor in tow. "Hello, Henry." The greeting made Wilson grin foolishly. Rose fixed her attention on the senator from New York. "This young man is the nephew of a dear friend of my late husband. Jarvis Tottle, the Honorable William Seward. Everyone calls him governor, Jarvis, in spite of his seat in the Senate."

"Pleasure, sir," Seward said in a voice grown hoarse from too many cigars. His clothes reeked of them.

Rose linked arms with the young man. "Jarvis is recently out of college in Kentucky. He wants to work in government. I told him you could open doors, perhaps find him a clerkship, since everyone says you'll head the new cabinet and be the de facto president." Long ago, Seward had predicted the "irrepressible conflict" between advocates of free and slave labor. Rose despised his Republican politics but welcomed him personally, as she welcomed others of his party for what they could do for her.

"I must warn you, however. Jarvis is known to sympathize with the South."

"There's a blue cockade on my hat, absolutely," Jarvis said

Seward adjusted the gentleman's traveling shawl drape
over his frock coat. "You're certainly not alone in Washing
ton. The *Star* claims we have twenty thousand secesh-minde
citizens in the District. A third of our white population. Man
work in government. Tell me about yourself, Mr. Tottle."

Margaret had been listening. Now she turned away, disap
pointed that Hanna wasn't present this evening. She ha
made many acquaintances since dipping into the waters c
Rose's social pond. Only one, Hanna Siegel, had become
friend.

Margaret and Hanna were the same age but were in othe
ways opposites. Hanna was European, fair, narrow-hippe
boyish. She dressed to conceal what little bosom she ha
Where Margaret was vividly dark, Hanna was straw blond
with blue eyes.

Margaret lived comfortably; Hanna was poor. Hanna's fa
ther was a former officer in the Austrian army. Asked abou
his reason for emigrating to America, he always replied wit
vague statements about "opportunity." He was seekin
preferment, a commission or a government job, like youn
Jarvis Tottle and hundreds of others.

Hanna was an actress. She ran with a crowd of theatrica
who were struggling just as she was; the sort of people Ca
houn Miller would dismiss as not respectable. Margaret had
picture of actresses as gregarious to the point of bawdines
and often brashly ambitious. Hanna was quiet, though quietl
determined. In the country less than three years, she retaine
only an echo of European speech. For eighteen months she'
hired out to the shrewish wife of an elocution teacher. Sh
washed dishes, scrubbed floors, carried slops, and in return th
teacher purged her accent.

They disagreed sharply on slavery. Margaret thought it a re
grettable system, but necessary for the South's survival. Th
Calhoun Miller view. Hanna wished one of God's lightnin
bolts would destroy every white man who practiced it. Hann
wanted to convert her friend. Margaret avoided the subject
she could.

Despite the differences, Hanna and Margaret were drawn to
gether by something stronger—a freedom of spirit they er

joyed in various ways. In good weather Margaret rented horses and they struck out north on the Seventh Street or Rockville roads, not sidesaddle, at a sedate walk, but astride, in full gallop. On occasion, feeling especially uninhibited, they wore trousers.

Margaret's feet in the stirrups showed a good amount of ankle under her trouser cuffs or flapping hems. She knew she had good legs and saw no reason to hide them. Men old and young admired the riders, and sometimes yelled propositions. Once an old woman tending a market garden on the Rockville pike pointed at them and cried, "Shame. Shame on girls like you!"

Which only made Margaret and Hanna laugh and gallop faster.

* * *

Rose's niece Adele arrived. Addie was the wife of Mr. Douglas, the Democrat whom Lincoln had defeated in November. They chatted amiably of inconsequential things. When would a new novel by George Eliot appear? What attraction would Grover's Theater show next? When would the Capitol dome be finished, the dreadful Washington swamps drained of their miasmic waters, the crumbling cobbles on shabby Pennsylvania Avenue replaced?

Everyone laughed when little Rose romped through the room in her short crinolines and full Turkish pantaloons. Rose Greenhow's daughter was seven or eight, a cheeky show-off whose behavior Margaret's father wouldn't have tolerated. Of course the Wild Rose herself was an exhibitionist, showing off her beauty, breeding, and influence at every opportunity.

Rose raised her arms in a theatrical way. "Ladies and gentlemen, refreshments are served. Tea, punch, and stronger libations for those who desire them." Senator Wilson said something to her but Rose ignored him and swept away to the dining room. Wilson tagged after her like a loyal dog. For certain men, Rose possessed a sexual attraction that was overpowering.

Shortly, Margaret found herself in conversation with a handsome, full-bearded Army officer who introduced himself as Captain Thomas Jordan. He wore the familiar drab dress uniform: a dark blue coat with a stiff standing collar and matching trousers with no seam stripe, the whole lightened only by brass buttons, a burgundy sash, and two gold bars on each shoulder strap. Jordan had an aloof, almost wary air. He watched the room while discussing the crisis:

"Now Georgia's gone, and Louisiana. Texas must go soon. How do you feel about the upheaval, Miss Miller?"

"I try not to feel anything. I have my own life and interests, as I should imagine you do. We don't need or want Americans killing other Americans. Don't you agree?"

"Only somewhat. My oath binds me to the commander in chief, yet I feel a contrary pull. My heart lies with my native state of Virginia. I wonder if Colonel Lee out in Texas feels that way? Perhaps we'll know soon, I understand they've recalled him." Robert E. Lee of Arlington was the nation's foremost soldier. He had led the Marine detachment that had captured John Brown at Harpers Ferry, bringing on a trial and execution that further divided the country.

"Well, I hope Mr. Lincoln has some skills or tricks that will bring about a resolution," Margaret said. "Why does the government need that old fort in Charleston harbor anyway?"

"I suppose they could survive without it, and all the other arsenals and forts as well. But to give them up willingly would be a sign of weakness. I believe we'll fight over it."

"I hope not. If it happens, I want no part of it."

"But if war comes, how can anyone remain neutral?"

"Believe me, Captain, I shall make every effort."

"I'm dismayed to hear you express such sentiments," said a familiar voice. Rose swept into view, no longer the smiling hostess. "You're an intelligent young woman, you come from Maryland—how can you possibly declare yourself unwilling to take part?"

Little Rose slipped up behind her mother and stamped her foot. "I'll go fight in her place. I'm the damnedest little rebel you ever saw."

Jordan laughed. Rose tweaked her ear. "We don't use that sort of language in polite company, dear." Little Rose marched away in a petulant imitation of a soldier.

Margaret didn't like being put down. "Isn't it rather silly to debate the question?" she said. "Captain Jordan may have to

ake a stand, join the quarrel, but what can a woman do, regardless of which side she's on?"

Jordan said, "I assure you that young women who are
above suspicion will be needed."

Margaret frowned. "Why above suspicion? Needed for
what? I don't understand."

Rose shot a look at the officer. His odd statement had annoyed her somehow. A faint redness sprang into his cheeks.
Rose spied a new arrival.

"Margaret, I believe your gentleman's here."

"Donal?"

"Yes. Were you expecting him?"

"For some time. He's been traveling."

Rose waved. "Here she is, Mr. McKee."

Margaret rushed to him. "Donal, thank you for rescuing
me. I had no idea when you'd return."

"The steamer docked in Baltimore yesterday. Your father
said to try the town house and if you weren't there, to come
here. How are you, my dearest?" Donal's black eyes shifted
briefly downward to the curve of her breasts. "I'd give you a
kiss and a crushing hug if we weren't in public. Is there any
champagne in the house?"

"This way." She led him toward the dining room buffet.
Sometimes Donal was a bother, but this evening she was
grateful for his presence. The exchange with Rose still stung.

Donal McKee was a slim, graceful man, severely grayed
by the cares of business though he was not yet thirty-five. He
was shorter than Margaret by an inch or two. He had delicate hands, curly hair, a receding chin that spoiled his otherwise strong face. She had met him at Newport two years ago,
when she and her father and Cicero were vacationing. A couple of jealous acquaintances, female, gratuitously informed
her that Donal was a womanizer. If so, he was circumspect.
In all the time she'd known him, Margaret had seen no evidence. She wondered if he'd dallied with anyone while he
traveled.

"How was your trip?"

"I don't enjoy poking through the books at the branches,
though it's necessary if we're not to be robbed blind. New Orleans was interesting because of this secession business. Ah,

thank you," he said to the white servant who handed him
champagne. Margaret declined the offer of a glass.

Donal slipped his arm around her waist. "I seemed to be
considered an expert on England because father came from
Leeds. I was repeatedly asked whether England would recog
nize the Confederacy. I said I wasn't privy to the policies o
Her Majesty's government, but I supposed so. British mill
need Southern cotton." He'd drawn her to a secluded corner
away from the clusters of guests. He finished his champagne
set the glass aside, and put both hands on her waist.

"Damn, Margaret, the sight of you always distracts me.
can hardly wait to claim you as my wife. Have you settled or
a date?"

"Not yet. But I'm thinking seriously on it."

"Not seriously enough. I'm an impatient man. I must have
another drink."

He strolled away, and in a moment fell into conversation
with Rose. She laughed and caressed his cheek a little too
fondly. Again Margaret felt the confusion of her relationship
with Donal.

When they'd first met, she was charmed by his worldliness
He was older, widely traveled, far more intelligent and urban
than all of the beaux of her own age who had drifted into he
life and been discarded. What confused and upset her was he
lack of romantic attraction to Donal. He excited nothing i
her except feelings of admiration and security—hardly a good
basis for marriage. This was the reason she continually de
layed choosing a wedding date. Watching Donal touch Rose'
arm in a possessive, even intimate way raised familiar ques
tions. Should she break the engagement? How could she face
her father, who was eager to see her married and settled, and
admit that she didn't love her fiancé?

All at once she was tossing in a sea of doubt and self
recrimination. It made all the blather about secession and wa
pale to insignificance.

6

February 1861

At Fourteenth Street, on the respectable north side of the Avenue, the hotel of the Willard brothers served meals to Washington's important people from daybreak till midnight. Between five p.m. dinner and the late supper hour, Willard's dining room offered a sumptuous tea. When Hanna had a night off in early February, she met Margaret there at half past seven.

As always, Hanna's friend was stylishly dressed. Hanna's own poor outfit shamed her. Over a heavily mended dress she wore her father's sack coat for warmth. A cloth workman's cap lay in her lap. Her one concession to femininity was black net stockings.

"I'm thrilled you have a part in *Twelfth Night*," Margaret said. "May I come see it?"

"If you care to watch unpaid actors do Shakespeare in a damp church basement, certainly."

"Viola's the young girl who impersonates the page Cesario, isn't she?"

"Yes. At least I have the figure for it."

"Stop. You mustn't think so poorly of yourself all the time." Hanna responded with a shrug and a rueful roll of her blue eyes. Margaret passed a gaudy handbill across the teacups and petits fours. "Here's a bit of theater for you. Father sent it in a letter yesterday."

The handbill from Baltimore's Halliday Street Theater announced: *Mr. J. W. BOOTH, Scion of the Famed Family of Players, In His Startling & Lifelike Personation of the Bard's Immortal Villain RICHARD III. Three Nights ONLY! Positively NO Extension!*

"Have you seen him?" Margaret asked.

"No, only heard about him. I don't believe he's appeared i Washington. He seems to prefer Charleston and the Souther circuit."

"A rebel at heart? I like him already. Father said he's a bet ter actor than his brother, Edwin, or the head of the family, Ju nius, when he was alive. 'Fire, dash, and a touch o strangeness'—that's how Father described young Mr. Booth Do you suppose he'll ever play locally?"

Hanna's tea had grown cold. She sipped the last. "I don' imagine he will unless someone opens a decent theater. A actor of his stature wouldn't play the music halls."

Hanna was familiar with those establishments. She worke several nights a week at the Canterbury, a music hall that pre sented a bill of beefy dancing girls, jugglers, performing dog: and blackface comics who told salacious stories. Though th work was hard, it helped Hanna and her father scrape by an allowed her an occasional nonpaying role with an amateu company. Hanna served ten-cent drinks and fended o loutish men who thought every girl in the place raised he skirts for a price. What an irony. Thus far in her life Hanna ha experienced three short flings and gotten no satisfactio physical or emotional, from any of them. Sometimes sh doubted her capacity to love a decent man.

Margaret's mind was still on Booth. "Father says he's de ilishly handsome, and has a reputation for chasing anything i skirts."

"I'd love to meet him and judge his talent. Onstage, you ur derstand."

They both laughed. Margaret laid the handbill aside. "Sinc I never read the papers, can you tell me when our new Pres dent will arrive?"

"Later this month. He's making a long ceremonial journe by train from Illinois. He can't get here too soon. I hope he' clear out all the Southern sympathizers."

Margaret's smile was devilish. "Fie, Hanna. Do you war me driven out? I like Washington."

"Of course I don't want that. We're friends. Sometimes forget where your heart lies."

"Not with either side, really. I hate the whole messy qua rel. I wish it would go away."

Gravely Hanna said, "It won't until it's resolved."

"But which way?"

"The right way, I trust." Hanna averted her gaze, aware of annoyance in Margaret's vivid dark eyes. Being too forthright about abolition had ruined several friendships for her. She didn't want this relationship destroyed.

The waiter delivered the bill on a silver tray. Hanna put her hand in a coat pocket. She didn't own a proper handbag.

"Please let me pay my share this time."

"You may contribute when some manager recruits a stock company to support a visiting star and you're engaged for a featured part, but not before. Oh, I forgot to ask about your father. Is there any news?"

"This afternoon he went to see the commandant of the Georgetown militia company. They advertised for an experienced drillmaster."

"I'm always curious about why he left the Austrian Army."

"He wasn't advancing fast enough, that's all."

But that was not all. The story was sordid; Hanna guarded the secret. It was true that Anton Siegel, a fiercely ambitious man, hated the slow advancement and meager officer's pay in Austria. As commander of his regiment he was in a position to fiddle with the books, and to squeeze Army suppliers for extra money under the table. One of them had turned him in.

The major never for a moment expressed remorse. Instead, furious because he was cashiered, he packed up his daughter and bought steerage tickets out of Hamburg. Thus ended Hanna's days in Vienna. All that was left of those times was a sad scrapbook of memories. Hot coffee with milk in one of the cafés on Stephansplatz. A luscious torte in the Sacher Garden. Quiet relaxation with a book under a leafy tree in the Stadtpark . . .

Father and daughter had reached Washington with no prospects and almost no funds. They nearly starved for three months, until Hanna found work. They weren't doing much better now.

"Papa's dreadfully melancholy these days," Hanna told Margaret as they stepped from the hotel to the Avenue's brick sidewalk. "He's drinking heavily again. I pray he had some success in Georgetown."

"Well, I'll gladly second that if it will take the strain out o
your face." Margaret gave a tip to the doorman, who whistlec
a horse-drawn cab from the corner. "Send me a note wher
you're free again. We must ride in the country as soon as thi$
dismal winter's over."

"Yes, we must," Hanna agreed. They embraced and Mar
garet left in the hansom, waving.

Hanna walked rapidly to Tenth Street and turned north. I
was a cold, cloudless evening, the stars sparkling like ice chips
She faced a long trek to the district called Nigger Hill—she
never uttered the offensive name—because paying for trans
portation was out of the question.

On her way up Tenth she avoided a drunkard vomiting over
everything within three feet of him; heard a volley of shots
saw two men brawling bare-fisted in front of one of Washing
ton's many "boardinghouses." Several daughters of Eve hung
from ground-floor windows, cheering the fighters on witl
foulmouthed enthusiasm. Prostitution was a necessary indus
try in a town filled with single and married lawmakers away
from home.

The Siegels rented a scabrous little shotgun house, three
tiny rooms, at the end of a dirt lane in a seedy section of towr
called the Northern Liberties. To reach it Hanna passed a nea
cottage owned by a black man named Spence, a porter on the
Baltimore & Ohio. Through a parlor window she saw Mr
Spence romping with his two little daughters. Hanna and he
father had never shared that kind of affection and compan
ionship. As a child roaming Vienna by herself, she'd hardenec
herself against wanting it, though occasionally she could be
bitterly jealous of people such as Margaret or Mr. Spence whc
were part of a loving family.

Hanna let herself in. The door was never locked. The neigh
bors knew the major kept a side arm and a saber close by a
all times.

The small front room, her bedroom, was dark. The$
couldn't afford to waste candles. The next room belonged tc
her father. There he slept, and stored his moldering uniforms
his Clausewitz and other books on the art of war. It too wa$
dark. A light showed in the back room. She moved slowl$
toward the feeble yellow glow.

The major slouched at the deal table. The top was scarred and filthy despite Hanna's efforts to keep it clean. A brick propped up a broken leg.

Siegel's cropped blond hair was turning white. His cheekbones were broad, his jaw strong. A long dueling scar from his cadet days marked his left cheek under his eye. He wore old uniform trousers, maroon with a gray stripe, but nothing else. His braces hung below his hips.

He heard her come in. He acknowledged her by extending his hand until the palm was two inches above the flame of the candle. Neither his hand nor his muscular arm showed a tremor. He was drunk; an empty schnapps bottle stood between his bare feet. A cockroach crawled around the bottle.

"Papa?"

Siegel withdrew his hand. With a smile he showed his palm, unhurt. Hanna took off her workman's cap.

"What happened in Georgetown, Papa?"

Because his English was imperfect they spoke in German. "Another got there before me." He groped under the chair, found the bottle empty, cursed, and threw it against the wall. It bounced and rolled.

"A stupid scarecrow half my age. Served in some rural militia company in Pennsylvania. But of course—of course!—he was an American. My experience counted for nothing. Also, behind my back, someone said I sounded too foreign. I hate this filthy democracy. I hate the mudsills who think they're equal to people of breeding. They aren't fit to clean up my shit."

Hanna wanted to weep. "Won't you please put on a shirt?"

"I'm not cold. Go to bed." When she hesitated, he beat the table with his fist. "Go to bed." His shout sent the roach scuttling.

"I will if you won't drink anymore."

"Tend to your own affairs. Close your door and give me some peace."

Hanna returned to the front room and shut the door. Before she undressed she went out to the reeking privy where she sat with her drawers around her knees. How she wished she could give her father greater support, greater comfort. But of course he wouldn't have it from her; she was a woman.

She remembered his drunken rages after her mother had died bearing her. "Liesl failed me. Your mother failed me. I wanted a son who could be a *soldier*." Hanna carried a deep wound of guilt and insufficiency, from hearing that so many times.

A year ago, in a secondhand bin at Shillington's popular bookshop, she'd discovered an 1844 novel, *Fanny, the Female Pirate Captain*, authored by some forgotten hack. The heroine was a buccaneer whose lover declared, "By my soul, thou shouldst have been a man."

Thou shouldst have been a man. She never forgot the line. In the story, it was ardent praise. Her father would scream it as accusation. She should have been a man. Sometimes she desperately wanted to be. Could that be why none of her short and clumsy love affairs had satisfied her?

She trudged back to the house and crawled in bed in her undergarments. The house was frigid; she couldn't buy stove wood until the Canterbury paid her for the week. Every night before sleeping, it was her habit to whisper all of Viola's speeches, but tonight she was too upset. Through the door she heard Siegel's mumbled litany of profanity. He cursed his luck, the Georgetown militia, American democracy—and he probably cursed her as well. She pulled a tattered blanket over her head and gave herself up to silent tears.

7

February 1861

Sledge worked his gold toothpick to the other side of his mouth. "God damn it, how long are they going to argue in there?" Lon couldn't help a twinge of guilt. His preacher father had been fierce about the sanctity of the Lord's name.

An Army officer, Captain John Pope, stood outside the suite to which Sledge referred. Lon and Sledge guarded the hallway between the suite and the staircase of the Jones

House in Harrisburg. Captain Pope watched them with un-concealed suspicion.

"Maybe forever," Lon said. "Colonel Lamon doesn't like the boss, that's plain."

Sledge bent his knee and rested his boot heel against the pale wallpaper, where it left a mark. Lon stretched and yawned, using the move to edge closer to the suite. Under the gas jets he and Sledge looked pasty and worn. They'd been up since day-break Thursday, when they left Baltimore for Philadelphia. They'd been ordered there to help protect Lincoln, his wife, sons, friends, and political cronies on the official train.

Because of death threats, Pinkerton wanted to spirit Mr. Lincoln to Washington immediately. Lincoln refused to cancel his Friday schedule. He'd raised a flag at Independence Hall to display the new star for Kansas and celebrate Washington's birthday. Following that he'd made a quick rail trip to Tren-ton, then came on to Harrisburg to meet with the Pennsylva-nia legislature and Governor Curtin. Lincoln had been summoned upstairs from the hotel banquet room at six o'clock, at Pinkerton's insistence. It was now half past eight.

Contentious voices were raised behind the double doors. Nicolay, the new President's secretary, was in there. Norman Judd, a stout Illinois politician, was in there, along with two more officers charged with guarding the President-elect. The argument had gone on since last night, when Frederick Se-ward had arrived at the Continental Hotel in Philadelphia with a letter of warning.

"I say we should implement the plan." That was Pinkerton, refusing to yield. "We had rumors of an assassination attempt as early as a month ago. Last night we had independent con-firmation, sent from Colonel Stone's Baltimore agents to General Scott, thence to Senator Seward, who dispatched his son with the letter. The evidence is strong, sir. I urge you to follow my plan."

Lamon interrupted. "No, I object. We still aren't sure."

"Ward, hold on." That was Lincoln. His was a thin, light voice that occasionally rose up high, most unpleasantly. Ward Hill Lamon was a lawyer, Lincoln's closest friend among all those riding the special train to Washington. "Nobody wants to see the President-elect sneak into town like a thief in the night. I don't. Since the election I've become familiar with death threats. I try to ignore them. But Seward and Scott are not alarmists. I do admit that both of them, and you, Mr. Pinkerton, could be reacting to the same set of rumors. Trouble is, we just don't know."

"I don't believe in a Baltimore plot and I never have," Lamon said.

"But the Baltimore gangs are notoriously lawless." That was old white-haired Colonel Sumner, regular Army.

"Doesn't matter. These so-called detectives are just promoting themselves with phantom conspiracies."

Pinkerton said, "Lamon, that's an insult. If duels were still allowed, I'd call you out. I've been undercover in Baltimore for a month, together with five of my best operatives. We were invited by Mr. Felton, president of the Philadelphia, Wilmington, and Baltimore, because of threats against his line. I've gained the confidence of leaders of the Southern faction, especially that barber at Barnum's Hotel, Ferrandini. He's part of a secret group called the Knights of Liberty. I have men planted inside the organization. Do you know what Ferrandini told me after I convinced him I was a secesh from Georgia? 'One thing will save the South. Mr. Lincoln's corpse.' "

"My, my," Lincoln said with a weary amusement. "Hotheaded, those Latins."

"The dago ought to be shot." That was the other colonel, Ellsworth. He commanded a regiment of Zouave militia.

Pinkerton's conviction strengthened his voice. "Ferrandini's an ignorant lowlife, but I take him seriously. In Italy he was allied with the man who almost killed Napoleon the Third. Furthermore, gentlemen, you don't know this slavery crowd as I do. No crime's too heinous to preserve their ungodly system. Hang every adult male in the South and we'd all be better off."

"Every one? That's a pretty uncharitable view, Mr. Pinkerton," Lincoln said.

"Nevertheless I hold to it, sir. I loathe and distrust the lot of them. The hour's late. We have a one-car special waiting, to connect with the eleven p.m. sleeper out of Philadelphia. My agent Mrs. Warne has reserved space in the last car. You will travel as her invalid brother. Mr. Felton's posted nearly two hundred men along the line, ready to signal if the track is sabotaged." It was the same plan Pinkerton had proposed last night. The President-elect had seen hundreds of thousands of well-wishers on his long rail journey from Springfield. The crowds were friendly. Baltimore was the feared exception.

Lincoln sighed. "All right. We can't slice this bacon any thinner. If ridicule is the only thing deterring us, I'm disposed to go along with the plan." Lamon started to object again. "No, that's it, Ward. I'll change out of this funeral suit."

"I have a hat and traveling shawl ready," Pinkerton said.

Lamon burst into the hall and strode away with a glare at the detectives. He was an imposing fellow, with a dragoon mustache and a self-important air. Lincoln liked his singing and banjo playing, especially his rendition of "The Blue Tail Fly." Lamon wore two concealed revolvers at all times.

Pinkerton rushed into the hall, flushed with excitement. He herded Sledge and Lon toward the stairs, away from the too curious Captain Pope.

"We'll be on our way in half an hour. No other rail traffic will be allowed out of town until morning. Men are standing by to cut the telegraph wires. By six a.m. I'll have the President safely at Willard's Hotel. The rest of the party will travel through Baltimore tomorrow as planned. You two will accompany them."

With his white tie undone, Lincoln poked his head out the door. He was a peculiar-looking man, almost ugly. He had sad, sunken eyes, straggly chin whiskers, and a rough, dark complexion. Woefully unpresidential, Lon thought.

"Pinkerton, I won't go until Mrs. Lincoln's told."

"I'll inform her personally, sir."

Lincoln disappeared. Lon and Sledge exchanged looks as the boss marched to an adjoining suite, knocked, entered. Lon liked to be charitable; his father had taught him it was a virtue. But a day in the company of Lincoln's haughty and sharp-tongued wife had overcome the training. They heard Mary Lincoln's hysterical cry:

"I won't have it. I won't, I won't!"

"Madam, he has agreed to go. He will be safe, I swear to you."

"And who are you? A tradesman. Nobody! I demand that Colonel Lamon accompany you to protect my husband."

"Acts like she's First Lady already," Sledge whispered. Captain Pope was rigid with embarrassment. They heard Pinkerton pleading:

"For pity's sake, madam, keep your voice down. I accede to your request. Colonel Lamon may come with us."

"And Robert." Bob was the Lincolns' oldest son, eighteen.

"No. Only Lamon." Mrs. Lincoln's shrill reply was lost under the voice of her son Bob trying to soothe her.

Lon wondered about Baltimore. It lacked a central depot, and an old ordinance prohibited locomotives from running through the central city. Passengers from the north had to travel a mile and a quarter from Calvert Street Station to catch the Baltimore & Ohio for Washington. Individual cars were pulled over horse-car tracks, but it had been planned for Lincoln to ride in an open carriage. In Baltimore, Pinkerton had been told that a group of conspirators would create a diversion, drawing off the police, while a smaller group closed in to shoot or stab Lincoln. The danger was heightened because of the police chief's open support of the Confederacy. Lon didn't sleep well that night.

*   *   *

"Must be a thousand out there," Sledge said.

"Two or three times that," Lon said as the passenger car creaked along the tracks. Lincoln was safe. An early-morning telegraph had brought word that "Plums," Pinkerton, had arrived in Washington with his charge, "Nuts." Lon laughed at the silly code names. Sledge said, "Careful, the boss probably made 'em up himself."

They'd just left Calvert Street with a mob trailing them. In the station the mob was relatively controlled. Their ringleaders organized three cheers for the Confederacy, three for its new president, Davis, and three long groans for Lincoln. At this Mary Lincoln collapsed on a plush seat and wailed. Bob, the Harvard student, vainly tried to comfort and quiet her.

A plodding team drew the car through the gray winter afternoon. Occasional spatters of rain streaked the windows, some of which were open because of the mild temperature. Men ran along both sides of the car, spitting, cursing, yelling.

"Kill the gorilla!"

'That's his wife in there!"

"Dirty whore!"

"Mama, what's that mean?" The Lincolns' youngest son, Thomas, called Tad, pressed against his mother's side, round-eyed. Mary Lincoln's powder had run down her face, melted by tears. She reminded Lon of a demented clown. She was a short, stout woman who might have been attractive once, in her days as a Kentucky belle.

A rock sailed in, ricocheting off a spittoon. "Close the blasted windows," young Colonel Ellsworth yelled, and proceeded to lower the first one. Old Colonel Sumner and John Nicolay sprang to help. The windows went down, bang, bang, and then the curtains were drawn, but not before men spat tobacco on several panes and smeared one with something brown that looked like feces.

Lon and Sledge stood at the car's rear door. The Army officers guarded the front. Lon's hand clamped tight on the Colt .31 in his pocket. Tad and his older brother Willie, ten, had pestered Lon incessantly till he showed it to them. They were handsome boys, but they were spoiled and undisciplined.

Someone beat on the car with a stick. Others joined in. Mrs. Lincoln pulled Tad and Willie against her bosom, clutching their heads and heaving out deep sobs. Colonel Sumner shouted at the man driving the horses from the front platform, "How much further?"

"Another two blocks."

"Go faster, Mrs. Lincoln's in grave distress."

Lon felt the car sway as the mob pushed the sides. Someone broke a window with a rock; glass fell out beneath the curtain. The chanting went on.

"Whore, whore!"

"He ain't gonna live to be president!"

"My God, they're madmen," Lon whispered, never even thinking of his father's disapproval.

Suddenly, through a small window in the door, Lon saw two men with mean faces and soiled clothes climb over the chain and mount the steps to the platform. A third stood on the rear coupler, ready to climb over the railing. Lon tore the door open, jumped outside.

The first man on the steps swung a billy. Lon jerked his head back, banging his skull painfully on the car wall. Sledge crowded past him, aimed his revolver at the man with the billy. The man immediately shoved his partner aside and leaped off the train.

Lon meanwhile was dealing with the man standing on the coupler. The man slashed out with a butcher knife, tearing Lon's trouser leg and raking his calf. Enraged, Lon pistol-whipped the man's face. The man fell off the coupler, his nose spouting blood. He lay across the tracks with his head at an odd angle.

On the steps, the last man watched Sledge extend his arm, point the Remington, and ask, "What about you, you son of a bitch?" The man jumped off like the first.

"Fucking cowards." Sledge holstered his piece. The car pulled away from the crowd surrounding the man on the tracks. "I think you broke his damn neck. Congratulations." Lon's guilt lessened when the fallen man was lifted to his feet, dazed but upright. "Better get inside and take care of that leg."

The flesh wound was more bloody than painful, but it seriously wounded Lon's purse. He couldn't afford to replace a pair of trousers right away. He bandaged the wound with cloth the porter found. He was still shaken from the fight.

The Pinkertons and the Army men kept the mob at bay until the car reached the other depot, where Mrs. Lincoln gradually calmed down. Rain fell steadily. As they crossed the border out of Maryland, Bob Lincoln led everyone in singing "The Star Spangled Banner."

Lon didn't sing with enthusiasm. Baltimore was a stinging lesson. The Southern partisans were a hundred times more violent and dangerous than Pinkerton had said. They had to be whipped, broken, prevented at all costs from spreading their murderous anarchy. He thought his father would have been proud of his resolve.

8

1836–1858

As a young man in Scotland, Mathias Price was attracted to the doctrine of God's universal love preached by John Wesley. It offered hope to the masses who lived without it in the rookeries of Glasgow, his home. He was converted at a revival in Bristol, England, and ordained before he was twenty-three. He chose to answer the call of Methodism in America.

He stepped onto American soil at Charleston and there saw a searing sight: a slave whose naked back had felt the whip many times. Stripes of scar tissue crisscrossed black flesh "like a relief map of hell," Mathias said.

In the 1830s the Methodist church in America was already reeling toward a schism over slavery. The Reverend Mathias Price would never serve in what he called the benighted South. He accepted a small pastorate in the village of Lebanon, Ohio, not far above Cincinnati. He'd been recommended by a first cousin, Dora Filson, and her husband, Silas, a prosperous farmer.

Mathias found a wife in the German community of Cincinnati. A year after their marriage, Christina Price died bearing their only child. The boy knew his mother only as a smudged pencil portrait made by an itinerant artist. His father kept it in an oval frame on his desk.

Mathias Price was a spare, strong man whose Christianity was as muscular as his body. He didn't preach comfortable complacency about the next world, but militant reform of this one. Prominent in the parsonage was an embroidery he'd asked Dora to sew. It was his amended version of a verse from Isaiah 58:

> Loose the bands of wickedness.
> Undo the heavy burdens.
> Let the oppressed go free.

He preached not only from the Bible, but from philosophers such as Emerson: "I do not see how a barbarous community and a civilized community can constitute a state. We must get rid of slavery or we must get rid of freedom." He quoted Wesley to condemn "that execrable sum of all villainies called the slave-trade." Southern sympathy was strong this close to Kentucky. Some in his congregation asked the bishop to remove Mathias. He fought back, held on, raised his son, Alonzo, to love kindness, intelligence, and above all, liberty.

Between Sunday sermons, the Reverend Mr. Price often disappeared for days. Sometimes he returned scratched and bruised, accompanied by black men or women he hid in the root cellar until the next morning, when they were mysteriously gone. Young Lon took this more or less for granted, and accepted it when his father avoided direct answers to questions.

When his father was away, Lon ate and slept at cousin Dora's farm. Silas, Dora's husband, came from Paducah, Kentucky. He opposed the Reverend's antislavery activity because the South couldn't survive without slave labor. Dora objected on different grounds. "He'll injure himself, or someone will kill him. It's dangerous work."

"But what kind of work is it?" Lon asked.

"Work that a man of the cloth shouldn't be doing." She would say no more.

The Reverend's small library was a place of refuge and happiness for the growing boy. He did his schoolwork there and read his father's books. He loved the chivalry and derring-do of Scott, the thrills of James Fenimore Cooper's Leather-Stocking Tales, the jollity and melodrama of Charles Dickens. He had a vivid memory of standing in a crowd with his father outside a Lebanon inn called the Golden Lamb as the great literary lion alighted for an overnight stop on his first American tour.

Lon discovered Edgar A. Poe, whose unusual tales appeared in obscure literary quarterlies that came into the house. Particularly fascinating were the adventures of Poe's Parisian detective, Dupin, who solved crimes with brainpower and observation. A Cincinnati newspaper article led Lon to the lurid memoirs of Vidoçq, founder of the Sûreté, the French criminal investigation bureau. Lying under a shade tree on hot summer days, Lon invented stories about himself as a clever policeman. In one of his first boyish love affairs— he was eleven, Patience ten—he said, "I want to be a detective like Dupin or the other one, I don't know how to pronounce his name."

He and Patience were strolling a country road. She said, "Are there detectives like that in America?"

"I don't know."

"Then how will you become a detective?"

"I don't know."

"If you don't know, Alonzo, why do you bother to think about it? You should be a storekeeper, or a farmer like Silas Filson."

"That would be too dull."

"Then what will you do instead?"

"I don't know," he cried, vexed. The romance soon withered.

Growing toward adolescence in the 1850s, Lon slowly reached an understanding of what his father did during his absences. Lon overheard people discuss something called the Underground Railroad, which wasn't really a railroad but a secret route to Canada for runaway slaves. Black men and women continued to appear for their brief residence in the root cellar. Sometimes they came with little darky children Lon would have liked to play with, but his father said the children didn't dare show themselves in daylight.

When Lon was twelve, he worked up the nerve to ask his father, "Do you work for the Underground Railroad?"

The Reverend gazed at his son by the light of a whale-oil lamp smoking on the parsonage desk. "Yes, I do. I'm what's called a conductor. This home is called a station. I've wondered when I should tell you."

"You think slavery's wrong."

"It is an abomination in the eyes of God."

"Cousin Dora says that what you do is dangerous."

The Reverend absently touched his left eye, brilliantly discolored by a purple and yellow bruise, a souvenir of his last trip. "Dora would like me to give it up. Silas thinks Africans are natural slaves, and the institution essential to the livelihood of all those misguided people down South. 'If we stop it,' they cry, 'what will we do? How will we survive?' I say find other work, or starve. Slavery is evil."

"Why, Pa? Aren't slaves happy?"

"No man can be happy in bondage. What if I chained you up so you couldn't go into the village for a licorice if you had the money? What if I kept you sweeping out the barn and cleaning the privy all the time?"

"I wouldn't like it."

"No, and that's slavery." The Reverend was silent a moment. "Come down to the cellar with me."

In the cool darkness, a black family ate from tin plates by candlelight. The Reverend asked the man to bare his back, and Lon saw a hideous mass of scars that glistened and smelled of strong ointment.

Mathias pointed to the scars. "That is slavery, Alonzo. Never forget the sight, or what it means. When we fight slavery, we do God's work."

* * *

One time Mathias Price came home on horseback, barely conscious, his arm in a bloody sling. Down on the Ohio River, Dora said, a slave-catcher had put a bullet in him. She was horrified. "It could have gone in his heart."

The national strife grew worse. People argued over the fugitive slave laws. Members of Congress attacked each other with words and even with canes. In "bleeding Kansas" men killed each other over slavery. Lon heard about something called secession, which Silas said was "coming for sure." Then one day in the winter of 1857, when Lon was eighteen, the Reverend returned from a trip with a high fever. Lying abed and alternately sweating and freezing, he explained to his son, "I waited six hours in an icy creek for the freight that was due from Kentucky."

"The freight?"

"The package. The shipment. Three Negroes. They never arrived. I don't know what happened. Oh, God have mercy, how I ache."

The doctor diagnosed pneumonia, which worsened. Without being told, Lon knew his beloved father was dying. One night when a blizzard howled, Mathias called him to the bedside. A lamp burned low. Lon kissed his father's stubbly cheek. It was hot as fire. Weak fingers sought his.

"Alonzo, I'm going to my reward. I will soon see whatever God has in store for us. You can make your way on your own. You're grown, you're smart, and there's goodness in you, so I have no fear. I want you to promise me that whatever you do with your life, you will always stand up for righteousness. Never compromise. Slavery must end. Work only for men who believe that. Abhor and fight those who don't. Promise me."

Lon's eyes filled with helpless tears. "I promise."

The feeble fingers squeezed again. The blizzard tore a shutter off the house with a crash. When the lamp went out, Lon stayed at the bedside. Soon after, with day breaking and the storm quieting, the feeble hand he held went limp.

Silas took charge of Lon. He was almost gleeful about giving the boy long hours of grueling labor on the Filson farm. Whenever Lon's work didn't satisfy Silas, the older man marched him to the barn and took a long hickory wand to his bare backside. Lon endured the punishments and the drudgery until the day Silas whipped him so hard his buttocks bled. Lying on his belly that night, he was struck with a new thought. He was no better than a slave. Slaves were treated the way Silas Filson treated him.

He thought of turning all the livestock out of the barn and setting fire to it. He couldn't bring himself to do it because he suspected that somewhere, somehow, the Reverend would be watching. So he just stole away up the moonlit pike to Dayton with a few possessions tied in a yellow bandanna. From Dayton he went to Chicago, a city rapidly becoming the beef, wheat, and rail center of the nation.

He found work mopping floors in a hotel, then unloaded canvas-covered wheat wagons at a grain elevator. His shortest job was night watchman at one of the abattoirs lining the lakeshore of the booming city. In a week the stenches and the bloody slaughter of the dumb cattle and swine drove him to quit.

He hired onto a work gang that maintained track in the yards of the Illinois Central railroad. It was brutal work, but it was outdoors, in the vigorous, progressive atmosphere of shuttling locomotives and freight cars loaded with grain and produce and manufactured goods. One day a vice president of the line, a Mr. McClellan, made an inspection tour with a smaller, more severe companion who seemed interested in testing the strength of locks and chains on freight cars. Lon asked his foreman who the man was. "Runs some new kind of private police agency. The line has him on contract to protect the yards and rolling stock."

That was all Lon needed. He saved every penny, slowly accumulated better clothes in a box under his narrow cot in the dank dormitory where he roomed with drunkards, drifters, and others of disreputable character. He associated with none of them.

When he had saved enough and bought a secondhand suit, decent shoes, and a clean cravat, he went to the address of the Pinkerton police agency, a second-floor office on West Washington Street at Dearborn. He was directed to a Mr. Bangs, whom he asked for a job.

"No, we have nothing. Not unless you have police force experience."

"That's the kind of experience I want to get, sir."

"Sorry."

He went back twice more. Each time it was "Sorry." The fourth time, Mr. Bangs looked him up and down. "Here again, Mr. Price? Determination is a worthy trait. How old are you?"

"Nineteen. Almost twenty."

"Can you read and figure?"

"Absolutely."

Bangs narrowed his eyes, a critical inspection. "We need a records clerk. I will set you up to see Mr. Pinkerton." Lon's heart beat like a bass drum in an Independence Day parade.

"Yes, sir! I'm ready."

Bangs actually smiled at Lon's enthusiasm.

9

1858–1860

Allan Pinkerton had clean, manicured nails, a precise part in his hair, a perfect knot in his cravat. Maybe Lon was just scared, but he felt like he was conversing with a block of ice. Pinkerton asked a few brusque questions to determine that Lon could read and figure and had ambitions to be a detective. Then he said, "Is Chicago your home?"

"No, sir. Southern Ohio. My father was a Methodist minister there after he left Scotland. He died last year. He caught pneumonia helping escaped slaves."

"Very admirable. What part of Scotland?"

"Glasgow, sir."

"Have you heard of the Gorbals?"

"It's a terrible slum. My father was born there."

"So was I. Was your father ever a Chartist?"

"No, sir. He told me he believed in the movement's goals for poor working people, but he said the Chartists were too violent."

"Some were not—the so-called moral force faction. I was a physical force man. When machines replaced decent men who were left to rot on the streets, there was no recourse but violence. The law was chasing me when I left Scotland. I don't know as I ever met your father, but I might have if he bought a barrel or cask from William McCauley's cooperage. I was apprenticed there."

"I can't say if he did or not, sir." Lon swallowed and took the leap. "I really would like to work for you and learn this business. I've read all about the man who started the Paris police force."

"François Vidocq. A scoundrel, but a pioneer." Pinkerton inked his pen, scratched something on foolscap. "We'll engage you for a month's trial. If you're honest, diligent, and I find no serious faults in your character, we will accept you as a permanent employee."

Lon jumped out of his chair and shot his hand out so energetically, he almost upset the inkpot. For the first time, Pinkerton smiled as he shook hands. Maybe there was a real person inside the block of ice.

*   *   *

The agency routine excited and fascinated Lon. The Pinkerton office was a kind of theater. Operatives used disguises and played roles to carry out assignments. Sometimes they went armed but often they didn't, relying on quick thinking rather than force. The four female operatives supervised by Kate Warne never carried weapons.

Unvaryingly, Pinkerton was at his desk by seven. The English detective Pryce Lewis told Lon that the boss rose before daylight, took a cold bath and a long walk, and was on his way to work by half past six. Lon liked Lewis, a cultivated young man who'd sold books before joining the agency. They discussed literature on their lunch hour if Lewis wasn't busy on a case.

Several times a day Pinkerton marched out of his office to meet clients, summon operatives, pile reports on this or that desk. Pinkerton wrote reports that almost qualified as short novels. The employees joked about it, but never to his face.

Working as a clerk, Lon soon changed his mind about the boss. Pinkerton was not forbidding so much as firm. He followed a rigid work ethic and expected it of others. Though Pinkerton was humorless and straitlaced, Lon decided that Mathias Price would have liked him because of his devotion to the abolitionist cause.

By the fourth week Lon was in a state of nerves. He feared he'd be let go. He'd made no major mistakes, but no one had commented on his record keeping, favorably or otherwise. It was almost an anticlimax when Mr. Bangs approached Lon's desk at closing time on Saturday. "Price, you're to come in Monday, and every day thereafter. Mr. Pinkerton authorized it."

A thrill raced up Lon's back. He wasn't aware that Pinkerton had noticed him at all the past month. The agency symbol, the unblinking eye that saw everything, was appropriate.

With a permanent job Lon could afford better quarters. He rented a clean room in the house of a couple in the Irish patch across the Chicago River. He acquired a second, better suit and soon had his sights on a different job, that of a regular operative. He mentioned it to Bangs, and to several others, with no result.

Lon and Philo Greenglass got acquainted. Lon and the ex-policeman were completely different but they liked each other. Sledge quizzed Lon about books, table manners, geography, simple mathematics—all apparently missing from his boyhood education. Where Lon was restrained, Sledge was boisterous, with a reputation for roughness. He almost always went armed.

Dreary winter gripped Chicago. Mountains of snow piled up. When it melted, the streets ran like dirty rivers. The wind off Lake Michigan was fierce and biting. It was a dark, depressing time for everyone except Pinkerton, who seemed unusually animated toward the end of February 1859. No one knew why.

On Friday evening, March 11, Lon was still at work at half past seven, finishing up the payroll ledger. Pinkerton burst out of his office. "Where is everyone?" He checked his pocket watch. The silent desks, the single lamp burning near Lon's inkstand, answered him.

Pinkerton handed Lon a sealed envelope addressed to Colonel C. G. Hammond, the general superintendent of the Illinois Central. "I need this delivered immediately. If Hammond's at home, wait for his answer and bring it to me at my house." Pinkerton paused before going on. "I needn't have the answer in writing. I'm sure I can trust you. I am asking Hammond to provide a special railcar to carry some people to Canada. They could be in danger if they remain in Chicago. That's why I need Hammond's response right away."

Lon reached for his cap and woolen scarf as Pinkerton added, "You know where I live?"

"Adams Street, near Franklin." Lon had never been invited to the house, but everyone knew the location.

"I'll wait for you, even if it's midnight or later."

Another storm was raging. The wind blew stinging sleet almost horizontally. Lon was stiff and frozen by the time he reached the Hammond mansion. The colonel was home. He told Lon to warm himself at the parlor fireplace while he read the letter. Finished, he destroyed it in the flames.

"You may tell Mr. Pinkerton he'll have his special car by five p.m. tomorrow. Do you know who is traveling to Canada?" Lon shook his head. "It isn't my place to tell you, but if he does so, you'll understand the urgency."

Once more Lon set out through the dark, nearly deserted streets. Chicago lay under a white blanket that muffled sound and created a false sense of peace. A half hour's trudge brought him to the clapboard cottage where the boss lived with his wife, their two sons, and a small daughter. Through the oval glass of the door Lon saw a startling sight: two black youngsters darting across the hall, playing tag.

Pinkerton answered the bell. "You're very prompt. Step in, Joan has a kettle on the hob. I imagine you need some tea to thaw out."

Lon craved hot tea but politeness compelled him to say, "That isn't necessary, sir. I'm not cold."

"Oh? Your lips are naturally blue? You'll have tea, no argument. What is Hammond's answer?"

"The car will be ready by five tomorrow afternoon."

"Splendid. Joan, some tea for Mr. Price," Pinkerton called to the rear of the house. "Take off your boots and come meet our guests. I will trust you not to reveal to anyone that you saw them."

"No, sir," Lon said. Boots left behind, he followed the boss to the parlor with a feeling of puzzlement.

The first astonishing sights were eight black faces. The five men and three women wore poor but clean clothes on their backs and looks of shy friendliness on their faces. They clustered behind a tall, bearded white man in a black frock coat and string tie. Blue-gray eyes sunk into his craggy face gleamed with reflections of the hearth.

"These people have traveled six hundred miles in a covered wagon," Pinkerton explained as his wife brought a steaming cup of tea to Lon. Joan was a plain, warm woman, from Glasgow; Lon had met her once at the office. "They were protected at every step by this gentleman, Mr. Brown."

Lon almost spilled the tea. He recognized the white man from magazine engravings. He was in the presence of John Brown of Kansas, the man who had killed proslavery men at the famous Osawatomie fight. Brown was a national figure, a hero to many. Others called him a murderer.

"Mr. Brown's companions are former slaves. They are going with him to Canada."

"Where I have established my provisional government," Brown said with an unforgettable madness shining from his eyes. "Then I have important work to do in the East."

"I've been raising money for that work, and for provisions for the trip," Pinkerton said.

Lon met each of the escaped slaves but was so overwhelmed by their leader that he couldn't remember the names. When he was ready to leave, Brown took his hand in huge, gnarled fingers.

"Young man, lay in your tobacco, cotton, and sugar because I intend to raise the prices. My revolution will bring the South to its knees and purge its sin in blood."

Lon didn't fully understand the statement until months later, when Brown's small force attacked the government arsenal at Harpers Ferry, only to be captured by Marines from Washington led by Colonel R. E. Lee. Brown was put on trial. The South called him a madman, the North a saint and martyr. Pinkerton frantically raised money for his defense but it did no good. Brown was hanged, and the boss was in a bleak mood for weeks.

*　　*　　*

In April of 1860, senior operative Timothy Webster was assigned an embezzlement case in Indianapolis. Adam Roche, a pipe-smoking German, was to go with him but fell ill. No other operatives were available. Bangs remembered Lon's ambition and sent him along with the Englishman. Lon wasn't permitted to carry a gun.

On the southbound train, Webster explained the case in his clipped English accent. "Twenty thousand dollars has vanished from the bank that engaged us. The vice president, a Mr. Thor Knudsen, is suspected by his employers. It's our job to locate some or all of the money so Knudsen can be turned over to the authorities and charged."

"Why is he a suspect?"

"Behavior. Knudsen was always a man of regular habits, with a passion for perfection, neatness. Then his wife of many years passed away. He brought a young Swedish girl to his residence as housekeeper. An affair is suspected. The bank president says Knudsen has grown secretive, erratic in his work and manner. The housekeeper may have inspired and encouraged his thievery."

In Indianapolis, Webster grayed his hair with theatrical powder and they drove out to the village of Carmel on a sunny Saturday. Webster carried a document that looked official but wouldn't bear close inspection.

They climbed down from the buggy in the crushed-stone driveway of Knudsen's large white house. Hedges and tree branches were showing buds; a smell of spring earth sweetened the air. Hard to believe they were chasing a criminal.

Webster observed carriages in both bays of the stable at the rear of the property. "We may have caught him home. I'd have preferred it otherwise. Keep a sharp lookout inside. Watch for anything unusual."

With the confidence of an experienced actor making an entrance, Webster marched up the porch steps and knocked loudly. A stocky young woman with a wide red mouth and enormous breasts under her white apron opened the door. Webster tipped his hat.

"Good morning, miss. I am Mr. Bainbridge from the office of the county building inspector. This is my colleague Mr. Harris. We're here for a routine inspection of this residence. Our credentials." Webster showed the official-looking document for all of three seconds. "Is the owner at home? A Mr. Knudsen, I believe?"

"Not here," the young woman said in accented English.

"Too bad. We'll try to make short work of this." Webster stepped across the sill, forcing her back before she could object. Lon noticed a small framed landscape hanging at a slightly crooked angle above the hallway umbrella stand.

Webster flashed a charming smile as he looked around. He indicated the dining room. "In there, Mr. Harris, if you please. I'll inspect the parlor. You're welcome to follow us, miss. This is really quite routine."

"Hurry up," she exclaimed, almost strangling on the words. She was frightened by guilt and fear of discovery, Lon guessed. That didn't mean they'd find evidence.

Every piece of dining room furniture was correctly placed and free of dust. Lon felt he was inspecting a museum. He went back to the parlor where Webster was jotting notes in a little book. "Everything satisfactory," Lon said.

"And here also. Let's inspect the—what is it?" Lon was staring at a portrait of an older woman in a dark dress.

"That's the second crooked picture. There's another in the hall. Everything else is in perfect order."

"Maybe I'll have a look." As Webster approached the portrait, the housekeeper bolted, crying, "Thorvald!"

Webster pulled the picture from its hook, turned it over. The brown paper backing had been slit along one edge. "Something was hidden in here and removed in a hurry. Check the other picture."

Lon heard a commotion upstairs: pounding footsteps, a man's angry voice. He inspected the landscape and ran back to the parlor. "Same thing. Do you think he hid the cash in the pictures?"

"Yes, and I'll wager there's more in others he didn't have time to cut." They heard noise and jumped into the hall. A stout man in his sixties was lunging down the stairs, his vest and collarless white shirt unbuttoned, his thin gray hair disarrayed. Lon and Webster were in the direct line of fire of his shotgun.

"Get out of my house," he yelled, taking aim.

"Knudsen, don't be a fool, you'll only harm yourself further," Webster said. Lon groped behind him for a small enameled ginger jar, whipped it over his head in a throw that broke it against Knudsen's forehead. Webster dove to the floor. Knudsen reeled against the stair rail, accidentally firing both barrels of the shotgun into the ceiling. Lath and plaster showered down. Upstairs, the housekeeper shrieked like a madwoman.

Webster tackled Thor Knudsen, who was flabby and no match for him. Lon cut open the backing of another small oil in the dining room and pulled out bills of large denomination. Webster held the shotgun on the sobbing banker while Lon ran for the authorities.

"You could have been killed," Webster said to Lon later.

"But I wasn't."

"Don't take chances like that too often. It isn't professional."

"I hear you, Mr. Webster."

"Tim," he said, a comradely arm across Lon's shoulder.

Back in Chicago, Pinkerton called Lon in. The boss congratulated him on his keen observation and quick thinking, which Webster had generously reported. Pinkerton gave Lon a handshake and an immediate promotion to operative. In the next few months Lon was almost too busy to see that sectional strife was pushing the country closer to a final confrontation over slavery.

10

March 1861

"Papa, I can't talk, rehearsal's at five."

"But I have excellent news." The major had bounded into the house with greater energy and zest than he'd exhibited for months. His boots were dusty from walking, but his old sky blue military greatcoat and cape were brushed and presentable. The monocle he kept in a cigar box was squeezed into his left eye. "A position. A clerkship with the Department of War in President's Park. I report next week."

Hanna leaped into Siegel's arms and hugged him. "That's wonderful. How did it happen? Didn't you apply there before?"

"Twice. I was treated like a cur. This is a new administration."

"Who hired you, the new secretary?"

"No, not Mr. Cameron. Two assistants. They liked my military background. The secretary has none. There are jokes that his greatest experience consists of stuffing ballot boxes in Pennsylvania. Lincoln put him in the cabinet because he helped secure the nomination. I don't care if he's Satan himself so long as he pays me adequately and—*ach*, Hanna. Your clothes. Why do you dress that way?"

The major was reacting to her shapeless gray wool coat and narrow trousers, castoffs given her by the wife of Mr. Spence, the black porter next door. Under her cotton chemise she'd wrapped and pinned strips of clean rag to flatten her bosom, and she'd cut her hair with old, dull shears, leaving it boyishly ragged around the ears.

"It helps me get into the part. I play a girl disguised as the page of Duke Orsino."

"Those theatricals, your friends, they influence you in strange ways." Shaking his head, he peeled off his old gauntlets. "I met a most interesting man while waiting for my appointment. A Mr. Baker, also seeking a position. In San Francisco, California, he led an informal military force he called vigilantes. They hung anyone who—"

"Papa, I must go. I'm very happy for you."

"For us. We can remove ourselves from this neighborhood of swinish Negroes. Be careful downtown, the city is a madhouse."

And had been for days, in preparation for Lincoln's inauguration on Monday, March 4. The hotels were full. Hundreds who couldn't find rooms slept in doorways or simply staggered up and down the streets all night. One paper said the National Hotel was serving twelve hundred meals a day. But she really hadn't appreciated the extent of the crowding until she reached Pennsylvania Avenue. Work gangs were scraping and raking the street for the entire length of Mr. Lincoln's ride from the Capitol to the Executive Mansion. People milled on the sidewalk. She suspected many came from Illinois because they wore coarse dark clothing and gawked shamelessly. The manager at the Canterbury said the prairie men were notoriously cheap, never leaving tips.

Hanna saw others, rougher men who swigged from bottles or flasks and pushed anyone who got in their way, women included. The town was flooded with the Baltimore plug-uglies come to disrupt the inauguration. When one stepped on her shoe, she glared and cursed him in her native language. He wasn't intimidated. He called her a filthy name and swaggered on.

A young man emerging from the National Hotel was mobbed by people with autograph albums. Hanna recognized Lincoln's college-age son from a lithograph she'd seen. Some wag had dubbed him the Prince of Rails. Bob Lincoln signed his name without complaint.

A bright flash drew her eye to the roof of a building she was passing. The March sun reflected from the field glasses of an Army officer observing the crowds. The director of her play said there would be sharpshooters along the parade route, because of death threats. According to one rumor, twenty ruffians from Texas armed with bowie knives were planning to slash a path through the District cavalry guarding the inaugural carriage and stab the President to death.

Other people said New York was about to declare itself a free city in order to trade with both governments. That President Lincoln would immediately call a peace conference with delegates from Montgomery, capital of the new Confederacy. That blacks were awaiting Monday in order to pay back their owners and employers. It was this kind of rumor that had sparked a regrettable exchange with Margaret when they last took supper together:

"My brother, Cicero, swears that the Negro housemaid of a friend said she was going to slap her mistress's face and spit on her as soon as Lincoln's in office."

"Margaret, how can you believe such nonsense?"

"I'm only telling you what I heard. My father says that once Lincoln and the black Republicans are in power, blood will run."

"What do you say?"

"As little as possible. I hate the idea."

"You can't sit on a fence rail forever. There's going to be fighting. I wish I could enlist. I wish I were a man, so I could help the cause."

"Your cause, not mine," Margaret said with obvious irritation.

Redness rushed to Hanna's cheeks. Both women looked away. Their waiter, a white man like all waiters in the fine hotels and restaurants, saw a spat in progress and went to another table.

Hanna laid her hand on Margaret's sleeve, a gesture of conciliation. Hanna's nails were blunt, broken in places, in contrast to the buffed perfection of Margaret's. Margaret spoke first.

"That was rude and thoughtless. Forgive me?"

Hanna said, "Of course."

"We mustn't get so heated. We're friends."

"Yes, indeed. Forever."

But friends, if they have character, take a stand, or they should, Hanna thought. Just as families, states, and the nation were dividing rancorously, so it was with Margaret. Hanna hated to see it and yet sensed a certain inevitability. They parted politely, without their usual display of affection.

* * *

Hanna's little company of amateur actors performed on a curtained platform in the basement of an Episcopal church behind the Capitol. The rector enjoyed theatricals and allowed the group to rent the basement so long as they kept it tidy. The church congregation teemed with Southerners and those who sympathized with them.

As usual, the actors were running about and cackling like barnyard chickens when she arrived. Today was their first rehearsal in costume. The director was a talented but rather prissy shoe salesman named Derek Fowley.

When Hanna walked into the dressing room, Zephira Comfort was in her underwear, struggling with her corset strings. "Oh, bother. Would you do me up, dear?"

"Certainly, dear." Zephira Comfort was fat, with bosoms like cannonballs. She was a poor actress, but Derek lived with her, so she was always cast.

Hanna loved the part of Viola, one of Shakespeare's women played by young men in Elizabethan times. Shipwrecked on the Illyrian coast, Viola disguises herself as a soft-cheeked male to protect herself from harm. Malvolio describes her as "not yet old enough for a man, nor young enough for a boy." Viola is soon in service as Cesario, page to Orsino, who sends her to the lady Olivia to woo her in his place. In the fifth and last scene of Act 1 Hanna made her first entrance in page's finery—a green silk coat and knee breeches, with tiny yellow flowers edging the coat lapels.

Hanna liked the snug feel of her white hose, the scent of her powdered wig. Zephira Comfort played Olivia in a heavy veil, until the text required her to reveal herself to the eloquent page.

Zephira clasped hands at her bosom and gushed. "How does he love me?"

Hanna's answer was more contained, realistic, and as a result, believable. "With adorations, fertile tears, with groans that thunder love, with sighs of fire! . . . If I did love you in my master's flame, with such a suffering, such a deadly life, in your denial I would find no sense."

At the end of the scene Derek leaped up from his stool, clapping. "Zeffie, you are superb. Don't let down. Dear little Hanna—that's a handsome outfit, but threadbare. A seam under the left arm is gaping like a chasm. Have the wardrobe girl sew it up."

"Yes, Derek."

"I do compliment your performance. If I met you as a stranger, I'd think you were a man. Pitching your voice lower helps immeasurably."

"Thank you, Derek."

"Five minutes, everyone. Then we press on."

Hanna went outside. The pale sun was sunk behind the unfinished dome of the Capitol to the west. Heavy shadows clogged the street. She heard horses approaching at a gallop.

She leaned against the church's brick wall and put a match to a handmade cigarette. Hanna liked the smell and sensation of tobacco. She spat a flake off her tongue as a half dozen cavalry, booted and spurred, charged through the purple gloom. Studying the way the darkness and their baggy uniforms tended to blur their individuality, she was struck by a new thought.

If I'm so convincing as a man, why couldn't I dress as one? Follow a regiment into the field? I'd like that. And Papa would have his soldier after all.

She was excited, though not a little fearful of the potential risks. But she was a clever actress, wasn't she? If she didn't strip naked, why couldn't she carry it off? She was so absorbed in the fantasy, she didn't hear Derek's call for Act 2. She had to be escorted inside by the grumpy stage manager.

11

March 1861

Inauguration day came in sunny but chilly. A gusty wind nipped the cheeks and numbed exposed hands. The military presence was enormous. District cavalry to accompany the parade and militia infantry to guard the route were supplemented by companies of regulars forming up in F Street, north of the Avenue, as Lon and Sledge started for the Capitol at half past nine. Militiamen with rifles perched on Avenue rooftops like so many vultures waiting for a corpse.

Felton, the railroad executive, had hired the Pinkerton detectives as a special patrol for the inauguration. It was a private act of patriotism. General Scott was in charge of security and wouldn't have authorized civilian intrusion. Old Fuss and Feathers lived on I Street. There, it was said, a French caterer supplied all his meals. Lon figured Scott ate five or six a day, because he was grotesquely obese, his arms and legs swollen by dropsy. He had to be hoisted into his carriage by noncoms. At seventy-five he was too old for supreme command, but he had it.

"Don't seem very happy, these people," Sledge said as they moved past civilians already crowding the curb. Lon had noticed the same thing. There was noise—boys hawking papers, vendors waving lithographed portraits of Lincoln—but not a lot of enthusiasm. He saw anger on some faces, anxiety on many more. Shutters on shops and upper windows were closed, probably as a protest.

They walked around the Capitol on the south side, to the east portico. Several hundred people were already waiting behind the reserved chairs set in front of the flag-draped platform. Under the platform, Pinkerton said, fifty armed soldiers would be hiding.

Lon and Sledge found Tim Webster in the crowd. He assigned Sledge to the northeast quadrant of the park, Lon to the southeast.

People shivered and complained about the wind. Lon turned up the velvet collar of his secondhand coat and held onto his black felt hat. He drifted, studying faces, watching for anything that might signal a demented person. He saw no one like that but still felt nervous. Why must an assassin look strange? Why couldn't he be handsome, or simply ordinary?

A few athletic types had climbed the park's bare trees. City police swarmed on the grounds, and a soldier with a rifle looked out of every window of both wings of the Capitol. Would any of them be fast enough to stop a determined sharpshooter?

The crowd grew to several thousand. Shortly after twelve, distant music reached them; the Marine band, marching up the Avenue. Lincoln and Buchanan had left Willard's in their open carriage, surrounded by their guards. According to the latest rumor, if the new President wasn't assassinated before he was sworn in, a squadron of Virginians would gallop across the Long Bridge and abduct him from tonight's inaugural ball.

Lon's eyes kept moving, searching for signs of trouble. Walking backward, he stumbled into a young woman and knocked a book from her gloved hand.

"Ma'am, I'm terribly sorry."

"I should hope so."

She was about his age, tall and handsome, with sparkling dark eyes and a full, rounded bust. Her clothes spoke of money and good taste. Over her skirt she wore a plush pelisse of dark amber. Her matching bonnet was trimmed with ostrich plumes. She was an inch taller than Lon.

He knelt and swooped up the book. *The Woman in White.* He brushed bits of winter grass from the cover.

"I haven't read this but I hear Wilkie Collins is a good writer. He and my favorite author, Charles Dickens, are friends."

She stared.

"I hear there's a detective in this novel."

She stared at his hat. Caught short, he swept it off. "Here you are, then. My compliments."

She took the book. "Thank you, but I don't need compliments from a Yankee."

Annoyed, he snapped at her. "What about accepting compliments from an American?"

Lowered lashes hid a flash of amusement. "My, you're full of sass. What does a man like you do for a living, may I ask? Slave in one of those dark, filthy factories under the illusion you're free?"

"No, and let's not start on how plantation slaves are better off than wage slaves, it's a specious argument. A factory hand can walk away. A slave walks away, they whip him, brand him, or worse." He should have ended it there, but her challenging eyes and haughty chin provoked him. "I suppose you disapprove of our new President too."

"I do. He's nothing but an uncouth rustic from Illinois."

"I'm from Illinois."

"Really. It's no recommendation. If Abraham Lincoln had so much as a thimbleful of common sense, he'd preach conciliation, not conflict."

"Not while the South's hell-bent on tearing up the Constitution to protect its peculiar institution. You secesh think your way's the only—"

"Sorry I left you so long, my dear." An older man who'd come up behind her grasped her arm. "Ran into an old friend. Do you know this gentleman?" The man had an affected way of speaking. Not British exactly, but crisp enough to establish his superiority and patronize a listener. He was smartly turned out in a long coat with brown velvet lapels, stand-up collar, bow tie, top hat, gloves, and a walking stick.

"No, Donal. The gentleman bumped into me and knocked my book on the ground. At least he had the courtesy to retrieve it."

"Well, thank you very much, sir," Donal said in a faintly sarcastic way that withheld sincerity. The man moved the young woman away, guiding with a firm hand on her arm. Lon wondered how such an attractive girl could be taken with a man with gray hair and a weak chin. He was probably rich. As she left, the young woman glanced over her shoulder. Lon couldn't say whether the look was inquisitive or scornful.

What galled him most wasn't her sharp tongue; matter of fact, he rather liked her spunk. He was infuriated with himself because he'd given antagonism right back, instead of trying to charm her into liking him. The moment he saw her, admired the curve of her cheek, the shimmer of her hair, he wanted her to like him.

Don't waste your time. That's a road you'll never travel.

Too bad. He couldn't say he'd fallen in love with the attractive stranger in such a short time, but something in his young man's heart had opened to the possibility.

Lon had never been in love. He'd enjoyed brief, superficial flirtations with a number of young women, and three episodes of sex. The last time, Sledge had taken him to a Chicago brothel and paid for the girl. Lon found it a mechanical, even sad experience. He didn't tell Sledge, because Sledge would have scorned him as a bookish romantic.

Walking away, he saw a colorful paper bookmark lying on the ground where she'd been standing. *Another good book from SHILLINGTON'S.*

He'd visited the popular bookstore. He picked up the bookmark, certain that it hadn't fallen out of the Wilkie Collins. Why had she dropped it? He searched for her in the crowd, as if by finding her he might find the answer. She was gone.

And he didn't even know her name.

He tucked the bookmark into an inner pocket and went back to work.

*   *   *

Shouts and commotion on the north side of the building signaled the arrival of the official party, bound for the Senate chamber and the swearing-in of Vice President Hamlin. Presently the official party of congressmen, Supreme Court justices, friends, and family emerged from the rotunda and came down the steps to the platform. There was Lincoln, sad-eyed as before, disappointingly ordinary. He took a front-row chair, his gold-knobbed cane across his knees. Senator Baker of Oregon stood behind a cheap little table to introduce him. Lon was fascinated by old Taney, the robed chief justice, seated to Baker's left. Taney had written the famous Dred Scott decision saying slaves were not citizens, therefore not entitled to protection of the law. Lon disliked the man without knowing anything else about him.

At the close of the introduction Lincoln stepped forward. He acknowledged the applause and laid his cane across the table. He took off his hat, moved as if to set it down, hesitated. A few snickered at his awkwardness. Up jumped Senator Douglas, the Little Giant. Smiling, Douglas took Lincoln's tall hat from him. He sat down with the hat held carefully on his knee. The crowd liked the symbolism of last fall's political opponents united.

The President's voice was no different on this occasion. It was thin, high-pitched, and, Lon hated to say, disagreeable. Yet Lincoln's rhetoric slowly drew him in.

Lincoln raised the issue of secession, then immediately said such a thing was impossible; the Union was perpetual. It could not be dissolved by individual states. The secession ordinances were null and void.

"And I therefore consider that, in view of the Constitution and the laws, the Union is unbroken. To the extent of my ability, I shall take care, as the Constitution itself expressly enjoins upon me, that the laws of the Union be faithfully executed in all the states."

The crowd held so still, you could almost hear the clouds sailing across the sky. A man behind Lon whispered, "Damn fool means to go to war if the South don't retreat."

Gravely, Lincoln told them there would be no violence or bloodletting unless it was forced on the national government. "In your hands, my dissatisfied fellow countrymen, and not in mine, is the momentous issue of civil war. The government will not assail you. You can have no conflict without yourselves being the aggressors. You have no oath registered in heaven to destroy the government, while I have the most solemn one to preserve, protect, and defend it."

His melancholy eyes held the crowd. "Though passion may have strained, it must not break our bonds of affection. The mystic chords of memory, stretching from every battlefield and patriot grave, to every living heart and hearthstone all over this broad land, will yet swell the chorus of the Union, when again touched, as surely they will be, by the better angels of our nature."

After the applause, Justice Taney brought out a Bible. He swore in the President and it was done. Without violence, thankfully. The phrase "bonds of affection" lingered in Lon's mind along with a sense of loss.

*   *   *

Before Allan Pinkerton and his men left Washington on Wednesday, Lon called at Shillington's bookstore. After almost a year as an operative, he could present a story convincingly.

"A young woman dropped a copy of *The Woman in White* in President's Park on Monday. I found it but she disappeared before I could hand it back. I'd like to return it if she wasn't an out-of-town visitor, but I don't know her name or where to find her. A bookmark from your store told me she must have bought it here."

Lon's guileless expression and his blue eyes overcame any suspicion on the clerk's part. He fetched a tin box. "We sold quite a few of the Collins since it was published last year, but we keep cards on local customers. Will you describe her?"

Lon did. The clerk found her card. "Miss Miller." Lon had trained himself to read handwriting upside down. First name Margaret. The clerk's thumb hid the address.

"From Washington?"

"Baltimore. But her family keeps a second residence in Franklin Square." The clerk showed him the number. Something jogged the clerk's memory hard enough to bring a smile. "She's not afraid to talk politics with some of our gentleman customers. She's a hot secesh."

"That's Baltimore," Lon agreed, tipping his hat.

He dashed away and after dark went to Franklin Square in a rainstorm, only to stand soaked and disappointed on the stoop. Not a light showed anywhere. He backed down the steps with rain dripping from his hat brim. She must have left. He was leaving in the morning. Damn. No chance to meet her again or even put his toe in the door.

*   *   *

On the westbound Baltimore & Ohio, the passenger car was overheated, the weather outside damp and dismal. Windows steamed up. Pryce Lewis sat next to Lon, going through the Washington and New York papers. "By God, they're rattling the sword down South. Listen to this from Arkansas. 'If declaring the Union perpetual means coercion, then Lincoln's inaugural means war.' The *Montgomery Advertiser* said, 'War, war, and nothing less than war will satisfy the abolition chief.' I fancy we're in for— Lon, what on earth are you doing? Who is Margaret?"

Lon smeared away the name traced in the steam on the glass. "Just a lady I met at the inaugural." He rested his chin in his palm and stared through the hole in the steam at rain falling on the winter woods. They looked as forlorn as he felt.

12

April 1861

The mob's blood was up, excited by blue militia uniforms, rifles with bayonets at shoulder arms. Margaret rammed an elbow into whoever was crushing her from behind. "For God's sake, stop pushing."

She slipped, would have fallen to be trampled under heels and hobnails if she hadn't held fast to someone's shoulder. She could scarcely breathe. She was trapped in a heaving mass of people who smelled of whiskey and anger. They were throwing things. Rocks, chunks of pavement.

Seven cars carrying soldiers had been pulled through town to the B&O Camden Station. Then the mob dropped a ship's anchor on the tracks, blocking three more cars. Young men of the Sixth Massachusetts jumped off the cars and marched in a lane between ranks of Chief Kane's police. Yesterday, companies of the Twenty-fifth Pennsylvania had passed through with only minor trouble. Cicero had promised more action today. She'd come down to Pratt Street to see the excitement.

The rain of missiles and obscenities continued. The militiamen looked to their officers for a command to defend themselves. A brickbat flung from behind hit Margaret's shoulder. Someone fired a gun. An elderly civilian fell down. The mob screamed.

A man near her drew a pistol. Other guns went off. A soldier flew back against a policeman, an inky red splotch blossoming on his overcoat. A captain clutched his face as a sheet of blood ran down. The gunfire became a din.

She put her hands to her ears. She still heard it. She closed her eyes a moment; she still saw smoky Pratt Street, soldiers and civilians falling. She ground her palms against her ears but the din only grew worse. A soldier with a fixed bayonet charged her, his pink face wild with rage. She threw herself backward but a wall of bodies held her. "Secesh slut," the boy screamed, stabbing her . . .

"*No!*"

Thrashing and crying out, Margaret awoke.

She realized she was safe. Trembling, but safe in her dark bedroom. Her nightdress was soaked through. In her dream she'd relived what she'd witnessed on Pratt Street yesterday, Friday, one week after the Charleston batteries had fired on Sumter, blasting away all hope of peace. On Monday, Lincoln had proclaimed an insurrection and called for seventy-five thousand state militia to defend Washington. What she had hoped would never happen to disturb the peaceful tenor of her life had come after all.

She looked at a clock on the mantel of the bedroom fireplace. Half-past nine. She threw on her robe and rushed downstairs. A foyer table was stacked with secession cards and broadsides. A copy of a two-page special edition of the *Baltimore Independent* lay at her father's place in the dining room. MURDER OF BALTIMOREANS BY FOREIGN SOLDIERY! THIRTEEN CITIZENS SHOT—FIVE REPORTED KILLED! OUR STREETS DRENCHED WITH BLOOD BY LINCOLN'S HIRELINGS!

Simms heard her moving about, pushed open the swing door from the kitchen pantry. "Breakfast, Miss Miller?" The elderly black man was solemn, depressed as she was by events of the past week.

"Just coffee, please. I have no appetite. Father and Cicero have gone?"

"To a big secession meeting in Monument Square, then some others, don't know where. Mr. Miller, he's het up, gray as a ghost. I fear for his health. Best you don't go out. When Clarissa come to work, she told me they're still rioting. It's terrible. It's all just so terrible."

Margaret threw a lock of rebellious dark hair off her forehead. "How was my brother behaving?"

"Coffee be here right away." Simms backed out of sight as if he hadn't heard the question.

The chicory-laced coffee tasted bitter. She couldn't swallow it. She'd come home a week ago Thursday, one of her regular visits, and been caught in Baltimore by the outbreak of war. Donal was in New York again. She had decided to stay in Baltimore on the assumption that it might be calmer than Washington. The assumption was wrong. Within hours, the mobs were parading. Secession pennants streamed from masts in the harbor. Fireworks displays celebrated the war.

Maryland's governor, Hicks, issued a proclamation calling for order. The response was derision; defiance. Well, Baltimore was known as Mobtown. Lovers of literature said the mysterious Mr. Poe had died at the hands of a mob during the municipal elections of 1849.

Margaret rested her elbows on the polished table and pressed her palms to her eyes. She recalled the broad-shouldered stranger in President's Park. He was puffed up with Yankee righteousness; quick to answer her gibes with some of his own. Thoroughly objectionable young man.

Then why had she thought of him often in the past weeks?

Well, he said he read novels. She knew a few Baltimore boys who did that, but they were fops. He had lovely blue eyes, but it was hardly a trait unique in the world. She couldn't explain it. He was the wrong sort, on the wrong side, and yet he stirred her somehow. No doubt he intended to muster in and kill Southern boys, and she'd never see him again.

She fretted about her father. Calhoun Miller had hardly slept the past two weeks, writing increasingly angry editorials and receiving strange visitors in the middle of the night. Virginians, he said, pumping funds into the state to help print the secession literature. Several times Miller had lost his temper with her over trivialities, something he never did. Either the secession effort was failing or going too slowly.

Her brother meanwhile hummed and bustled about the house with unusual good cheer. He even told her the name of his secret group, the Knights of Liberty. He said they would resist the Northern aggressors not with platitudes and printed material, but with explosives, flammable oil, stolen arms. Cicero liked the terrible upheaval.

She feared for his safety in the streets, but she feared even more for the safety and well-being of her right-minded father. When night fell, neither he nor Cicero had come home.

* * *

The warehouse smelled of fish and the damp wool clothing of the two dozen men gathered there. When another arrived, a burly doorkeeper stopped him. Passwords in Latin were exchanged.

A small table held two lamps, the only illumination. Crossed sabers and a Bible lay between them. Six feet behind the table a state flag hung from a beam. Cicero Miller stood to one side, eyes darting over the band of righteous men listening to his father speak.

Calhoun Miller's linen looked soiled. His eyes were gritty with weariness. He'd addressed the public rally at the municipal monument to George Washington, then two other meetings, before this one. Cicero maintained a sober expression but inwardly he was elated. For the first time, events had persuaded Calhoun Miller to speak to the Knights.

"Last year, with pride and hope," Miller said, "I took part in the nominating convention of the new Constitutional Union party. Before the November elections, we presented ourselves as the alternative to the Douglas Democrats, Southern Democrats, and the despised Republicans. Ours was the party and platform of compromise and moderation."

Hearing that, some of the Knights grumbled. In the harbor a ship's bell rang. A wagon horse clip-clopped outside, then stopped.

"Our candidates, Mr. Bell and Mr. Everett, were pledged to reject the radical philosophies of both sides. We wished to preserve the Union"—someone objected with a loud "No!"— "but also to protect Southern interests. The ascension of Mr. Lincoln has shown me we were in error. There is no spirit of compromise on the other side, so there can be no moderation on ours." Cicero watched a pair of rats dart through the darkness behind his father.

"The institution of slavery has prevailed in Maryland for

generations, and we proudly say we are Southern in practice, Southern in temperament." Cicero led the applause. "Our timid governor has finally addressed the crisis by ordering rail bridges destroyed north of the city, so no more foreign troops can pass. But much more is required. Maryland must join her sister states of the Confederacy. I charge you as patriotic citizens to make it happen, speedily, using any and all necessary methods, before the egalitarian hordes enthroned in Washington overwhelm us. Peace is no longer possible. Restraint is no longer possible. Very well. I prefer to die defending the Constitution as revered and maintained by the South than to live one hour under what has been revealed as the fanatical tyranny of the North."

"What we supposed to do, kill anybody who don't want to secede?"

Cicero turned, identifying a man named Scully, who'd recently joined the Knights. Bill Topping, a stouter man who'd joined at the same time, stood next to him.

Calhoun Miller said, "I reluctantly answer yes, if that be necessary."

"Can't go along, sorry."

Cicero's crippled foot scraped as he moved to confront the naysayer. "You took an oath of loyalty when you joined this organization. You can't go back on it whenever it suits you."

Scully said, "Wrong. You men are inciting to riot. This meeting is over."

"Who the hell are you to issue edicts?"

"You know my name. John Scully." He pulled a pistol from his jacket. "Of the Pinkerton organization. Bill, call the men from the police wagon."

Topping rushed for the warehouse door. He had a gun too. Voices clamored:

"Bastard said he was from Alabama."

"How'd he get the passwords?"

Cicero's was loudest: "Seize them."

Topping rolled back the door on its rusty track. In the street, haloed by lamplight, Baltimore police stepped from behind their wagon. Enraged, Cicero limped to the table, blew out one lamp. Someone fired a shot that struck the other one, shattering the chimney and spattering hot oil. Policemen charged into the warehouse swinging clubs.

One of the Yankee detectives fired shots; one of the Knights fired back. Instantly there was a pandemonium of shouts, weapons going off, men running, fire spreading from the lamp on the floor. Cicero dragged himself to his father.

"We have to get out. That way." Practically at his ear, another gun went off. Miller looked startled. Then he fell.

*   *   *

"Simms." The voice downstairs belonged to Margaret's brother. "Simms, you lazy nigger, get up here!"

Margaret threw her book aside and ran downstairs as Simms stumbled up from his cellar room, emerging through a small door under the staircase.

"Get dressed, get the carriage." Cicero was leaning against the wall, disheveled, sooty-faced. Margaret froze at the sight of a long smear of red on the wallpaper behind him.

"Why do you need the carriage at this time of night?" she said.

"To bring a body back to the house."

"Body? Oh my God, not—"

"Yes. Police broke up our meeting. A man who pretended to hail from Alabama sold us out. He was really a Yankee detective. I don't know who fired the shot at Pa, but they killed him."

"I'm going with you."

Simms lashed the horse through smoky streets where ragged boys stoned pedestrians and set off squibs that hissed and fumed. Bonfires burned unattended, consuming fixtures from looted stores, discarded clothing, an overturned pony cart. Bands of rioters fled past the rockaway like hounds on a hunt.

In the wharf warehouse, two city patrolmen guarded the supine body of Calhoun Miller. Margaret sank to her knees beside her father. She touched his white face. "No, Papa. Oh, no."

"Mayor Brown's coming to inspect," a policeman said.

Cicero snarled, "Let him." Brown was antislavery. "For Christ's sake stand back, where's your respect? This is Calhoun Miller, the newspaper editor. He was shot down at a peaceful gathering. Help me roll him in the blanket, Simms."

In the rockaway with the sad heap of Miller's corpse lying on the opposite seat, Margaret wanted to weep and rant, but she wouldn't allow herself.

Cicero clutched her hand. "They'll pay for what they did, I'll make sure."

Margaret looked into her brother's gleaming eyes. He might be half-mad. But the murder had made them allies. She squeezed his clammy fingers.

"So will I. We'll both make them pay. I was a fool to say the struggle didn't matter."

Part Two

SPIES

13

May 1861

Washington was a carnival or a cesspool, according to your politics. Margaret thought it the latter. After a perilous April week of railroad bridges burned and telegraph wires cut, a week that had left the city trembling with fear of invasion, the wires were spliced, the trestles repaired, and southbound trains again delivered soldiers to the capital.

She thought of them as Attila's Huns. They sneered at the muddy, dilapidated city they were called to defend. They slept and built cook fires in government buildings. They disfigured open spaces with sprawling tent villages. They were serviced by greedy sutlers and enterprising soiled doves arriving on every train from the West. They held target practice on the Smithsonian grounds with no thought for civilians close by. Whether ruffianly Zouaves from Brooklyn fire engine companies or kid-glove playboys from the Seventh New York, they savagely beat citizens for any fancied slur or slight.

They drilled, drummed, and bugled at all hours. They brawled and rioted in the taverns and the streets until the provost guard subdued them with fire hoses. They presented regimental band concerts under the trees of President's Park. They protected the Potomac bridges with mounted sentries. They refused to dig latrines and urinated and defecated wherever they chose. With its fouled canals and sewage-ridden river, Washington had always smelled; now it stank unspeakably.

On a mild May afternoon, Margaret left Franklin Square in her smart little piano-box buggy. When the buggy stalled behind a broken-down dray, one of the Yankee vulgarians lurched off the curb to accost her, heedless of her black bombazine dress, black gloves, black hat.

The man had yellow chevrons on his blue flannel shirt. His

breath smelled like gin-soaked garbage. He laid a hand on her leg and asked wouldn't she sleep with a defender of freedom?

She slashed his cheek with the buggy whip and drove through a narrow lane that opened next to the dray.

With a shaky hand, she returned the whip to its socket. A thread of bright blood stained the shaft. She hadn't known so much accumulated rage was still buried within her.

She tied the horse to a ring post in front of the brick manse at Sixteenth and I Streets. Her face, powdered carelessly, resembled a grotesque white mask in the sunshine. She noticed unweeded flower beds. The Negro gardener who tended them must have abandoned his job.

When the door opened, Margaret said, "Rose, do you know the Yankees killed my father?"

"Yes, I heard. I am so terribly sorry."

"I'm here because I've been indifferent to important things. That was wrong. You're acquainted with so many people who must be in sympathy with Mr. Davis and his new government. Is there any way I can help them?"

Rose Greenhow smiled in a slow, warm, almost seductive way. "Of course. Come in. We'll talk."

*   *   *

Rose's parlor had an airless and dusty feel. Only thin blades of sunshine slipped between closed draperies. Margaret heard no one in the house except little Rose, who was stomping upstairs.

Rose looked stunning in dark red silk with pagoda sleeves and a tightly fitted bodice that flattered her ample figure. When she sat down, Margaret glimpsed scarlet stockings.

"I'm sorry you have been through an ordeal," Rose said. "Will you tell me the tragic details?"

Margaret related the story. "I've worn these weeds for a month. It's time I put them away. My brother, Cicero, left for Richmond last week."

"It will soon be the capital of the Confederacy, I hear. Montgomery will be abandoned."

"Cicero's determined to help the cause, as I am. With his infirmity he'll never be a soldier, but he's clever. He'll find a place."

Little Rose flounced into the parlor. She darted behind her mother and deliberately tipped a vase of tulips. Water ran over a fine inlaid table. When Rose scolded her, little Rose bawled, threw herself on the carpet, and bit a table leg, leaving deep teeth marks.

"Excuse me, Margaret." Rose dragged the screaming child upstairs by the ear, locked her in her room, and came down again.

"When I deny the little imp anything at all, she retaliates for hours. I'm afraid she has the true rebel spirit."

Margaret smiled. "I've closed the house in Baltimore. Simms, our colored man, will continue to live there as caretaker. Father's estate will pay him. I don't intend to go back to Baltimore until the war's over in ninety days or so."

"That may be optimistic. Captain Jordan—do you remember him?" Margaret said she did. "He's back and forth to Richmond, and he says Beauregard will soon come up from Charleston to take command of the Alexandria line. Did you hear that Lincoln offered command of the Army to Bob Lee and Lee turned him down? He's joining Virginia."

"Will the armies fight there?"

"Undoubtedly. It will be crucial for Beauregard to have information about enemy strength. Let me show you something."

Skirts rustling, Rose took Margaret into a small library where she displayed a sizable stack of newspapers. "*New York Herald. Washington Evening Star.* Here's the filthy rag the local Republicans publish. The editors have one thing in common. Great generosity with reports of the Yankee regiments, where they are, where they're going, in fulsome detail. Until our Northern friends realize how stupid that is, we are in their debt. Captain Jordan takes care of forwarding papers to Richmond. He's resigning his commission, by the way."

"Isn't he a West Point man?"

"What of it? Some of the best graduates of that place have already come over. Lee is the most brilliant of them. If only Jeff Davis will give him his head! Davis graduated from the Academy and served in Mexico, so he mistakenly fancies himself a supreme strategist."

Rose shut the library door and they returned to the parlor.

Margaret realized the house was deserted, the Negro servants gone, for a more subtle reason than a desire for privacy.

"If you join us, you'll learn of some other work the captain's doing," Rose said.

"Then there's a place for me?"

"Yes, in a small, select circle of refined ladies and gentlemen who will take on the clandestine task of supplying military information to our generals in Virginia. The South needs far more than newspaper subscriptions." Margaret's heart began to beat hard in her breast.

"The work will call for keen wits, and the courage to face down some of these Yankee ruffians in an emergency. We do have an advantage. Most of them are ignorant peasants. Will you take a day or two to think about it?"

"I don't need a day, Rose. I came to you hoping for something like this. What you've told me exceeds my hopes."

Rose swept to her feet. "Be very sure of your decision."

"I am."

"You are pledging yourself to loyalty and secrecy, no matter what hazards may arise. You must obey instructions without question or hesitation."

"I will."

Rose embraced her warmly. "Then you'll be a great asset. Attractive young women won't be suspected by these Yankee clods. Do you have servants here in Washington?"

"Only a marvelous cook who's a perfectly awful and lazy housekeeper."

"Discharge her. Colored people can't be trusted. Not in these times. The paramount thing to remember is this: We're at war. We must win the war even if we sink to behavior none of us would have contemplated before."

*   *   *

Two nights later, Margaret returned to Rose's house and repeated her declaration of intent to Captain Thomas Jordan. At the end she asked, "Did it cause you pain to abandon your commission?"

Jordan snorted and tugged his beard. "General Scott's staff was a fine source of information for a while, but my sentiments were known, and they began to restrict what I could see. Otherwise I have no regrets. The volunteers backslap their commanders, address them by first names—won't obey an order if they don't happen to like it. They elect all officers but the colonel according to popularity. That isn't an Army—it's a rabble. I'm glad to be free. Furthermore, within our new organization, Captain Jordan no longer exists. I'm Rayford. Assumed names are a necessary protection."

Jordan told her he was establishing safe houses in southern Maryland and recruiting watermen to ferry couriers across the Potomac to Virginia. Rose's men and women would be called on to carry coded messages out of the city to the couriers waiting at the safe houses.

"Do you know anything about codes and ciphers, Margaret?"

"Just what little I came across in Edgar Poe's stories."

"Let me show you one cipher we'll use. It's called the pigpen cipher, or sometimes the Rosicrucian cipher, because the sect used it for secret documents. It's very old, but once you understand it, you'll find that you can easily encrypt a message."

He spread writing paper on the lamplit table. "It's a symbol cipher, not a substitution code that uses patterns of words to stand for other words that are the nulls and clears."

"I beg your pardon. Nulls and . . . ?"

"Clears. Nulls are words in an encrypted message that have no meaning. Only the clears reveal the content. Here's the pigpen." He drew two horizontal lines, crossed them with two verticals, creating an open-sided grid of nine boxes. Starting with ABC in the upper left box, he filled each with three letters. The lower right box held only Y and Z.

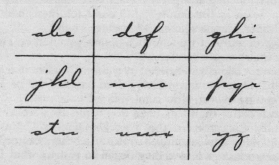

"Because the grid's open on all sides, no two boxes are alike. For a coded message, you draw the shape of the box required for the letter you want, then put in one dot for the second letter in that box, two if you want the third letter, or if it's the first letter, none. You repeat the process for the rest of the letters in the message. I'll write the word *cat*."

Jordan laid his pencil beside the paper. "You can see it isn't sophisticated. Hardly worthy of an Army in the field. But we aren't yet an Army, so we make do. We will be an army soon. This house will help bring that to pass. Therefore let me say welcome."

He offered his hand. Margaret took it, shivering with uncontrollable excitement.

*   *   *

Next day she was browsing among Shillington's books when a voice startled her. "Margaret?"

"Good heavens. Hanna." Her friend was unflatteringly dressed in trousers and a mannish frock coat. Her blonde hair was barbarously short. A clerk stared; two patrons whispered.

Margaret wrapped Hanna in a hug. "How are you? It's been ages since we've seen each other."

Hanna touched Margaret's black silk sleeve. "Has there been a death in the family?" Margaret told her about Calhoun Miller. Hanna squeezed Margaret's hand.

"How dreadful. I remember meeting your father. He was such a smart, polite gentleman."

"He was callously murdered by a pair of Yankee detectives, though I don't know which one fired the shot. I'll be a long while getting over it. How is the major?"

"Much better than he's been in a while. He's working for Secretary Cameron in the War Department." Margaret thought of her new allegiance to Rose and "Mr. Rayford." All other relationships had to be scrutinized in light of it.

"He's happy to be in the center of the war," Hanna went on, "but of course he's dissatisfied with the pittance they pay him. He'll never rest till he makes a fortune, though I don't see how he will in Washington. Is Rose still conducting her salon?"

"Occasionally. Not as often as before."

"Well, given her politics, I don't care to go back. May we ride some afternoon?"

Margaret couldn't reply with an enthusiastic yes, as she wanted. "Oh, I'm afraid not. I'm dreadfully busy with other things. The estate . . ." It trailed off, lame and cold.

Hanna peered at her with something close to suspicion. "I see. Well, good-bye then. Until we meet next time."

Hanna left the store. Margaret slid a book back on the shelf, hating what she'd done. The guilt passed quickly. In wartime, didn't friends sometimes find themselves on different sides? Hanna was now the enemy.

14

June 1861

Half a mile distant, a B&O engine whistled. The Ohio Valley's link with western Virginia was open again. Two weeks ago, three Federal columns had entered and secured Grafton, the junction of the line's branches to Wheeling and Ohio. Five days later, in the rain, General Morris had surprised a small Confederate force at Philippi and sent the rebs running, some with pants still around their ankles. The substantially pro-Union counties of western Virginia cheered "the Philippi Races." The man who had sent the three columns across the Ohio River was newly commissioned Brigadier General George McClellan.

In the Kanawha Rest, a public house in Parkersburg, where the B&O approached the river, Lon and his partner sat by a grimy window, keeping watch on a warehouse across the street. They'd watched it for three days, daylight and dusk, with no result.

Lon scratched a fingernail back and forth on the plank table. The sleeves of his gray work shirt were rolled up, the brim of his old straw hat pulled down. No one paid attention, which was the point of looking dull and ordinary.

Sledge puffed a corncob pipe and idly turned pages of a local paper. "Appears they're about to form a pro-Union government up in Wheeling. Don't want to be part of a slave state anymore."

"That right. Well." With no warning, a memory clicked in. "Oh, hell's fire." Lon whacked his whiskey glass on the table and startled the tavern keeper. "We left Cincinnati so fast, I forgot to pay my rent."

Sledge's owlish gaze reflected his three whiskeys to Lon's one. "Not like you, partner."

"My landlady's one of those Cincinnati Germans. Expects everything on time, if not sooner. I suppose she'll heave my belongings into the street."

"Threaten her. She'll heave 'em right back."

"That's your answer to everything. A fist."

"Works. Not so loud, hey?" Sledge eyed three farmers at the bar. "You're goddam touchy, you know that?"

"Why not? Our colleagues are in Kentucky, Tennessee, gathering useful information, and we're in the backwoods, watching a damned warehouse full of old flintlock muskets left over from Bunker Hill. Good for nothing."

"With rifling and new percussion caps they're good for plenty. That's why they've been busted out of other warehouses around here."

"Not by rebels. By common thieves."

"The rifles and ammunition are Army property. McClellan wants the ring broken up. You're in the war, partner."

"I don't think so," Lon said with a sourness not typical of him. While the war went forward, his life went the other way.

Just as the boss had predicted, G. B. McClellan had been recalled to the colors. In fact, three states, New York, Pennsylvania, and Ohio, had tried to recruit him. He chose to command the Army's new Department of the Ohio. He immediately telegraphed Pinkerton, asking him to organize a bureau to gather military information. He called it a secret service department. He would bear all the costs. The Army had no such operation, and no budget for one. McClellan had been impressed by similar bureaus when he was overseas as an observer in the Crimean War.

Although Pinkerton and Brigadier General McClellan were a mile apart on slavery—the general was a Democrat, tolerant of it—the boss felt it his duty to serve. He was ready. In April he'd offered the resources of the agency in a letter to the President. Invited to Washington, he sat through a long meeting, received promises, went home to Chicago, and heard nothing more. He made no secret of his anger.

He had scaled back Chicago operations and moved his most capable men and women to McClellan's headquarters city, Cincinnati. In a dusty downtown office building, with no name on the outer door, "Major E. J. Allen" presided over his new bureau. Allen was the boss's *nom de guerre*, a phrase Pinkerton explained when Lon asked.

Singly and in pairs, the other operatives had been sent to rebel territory. Pinkerton himself undertook a risky journey all the way to Memphis, presenting himself as an expatriate from Georgia, the role he'd played in Baltimore. Lon and Sledge were dispatched to chase petty thieves. Lon hated being so far from the real war, and Washington, where he'd met Margaret Miller. He thought of her a lot.

The summer twilight, dusty orange, faded from the street. In the gloaming June bugs buzzed and lightning bugs winked. The tavern keeper struck a match for a ceiling lamp. As the farmers drank more, they told scurrilous jokes about Jeff Davis. Then one of the farmers brought out a mouth organ and played "Columbia, the Gem of the Ocean." Another whooped and clumsily danced around the floor. The tavern keeper said, "Don't break any chairs or you pay for 'em."

Lon's ears caught a sound in the unpaved street. He wiped the greasy windowpane with his sleeve. Four roughly dressed men rested their lathered horses outside the warehouse. Lon grabbed Sledge's arm without looking. Whiskey splashed his hand.

"Jesus, Lon, you spilled half my—"

"Look there. The man in the middle—the one with the

huge head. I saw him in West Union six days ago when we were riding the line."

"Recognize the others?"

"No. But I remember him." So might anyone; he was a giant, a cruel burden on his swaybacked horse. His head was shaved, emphasizing his gnarled ears, swollen cranium, bulging forehead, eyes buried in fat and almost invisible. Like the other three men, he wore holstered pistols in plain sight.

"Where are they going? Is there a back door to the warehouse?"

Sledge said, "Yep. Saw it when I looked around earlier."

"Why didn't you tell me?" Lon jumped up, overturning his chair, interrupting a rendition of "The Girl I Left Behind Me." He yanked his hat on. "Let's go."

The horsemen disappeared single file at the right side of the warehouse. Its wide street door, locked and chained, remained undisturbed. Lon ran across to the building's left side, stole along the wall in purple shadows. At the corner he pulled his Colt .31 from under his shirt. The B&O whistled again. The long wail made him think of death. He began to sweat. He heard voices.

"Where's the fucking wagon?"

"Next street, I'll bring it when it's time."

"Saw that chain, we ain't got till next year."

"Shut up, Grier, I'm goin' fast as I can."

Lon heard the rasp of something working on metal.

"The fuck I'll shut up, this is my minstrel show, don't you forget it."

My minstrel show, Grier. Was Grier the leader?

A clank, a rattle, then a man whooped softly as the chain broke. They wrenched and tugged at the door, probably the end without the padlock. Grier gasped, "I can squeeze through but go ahead and bust the lock. We need the door wide open to haul the goods out."

"It's got too dark, Grier. Can't see."

"Use the fucking lantern. Let the idjit hold it."

As best Lon could figure it, two men had gone inside the warehouse leaving two behind. One was attacking the lock hasp. What did they call the other? Idiot? A fine bunch.

With whispers and hand signals, Lon and Sledge set themselves. Lon counted three and jumped out from the corner, far enough to leave room for Sledge. The man chiseling the lock spied them first. The man with the bulbous head was staring at the stars. The lantern in his hand looked toy-sized.

"Grier," the first man yelled, hurling his chisel. It caught Sledge's forehead, stunning him. The giant turned his slitted eyes on the detectives and threw the lantern. Lon dodged. The lantern broke in a pile of kindling and firewood. The kindling ignited. Lon aimed at the other man.

"Put them up high, partner. High as you can."

The area behind the warehouse grew bright as the kindling blazed. The man at the lock obeyed Lon, but the giant reached out, grabbed the man's arm, whipped him around, and threw him into Sledge, who was bleeding from a three-inch gash to the forehead. Sledge caromed into Lon. Lon pushed him off, but by then the giant had him by the throat.

Lon went to his knees. The giant choked him, smirking like a child. In the warehouse, men shouted questions. Lon's eyes blurred. The giant hands crushed his windpipe and starved him for air. Grier and the fourth man were kicking and pushing the loose end of the door to get out. Lon had a vague thought that he'd die in Parkersburg, ignominiously, with never a chance to do something fine for his country.

A pistol cracked. The giant gasped, rose on his toes, and convulsively squeezed harder. Everything darkened. Sledge put three more shots into the giant—back, legs, head. The swollen skull exploded like a rotten pumpkin dropped off a roof. Blood and gray matter drenched Lon as he ripped free of the constricting fingers. One man had escaped the building. Though the firelight was bright, raising a clamor at the public house, Lon was too dizzy to see the man's face clearly. But he saw a target clearly enough to shoot it. One bullet; the man went down on his face.

"Oh, Godamighty—Grier? *Grier?*" That was the man chiseling the lock. He fled, vanishing between some shanties on the next street. The man left inside retreated and moments later kicked down a side door. Lon ran around the building but the man was gone into the dark.

Men appeared, with lanterns. The tavern keeper shouted, "Fetch water buckets or it'll burn the whole neighborhood."

Lon swallowed sour bile that burned his throat. He nudged Grier with his boot, rolled him over. Lon's shot had taken the gang's leader in the chest. Grier's mouth was open, his eyes too. His expression was curiously innocent, bewildered.

Lon wiped his forehead. "Anyone know this man?"

One of the farmers bent over the corpse. "Name's Decimas Grier. Hails from over Clarksburg way. Known to steal anything laying loose. The other, that thing with half the head gone, I don't know him at all—oh, Jesus, Mary, and Joseph." The farmer reeled off to throw up.

More townsfolk arrived, including a couple of youngsters excited about the mayhem and dead bodies. Buckets of water emptied on the fire reduced it to embers. Sledge worked the blood off his face with his shirttail.

"Thanks for getting him off me," Lon said. "I was about done."

"That's why I plugged him, partner. If this Grier was the boss, maybe we broke the whole ring. Mr. Pinkerton would be happy to report that to the general."

Lon couldn't calm down. It had been a near thing. Grier and his miserable thieving cohorts could have left him dead in the dirt in this backwater.

Sledge noticed his look. "What's wrong now?"

"If I'm going to lose my life, I should make it count. I should be in uniform."

"Killing's killing."

"Not to me."

"Ah, sometimes I think you're crazy." Sledge walked away.

Lon wasn't deterred. When he was back in Cincinnati, he'd resign. This time he'd make it stick.

Suppose he traveled all the way to Washington to enlist. He might find that girl, unless she'd boarded up her town house and left. He could certainly conduct a search. The idea cheered him up considerably.

15

June 1861

Summer brought long days, abundant heat, the sudden death of Stephen Douglas, and excited speculation about a movement against the rebels massing across the Potomac at a rail junction less than a day's march from the city. Brigadier General Irvin McDowell of the adjutant general's office was given command of the Department of Northeastern Virginia. McDowell set up headquarters in the abandoned Lee mansion in Arlington. Robert E. Lee and his family had gone South.

Rose Greenhow concluded her period of mourning and began to leave the house frequently. She also continued her evening salons. Here Margaret met Augusta Morris, an attractive widow, and a pretty young woman named Bettie Duvall. Introductions were performed by Mr. Rayford, né Jordan, who told Margaret privately that for the security of all, Mrs. Greenhow preferred that the ladies not socialize, except on occasions she arranged.

A curious assortment of gentlemen attended the salons Rose continued to invite Republicans, chief among them her rumored paramour, Senator Wilson of the Military Affairs Committee. There was Mr. Donellan, a former employee of the government Land Office, and Mr. Butler, proprietor of an exclusive china shop on F Street. There were young clerks awed by Rose's importance and willing to do anything she asked and an occasional officer such as Captain Boyce of the First Rhode Island. Rayford said Boyce was heavily in debt to one of the city's gambling hells, hence "malleable."

Hanna never returned to the salon. Margaret hadn't expected it after their last encounter.

One pleasant Saturday, Rose organized a picnic. In several carriages, half a dozen ladies and gentlemen drove out to a grassy field near one of the new redoubts under construction. Washington's defenses consisted of a ring of similar fortifications. The object of interest this day was Fort Ellsworth, named for the late colonel of the Fire Zouaves. Ellsworth had been shot as he pulled down a Confederate flag defiantly flying from the roof of a hostelry in Alexandria.

They picnicked on catered baskets of cold chicken, pâté, cheese, French baguettes, white grapes, and iced champagne. While the group chattered on innocent topics—the thespian talents of Joe Jefferson, high prices caused by the war, the dreadful melees that broke out every time the soldiers were paid—Mrs. Greenhow peered at the construction site through a small spyglass and penciled notes in a diary covered in red leather. Margaret enjoyed the outing, but she chafed at the inaction. So far she'd been given nothing to do but await a summons.

It came the following Saturday. Mr. Donellan asked her to drive to an address near the Navy Yard and acquaint herself with the person and house of Dr. Whyville, a physician. The doctor was a jolly, avuncular graybeard. He welcomed her into his smelly surgery and said they would soon be working together.

Making sure the waiting room was empty, he said, "Donellan is setting up a doctor's line to Richmond. This is the northern terminus. Physicians are sacred figures, you know." He winked. "Peripatetic—always riding somewhere to tend a patient in distress. No one will question a doctor's movements or insist on searching his black bag. Excellent concealment, wouldn't you agree, Miss Miller? Next time perhaps you'll bring me a message for Richmond. I shall enjoy that." He shook her hand and she departed.

On her way home she saw bands of uniformed men roistering in the streets. Shouts, the pop of pistols, a baker's wagon overturned and set afire, told her it was another payday. She went out of her way to avoid confrontation.

That night, in the midst of a thunderstorm, she was wakened by a hellacious clamor at the street door. She wrapped herself in her gown and sleepily stumbled downstairs. Through the side glass of the door she saw three soldiers hunched in the rain. The biggest hammered the knocker again. Margaret stood in the opening. "What the devil do you want?"

"Hoo-hoo, I'll buy her right off," said one of them with a wheezy glee.

"Evening, Madam Ann," the biggest one said, taking off his cap and grinning like a fool.

"My name isn't Ann, and you've got the wrong address."

The big man examined a sodden paper. "Ain't this Madam Ann's boardinghouse?" *Boardinghouse* was Washington code for bordello. "Lafayette Square?"

"You drunken fool, this is Franklin Square. Good night."

"Listen, woman, we're soaked, we're hot as roosters, we come to buy some sweet flesh. We'll step in to make sure you aren't lyin' to us."

Terrified, Margaret used all her weight to shut the door. The big man reacted too slowly. She shot the bolt and leaned against the wall as the soldiers yelled and pounded with their fists and elbows. What if they broke a side glass? Reached in . . . ?

They didn't. The rain dampened their zeal and they staggered away in a glare of lightning.

Next time she saw Rayford, she told him she needed a pistol. He directed her to a gunsmith who sold her a handsome little sleeve gun, .44-caliber, from the factory of Henry Deringer. In a fenced yard behind the shop, the gunsmith steadied her arm while she took her first shot at a blue bottle. The kick was substantial, but amazingly, the bottle burst into fragments. The gunsmith grinned.

"Deringer makes one-shot pieces exclusively. But one's all you need at ten to twenty feet. Lots of ladies are equipping themselves with this little number. These are dangerous times."

"Yes," Margaret said fervently. "I'll need a supply of ammunition."

*   *   *

Rose Greenhow summoned her by messenger on a Tuesday. She was told to enter at the back of the house. Rose took her to a parlor window, parted the draperies, showed her a man in a planter's hat and white duster in a covered buggy across the street. He seemed perfectly relaxed, as though he always stopped outside a church to read his newspaper.

"That gentleman has been watching this house for the past two days. I'm sure he isn't friendly. Mr. Tobias is in the library. He's about to leave for Port Tobacco with a message hidden in a hollow cane. I don't want him detained or followed. Will you drive out and speed away so the man sees you? It may divert him. Five minutes is all we need."

Margaret said of course. She raced her piano-box buggy from the alley into I Street, drove past the stranger as she went north on Sixteenth. She could see little of the man beyond a luxuriant mustache and beard.

He snatched up the reins to follow. Nervous and exhilarated, Margaret touched the horse's croup lightly with the whip.

After ten blocks she turned in the middle of the street and clipped south, giving the stranger a saucy smile as she passed. He saluted her by tipping his planter's hat, turned around, and chased her.

Margaret swerved to the curb in front of Rose's house. She composed herself and waited in the shade of the buggy top until the stranger arrived. He returned to his original spot, wrapped his reins around a dashboard post, and strolled across the street. He seemed a well-set-up gentleman, on the short side but strong looking. His ruddy cheeks were dry in spite of the heat. She wasn't fearful until she saw the coldness of his gray eyes.

He swept his hat off and bowed. The June sun struck highlights from his long sandy hair. She judged him in his thirties. "A handy bit of driving, ma'am. I realized too late that you were deliberately leading me away from this house for a reason."

"The reason is simple. I wanted to take the air for a few minutes. I don't know why you're interested. I've never seen you before."

"Excuse my impoliteness. Colonel Lafayette C. Baker, at your service." His eyes darted to the brick house. "Do you come here often?"

"What if I do? You call yourself colonel. Do you have credentials?"

Baker responded with a grudging smile, as though he hadn't expected resistance from a pretty young woman. "Not yet, ma'am. My interest is that of a patriotic citizen who sees a possible nest of treason."

"Treason? Here? What nonsense." She lifted the reins. "Excuse me."

Annoyed, Baker seized her arm. He didn't mind exerting enough pressure to hurt. "Everyone knows the woman living in that house is a hot secessionist. Why not her friends? There are comings and goings at all hours."

Margaret wrenched out of his grasp. "I find you offensive. Are you spying, Mr. Baker?"

He slapped his hat against his leg. "Colonel."

She could deliver a look of splendid disdain when she wanted. "I have only your word for that."

Lafayette Baker reddened but held back whatever furious reply he wanted to make. "I regret to see a woman such as yourself mixed up with Greenhow, Miss . . ." A pause left room for her to give her name; she didn't. "You're an attractive creature, though I guess your sympathies are similar to hers. The secesh are high and mighty in Washington these days. There'll come a time when they won't be allowed to spit in the face of the established constitutional government. You'd be wise to disconnect yourself from that woman." He laid a finger on Margaret's left hand and stroked gently. "We might discuss it further some evening."

"Mr. Baker, will you take your hand away, or do you want this whip in your face?"

Baker stepped back. "If I were a man given to cursing, I'd call you the name you deserve."

"Good day, sir." Margaret whipped up the horse and left Baker in a cloud of tawny dust. She felt alive, worthy—important. She had always loved games: whist, patience, even the scandalous game of craps. Once she'd wheedled and nagged Cicero until he took his dice from a drawer and gave her a lesson. This game of chase and deception was the grandest game of all.

Next day she reported the substance of the encounter to her mentor and told her the stranger's name was Baker. It meant nothing to Rose.

*　　*　　*

Hanna called on Margaret. They sat in the parlor, stiffly formal, as though their outings on horseback and their other exchanges had never occurred. In the square, soldiers and sutlers' wagons made a great racket. The Twelfth New York was making camp, covering the grass with its white tents.

"Margaret, I'm sorry to speak of this but it's necessary. My father says there is suspicion that you're doing more at Rose's house than socializing. I'm not at liberty to tell you how the department found out—"

Margaret broke in. "I know how. A man named Baker. Is he connected with the War Department?"

Hanna's blue eyes showed her discomfort. "He'd like to be. He's trying to attach himself."

"Frankly he scares me. He's a snake."

"No argument there. I've met him."

"But many other things scare me, and I don't run away from them. My father's murder left me with a debt to pay."

"Oh, Margaret, you're no match for some of these men who are coming into town. My father's brave, but he's taken the measure of Baker and doesn't treat him lightly. Baker was a San Francisco vigilante. He hung men without a trial. He brags on it. He or someone like him will close in on Rose. She's too open about her loyalties, too bold in her maneuvering. The authorities won't tolerate it forever. If you're involved with her, get out before you're dragged down too."

Margaret folded her hands in her lap. It hurt to reject this young woman who'd been her friend, but the boundaries were drawn. "Let's talk of other things. Shall I brew some tea?"

After a sad, searching look, Hanna shook her head. "I'll go. I'm sorry you won't listen."

Hanna rose. Margaret moved toward her for a sisterly kiss. Hanna saw her intent, shook her head, and ran out the front door into the hot summer sunshine, leaving Margaret in the dim parlor, twisting a handkerchief and frowning.

16

July 1861

How delicious it was, the impersonation. Far more pleasant than prancing about the stage in Cesario's tights and struggling to remember the Bard's lines during three awful performances, each more foul than the last thanks to Zephira Comfort's chewing the scenery.

She chose Thursday because the whole city was mad with patriotism; soldiers everywhere. Hundreds of flags hung out in a show of loyalty. Artillery batteries across the river and behind the city pounded the sky with salutes. Citizens threw streamers and dodged firecrackers tossed from balconies. Twenty thousand New York troops paraded on the Avenue, just a fraction of those quartered in and around Washington.

Soldiers not employed in martial displays loafed in the tents that covered every square yard of open space, or they wandered drunkenly, accosting strangers for money to get even drunker. The public was elated by news from western Virginia. A brave young general named McClellan, a true star of the West, was marching and countermarching to drive the rebels back over the Alleghenies. So far the North had experienced no significant battlefield losses; the capital was primed to celebrate. Hanna wondered what Margaret would do when the sun went down, the public squares blazed with Chinese lanterns, and the soldiers shot off fireworks all night long.

Uniforms of the regulars and the three-month militiamen who would soon go home were a hodgepodge of color and design. With Derek's permission, Hanna rooted in the drama society's costume trunks and assembled an outfit of gray harem pantaloons—passable as Zouave trousers—a navy blue jacket with tarnished buttons and worn gold piping, cheap

Massachusetts-made shoes that fit either foot, and a gray cap with an embroidered design on top, left over from a French comedy. To this she added a havelock obtained from a friend who, along with other ladies of her church, was sewing them relentlessly for the Army. Hanna spent half the night of July 3 picking the embroidered fleur-de-lis off the cap, polishing the buttons, trimming the rattiest threads from the piping. The havelock, heavy white drill pinned into the cap to protect a soldier's neck from sunburn, was an import from the British Army in India.

While President Lincoln, General Scott, the cabinet, and senior Army staff reviewed the Pennsylvania Avenue parade, Hanna walked confidently toward the Long Bridge. Her stomach was fluttering and had been ever since she stole out of the house while the major snored. Stage fright was useful. Properly controlled, it lent an edge that improved a performance. She had pinned her chopped hair inside her cap, tugged the bill low over her eyes, and smeared dirt on one cheek. A two-cent cigar, purchased at a shop by means of a lot of grunting and pointing, hung from her teeth. She'd smoked half the cigar in an alley, choking the whole time. Anything for art. She hoped the unlit cigar stub enhanced the illusion of maleness.

Friendly soldiers greeted her on the approaches to the Long Bridge. Her response was the same each time: "Yo."

The planks of the bustling bridge were smeared with the droppings of cavalry horses jogging back and forth from the city. The homes and shops of Arlington showed appropriate Union flags, limp and hazy in the ripening heat. Perspiration soaked Hanna's underclothes. The havelock was too heavy and scratchy. Surely the three-month men would be happy to see the last of their improvised uniforms. The major said the War Department was alarmed by the number of men whose enlistments expired in July, when a great battle was expected.

As she passed around two inbound sutler wagons, great canvas-topped freighters driven by men who foully cursed the foot traffic, Hanna realized someone had fallen in step beside her. If she didn't speak, he'd be suspicious. She turned her head an inch or so.

"Yo."

The man wore a blue flannel shirt with an inverted U of buttons on the front, gray trousers with a blue stripe, a neckerchief and fatigue cap. His russet beard was long and thick. "Where you headed, soldier?"

"Yonder. Arlington." Hanna pitched her voice low; chewed the slimy cigar.

"McDowell's at Arlington House, y'know. I mean not today, but it's his headquarters."

"Yup. Goin' to see it."

"My name's Cole. Reliance Cole. First Rhode Island. They finally moved us out of that damn Patent Office to some swell's estate north of town." Hanna nodded and made small noises to signal interest. "What's your name?"

She blurted, "Smith." Realizing the inadequacy, she tacked on, "Bethlehem Smith."

"Pleased to make your acquaintance. What's your unit?"

She'd anticipated that one. "Eleventh Indiana."

"Didn't know there were Westerners here."

Hanna nodded again. She hadn't visited a privy since early morning. Pressure was building. Cole chuckled. "Hanged if you look old enough to soldier, Bethlehem. You started to shave yet?"

She rubbed her dirty cheek. "Beard never shows. Fair skin."

"Fair to invisible." Cole laughed. They left the Long Bridge, and the guard posts where bored men stared sullenly at those off duty. "Up ahead there's a good Union tavern. Better'n the Marshall House in Alexandria where Ellsworth bought the farm. 'Least they killed the cowardly innkeeper who shot him. 'Spect I can stand a beer in this heat. You?"

"Oh, no, I don't think—"

"Sure you can, c'mon." Cole wrapped a thick arm around Hanna and squeezed.

A hundred yards along the rutted road, the tavern he'd pointed out had a good crowd of soldiers and civilians, some lounging outside with glasses and tankards. As they strolled up, Cole pulled at his crotch. "Gents, where's the shitter?"

"Trench, out back."

"Got a bellyache," Cole told Hanna as he started away. "Figger it's the bad water. Need to piss?"

"No, no, I'll wait here." The pressure had increased; she was suffering. She rested against the tavern's painted siding, sweat in her eyes, heart beating unnaturally fast. This was the hardest role she'd ever played. In broad daylight too. She felt proud of herself, but anxious. The day was far from over.

Cole reappeared, buttoning up. "Let's have that cooler."

They marched into the smoky taproom. Cole ordered two glasses of lager. Hanna was too full for beer but she sipped it to soothe her nerves. Cole delivered himself of opinions on the President's unattractive phiz, possible diseases carried by whores he'd plunked in the District, the beauties of summer at Little Compton, Rhode Island, which he sure-God hated to be missing. Hanna drank a quarter of her beer in the time it took him to consume two glasses. The beer made her feel better, although the pressure to relieve herself was almost intolerable.

"Let's see Arlington," Cole said, and away they tramped, to the sloping green lawns crowned by the white-columned house where Lee and his family had lived until, as Cole put it, "he sold out the country what educated and trusted him." Guards stood outside four large tents in front of the mansion, headquarters flags flying above them.

After they had their fill of gazing at McDowell's headquarters, Cole said, "Heard there's a pretty fine cathouse 'bout a mile or so on. Want to go?"

"Nah. Have to get back to camp."

Cole fingered his russet beard. "Bethlehem, you're the oddest soldier I ever seen in my twenty-five years. Sounds like you'd sing soprano in church choir."

"Tenor."

"Got no beard, got a voice like a piping bird—" Rooted to the earth, Hanna waited for certain exposure. Cole farted loudly, pulled his pants away from his seat, and shrugged. "Reckon an Army takes all kinds. Pleasure to make your acquaintance." He offered a hand.

Hanna had to shake. Cole said, "What do y'do out in Indiana? Them soft hands sure don't work a plow."

"Music teacher. Piano and singing."

"Shoulda guessed. Tenor in the choir. It does take all

kinds," he repeated as though it were heavy philosophy. Hanna's bladder was ready to burst. She gave a little salute, about-faced, and marched hurriedly in the direction of the bridge. She hadn't gone forty steps before she darted into an airless lane between small houses with gardens already parched by summer heat. Frantically she hunted for an outhouse. Then it was too late.

She leaned against a toolshed, making a sound somewhere between a laugh and a sob. This was the strangest but most exhilarating day she'd ever spent. She could say that even with her pants wet.

She loitered in the lane until the spot began to dry, then set out again, feeling vastly better. Despite the hot wool, the shameful dampness, the way she'd nearly died a dozen times as Cole fired questions, she was excited and proud of herself. A rush of sensation that was almost sexual buoyed her all the way back to the Northern Liberties.

She slipped into the silent house and changed clothes as the sun was going down. She tied on a faded but feminine apron and pondered her next goal. A battlefield, in or at least near the fighting . . .

She tidied the house, straightening the broken and mismatched furniture as though it were actually worth something. She hummed as she worked. She was still humming when the major booted the front door open shortly after dark. He smelled of cigars; better ones, no doubt, than the weed she'd chewed on all day.

Siegel never paid attention to where he discarded his clothes. Hanna picked up his cape. He said, "You smile sweet like that when you've been playacting."

"Yes, I was playacting today. I was very good too."

"I don't understand playacting on a holiday."

"Derek's a taskmaster. Have you eaten supper?"

"Stopped at the National with some fellows from the department. Some of the regular waiters are joining the Army. The hotel is replacing them with *Negerin*. It's a disgrace, having colored men handle a white man's food." He shook his head at the seriousness of it.

"Papa, isn't the National Hotel terribly expensive?"

"So we're on short rations for a week. They pay me a serf's

wage but I won't live like one. Got to keep up appearances until I can do better."

In the kitchen Hanna found a crust of bread spotted with mold. She picked off the mold and chewed the bread, struggling to recapture the ecstatic feelings of the afternoon.

17

July 1861

On July 6, a Saturday, Margaret carried a message to Dr. Whyville. The following Tuesday she carried another. Each delivery consisted of a sealed oilskin packet no larger than a silver half-dollar. The thickness suggested a sheet of paper folded small. Rose handed the packets to Margaret with cautionary words about their importance.

On her trips to the doctor's house, Margaret was struck by the atmosphere of the city. Yes, Washington was crowded with strangers, tents everywhere, wagons tying up traffic, provisions and materiel piling up on the Potomac wharves where small schooners and steam-driven vessels docked and departed all day and all night. Work crews pulled insulated wire from huge wooden reels, stringing telegraph lines to government buildings, the bridges, the camps across the river. Merchants from out of town rented empty stores and kept late hours offering everything from poultry to photographic portraits. War had brought sudden prosperity, but there was more to it. Washington exuded confidence; a certainty that the first great battle of the war would be the last one.

Newspapers blandly declared that Irvin McDowell would advance to Fairfax Court House by mid-month. Broadsides and posters trumpeted editor Horace Greeley's cry of "Forward to Richmond!" The new Confederate congress was scheduled to convene there on July 20. Loyal Unionists expected the South to be crushed on the battlefield by that date or soon after.

At half past seven in the morning on Friday, July 12, a white boy brought an urgent note to Franklin Square. Margaret arrived at Rose's shortly after eight, wearing a cool dress of white linen lawn and a floppy straw hat.

"Dr. Whyville is incapacitated," Rose said. "Typhoid fever. This must be carried down the doctor's line before the day's over. Will you take it? There's no one else."

"Of course I will."

"Let me show you how important it is." Rose reached behind a row of books and brought out a map drawn in black ink. Margaret recognized the curving Potomac and the area around Washington. Black circles without labels indicated Virginia towns. A line of red dots ran from cross-hatching that represented the city down to a small Maltese cross. Rose touched the cross.

"This is Manassas Junction, where the Orange and Alexandria joins the Manassas Gap line to Winchester." Beauregard's army was reportedly assembling there.

"And here"—the red dots—"this is the probable route McDowell will follow to move his five divisions into battle."

Little Rose poked her head into the library, whining for candy. Her mother stamped her foot. "Not at this hour. Get out of here." The child recognized the stress in her mother's voice and vanished.

Margaret said, "Is the map reliable?"

Rose smiled. "As reliable as any copied from the original at the War Department." Margaret's pulse quickened with excitement. Had Rose gotten the map through Senator Wilson? Was he betraying his government in return for her favors? She knew better than to ask.

"This piece of information is second in importance only to definite word of the day and hour that McDowell will move on Manassas. I'm working to learn that. Meantime, this must be rushed to our friends."

Margaret's assignment required a buggy ride to a Maryland hamlet called Surrattsville, roughly ten miles south of the Potomac's East Branch. "A half mile beyond the tavern there's a dead hollow tree of some size. It's on the left as you approach.

On the side away from the road you'll find a hole about three feet above the ground. Leave the map there. One of Dr. Whyville's colleagues will retrieve it and take it further."

"How should I carry it?"

"Come to the dressing room."

Margaret sat with hands in her lap as Rose carefully folded the map inside one of the small oilskin packets. She lifted Margaret's hair in back and pinned it up, concealing the packet. With her hands on her hips, Rose studied her work.

"All secure. On your way, then."

"I have a pistol at home. Should I get it?"

"No time. You must leave now." Rose kissed and hugged her, and within an hour Margaret was across the East Branch into Maryland, jogging her buggy around farmers' carts coming to the city with melons and cabbages and potatoes. The fields and woods shimmered in the heat. The buggy horse raised dust from the winding road; Margaret's face and hands were powdered with it.

As she saw no one but residents of the bucolic countryside, her tension began to ease. She was congratulating herself on an uneventful trip when she heard a horseman. The pale blue ribbons trailing from her hat were sometimes called follow-me ribbons; the term was damnably appropriate.

She peered behind, wondering whether she'd heard two horses. She saw only one, ridden by a blue-clad soldier. Her first impulse was to whip up the buggy horse and race off, but that would only make her suspect. The rider broke into a trot and quickly drew up beside her. He raised his gauntlet to signal her to pull off the road.

The man was older, spindly, with homely features. He wore a holstered revolver and carried a shotgun in a saddle scabbard. He touched three fingers to his hat and she thought, *Polite. Old-fashioned.*

"Greetings, ma'am. Snell's the name. Washington provost guard."

"Aren't you far from your jurisdiction, Sergeant? I thought the provost guard only policed the District."

"In wartime, ma'am, everything is our jurisdiction." Margaret felt a trickle of perspiration on the nape of her neck below the hidden packet.

"What is it you want? I'm in a hurry."

"Ma'am, I don't mean to be offensive. This is my duty. There's reason to believe you're carrying a piece of confidential information."

"How did you come by that ridiculous conclusion?"

"We did, that's all. We expect the information is hidden somewhere on your person."

"What do you propose to do? Lay hands on me to find it?"

"Ma'am, I really don't want to do that. But I'm required."

"I've never heard anything so vile and uncivilized." She hoped her glance and her tone were sufficiently fiery.

He mumbled his answer. "Sorry, ma'am. It's orders."

Heart thumping so hard she fancied he must hear it, she pulled off her sun hat and laid it beside her. She patted the back of her head, loosening a pin. "Please avert your head while I climb down."

Inviting him to look away, she suspected he wouldn't. She raised her skirts to show a few inches of ankle, calf, and stocking as she descended to the ground using the buggy step. Snell's face was blazing red. She snapped at him. "Sergeant, I ask you again—will you kindly look away?"

This time he did. Turning so her right side was hidden, she snatched the packet as she shook out her hair. She tossed the packet into weeds on the road shoulder. "You may conduct your business."

Still flustered, Snell said, "I'd like to find some shelter. Where you wouldn't be embarrassed."

"Embarrassed? I'm furious. If you insist on this unspeakable behavior, you might as well search me in front of God and everybody. I hope people come along to see how the Yankees make war on women."

Snell dismounted, hesitating. "Hurry up, Sergeant. I haven't got forever."

He blushed again. "Ma'am—I can't. I can't lay hands on a gentlewoman."

"You have more breeding than I thought. Am I free to travel on?"

"Yes, ma'am, I guess you are."

She took her seat in the buggy, making sure to give him another glimpse of leg. In adolescence, her female friends had criticized her for being too forward, too open with men. Those qualities had saved her from Sergeant Snell. There were advantages to being a woman of modern temperament.

As she took up the reins, Snell walked his horse to the other side of the road. She was startled to glimpse a mounted man half hidden by the branches of an enormous willow. When Snell lifted branches to ride underneath, Margaret clearly saw a second horseman wearing a white duster and a planter's hat that shaded his face. The willow branches settled, hiding both men.

She raced the buggy to Surratt's ramshackle tavern and stopped there to collect herself. A young man introduced himself as the owner's son. He apologized for the crudeness of the establishment. It was mostly for men. Would she take coffee and a bowl of Mrs. Surratt's barley soup if he pulled a table to the porch? She would.

When she finished, she drove back to the spot where Snell had confronted her. The road was empty, the packet easily found in the weeds. Turning south again, she reached the hollow tree with no difficulty.

A farmer and a barking collie appeared, herding some sheep in the direction of Washington. From the buggy parked in the shade, Margaret gave him a polite smile. He touched his forehead shyly and didn't speak. When he was gone, she looked around. She saw nothing more threatening than a distant barn. She walked behind the tree, dropped the packet in the hole. Traveling north again, she passed the herder and his bleating flock.

She let the weary buggy horse walk awhile. Heat blurred the landscape with a whitish haze. She felt better. She'd played the game and won. She began to sing softly to herself. Moments later she realized the song was "Dixie."

*   *   *

On Wednesday, the seventeenth, Rose called her trusted ladies and gentlemen together for tea. Rose's color was high. She wore a burgundy gown with a daring neckline that showed cleavage. Mourning was definitely over.

"I have news," she announced. "Our friend Thomas Rayford won't be with us in the future. He's gone to join General

Beauregard's staff, under his rightful name. He served us splendidly by setting up our codes and courier lines."

Rose smoothed her skirt. In the hall, little Rose was whistling and marching. "Mr. Donellan is also absent. He came over from Virginia on Monday evening and returned the same night with the most important message thus far sent from this house. Nine words." She stretched the moment. "'Order issued for McDowell to march upon Manassas tonight.' A friend at the Capitol has verified that McDowell is already in or near Fairfax Court House, but General Beauregard had the news in advance."

Bettie Duvall sighed. "Oh, how fine." Mr. Butler, the china dealer, applauded and asked how Rose got the information.

"It's best if that remains confidential."

Little Rose ran in and thrust herself in front of her mother. "Mama, does that mean the Yankees will be killed?"

Rose laughed. "Yes, if all goes well for our side, that's what it means."

"Hooray." Little Rose turned a cartwheel that nearly toppled a Chinese jar from its pedestal.

* * *

During the next three days, Washington lived on signs and rumors. Smoke columns rising in Virginia came from campfires, houses put to the torch, or artillery, depending on your informant. On Friday, the butcher from whom Margaret bought meat said there was "desperate fighting," though when pressed, he was vague about details.

In the afternoon, when Margaret continued her shopping for household necessities, she learned that the whole town expected the great battle to be fought on Sunday. In the Willard, where she ate an early supper, the catering desk was besieged by gentlemen ordering picnic baskets. She asked her waiter about it.

"Why, ma'am, they're going to drive out and watch McDowell whip the rebs. You can't find a rig or a saddle horse for rent at any price." Margaret thought the idea of having a picnic while men slaughtered each other was bizarre. Death was inevitable in wartime, but she saw no reason to enjoy it as a spectator.

Throughout Saturday the city remained quiet except for a faint and far-off rumble of heavy guns. She woke on Sunday hearing the rumbling again, louder this time.

She was too restless to stay home. Her bed unmade, her breakfast coffee grounds still in the pot, she dressed and hurried to the Avenue. During the morning and into the afternoon she wandered among thousands of others awaiting news. At the newspaper offices, chalkboards used for bulletins remained blank. Occasionally a rumor flashed through the crowd. McDowell was victorious. No, he was beaten, his Army in wild retreat to Centreville. No, to Fairfax. No, the Potomac. As the sun went down, she was still drifting in the sea of men and women, all curiously subdued. If McDowell had won, wouldn't news have reached them?

She walked to the War Department, hoping she might learn something. Every window in the building was alight. She heard a great hollo on the Avenue, ran with others to see a bedraggled couple in a barouche surrounded and unable to move. The woman's face was pale with fear. In her lap she held a picnic hamper with its lid gone. Questions were shouted. The man shouted answers:

"Joe Johnston's Army came in on the Shenandoah railroad to reinforce Beauregard. Our troops broke and ran. The roads are swarming with cowards trying to save themselves. People had their carriages wrecked or stolen. We were lucky to get through."

Someone cried, "Hurrah for Beauregard, hurrah for Jeff Davis!" With oaths and yells, others leaped on the man, beat him to the ground, and kicked him.

Thousands stayed on the streets all night as more civilians arrived by moonlight, telling their version of the same tale of defeat and flight. Margaret was weary in every bone, and yet she stayed. The night sky clouded over. Just before daylight, a thin drizzle began. The first soldiers appeared from the direction of the Long Bridge.

Dirty, bloodied, many without their weapons, they dragged along by twos and threes, their units broken and scattered. Some of them pushed their way into President's Park and lay down to rest under the dripping trees. Though Margaret rejoiced in the Confederate victory, the aftermath wasn't pretty.

You might celebrate a wartime triumph, but how could you celebrate the death and injury that went with it?

She trudged home at half past seven, tumbled into bed, and woke before noon. Returning to the Avenue, she heard angry men and women blaming Scott and McDowell for the defeat, or the West Point officer clique, or the three-month militiamen who ran. She walked to the Long Bridge and watched a dozen Confederate prisoners march into the city under guard. Women and children flung stones, spat on them. *"Kill the traitors!"*

"Where are they going?" Margaret asked a corporal marching with the captured rebels.

"Prison. The Old Capitol." The soldier looked as frightened as the prisoners. The screaming was incessant.

"Hang them!"

"Shoot them down!"

Then came the ambulances, twenty of them, forty, fifty, in a long, slow procession. Crude two-wheeled affairs with canvas side curtains, they rocked back and forth, jolting in and out of potholes. Every bump and lurch made the unseen wounded cry out. The chorus of pain finally drove Margaret back to her town house. In her dreams that night the ambulances rolled on, stretching for miles to the horizon. She woke dry-throated, the images fading, but not the awful screaming.

18

July 1861

Lon rode the B&O in a downpour, unable to sleep. Finally, on the other side of the streaked glass, white Army tents appeared along the right-of-way. From the end of the car the conductor announced, "Beverly, Ohio. The stop is Beverly."

Lon climbed down to the depot platform. Even in the middle of the night the little village on the Columbus–Parkersburg line blazed with lights. Three days ago, less than twenty-four hours after the disaster at Bull Run, the secretary of war had telegraphed General McClellan, summoning him to Washington to command the Department of the Potomac in place of the disgraced McDowell. McClellan's star was high after his successes at Grafton, Philippi, Rich Mountain, Corrick's Ford. The roads and rivers and railways of western Virginia were safely in Union hands, a base from which the eastern part of the state could be attacked.

The rainy air helped revive Lon. He slogged through the mud, asked questions, dodged the charging horses of Army couriers. In a complex of wedge tents, he found a disheveled officer to whom he'd been directed.

"Lieutenant Jeter? I'm supposed to see the general."

"General's got no time for civilians. He's due out of Wheeling in the morning. A special train's taking him to Washington, you know." He said that as though Lon were some backwoods idiot.

Testy, Lon said, "I know all about it. The general sent for me. Take a look." He handed his note to the lieutenant.

"Major Allen of Cincinnati? Never heard of him."

"The general knows him. Damn it, I'm telling you he sent for me."

With a look that called him a liar, the lieutenant left the tent. Rain dripped on the canvas. From the pocket of his bedraggled coat Lon pulled a bottle of vegetable tonic and a chunk of hard biscuit, the remains of last night's meal. Shortly the lieutenant returned, looking cross.

"Hanged if you aren't right. He'll give you ten minutes. Follow me."

Major General McClellan had a large wall tent to himself. He stood up behind a field desk papered with memoranda, reports, yellow telegraph flimsies. An ambrotype on a small easel dominated the clutter—his pretty wife, Ellen.

"Mr. Price. Greetings. I remember you from Chicago." McClellan shook with a powerful grip. Lon marveled at the man's alertness and vigor at half past four in the morning.

George McClellan wasn't tall, yet everything about him seemed formidable, heroic. His auburn hair was combed, his reddish brown mustache and imperial trimmed. On his blue

wool blouse there were no shoulder straps; no indications of
rank at all. No wonder that at thirty-five, McClellan was already something of a god to his men.

The general pointed to a camp chair. Lon sank down grate-
fully. "Bit hectic, this past week," the general began.

"I'm sure that's true, sir. Congratulations on your new
appointment."

McClellan smiled in a pensive way. "It's flattering to think
you're called upon to save the nation, which is what some of
the papers are saying. I have no intention of becoming a military dictator such as they had in the Roman empire. But my
assignment's clear. There's a rabble in Washington calling itself an army. I'm to whip them into something worthy of that
name. What happened last Sunday was a disgrace. I hold Scott
rather than McDowell responsible. If you're charitable, General Scott is simply too old. If you're not, he's incompetent.
But you've come a long way, Mr. Price. Let's get to business."

"Major Allen asked that I speak to you."

"About your resignation."

"Yes, sir. After I returned from western Virginia—"

"You and your colleague broke the ring of thieves making
off with our supplies. A day after you got back to Cincinnati,
you quit, is that correct?"

"Yes, sir. I quit in order to enlist and fight. I hope I don't
sound pretentious, but I believe in this war. My father was a
preacher. He worked for the Underground Railroad. He
thought Negroes should be free."

"Well, I suppose that's commendable. Personally, however,
I wouldn't give you ten rusty nails for the right to entertain
black people in my home. I can't imagine they'd want to come
there, either. This war is being fought to preserve the Union."

Lon would have argued but it wasn't the time or place.

"Major Allen says you're a top man. One of his best. He
doesn't want to lose you. I appreciate your desire to serve, but
you should realize that if you're with the major, you're already in the Army."

"Sir?" Lon said, puzzled.

"As soon as practicable I intend to bring Major Allen and
his entire organization to the capital, to perform the same intelligence work for me and my staff that you have been doing

in Cincinnati." Lon was stunned. McClellan continued, "You won't drill, you won't carry a rifle or wear a uniform, but you'll be a soldier, with an indispensable task. How can we fight the rebs if we don't know where they are? How many men they have? How they're deployed? We need trained agents to ferret out answers to those questions. You'll see your share of battle and danger, of that I'm confident. And you'll be serving your country as fully as any man marching in the infantry."

McClellan stood again; time had run out.

"I recommend that you change your mind, Mr. Price. Change your mind and withdraw your resignation."

Lon was dazzled by the opportunity McClellan put before him. He thought suddenly of Margaret and hardly hesitated.

"Put that way, General—I will."

"Then this was time well spent. Find Lieutenant Jeter, have him set you up in the officers' mess. The train for Columbus won't pass through till half-past seven."

"Yes, sir. Thank you, General."

McClellan tossed off a casual gesture, part salute, part friendly wave. He was already back to work at the field desk.

Lon went out into the rain. He and McClellan obviously didn't think the same way about slavery, but that didn't matter. Serving with Pinkerton in the new capacity McClellan had described, he could fulfill his promise to his father.

Over the eastern hills watery gray light was breaking. Lon felt more alert and cheerful than he had since leaving Cincinnati.

*   *   *

In a beer garden in Over-the-Rhine, Cincinnati's German district, Lon told Sledge about his interview. Sledge said, "Glad we'll still be partners." He wiped away a foam mustache and waved his empty stein at a passing waiter. In another part of the garden, four men in lederhosen played a schottische. Lon and Sledge had both drunk more beer than was good for them. Under glowing paper lanterns, with paper flowers brightening the white trellises around them, the war hardly seemed to exist.

"I know why you did it," Sledge said as new steins arrived.

"To fight for the Union, and the end of slavery."

"Sure, sure. A glorious crusade for Gentleman Lon. Listen. I'm not the smartest boyo, but I know this. The work we do now is dirty work, and it'll be the same where we're going. I know you don't believe that, but one day you will. You will. *Prosit.*"

They drank in silence. Sledge belched so loudly, other patrons stared. "Meantime, boyo, let's have a good time. Knock some heads, meet some girls—oh, I forgot. For you there's only one. In Washington. *That's* why you changed your mind."

Lon's red face was a silent confession.

19

August 1861

Pinkerton's men and women moved to Washington quietly. They hid away in obscure rooming houses around town. Lon and Sledge rented from an Irish widow on K Street, under assumed names. The boss hardly needed such excessive caution. The city was focused on the man he idolized, the dashing commander in charge of the force renamed the Army of the Potomac.

McClellan did his best to stay visible, to raise the morale and improve the fighting readiness of the three-year volunteers arriving to replace the ninety-day men. He operated from headquarters at Nineteenth and the Avenue, a house rented from a Navy officer. It had no mess. He and his staff took meals at an I Street café run by a popular mulatto caterer. McClellan worked at headquarters mostly at night. Several times when Lon had business in the building and passed the open door of McClellan's office, he saw the President, usually in a shiny black suit and leather slippers, telling law stories to the fastidiously dressed general, or listening to theories of training and strategy.

McClellan spent his twelve- and fourteen-hour days charging somewhere on his big bay horse Dan Webster, astride the kind of saddle he'd seen in the Crimea and recommended the Army adopt; the Army had named it after him. He set a hard pace for staff officers and the dragoon guards who rode with him. He inspected every one of the forty-eight defensive forts, redoubts, and batteries ringing the city. He galloped across the Potomac to visit the encampments that sprawled from Arlington down to Alexandria. Beauregard was still at Manassas. Pinkerton said the general feared an attack on Washington, but McClellan's good cheer and élan hid that from the rank and file. Soldiers waved their caps and holloed to "Little Mac" or "General George" when he rode by. He rose in his stirrups and waved his cap to salute them.

He wasn't so popular with a minority that tasted his discipline. His patrols swept the streets of drunken or abusive soldiers. Offenders were bucked and gagged, or forced to stand on a barrel for hours holding a sack of bricks. These public displays were meant to discourage others inclined to err.

Every patriotic citizen wanted McClellan's photograph. He posed in Mathew Brady's studio on the Avenue. The most popular print showed him with his right hand inside his jacket, a pose much favored by senior officers. The papers and the public began calling him Young Napoleon.

Pinkerton sent Tim Webster and Hattie Lawton back to Baltimore, where the secret societies were reappearing. Pryce Lewis was in Washington, along with several other operatives. One was Sam Bridgeman, a Virginian whose air of gentility belied coarse habits. He picked his nose in public and spat wherever he pleased, though he'd successfully played a footman on a daring reconnaissance mission in Virginia in the summer. Pryce Lewis had been with him, posing as an English lord out to see America. Lon didn't like Sam Bridgeman.

One night in the Ebbitt Grill, Lon was drinking with some of his colleagues at the mahogany bar. Since Parkersburg he'd acquired a taste for sour mash whiskey. It was stronger and faster than beer for dulling bad memories such as the moment Sledge's bullet blew the giant's head to pieces in Parkersburg.

An operative named Frank Ellis brought up the situation in Maryland. Secession was still discussed, but less fervently because of the threat of armed intervention by Federal troops. Sam Bridgeman bragged that he'd broken up one of the Baltimore secret societies.

"Knights of Liberty. There was a lot of shooting. A seditious bastard named Miller died on the spot. I don't know if it was my bullet, but I like to think so."

Bridgeman pushed away from the bar and spat brown tobacco juice on the floor. Standing on Bridgeman's left, Lon concentrated on his empty glass. Miller. That was the girl's name. From Baltimore.

He didn't like to admit that Sledge might be right about their work. He just hoped a lot of dirt wouldn't rub off on him.

Later that night he walked to the town house in Franklin Square. Lamps burned on the lower floor. Another lamp moved in the foyer, lighting up the fanlight glass like a firefly passing. She was there.

How could he see her? If he tried, would she slam the door in his face? Cuss him out for a Yankee? It was worth the risk.

*   *   *

Pinkerton gave him no opportunity. McClellan wanted to know the strength of Beauregard's army. Pinkerton sent Lon, Sledge, and Sam Bridgeman into the enormous tent city over in Virginia. Everyone who fled across Confederate lines—deserters, refugees, slaves—was to be questioned. Pinkerton chose Lon to interrogate contrabands, as runaway slaves were called. He said he gave Lon the assignment because he knew Lon had sympathy and concern for the Negroes.

"Which I am sorry to say the general doesn't share. I don't know how he will treat any information we obtain from Negroes. That doesn't relieve us of our obligation."

Lon set himself up in a wall tent in a camp near Baileys Crossroads. He spent the hot August days patiently asking questions of a procession of mostly illiterate black men who had risked their lives to escape their owners.

The Negroes came shyly, often fearfully, into the tent. Usually they wore ragged clothing, or something not much better. They scraped their feet and knuckled their foreheads, and Lon grew angry all over again at the conditions in which these men had been forced to live since childhood.

The tent stank of sweat, and of nearby latrine trenches. The contrabands sat on a stool in front of a table piled with reports to be handed to Pinkerton, who already had so many to handle, he said that he felt like a one-armed Polyphemus.

Lon asked the same questions of each contraband. "How many men, how many white soldiers would you say are camped around Manassas Junction? A few? A lot?"

"Thousands," the contraband would answer with wide-eyed sincerity. Or, "More'n I could count." Or, "Cap'n, they was all over the ground far as these old eyes could see."

"At Bull Run, the rebs brought in their black horse cavalry. It frightened a lot of the militia, so they ran. Did you see any cavalry? Did you count any black horses?"

"Black horses everwhere," they'd say. Or, "That's all they got, sir, nothin' but black horses." Or, "Oh, my, must be a whole lot of black horses—how big's a million?" They wanted to help, but routinely, when Lon laid aside the sheet headed "Plato" or "James" or "Amos," there wasn't a single useful answer on it.

Then a different sort of man walked in. He was thin as a stick, dressed in clean drill trousers and a work shirt with the sleeves torn off. The gray wool on his head said he was older than he looked, which was about thirty.

The man had a long jaw, a narrow face. Bushy eyebrows jutted over deeply recessed dark eyes. His skin was a beautiful golden color. Lon supposed he was a mixed-blood of the kind called high yellow.

The man was too big for the stool. He hunched over and folded his hands on his knees, and instead of grinning at Lon, or repeatedly saying "sir" to show his eagerness to cooperate, he waited for Lon to begin the conversation.

"It says on the roster that your name is Zachariah Chisolm."

"Says that because it is."

"My name is Alonzo Price."

"All right." No approval, no disapproval, just "all right," and silence.

"Can you read, Zachariah?"

"Some."

"Cipher?"

"Enough to keep from being cheated."

"Where and when did you escape?"

"From the camp of the Wade Hampton Legion, night before last. There was no moon. I figured I had a chance."

"The Hampton Legion of South Carolina?"

"I was a house nigger for Captain Tyree Broom. He brung me up from Summerville to cook his meals an' tend his clothes while he soldiered. Lots of us got brung up north by our masters."

"Was your master a kind man, or unkind?"

"Mostly kind, but it don't make no difference. He was master. Wasn't too smart, though. He carried me most all the way to freedom and he didn't think I'd go the last mile. I was just waiting for my chance. Night I left, Captain Broom drank too much claret wine an' shot himself in the foot while he was cleaning his pistol. Caused a lot of excitement. After his friends hauled him off to the surgeon, I jumped."

Lon inked his quill and scratched a couple of lines on the sheet headed *Chisolm, Z.* "What can you tell me about the size and disposition of the Confederate army?"

"Dispo what?"

"Where the regiments are placed."

"Can't tell you much. I don't know how to reckon the size of Armies. There's just a hell of a lot of soldiers. You give me a map, I ain't sure I could draw an X to place the Hampton Legion."

"Some of the Negroes who've sat there have given me numbers. Large numbers."

"Well, sure, doesn't surprise me. They want to please the white man. They fear if they give the white man the wrong answer, he'll be mad with them and send 'em back. That's why they make up things."

"Frankly not very useful things. Why don't you make up answers?"

Chisolm seemed saddened by the question, or perhaps disappointed with the man asking it. "If I did I'd be lyin' to you. What good that do either of us?"

Lon sat back and scratched his face where a biting fly had deviled him. A bugler blew a call. Men marched by outside, drilling.

"I like you, Chisolm. You're not a damn bit of help, but I like you." Chisolm let his lips twitch in the beginning of a smile. Lon had a sudden thought.

"Would you go back into enemy territory?"

"You think I'm dumb as Captain Tyree Broom? Hell, no."

"Would you go back if you were sent back, maybe with someone like me, to gather information that would help our side? Because of your color, you could move easily behind enemy lines."

Chisolm squinted at Lon as though trying to detect a snare. "That way, yes, maybe I would."

"I'm glad to know." Lon capped the inkwell and reached for his hat. "Where are they keeping you?"

"Contraband camp, mile or so that way. Bunch of them little bitty pup tents."

"Make sure you stay there so I can find you. Make sure they don't send you somewhere else. Let's get out of this oven and find a cool drink."

They walked down the lane of tents in the broiling sun. A young redheaded soldier sat outside his tent, bare-chested, polishing buttons of his blouse. The soldier watched them. After they passed Lon heard him spit.

Lon took out a tobacco pouch, rolled a cigarette, and lit it. Ahead, where the trampled lane rose to a slight crest, a patched tent with a plank counter sold necessaries but, as a sign warned, NO LIKKER TO SOLDIERS. A larger sign at the tent's peak advertised J. O. HOBHOUSE SUTLER, 2ND MAINE. The Second Maine had felt McClellan's fury in a dispute over the term of enlistment. Sixty-some men who'd rebelled and rioted had been shipped away to prison in the Dry Tortugas wearing manacles and leg irons.

The sutler's counter displayed cheap razors, shaving soap mugs, writing materials, little sewing kits called housewives. The sutler was a small, sly-looking man. Lon tapped a coin on the plank counter.

"Got any lemonade in those barrels?"

"I can sell you a glass, but not him. No niggers served."

Lon tossed his cigarette in the dirt. "Suppose I buy two glasses."

The sutler laid a long bowie knife on the counter. The cutting edge bore rusty bloodstains. "You try to serve him one, we'll have a problem, mister."

Lon took a breath of stale air, trying to decide what to do. The sutler's hand moved spiderlike toward the knife hilt. Behind Lon, Zach Chisolm said, "I ain't thirsty."

Lon bridled his anger, tugged his hat down over his eyes, and wheeled away from the counter. "I'm not either." As they walked off, the sutler said, "Nigger lover."

Chisolm hunched his shoulders, his hands in his pockets. "Guess I was wrong about the North. Thought men of color would be treated fair. Same as white men."

"A lot of good people want it that way, Zachariah. I fear a lot of others aren't ready for it. They will be one day."

"Liable to be dead by then," Zach said with sullen anger. Lon had no answer for that.

* * *

In Pinkerton's second-floor office at the headquarters house in Washington, Lon presented his idea. The boss was enthusiastic. "Let's not lose sight of this Chisolm. We'll bring him over here, find him a job till we can use him. I'll send Frank Ellis."

"I can go," Lon said.

"No, you and Philo and Bridgeman and Lewis have a new assignment. It came through Tom Scott, the assistant secretary at the War Department. We're ordered to watch a suspected traitor named Rose Greenhow."

20

August 1861

"No cursing, no spitting, no blasphemous behavior of any kind," said the rector of St. John's Church, I Street. "This is a house of God."

The elderly rector had loaned his storeroom to Major E. J.

Allen, with the endorsement of the War Department. Lon found the room eerily reminiscent of his childhood, but there was an irony in doing war work amid shelves of hymnals, prayer books, and Sunday school lessons promoting meek and mild Christian behavior.

He opened the window. The heat of the August morning boiled in from the dusty street. Big blue flies followed. They were swarming on manure heaps left by coach and dray animals. Sledge arranged a small table, two chairs, a jug of water, a drinking glass, paper, pencils. Their shift lasted until dark, when Lewis and Bridgeman would take over.

Across the street, framed by unattractive ailanthus trees planted on the curb, Mrs. Greenhow's two-story brick manse drowsed in a yellow haze. The boss had been called to Washington to gather intelligence for McClellan, but a second, quite different mission had been thrust on him. Counterespionage, Pinkerton called it. The operatives were charged with noting and describing every person entering or leaving Rose Greenhow's.

"Beauregard knew the date of McDowell's advance ahead of time," Pinkerton said. "Mrs. Greenhow is regularly visited by officers with access to confidential material. She's a logical suspect."

For the first three days, callers were few: tradespeople; a low-level State Department clerk; a regal young woman Lon followed from the house to a milliner's, then to her residence near Rock Creek Park. The driver of an ice wagon identified the woman as Mrs. Philip Phillips. "Secesh to the bone. Husband was an Alabama congressman. He's gone south. You tell me why a wife'd stay behind if it wasn't to help the damn rebs."

That fitted Mrs. Phillips into Rose Greenhow's circle, but was hardly evidence of treason. "We'll find the evidence," Pinkerton assured Lon when he reported. "The Rebel Rose will slip, and when she does, we'll be there to catch her. With handcuffs."

Near the end of the third week of August, Lon was rotated to night duty. As he sat sweating in the darkened storeroom, a handsome piano-box buggy tied up in front of Rose's house. A woman climbed to the high stoop. The bell carried clearly in the stillness.

Revealed by a spill of light, the mistress of the house greeted her visitor. Lon sat up, jolted. The caller was the pretty young woman from Franklin Square, Margaret Miller. He knew her sympathies lay with the South, but he never imagined she'd be involved with spies.

Sledge had sneaked off to visit a brothel for an hour. Margaret drove away before he returned. Lon kept mum about the visit. He debated courses of action most of the following day, Saturday. Mrs. Greenhow was suspected of treason, but did that implicate Miss Miller? What if she was merely a social acquaintance? The questions justified what he decided to do in order to see her again.

In the late afternoon he tied on his best cravat, whisked the dust off his boots, and put on a brown beaver top hat borrowed from Pryce Lewis, who owned three. The city sweltered under a menacing copper-colored sky filled with reverberations of distant thunder.

He knocked at the door of the town house in Franklin Square. He hoped he wouldn't find the young woman with Donald, or Donal, or whatever his name might be. Their short meeting had generated a fierce dislike on Lon's part.

He heard someone in the hall. The door opened and there she was, lovely as a rush of cool air after a summer storm. He couldn't explain why her brown eyes, her wide red mouth, her imperfect but still lovely face, and full figure spoke to him, made him yearn, but they did.

"Yes, who—?" Recognition then. "Well. President's Park. Wilkie Collins."

"Don't forget Illinois rustics. I'm flattered that you remember, Miss Miller."

"Oh, I never forget a good adversary." Was there a hint of mockery? "May I ask what this is about?"

"It isn't a social call. I have a bit of important business to transact, if it's convenient."

"As a matter of fact it isn't, but you may come in. Briefly." She stepped back. The rustle of her hidden petticoats caused an immediate physical reaction. He hoped his condition wasn't obvious.

She led him to a parlor tastefully but not lavishly furnished. Plants in small tubs relieved the somber monotony of dark wood. Margaret settled herself on a love seat, arranged her green taffeta skirt, dabbed a streak of perspiration off her cheek with a lace handkerchief. A small gold palmetto tree on a chain rested on the bosom of her dress. The palmetto was the symbol of South Carolina. She didn't hide her loyalties.

"I'm afraid you have the advantage, sir. I know you're a Yankee, but that's all I know. Since you have my name, may I have yours?"

"It's Price, Lon Price. Short for Alonzo." He sat down opposite her, holding his tall hat like a drowning man clutching a life preserver; her face and demeanor did that to him. "It was important that I see you, so I went to some trouble to learn your identity and whereabouts."

"May I ask how you did that?"

He reached inside his coat and laid the bookmark on his knee. "You dropped this when we met. I followed the trail to Shillington's."

Her eyes shifted away for an instant. "It must have fallen out of the book."

"No doubt," he said, his expression bland.

"Are you a policeman, Mr. Price? They've hired a hundred and fifty for the new District force."

"True, but I'm not one of them."

"Some other kind of detective?"

"My occupation doesn't matter." He put the bookmark away. "I came to advise you in confidence that your friend Mrs. Greenhow is under suspicion of disloyalty."

"Rose? Disloyalty to whom?"

"The government."

Her fist closed. If the hanky had been a rock, he fancied she might have hurled it. "So you are a detective. Some kind of damned spy for Lincoln, Cameron, that crowd?"

"If you'll let me expla—"

"Permit me to finish, if you please. Rose Greenhow is a good and valued friend. You're a fool to try to turn me against her. The men who sent you are fools."

Lon jumped up, heat and redness in his face. "No one sent me. No one else knows about this."

She reacted with silent doubt. The parlor had grown significantly darker. Black clouds tumbled over nearby rooftops. Thunder boomed.

"It isn't my intention to turn you against a valued friend," he said in a calmer voice. "Your welfare was my only reason for coming here. You're putting yourself at great risk by associating with the lady, however much you like her."

Her anger melted into a wary puzzlement. Lon sat down again. She dabbed her forehead. "Why should my welfare be your concern? We've met only once, and not exactly cordially."

"No, but you did get your book back."

"Mr. Price, don't bandy words with me, I'm not some adolescent in the schoolyard. You must have a reason for this visit other than sheer kindness. Kindly state it."

Lon knew he could pull back, leave, save himself embarrassment. But she seduced him with the sweet curve of her cheek, the dark waterfall of her hair, the hint of ankle and petticoat showing above her button shoes of red-dyed leather.

"All right, I'll tell you the truth, though I suppose you'll throw it right back in my face. Here it is anyway. As you said, when we met, we exchanged words—"

"Some call it fencing." She almost smiled.

"Fencing," he repeated. "And you jabbed me pretty hard. In spite of that, I went away thinking you were an intelligent woman, and very attractive. That's why I searched out your name and address at Shillington's. I wanted to see you again."

"Well, you have. Is that all?"

A black vendor hawked strawberries in the street. His head, a straw basket perched on it, seemed to float past the window. The room's hothouse atmosphere grew heavier.

"No, and this isn't the meeting I imagined or hoped for," he said as he stood again. "Since my visit to the bookstore, the matter of your friend Rose Greenhow has come up."

"How?"

"Never mind that. I simply want to warn you about your relationship with that woman."

"Mr. Price, let me say again that Rose Greenhow is a friend and will remain one. We have common sympathies."

"Obviously. At this time, in this political climate, they can get you into trouble."

With a whoosh of petticoats and a fire in her eye, she walked right up to him. "Are you threatening me?" A blinding white glare opaqued the windows. A thunderclap rattled the glass. "Who do you work for? Who is paying you? I demand to know."

"Well, if that might convince you that my message is worth heeding, I work for the War Department."

"So you are a dirty spy." She slapped him.

Lon stepped back. Her handprint faded from his ruddy cheek. "I'll overlook that, Miss Miller, and I'll tell you once again that by associating with that woman you're putting yourself in danger."

She stormed into the hall; flung the front door open. Dust flew on the gusting wind. Lon clapped his hat on his head. Moved toward her with slow, deliberate steps; a kind of taunting. She stamped her foot.

"Will you get out of here or shall I run into the street and scream for help? I have strong lungs. I can bellow like a heifer, and I will."

It made him laugh. "I'd expect no less, Miss Miller."

He thought she wanted to respond with a smile, perhaps a truce, but she didn't. They simply stared at each other while the wind snarled and whined. Then, impulsively, he took hold of her forearms and kissed her.

He savored her moist mouth, the shape of her body. After a few seconds he stepped away, expecting she'd slap him again. She was, instead, frozen and speechless. She started a sentence, faltered. "Mr. Price, you—you have the most infernal gall of any human being I've ever met. Another damned Yankee trait, I suppose."

"Probably. I told you, I liked you the moment I saw you. If that's a criminal offense, I'm guilty. Good afternoon, Miss Miller. Please remember my warning."

He ran down the steps into blowing clouds of dust and debris. She slammed the door. Across the street an old gentleman struggled to open an umbrella. The wind snatched it and sailed it away. At the curb, Lon rubbed his cheek. That was the end of that.

Striding off, he saw a curtain move at one of the town house windows. He couldn't see her but he knew she was watching. What a contradictory creature she was. It was part of her fascination.

He jumped to catch the old gentleman's umbrella rolling in the gutter. He crossed the street and returned it to him. When he looked back at the town house, the curtain was still. He shook his head and went on.

*   *   *

Sledge was waiting for him at the Willard Hotel dining room.

"Gentlemen, your order?" The tall, yellow-skinned waiter looked quite professional in his starched white shirt with sleeve garters, black string tie, and waiter's apron. Zachariah Chisolm was the third Negro hired to replace white waiters leaving for the Army.

Sledge sent Zach for two whiskeys. "What's biting you, partner? You look like a rooster whose comb got clipped."

"I feel like that. Today I went to see a woman I met in President's Park on inauguration day. I saw her calling on Rose Greenhow last night."

"Where was I?"

"Enjoying the favors of Pearl, or Maude, or one of their fallen sisters." Lon explained his attempt to warn Margaret about the suspected spy.

"Jesus, what were you thinking? Anyone who associates with Greenhow has to be a damn traitor. Trust any of 'em, including this lady, and sooner or later they'll sell you out. Kill you, if need be."

"I can't believe she's like that."

"Then you're a naïve damn fool. Don't you listen to the boss? Greenhow and her friends are soldiers, never mind that they wear paint and powder. You've got a lot to learn, partner."

Zach hovered again, his pencil and waiter's pad ready. Thunder shook the dining room chandeliers. Sledge stuffed his napkin into his collar. "Come on, order, or we'll be late. The boss said he'd look in tonight."

*   *   *

Pinkerton arrived at the church just before ten o'clock, with Sam Bridgeman. "Anything so far?

"Quiet as a grave, sir." Lon pointed across to the darkened

manse. "No lights showing since half past nine. I expect she's retired."

They settled down to watch. About ten-thirty, a tall man wearing a general officer's hat and rubber poncho arrived on foot. A glitter of lightning shone on the brass eagle pinning up the hat brim.

"Who is it, anybody know?" Bridgeman asked.

"I have my suspicions," Pinkerton said as the stranger climbed to the stoop and knocked. "Someone's been copying plans of the city fortifications. A clerk found a smeared copy half-burned in a stove at the provost marshal's headquarters." A lamp in the downstairs hall silhouetted Rose Greenhow admitting her visitor. "This may be our bird. Follow me!"

They cracked their shins and bumped each other going down the dark stairs. The rain had driven people indoors; they crossed the street unnoticed and crowded into the space under the steps. Pinkerton stared at the first-floor windows above his head. Lamplight shone behind the curtains.

"She's taken him in the parlor. Lon, Sam—bend down so I can stand on your backs." Pinkerton pulled off his boots.

They crawled from under the steps, stood, and positioned themselves. Sam Bridgeman said, *"Oof!"* as Pinkerton climbed on their backs. He held the parlor windowsill to steady himself. Lon spotted a hackney coach approaching in the next block. If lightning flashed as the coach went by, they'd be seen. Before he could warn the others, the hackney turned right into K Street, gone.

He braced both hands against the bricks. Pinkerton's weight was considerable. A faint squeak said the boss had pried up the sash to peer through the curtains. Bridgeman groaned. "I can't take much more." Lon spied a man and woman hurrying down the block under an umbrella. "People are coming!"

Pinkerton jumped down, spattering mud on the others. "Everybody under the steps." The four jammed into the space under the stairs until the couple passed. The rain was heavy, which helped conceal the detectives. Lon's back ached.

The couple disappeared. Pinkerton whispered, "I recognized the man in the parlor. Captain John Elwood, Fifth Infantry. Attached to the provost marshal's office. He was sitting this close to her"—Pinkerton showed his hands, the palms an inch apart—"going over drawings. A dollar says they're plans of our fortifications. Wait, the lamp's out in the parlor. She's in the hall. She's taking him to the second floor."

"For what?" Bridgeman said.

"What do you suppose? She's rewarding him the way she rewards all of them."

The storm muttered on. Five minutes became fifteen, fifteen became a half hour. Sledge tilted his pocket watch to check it in a flash of lightning. "Been up there nearly an hour. How long do we—?"

Pinkerton clamped his hand over Sledge's mouth. Lon heard Rose's voice, and the officer's, and then what sounded like a kiss. Rose whispered, "Good night, my dear." The officer ran down the steps and headed toward the Avenue.

"Sam, come with me," Pinkerton exclaimed. "You two wait here."

"For how long?" Sledge's question went unanswered; Pinkerton and Sam Bridgeman were already gone in pursuit of the officer. Pinkerton had left his boots behind.

Lon knelt on the damp ground beneath the steps and rubbed his back. "This is crazy. We're acting like circus clowns."

"No argument there," Sledge said.

A farmer's wagon loaded with milk cans clattered by. Down the block, a first-floor window flew open; a householder tossed a mewling cat into the rain. Rose Greenhow's house remained dark. Time ticked by.

At two o'clock, Sledge said, "Let's give up. They aren't coming back."

"One more hour," Lon said.

At three, they trudged to their boardinghouse. Lon threw off wet clothes and caught a couple of hours of sleep. He was awake at half past seven. By eight he and Sledge were in Pinkerton's second-floor office at McClellan's headquarters. The boss wasn't there.

Lon read the latest *Evening Star*. Accusations were were still flying about the Confederate victory at Wilson's Creek in Missouri twelve days ago. The North had lost the second big battle of the war. In St. Louis, pro-Southern newspapers were being suppressed by General Frémont. In U.S. circuit court in

New York, the *Brooklyn Eagle* and the *Daily News* faced charges of disloyalty. There were brief descriptions of cavalry skirmishes in Virginia and Maryland.

Around half past nine, boots thumped on the stairs. Pinkerton appeared, hatless, bedraggled, his eyes slitted from weariness. Lon said, "Sir, what happened?"

Pinkerton threw off his sodden overcoat. "Bridgeman turned his ankle and I had to leave him. I followed our man to barracks. Elwood called out the guard to arrest me. I identified myself as E. J. Allen and stood pat. Elwood had me thrown in a cell. This morning he dragged me to see Tom Scott at the War Department."

Pinkerton treated them to a rare smile. "Scott told Elwood who I was. I asked Elwood if he'd visited Rose Greenhow last night. He denied it. I told him I was there, with witnesses. He changed his story. Claimed it was a social call. Then I told him I'd seen him pass a diagram of fortifications to that woman. He broke down. Admitted he delivered not only plans but a list of armaments. I didn't mention the hour they spent upstairs. The confession was humiliating enough. Elwood's in the guardhouse. He was crying when they led him away. I told them to take his belt, braces, anything he might use to harm himself. Have you boys had breakfast?"

Sledge said, "Not yet. I guess we should say congratulations." It seemed incredible that last night's antics had resulted in the arrest of a traitor.

Pinkerton's eyes were dancing. "Let's have steak and eggs somewhere, to celebrate. Elwood's confession is exactly what we need. Our Rebel Rose is finished. Her friends will be next."

21

August 1861

On the same stormy afternoon of Lon's visit to Margaret Miller, Hanna arrived at the Capitol out of breath. She heard cannon booming when she was still west of the building. By the time she reached the commons on the east side, a band was blaring "Columbia, the Gem of the Ocean." The brass rose bright and strong above the pounding of the snare drums. She picked up her skirts and ran. The major hated tardiness.

She raced behind a long row of carriages. Families stood in them or beside them, waving small flags and cheering the units marching by. General McClellan had transformed the trampled commons into a parade ground. His grand reviews lent an air of confidence and gaiety to a city badly shaken by McDowell's defeat. It was widely accepted that on the night of the Bull Run retreat, the Confederates could have captured Washington had they pressed on instead of holding their positions.

Hanna searched for her father in a crowd of several hundred standees. She spied him in conversation with a gnome-like man of middle years whose sour face, wire spectacles, and full chin whiskers were tantalizingly familiar.

Her father's clothes witnessed to his improved station. His gray double-breasted coat and trousers were fine British wool. The coat pockets were expensively edged with silk braid. The gray was enlivened by a scarlet waistcoat and matching bow tie. Of course he had a top hat. Siegel spent most of his small salary on himself. Anything Hanna wanted, down to a spool of thread to mend a skirt or a stocking, she paid for out of her Canterbury wages.

They had exchanged the mixed neighborhood on the north side for a rented cottage in a district of white artisans and office workers behind the Navy Yard, near the East Branch. The major considered it merely another way station. He promised Hanna a larger, finer house in the suburbs or one of the fashionable squares as soon as he earned more than his meager government salary. He called it "a pittance," unworthy of a man of his education and experience. Still, he was delighted that his clerkship involved him in important work and brought him into contact with important people.

The white-gloved companies marched and countermarched to the music of regimental bands. Shouldered bayonets gleamed like silver spikes. The colors stood out stiffly in the rising wind. Streaks of lightning lit the black sky.

"Certainly I know the President," the gnomelike gentleman was saying as Hanna approached. "Some years ago he and I represented Cyrus McCormick in a lawsuit. I insisted on being lead counsel because Mr. Lincoln was an unskilled country lawyer. I don't see that he's changed greatly."

"Ah, here's my daughter," Siegel said. "Hanna, may I present the attorney general, Mr. Stanton?"

Edwin Stanton; she had seen his picture. She smiled and offered her hand. "How do you do, sir?"

"Charmed." The top of Stanton's head barely cleared her shoulder. His legs were stumpy. His disagreeable expression reminded her of a pug dog.

"You are late, my dear."

"Duties, Papa." She'd rushed from the Canterbury. She didn't want to embarrass the major by saying she'd spent the afternoon scrubbing floors.

A man strolling along in front of the crowd, studying faces, caught Siegel's attention. "Colonel!" The man came over, sweeping off his planter's hat. The skirts of a white duster snapped in the wind.

"Major Anton Siegel, sir. We have met before."

"Yes, we have, how are you?"

"Fine, sir. Do you know Secretary of War Cameron's legal adviser, Mr. Stanton?"

"Only by his excellent reputation. Lafayette Baker, sir. Your servant."

"Pleasure," Stanton said with his lip still curled. Hanna

wondered if he liked anyone besides himself. "Are you in the military, Colonel?"

"In my own way, yes, sir. I've been fortunate to be given a roving commission in the State Department. I'm charged with the investigation and discovery of disloyal citizens."

"It's wasteful and unproductive to have that activity divided between two cabinet departments," Stanton said. "Mr. Seward is too lenient with suspected traitors, Mr. Cameron too disorganized and inexperienced to effectively counter them. The effort needs to be centralized under a strong secretary of war." Listening politely, Hanna decided she didn't like the dogmatic and scornful attorney general. She liked the icy Colonel Baker even less. She caught him brazenly studying her flat bosom.

Baker looked away without embarrassment. "I agree the situation's highly confusing. But not the objective. We must root out enemies of the state and render them harmless. The President's suspension of habeas corpus near military camps was helpful, but it should be greatly broadened. A rope thrown over a tree limb is very effective too." He smiled as though he'd just said something humorous.

"An extreme view, Colonel." A drop of rain struck Stanton's spectacles. "I am not entirely out of sympathy with it, however."

Baker made a respectful bow. The sky burst. After hasty good-byes, Hanna and her father ran from the field, avoiding carriages hurtling past with cargoes of shrieking children. They fled into the Capitol as the storm worsened. Hanna unburdened herself in German:

"That Mr. Stanton is disagreeable."

"But a brilliant attorney, they say. An able administrator, and a bitter foe of the rebels. Everyone believes his star will rise."

"What about the other man, Baker? He looks like a schemer."

"All to the good, given his task. I met him when we both applied to the War Department. When lines of responsibility are clearer, it would be good to have him with us."

"You're swimming with sharks, Papa."

Major Siegel laughed. "Better than swimming with the tiny

minnows." As quickly as it began, the deluge slackened. "Your skirt is muddy," the major said as they left the building.

"I'll clean it when we're home."

"I have been meaning to speak to you about your appearance. Can't you buy better dresses? When you look shabby, it reflects badly on me."

Tears sprang to her eyes. He didn't notice. He'd spied a man he knew and dashed off to slap his back and greet him.

22

August 1861

At eleven a.m. on Friday, the day after Captain Elwood's arrest, a two-seat spring wagon with fancy black paintwork, black leather seats, and a fringed canopy moved slowly north along Sixteenth Street. Lon held the reins, with Pinkerton next to him. Sledge nearly crowded John Scully off the rear seat. Scully must have brushed his teeth with gin, but the odor didn't hide his need of a bath. Except for Scully the operatives looked like respectable bureaucrats out for a morning ride.

They passed the Greenhow mansion, its curtains closed against the heat. Pinkerton scanned the sidewalks ahead of them. "There she is." Near the next intersection, a woman with a parasol strolled arm in arm with a gentleman. Lon drove past a pony cart and quickly caught up to the couple. He reined the gray to a walk.

Rose sensed their presence, whirled, and gave the detectives a sharp look. Pinkerton jumped down. He swept off his broad-brimmed black hat.

"Major E. J. Allen, Mrs. Greenhow."

"I know who you are. The little Jew detective."

Pinkerton almost smiled. "You're wrong about the religion, but the profession is correct. May we return to your house?" He ignored the small, dapper man blinking and fretting in the shade of Rose's sun umbrella. Lon rested his boot on the wagon dashboard. The pocket Colt in his belt gouged his stomach.

Pinkerton said to Rose's companion, "Make yourself scarce if you please, sir."

The man had a small waxed mustache and florid cheeks. He stamped a tiny shoe. "Do you know who I am?" A heavy accent fractured his English. "Étienne Chambord, of the French legation. You have rudely interrupted a private conversation."

Pinkerton fanned back the skirt of his black frock coat, showing off his holstered revolver. "This is United States government business. Leave."

"Disgraceful," the diplomat cried. "Your President entertains Prince Napoleon, the emperor's cousin, at a state dinner, with all courtesies, and you treat the accredited representatives of France like criminals. I shall not be moved from this spot." A housemaid leaned out a first-floor window, interested in the standoff.

Pinkerton said, "Mr. Greenglass, see if you can change the gentleman's mind."

Sledge dropped from the wagon, grinning and flexing his fingers. He smiled down at the Frenchman, who was a head shorter. "Ready for ten rounds bare-knuckle, Frenchy?"

Rose stepped between them. "Don't involve yourself with this Yankee trash, Étienne. We'll discuss diplomatic recognition for the Confederacy another time."

Chambord slapped his high-crowned felt hat against his leg and marched away. Pinkerton said, "Mrs. Greenhow, I am placing you under arrest. I ask that you accompany me to your house, where you will be detained."

"On whose authority? Show me your warrant."

"I don't have a warrant. I'm acting on verbal authorization from the Departments of War and State. Will you walk peaceably? I don't relish the idea of mistreating a member of the gentle sex."

"The hell you don't, you insignificant worm." Rose aboutfaced and strode off. Pinkerton signaled Lon to turn the wagon in the street.

Rose carried her parasol in her right hand; an embroidered reticule swung from her left arm. Her stride and up-tilted chin shouted defiance. Scully muttered, "They must have carved that bitch out of marble."

Lon kept pace with Rose and Pinkerton, who walked two steps behind. Near her house, Rose suddenly darted forward, widening the gap. At the foot of the high steps she dropped the sun umbrella, reached into her reticule, thrust something into her mouth, and chewed. Pinkerton grabbed her arm.

"Madam, spit out that paper."

She showed her teeth and tongue; she'd swallowed it. Lon couldn't help laughing. Pinkerton snatched her umbrella off the ground and shoved Rose up the steps. "Touch anything else, in your handbag or in the house, and I'll handcuff you."

Lon tied the gray and ran up the steps after Sledge and Scully. Pinkerton was already inside with his prisoner. A ferocious wail said that Rose's daughter had grasped the situation. Lon had observed little Rose from the church storeroom and decided she was a spoiled hellion.

In the gloomy foyer, Pinkerton yelled, "Bring that child back here, Mr. Scully." Little Rose was too quick. She fled through the kitchen into the rear garden and shinnied up an elm tree. She leaned from the lowest fork, just out of Scully's reach, shrieking, "Mother has been arrested. Mother's arrested by the damn Yankees!" An elderly black gardener came running from the adjoining property. He turned around when Scully showed him a four-barrel hideout pistol.

"Stay up there till you starve," Scully shouted. Little Rose spit on him. Watching from the kitchen, Mrs. Greenhow was deliciously amused. Pinkerton forced her into a wooden chair. "Mr. Greenglass, you and Mr. Price search the place. I want papers, letters, anything that looks important." He called into the garden. "Come in, Scully. If the little brat runs off, so much the better."

Scully trudged to the house, leaving Rose's daughter in the tree, bewildered by the abrupt lack of interest. She climbed down and followed Scully to the kitchen. Pinkerton dragged her to her mother. "Keep her quiet or we'll lock her in a closet."

Sledge was already headed for the parlor. He threw the drapes open with a clash of rings as Lon walked in. Sledge pulled a tall secretary away from the wall, tipped it forward so it fell with a crash. Papers flew. An inkwell splattered black ink on the Oriental carpet. Sledge grinned at Lon, who was appalled. He remembered how Mathias Price had once defined the essential evil of slavery. *The owners have too much power. There's no way to check it.*

Suddenly, a cry of "Stop her!" whirled him in time to see Rose's heels flying upstairs. He ran after her, climbing steps two at a time.

Rose darted into a bedroom; snatched something from the mantel of the white-painted fireplace. Swinging around, she pointed a Smith & Wesson revolver at Lon's forehead. Though she held the revolver with both hands, the muzzle wavered unsteadily.

"You Yankee vermin, I'm going to kill you."

Lon drew the pocket Colt from the waist of his trousers. "All right, Mrs. Greenhow, but you'll have to cock the gun first."

She was stunned, giving Lon enough time to reach her, grab the revolver, and throw it without regard for where it landed. It broke a window and sailed off in the sunlight.

He prodded Mrs. Greenhow downstairs at gunpoint while Sledge, Scully, and Pinkerton yanked drawers out of sideboards, overturned china cabinets, trampled on silver and broken dishware, ripped paintings from the walls, slashed the canvas, and snapped the frames apart. At the top of her lungs, Mrs. Greenhow revealed a formidable command of obscene language. Pinkerton forced her arms behind her back, slipped iron cuffs on her wrists, and flung her on a sofa. From there she watched the carnage with horror and outrage. Little Rose huddled against her mother's bosom, snuffling.

Lon dug his fingers into the soil of a potted palm, hunting for buried objects. "Turn it over, spill the dirt," Scully said as he took several cardboard file boxes to Pinkerton. The boss was studying a small book covered in red leather. He seemed pleased. Lon left the miniature palm standing in its Chinese jar and ran to the library where Sledge was spilling books from the shelves. Sledge inspected a book, riffled the pages, then with a grunt of effort tore the front from the spine and threw the pieces away.

Too much power. No way to check it . . .

"Are you tearing them up for the hell of it?" Lon said. Sledge had a second book, tooled leather and gilt-stamped. Lon wrenched it from him. "You don't have to ruin them to see if anything's hidden."

"What's it to you? The woman is secesh."

"This is personal property. Where do we get the authority to destroy it?"

Sledge knocked the book out of Lon's hand with a rock-like fist. He shoved Lon's shoulder. "Whose side are you on, partner?"

"Don't do that."

Sledge clenched his jaw and shoved again. Lon slashed out with the pocket Colt. The gunsight gashed Sledge's hand, not deeply, but enough to bring blood. Sledge cocked his huge fist; Lon aimed the Colt. Suddenly, with a bewildered shake of his head, he stuffed the pistol in his pants and stared at his partner.

Sledge's fist opened. He lowered his hand. The anger in both of them ebbed quickly, but something new and ugly remained. Lon gave voice to it:

"What the hell are we turning into?"

He walked away. Behind him, Sledge ripped another book. Scully sang as he broke dining room furniture. If this was meant to be a lesson to Southern sympathizers, it was the wrong lesson.

23

September 1861

Margaret learned of Rose's arrest two days later. Mrs. Philip Phillips, a woman she knew through Rose's circle, called on Sunday afternoon to impart the news. She interrupted Margaret at her writing desk where she was composing a letter to Cicero. She hoped to send it to Richmond by courier. Regular mail service to the South had ended in May. Margaret hadn't heard from her brother since he'd disappeared from Baltimore.

Mrs. Phillips was agitated and angry. "Rose is surrounded by detectives working for a Major Allen. His men ransacked her house when they arrested her. The same men have worked for the Yankees since the Baltimore riots."

Margaret grew pale. Was it possible some of them had a hand in her father's murder?

"Are they treating Rose decently?" she asked.

"She's confined to her bedroom. She isn't permitted to close the door, not even when she sleeps. Can you imagine a woman being abused that way?"

"By Yankees, yes. How do you know all this?"

Mrs. Phillips managed a sly smile. "Rose is smarter than any ten men. And she has a slew of admirers she doesn't even know. When I passed the house yesterday, a crowd was gathered outside, showing support for her. Rose smuggled a note to one of them."

"Is she allowed visitors?"

Mrs. Phillips said no and took her leave. Margaret was in turmoil. First Cicero to worry about, now her friend. The Washington press began to report significant developments in the case of the notorious Mrs. Greenhow. Soldiers from the Sturgis Rifles, General McClellan's personal bodyguard, replaced the civilian detectives, and the house was promptly dubbed Fort Greenhow. Margaret was horrified to read that Mrs. Phillips, her two daughters, and her sister were likewise arrested for "disloyalty" and imprisoned at the house. She began calling there every afternoon. Each time, an armed soldier turned her away. Then, one sultry day in September, she was admitted, without explanation.

She expected to find the house in ruins. Instead, neatness and good order had been restored, damaged furniture replaced by new pieces. A handsome and personable Army officer introduced himself as Lieutenant Sheldon, in charge of the guard detail. He directed Margaret to the music room adjoining the parlor. Someone was playing "Maryland, My Maryland" on a pump organ. The song, written by a Baltimore expatriate after the riots, was a new rebel anthem.

Puzzled by the secesh music and the friendly behavior of the soldiers, Margaret stepped into the parlor. She was stunned to see not just Mrs. Philip Phillips, but Augusta Morris, another of Rose's agents. Augusta put down her Walter Scott novel and gave Margaret a sharp look. Margaret presumed it was a warning to be careful of what she said.

She knocked at the open door of the music room. Rose broke off in mid-phrase. "Margaret! How grand to see you." They embraced.

"I don't know what to make of all this, Rose."

"Typical Yankee bestiality. I feel like Marie Antoinette in the Bastille before they guillotined her. Things have improved slightly since that detective left."

"Major Allen?"

"His real name's Pinkerton." In a whisper: "He has arrested Walker, and Colonel Empty. They're jailed in the Old Capitol." Walker was a valued agent, a clerk at the post office. "Empty"—M.T., for Michael Thompson, a South Carolina lawyer—was another. "Pinkerton found my diary with Tom Jordan's ciphers written down, but I have other ways to communicate with the outside."

"You mean the soldiers cooperate?"

"Some do. If they're gentlemen and look the other way when I ask, I'm happy to consider them friends. If they deny my little requests, they get the back of my hand." Margaret was in awe. Rose's charm and determination hadn't failed her.

"I may have an errand for you soon." Rose was interrupted by a bellowing contralto in the parlor. *"Good morning, ladies."* No one returned the greeting. Mrs. Phillips gave the newcomer a disdainful glance and went back to her needlework.

The woman sat down huffily. She was large, with a round, coarse face. Rose whispered behind her hand. "Mrs. Onderdonk. Thoroughly, unredeemably canaille. Lieutenant Sheldon won't say why she's been detained. I suspect she was planted to spy on us. I refuse to eat at the same table with her. Come upstairs. I'll show you a letter I'm writing to Secretary Seward to protest this mistreatment."

When Margaret returned two days later, Rose showed something else she'd been working on: a cloth bookmark embroidered with tiny flowers of different colors. "I would like you to take this to Dr. Whyville."

"Is he well again?"

"Yes, though he's rather weak."

"And he needs a bookmark?" Margaret said, amused.

Rose looked swiftly at the guard in the hall, a blond boy immersed in the *Police Gazette*. "The colors of the different threads convey a message the doctor will understand and pass on. The detective may have confiscated my cipher book, but he didn't steal my brains."

Margaret drove to the physician's house that afternoon. She carried the bookmark and her letter to Cicero, addressed care of general delivery, Richmond. As she went in, she noticed a carriage parked in deep shade in an alley across the way.

Dr. Whyville had lost a great deal of weight. He looked cadaverous and wan. Margaret stayed less than three minutes. When she stepped back into the hot September daylight, Lon Price was striding toward her from the alley entrance.

The emotions she felt were powerful but conflicting. With mingled guilt and pleasure she remembered the taste and passion of his kiss. To her astonishment, it had stirred something profound within her. Yet the man might be part of the organization responsible for her father's death. She dared not forget that.

"Mr. Price." She hid her nervousness behind a cool nod. "Why are you snooping in this neighborhood?"

"That's a mighty harsh term, snooping."

"Isn't it what you do? Aren't you paid by a detective named Pinkerton?"

His blue-gray eyes revealed nothing. "I work for Major E. J. Allen of the War Department."

"I suppose one name's as good as another for a spy." She expected anger and was surprised by his rueful smile.

"You're something, Miss Miller, you surely are."

It shamed her. She drew a breath. "I do owe you an apology."

"Why's that?"

"The last time we met, I raised my hand to you."

He shrugged. "The fencing got a little rough, that's all. Let's discuss the man who lives in this house. Dr. Whyville is a known Southern sympathizer, and a suspected Confederate agent. I'm sorry to see you visiting him. It connects you with the wrong people again."

"Dr. Whyville is a fine physician. I see him whenever I'm not feeling well."

"And he diagnoses and treats you in less than five minutes? Somehow I doubt that." Before she could reply he said, "Obviously my first warning went unheeded. You just don't understand the realities. Arrests are being made. People are being locked up."

"And damned unjustly." She was stunned by her own unladylike profanity. So was a black boy rolling a hoop in the dusty street.

"Justice is in short supply in Washington, Miss Miller. The President's suspension of habeas corpus is interpreted very broadly by the authorities. If it's decided that someone's behaving suspiciously, due process is forgotten." With his back against Dr. Whyville's sturdy picket fence, he scanned the street. It was deserted save for a white-haired woman tending a withered flower bed three houses away.

"I was assigned to watch the doctor's residence, but someone else may have trailed you here."

"I didn't see anyone." The thought alarmed her.

"I implore you. Go home. Please. Don't involve yourself any further."

"Why are you saying all this?"

He responded with a smile that struck her as genuine, without dissembling. "Haven't I told you? I wish I were bright enough to spout some poetry to explain, but I'm not. I'm just a fool chasing moonbeams. I know you don't care about me."

How cruel it was that she liked this man. He was the enemy. She said, "You're mistaken, Mr. Price. I do care about you, especially your past. In April, in Baltimore, detectives attacked a man speaking at a private meeting of a group called the Knights of Liberty." Wariness stiffened and then obliterated his smile. "Did you or your organization have anything to do with it?"

"I'm not permitted to say where we go or what we do."

"My father was killed at that meeting. Shot down like a common thief. He was unarmed."

"Maybe he was inciting the group to unlawful acts."

"Go to hell, Mr. Price. You just go to hell. I think you've all but admitted you know about it."

"The Knights were dedicated to terrorism against the government. They've been broken up. I'm aware that a man named Calhoun Miller died at one of their gatherings, but I didn't connect him with you. I'm very sorry for the tragedy. That's all I can say. Now please go home and stay there. Nothing else will protect you."

He walked swiftly toward the alley, kicking up yellow dust as he went.

*   *   *

A week later, a Thursday night, Donal was back in Washington. He had tickets for a performance by Joe Jefferson in his perennial role of Rip van Winkle. Margaret had seen the great actor play the title character, but she was quite willing to see him a second time. Jefferson's acting might compensate for the dingy atmosphere of the old Washington Theatre at Eleventh and C Streets.

The box Donal booked was infernally hot. At intermission, Margaret was glad to escape to the portico. Hissing gas fixtures above the main doors showed up the peeling paint on tall white pillars. Donal watched a couple of soldiers cavorting in the street with two painted ladies. Fastidiously, he wiped his lip with a handkerchief.

"I don't like the atmosphere in this town. I'd be much happier to wait out the war in New York City or Nassau. I'd like you to consider it seriously, Margaret, for the sake of your own safety and contentment. We could be married. You've agreed in principle."

"Donal, this isn't the time."

"You still won't settle on a wedding date? Why not?"

A hackney coach pulled up across the street. The door opened and Lon stepped down. Sudden dread gripped Margaret as he paid the cabman.

"Because I have a duty. Rose is being held illegally. She needs her friends standing by." It was a quick, blessedly convenient way to slip past the marriage issue. Lon strode toward them, his face grim. He greeted them with a polite tip of his hat.

"I'm afraid I must spoil your evening, Miss Miller. I have to take you into custody."

"Custody? What the hell do you mean?" Donal's shout drew stares from other theatergoers.

"It's War Department business. I asked to be the one to do this because I wanted Miss Miller spared the treatment some of our men give to prisoners." To Margaret he added, "An agent named Scully did follow you to the doctor's house."

Donal said, "What's he talking about, Margaret? What are you mixed up in?"

How strange she felt. Frightened, yet oddly elated that, of all people, Lon Price had reprieved her from consideration of a wedding she didn't want.

"I've only been doing what I thought was right," she said. "I'll be safe with this gentleman. He's a Yankee, but someone taught him good manners." She slipped her arm in Lon's, her breast pressing his coat sleeve. Though it wasn't intentional, she took unexpected pleasure in it.

Donal shouted again, perhaps hoping others would intervene. "You can't arrest someone without a warrant."

Two portly gentlemen approached, their faces bellicose. Lon opened his jacket to show a pistol in his waistband. "I wouldn't interfere."

The men pulled back. Lon spoke to Donal. "You're wrong. Washington is under martial law. Anyone can be arrested, anytime, for anything. Miss Miller?"

Arm in arm, they stepped into the street. Donal McKee watched with an expression of stupefied rage.

24

December 1861–January 1862

"How are you doing, Zachariah?" Lon asked in the alley behind the kitchen of Willard's. Their cigarettes glowed in the December dusk. Spits of snow mixed with a rainy drizzle.

"Staying alive," the tall man said. "Got me a decent room with a widow lady of color."

A poultry wagon pulled up in the churned mud. The driver unloaded his delivery—plucked chickens strung from a pole. Going in, he bumped Zach. "One side, nigger."

Lon said, "Do you get much of that?"

"More'n I expected, an' plenty enough to choke on. If I was to fight every white man who called me a nigger, I'd never eat or sleep. You goin' to need a black man to go into reb country, like you said once?"

"If the Army ever moves."

George McClellan's star had risen higher than ever thanks to his deft maneuvering after the October fiasco at Ball's Bluff. On the Potomac northwest of Washington, a small engagement—some seventeen hundred men on each side—had turned into a Union rout. Most of the men on the Confederate side were already blooded. The Federal troops were not. The minor battle became a major embarrassment for McClellan, who kept a personal printing press churning out proclamations. The one just prior to Ball's Bluff had said, "Soldiers! We have seen our last retreat! We have seen our last defeat!"

Congress wanted a scapegoat. McClellan convinced some important senators that the fault lay with Winfield Scott. The general-in-chief was too old, too tired, too sick with dropsy and gout to be effective. The ploy worked. Congress absolved McClellan and assigned blame to the commander at Ball's Bluff, Brigadier General Stone. On November 1, on Lincoln's order, McClellan replaced Scott. Washington celebrated with a torchlight parade of Blenker's German divisions, and red, white, and blue rockets over the Capitol.

As Christmas approached, McClellan's troops drilled, huddled in rain-drenched camps, and waited. The line from the government's daily bulletin, "All quiet on the Potomac," was spoken derisively. Congressional radicals found Lincoln too patient. They organized a joint committee to investigate conduct of the war. Secretary Cameron's chief counsel, Edwin Stanton, was scathing about McClellan's torpor and luxurious living: "The general's champagne and oyster suppers must stop."

Lon said, "Came for some advice, Zachariah. I need a Christmas present for a lady. She's locked up in a house with seven other women. The government claims she's a spy. Food is the only gift she can receive."

Zach tossed his cigarette in a puddle. The music of a street band playing "Adeste Fidelis" floated to the alley. Despite the weather, and the war, Washington was enjoying the season. The city teemed with inventors and pickpockets, arms dealers and horse wranglers, undertakers and surgeons, all looking for business. The famous novelist Mr. Trollope came to town. And every day, more whores.

"This lady mean something to you?"

"When I'm on duty, no. Otherwise . . ."

The unfinished sentence made Zach smile. "Cloved ham. Big cloved ham'd be good. Fancy, but not too friendly. Her jailers'd like it too."

"Can I buy it from the hotel?"

"See if I can fix it with the chef. I got to go now. 'Member what I said. I want to do something to smack the rebs."

"So do I. I'm sick of questioning deserters."

*　　*　　*

On Christmas Eve, Lon called at Fort Greenhow with the ham wrapped in gift paper. Margaret's healthy color was gone. She looked thinner, though no less desirable. He wanted to reach out, hold her. A guard was watching them.

A few greens were strung in the parlor, the only sign of a celebration. Three of the female inmates sat cocooned with their thoughts. According to Margaret, the newest, Mrs. Baxley, could be depended upon for a fit of hysterics at least once a day.

"How grand of you," she said when Lon presented the gift in the library. "There's no way I can repay your kindness, Mr. Price."

The sweet aroma of the ham seeped through its bright wrapping. In the corner, little Rose was searching for a book. "I'd like you to call me Lon, though I expect you call me other things." She laughed. "How are you faring in here?"

"The days pass slowly. Nights are the worst. I'm squeezed in an attic room with two cots and Mrs. Onderdonk, who snores."

Little Rose stuck out her tongue. "Mama says she's a pig and a dirty informer." Oink-oinking, she skipped away with her book.

"It would be a lot worse for you in Old Capitol," he said.

"Are they thinking of moving us?"

"That's the rumor. Secretary Cameron is on shaky ground. There's talk of a forced resignation, and Stanton's mentioned as the likely candidate to succeed him. Mr. Stanton takes a hard line on enemies." And on slavery, which would pit him against Pinkerton's patron. The boss was already grumbling about anti-McClellan cliques.

"Major Allen feels security's poor in here," Lon continued. "Mrs. Greenhow is still smuggling messages to the outside."

"She's a popular woman. She has many friends. Senator Wilson still calls, though he tells everyone he's investigating for some committee. *He* doesn't consider us traitors."

"You hold me responsible for what's happened, don't you?"

"How could I not? I understand you don't give the orders. You're a good soldier. I just wish you weren't. I wish you were on my side."

"I am, more than you know. I care for you, Margaret."

"I'm engaged to be married."

"To that McKee fellow. It doesn't change my feelings."

A clock ticked in the silence. Margaret sank down on a library stool, looking soft and vulnerable in the lamplight. "God, I don't know whether we're living in a comic opera or a bad dream."

"A war, Margaret. Like none ever before experienced in this country. Cousins and brothers and friends are fighting and killing each other."

"When do you suppose it will end?"

"Springtime, if General McClellan takes the field when the roads are dry. The President wants him to move and capture Richmond."

She looked at him intently. "I want to know who murdered my father."

"I can't help you. I've said that."

"So we're still enemies."

"I hope not."

She was silent. The wall between them was as high as ever. Discouraged, he wished her merry Christmas and left.

*   *   *

Old Capitol Prison at First and East Capitol Streets consisted of several buildings, some straggling a whole block north to A Street. Board fences built since the start of the war created a compound where prisoners could take the air in good weather. But there wasn't any; rain fell constantly through New Year's into January. McClellan remained inactive, recovering from an attack of typhoid.

On Monday, January 20, Pinkerton sent Lon to the Old Capitol with a sealed envelope for the warden, a scurvy little man named William Wood. Lon didn't expect to share the boss's every thought and decision, but it struck him that Pinkerton had grown more secretive since Stanton was appointed secretary of war the previous week.

Rain dripped from Lon's hat and poncho as he tied his horse outside the prison, three stories of brick elegance that had become a temple of filth and misery. Members of the Congress and Senate had once passed through the main door, to do the nation's business. Now the second-floor legislative halls were chopped into five large rooms holding Army officers awaiting court-martial, assorted Virginians and Marylanders arrested for aiding the enemy, and in Room 16, the largest, men and women whose political views were deemed dangerous. Elsewhere in the prison, black contrabands were kept as charity cases.

Pinkerton's men joked about the Old Capitol as "a rattrap with many holes leading in but no hole leading out." Lon loathed the dirt, the scabrous whitewashed walls, the stench of the overflowing open-air latrines. Two enclosed sinks for officials were available with appropriate bribes to the jailers. The warden planted paid informers among the prisoners, adding another layer of deceit.

Lon showed a pass to the soldier standing guard outside. Two noncoms emerged carrying a litter. A soiled sheet draped a man's body. Lon asked the sergeant, "Who's that?"

"Captain Elwood. He finally got hold of rope. Hanged himself last night." Rain plastered the sheet to the dead man's nose, chin, and gaping mouth. Lon shuddered, remembering the night under Rose Greenhow's steps.

The duty sergeant in the anteroom said Warden Wood was in the basement, interrogating a prisoner. Stories of Wood's methods had reached the Pinkerton office. Lon started for the stairs. "You can't go down there." Lon paid no attention.

The badly lit lower hall smelled of urine. Something scampered across Lon's toe as he approached the only door with light showing beneath it. He heard a wheedling voice he recognized as Wood's. He knocked. "Message for the warden from Major Allen."

The door was opened by a prosperous-looking man in a knee-length overcoat of gray tweed with a bold red handkerchief spilling from the breast pocket. The man wore smart leather gloves and a gray felt bowler. Lon didn't know him.

"I'll take the message."

"I'm to hand it to the warden personally."

"Let him in, let him in, we're almost done with this fish." Wood stepped away from an Army officer slumped in a chair with his wrists tied behind him. The warden was a small, ugly man, with uneven teeth and sprouts of hair in his ears. His waistcoat, shirtsleeves, and trousers were stained and speckled by food and drink. The warden always reminded Lon of a Dickens villain.

Lon gave him the letter. The bleary officer raised his head. "For Christ's sake, you haven't fed me or let me sleep for two days. I'm sitting in my own shit."

"I'm sorry, I'm very sorry," Wood said, bobbing his head and dry-washing his hands. "I'm just a humble fellow like yourself, doing as I'm told. I want to be your friend. I want to help you. All you have to do is sign the paper."

"Told you, I won't sign a goddam blank confession. I'm not guilty of anything except disliking the President and saying so publicly."

"Then I'm sorry, you'll just have to stay awake and go hungry a while more. If you change your mind, I'll be the first to help. Serve you breakfast myself, yes, sir."

The well-dressed man seemed greatly amused. Wood patted the prisoner's head, waved the others into the hall. When he shut the door, he discarded his geniality like a mask. "He'll sign. We'll break the son of a bitch before dark."

He ripped the envelope with a dirty fingernail; read the message. "Quite a piece of news you brought. Do you know my colleague from the War Department, Colonel Lafayette Baker?"

"Lon Price. I've certainly heard of you, Colonel." This was the mysterious free agent who had circled round and round the cabinet departments, ingratiating himself to secure a job. The boss said Baker had taken a dangerous trip to Richmond on his own, to impress Stanton.

They shook hands. Baker's grip was powerful. "You're with Major Allen, Mr. Price?"

"That's right."

"So you're really working for McClellan."

"I'm working for the Union."

"Secretary Stanton has little faith in your general. If he doesn't engage the enemy soon, he'll be back running some hick railroad. I mention it because I've heard you're a top operative. Don't back the wrong horse."

Lon wanted to plant a fist in the middle of the smug face. "Any reply to the message, Warden?"

"Say that we'll do our utmost to accommodate the guests in a style that befits them. Did Allen share the news with you?"

"No."

Wood bared his stained teeth, a troll's grin. "He's persuaded the higher-ups to close Fort Greenhow. All the lovely inmates will reside here starting tomorrow."

25

February–March 1862

Pinkerton had two dozen operatives working in Washington. During the winter several slipped in and out of Richmond. They bought drinks and wheedled information out of army malcontents, observed and made drawings of fortifications, gleaned what they could from random gossip. One agent, Elvin Stein, managed to stand close to Jeff Davis at his inauguration in the Virginia capital.

Tim Webster made the dangerous trip several times, with Hattie Lawton posing as Mrs. Webster. Lon envied the men. Their work behind enemy lines fueled resentment of his monotonous job. *What was the name of the regiment? Did you count the huts? What were their rations? Describe their morale.* Deserters and contrabands continued to exaggerate to please their new friends. When Lon turned in troop strength estimates, Pinkerton increased them:

"Always add ten percent to make up for regiments lost in the counting. If the general's to succeed, the Washington cabal must give him adequate manpower. Unless the enemy numbers are significant, they won't." The phrase *Washington cabal* referred to Secretary Stanton and the congressional radicals, "secret enemies" who were "trying to prejudice the President's mind against his commander."

They seemed to be doing a good job. In the autumn, when Little Mac was drilling his men seven or eight hours a day to create a trained fighting force from a disparate array of three-year volunteers and old Army men, Lincoln had given him his head. The general was not to be hurried. But in January, perhaps swayed by the radicals, Lincoln grew tired of waiting for McClellan's frequently promised "one great blow that will fatally crush the rebellion." The President's evening visits to headquarters for story-swapping stopped. Through Pinkerton, Lon heard of special, secret war orders from Lincoln that laid down irrevocable dates for the army to take the field against Joe Johnston's Confederates dug in at Manassas and Centreville.

Pinkerton said McClellan was "enraged and humiliated" by Lincoln's amateurish interference in military affairs. At the same time, Little Mac was promoting his plan for taking Richmond. It called for moving the Army by water down to Chesapeake Bay and then to Urbanna on the Rappahannock. From there he would strike out overland for the last fifty miles. Lincoln hesitated, withholding approval.

The radicals resurrected Ball's Bluff, where one of the Senate's own, Baker of Oregon, had died in the fighting. Brigadier General Stone was dragged before the Joint Committee on Conduct of the War and accused of "consorting with the enemy." Charges were based on testimony of a deserter named Jacob Shorb. He swore to the truth of earlier, unsubstantiated stories of secret negotiations between Stone and Confederate officers. Pinkerton called Shorb's statement unreliable, but he passed the report to McClellan, who sent it to Stanton. General Stone denied the charges and defended his honor and loyalty. He was arrested and packed off to prison in New York harbor, his career ruined. The point wasn't lost on the boss:

"General Stone is a conservative Democrat, tolerant of the South, like a certain high-ranking officer of our acquaintance. The Republicans choke on that. They're hell-bent on weeding out men who don't embrace their views one hundred percent. Being an emancipationist is fine, laudable. I'm an emancipationist. But the way the emancipationists in Congress promote their agenda is vicious and unprincipled. It isn't idealism, it's politics."

Reports of new victories came from the West. Fort Henry on the Tennessee River fell, and Fort Donelson on the Cumberland. Nashville was occupied. Why, then, was it still "all quiet on the Potomac"? The word *cowardice* was whispered in connection with McClellan.

*   *   *

Lon brought reports into the city every few days. He was caught there when a snowstorm struck. He was crossing the white wasteland of Treasury Park, bent against the wind, when a scarecrow figure loomed too abruptly for him to step out of the way. They collided. A blue-caped soldier following the tall man drew his side arm. Lon exclaimed, "Mr. President, I'm sorry, I didn't see you."

A muffler covered half of Lincoln's sallow face. Sunken eyes seemed to shine feverishly under his stovepipe hat. He signaled the soldier, who put his pistol away. Lincoln bent to peer at Lon. "We've met before, sir."

"Harrisburg, Mr. President. My name is Price. I'm with Major E. J. Allen. I'd like to say I was mightily sorry to hear about your loss."

"Willie was a fine boy. Spoiled, I guess, but he'd have grown out of it. Doctors called it bilious fever. It's always bilious fever if they're ignorant of the true cause."

"A terrible loss for you and your wife."

"We all bear burdens. The nation bears the heaviest one. Many families will lose beloved sons. We'll come through it. I pray the same for you in your important work. My regards to your chief."

Bony fingers, cold but strong, clasped Lon's hand. Then the President and his bodyguard proceeded down the path, quickly lost in the snowstorm.

The President looked sad, and whipped. The war was at a standstill. His wife was suspected of disloyalty because of her Kentucky relatives—"Two-thirds slavery, the other third secesh," they said of Mary Lincoln. Lincoln's general-in-chief alternately snubbed him, rebelled at his interference, or wooed him for whatever military purpose he had in mind. As Lon tramped on toward the Avenue, he reflected that the gaunt and gloomy man from Illinois bore the greatest burdens of anyone.

* * *

Sledge rode out to Fairfax Station one evening in late February. The weather had turned warm, melting the snow. Sledge and Lon walked among soldiers' log huts near the Orange & Alexandria railway, then up a low hill with a black shell crater gaping in its southern slope. Lon twisted a telescope into focus. He hoped to see Joe Johnston's campfires. The terrain was too hilly. All he saw, low on the horizon, was the bulbous silhouette of one of the new Federal observation balloons. A telegraph wire ran from the basket to the ground. Against a background of deep blue twilight and emerging stars, the balloon was descending slowly as the aeronaut valved off its lighter-than-air gas. Unseen below it, a ground crew held fast to heavy guy ropes to protect the balloon from chance wind gusts.

Sledge lit his corncob pipe. "Lewis and Scully headed for Richmond yesterday. Tim Webster's bad sick in some hotel down there. Crippled with arthritis. One too many trips across the Potomac in icy weather, I guess. Hattie's tending him. Pryce and John will take over, maybe try to bring him out."

"Lucky bastards." Lon snapped the sections of telescope together.

"You think so? Pryce says Richmond's crawling with detectives working for the Confederate provost marshal, Winder. He plays a rough game. Rougher than ours."

"I'd still like to be in it."

Sledge sucked on his pipe and blew smoke into the night air. He'd largely given up trying to persuade Lon that they weren't knights jousting with chivalrous opponents. He settled for an occasional prediction that Lon would get his eyes opened someday and, being the person he was, Lon wouldn't like what he saw.

*   *   *

When Lon returned to Washington with another valise full of reports, steamers, tugboats, and barges were crowded together in the Potomac basin: the flotilla McClellan was assembling for the voyage to Urbanna. Residents of the city still feared invasion. General Tom Jackson, called Stonewall after a heroic stand at Bull Run, was abroad in the Shenandoah valley with a force estimated at twenty to thirty thousand. Jackson was the capital's nightmare. If McClellan moved most of the army toward Richmond, the city would be vulnerable to a strike by Jackson's fast-marching "foot cavalry."

Pinkerton said that when the army did move, he would follow, doing intelligence work from the field. "I know you've chafed at all those hours of asking questions, Alonzo. I expect to take Mr. Bangs as my field assistant, and twelve other men besides. You will be one of them. See to your kit, make sure you have a weapon, and take any precautions that might be necessary in case you should be killed or captured. A will is a good idea."

"Thank you, sir, but there's no one to inherit anything." Admitting that brought frustrating thoughts of Margaret.

He and Sledge discussed Pinkerton's remark about capture. Lon thought of something that might be useful, so he took Sledge to the Mathew Brady studio on the Avenue. Brady, a feisty little Irishman with a bushy beard, was a popular Washington photographer. He kept a storeroom of martial properties for soldiers who wanted portraits to send home.

"We work for Major E. J. Allen," Lon began.

"I've heard the name." Brady's expression suggested he'd heard more than that.

"We want to be able to prove we're rebs if it's necessary."

"Wait here."

Brady returned with a large flag, four feet square; the Confederacy's new battle flag, a red field and a blue St. Andrew's cross holding thirteen white stars, eleven for the seceding states, two more for Missouri and Kentucky. The flag was pristine, the colors vivid.

"Where'd you come by that?" Sledge asked. "Looks brand-new."

"A gent from the vestry of one of our fine Episcopal churches came in for his portrait last week. He brought the flag as a backdrop. Said he purchased it from a shop here in town." Brady's smile was sardonic. "He didn't identify the shop, and I won't identify him. You're liable to arrest him."

"The flag's perfect," Lon said. "If we're captured, we're loyal sons of the South, with a picture to prove it."

Brady posed them in head clamps, Lon sitting, Sledge standing, against the flag and a potted palm. He dodged under the black head cloth, made the long exposure, and told Lon to come back tomorrow. Lon picked up two small metal cases, each holding a pale brown image of two heroic Confederates with jutting jaws and warlike scowls.

The next day Lon took his picture to Old Capitol, to show

Margaret. On the second floor, Room 16 was home to some two dozen men and women of varying age and appearance. It was a filthy, squalid place, with bunks ranged around the walls, and no privacy. Most of the bunks overflowed with small trunks, hatboxes, shoes, books, and other personal items.

"Why do they use the beds for storage?" Lon asked the guard.

"Ain't no good for sleeping. We got more bedbugs than McClellan's got soldiers. At night they put pallets on the floor. Some pull those tables together and spread blankets on 'em." Lon spied Margaret deep in conversation with someone partially hidden by another prisoner. He started through the tables of letter writers and penny poker players, only to stop when the prisoner moved and he recognized Margaret's fiancé, McKee. Stung with jealousy, he about-faced and left.

* * *

Through the winter, Lon had prepared for the possibility of capture in another way. He crammed his head with everything he could read and memorize about codes and ciphers. In enemy hands, a spy might need a safe means of sending a message to his commander.

Back in Cincinnati, the boss, General McClellan, and a telegrapher had developed a word-transposition cipher they used frequently. It depended on code sheets that could incriminate anyone caught with them. Lon wanted something workable but less dangerous. He found it in a translation of the otherwise turgid *Treatise on Secret Writing* by the French nobleman Blaise de Vigenère.

What he found was the Vigenère tableau, a classic grid of letters of the alphabet that anyone could remember, and use, without special skills, apparatus, code books, and the like. The cipher substituted letters in a chosen keyword for letters of the message, and based on these, the message was easily encoded and decoded using the tableau.

```
ABCDEFGH I JK LMNOP QRS TUVWXYZ
Aabcdefgh i jk l mnopqrstuvwxyz
Bbcdefghi jklmnopq rstuvwxyza
Ccdefghijklmnopqr stuvwxyzab
Ddefghi jklmnopqrs tuvwxyzabc
Eefghijklmnopqrst uvwxyzabcd
Ffghijklmnopqrstu vwxyzabcde
Gghijklmnopqrstuv wxyzabcdef
Hhijklmnopqr stuvwxyzabcdefg
Iijklmnopqr stuvwx yzabcdefgh
Jjklmnopqrst uvwxy zabcdcfghi
Kklmnopqr stuvwxyz abcdefghij
Llmnopqrs tuvwxyza bcdefghijk
Mmnopqrst uvwxyzab cdefghijkl
Nnopqrstuvwx yzabc defghijklm
Oopqrstuvwxy zabcd efghijklmn
Ppqrstuvwxyzabcde fghijklmno
Qqrstuvwxyzabcdef ghijklmnop
Rrstuvwxyzabcdefg hijklmnopq
Sstuvwxyzabcdefgh ijklmnopqr
Ttuvwxyzabcdefghi jklmnopqrs
Uuvwxyzabcdcfghij klmnopqrst
Vvwxyzabcdefghijk lmnopqrstu
Wwxyzabcdefghijkl mnopqrstuv
Xxyzabcdefghijklm nopqrstuvw
Yyzabcdefghijklmn opqrstuvwx
Zzabcdefghijklmn opqrstuvwxy
```

First, the sender wrote his keyword above the words to be transmitted, as many times as necessary. For practice, Lon wrote

PINKERTON
messenger

with *Pinkerton* the keyword. Going down the tableau's vertical P column to the intersection of the horizontal M linc gave him *b* as the first letter of the encoded word. For the *e* in *messenger*, he went down the I column, to the intersection with the horizontal E line, which gave him *m*, and so on. The entire word *messenger* encoded was

b m f c i e z s e

The decoder needed to know the sender's keyword, but that was all. Lon was delighted by this newest piece of spy equipment. He made sure both the boss and George Bangs knew his keyword, *preacher*.

* * *

On March 7, Friday, Lon tumbled out of bed to the sound of drumming and bugling in the streets. All day long, avenues and bridges were filled with regiments of blue-coated soldiers marching into Virginia, where smoke smudged the sky in the direction of the Confederate works at Centreville and Manassas.

The boss ordered Lon to follow the troops and report after the fighting. But there wasn't any fighting. On the Long Bridge, an officer galloping to the city shouted to anyone who would listen, "Joe Johnston's gone. The whole reb Army slipped away south."

In Centreville, Lon beheld astonishing sights. The black iron corpse of a locomotive sat on the tracks. Charred skeletons of freight cars had collapsed behind it. Johnston's men had burned their huts, their stores, everything but their fortifications. Long gun barrels painted black jutted from the embrasures. Gleeful soldiers were already using knives to cut slivers and chips from the wooden guns.

Lon fell into conversation with a stout British journalist named Russell who summed it up scornfully: "Little Napoleon's been humbugged by the rebels and their Quaker cannon. What's his next mistake?"

* * *

The following day, Washington was excited and alarmed to hear that a Confederate ironclad, *Virginia*, had sunk two frigates in Hampton Roads. She was the old Union frigate *Merrimac*, captured and converted. A day later she fought a standoff battle with a queer new vessel called the *Monitor*.

Lon saw an engraving of the Union ship. She resembled a shallow tin can on a wood slat.

With an enemy ironclad in the waters of Chesapeake Bay, and Joe Johnston's Army reported to be digging in below the Rappahannock, the Urbanna plan was dead. Pinkerton assembled his men chosen for the field. One was his son William, recently arrived from college for courier duty.

"Be ready at any hour," Pinkerton said. "We'll steam down the river to Fort Monroe with the Army."

"Does that mean fighting on the Peninsula?" one man asked.

"I believe that to be the general's intention."

McClellan no longer had the rank of general-in-chief. Lincoln had relieved him of all duty except command of the Army of the Potomac. The President said it was a boon; McClellan could concentrate on the campaign. The boss saw it differently:

"Another stab in the back by the Washington cabal."

Lon was bothered by the boss's harping on the cabal idea. Did a secret clique exist, or was it imaginary, a product of Pinkerton's unwavering devotion to their vain and prideful general? Lon knew of warring factions inside the government, but he thought they should work together, not savage each other like bloodied gamecocks.

As the meeting broke up, Pinkerton called him aside. "That contraband of yours—what was his name?"

"Zachariah Chisolm."

"Will he come with us?"

"If you want him, I'm sure he'll quit his job in a minute."

"See to it. We may have use for a man of color."

*   *   *

Lon closed out his account with his landlady. She promised to have a room when he returned. "You be careful with yourself, Alonzo. You're a fine young lad. Come back safely."

"No doubt of it," he said. He didn't underestimate the hazards of war, but this was what he'd lived and hoped for through the long, dreary winter. A renewed sense of purpose overcame his anxieties.

The operatives were paid six dollars a day in addition to an expense allowance. Lon had saved money regularly in a coffee can under his bed. He used the fund to equip himself for the campaign. The Pinkertons weren't supplied by Army quartermasters, something of a blessing since clothing and food sold to the government by private contractors was often shoddy or tainted.

Preparing for this moment, Lon had talked to some veterans of the regular Army, to learn what was useful in the field and what wasn't. Into a new knapsack he stuffed an extra pair of socks, an extra pair of drawers, an extra shirt, boxes of ammunition for his Colt, an ivory-handled jackknife, tobacco, cigarette papers, matches in a waterproof tube, his Bible, a razor and shaving soap, and a tin of tooth powder applied with any green twig that was handy. For a canteen he substituted a heavy tin cup that could double as a coffee boiler. Mess gear for the operatives would be carried in a camp chest in a supply wagon.

The knapsack weighed about twenty pounds. On top of it went a blanket roll and half of a shelter tent folded inside his rubber poncho. The poncho could serve as the tent floor.

He bought a new coat of heavy denim, knee-length, without markings. On the advice of an infantry sergeant he abandoned boots for stout walking shoes—brogues with thick soles and flat heels. Corduroy pants and an unmarked forage cap completed the uniform. Throw the cap away, he could pass for a farmer.

On St. Patrick's Day, a Monday, the Potomac was black with two or three hundred hulls of the transport flotilla. Steamers hooted and the tugs threw towlines on the barges. The first companies of Heintzelman's Third Corps marched to the wharves at Alexandria to board *Ocean Queen* and *Constitution*.

It was two o'clock when Lon called at the Old Capitol. He found Margaret in Room 16, sitting at a deal table with a male inmate. Cards and a cribbage board suggested a game of muggins in progress.

The sleeve of Margaret's yellow silk dress had been patched with blue flannel. Dirt marked her wrinkled skirt, as it marked the clothes of the young man with her. He was sallow, with big ears and a phlegmatic expression. His pale blue waistcoat bore a sizable wine stain. Both of them had left their noon meal uneaten; it was a pasty white mess of boiled beans, rice, and lumps of gray meat. Only reckless fools ate the meat served in the prison.

When Margaret saw Lon, she folded her cards and jumped up with a smile that was warm and genuine, or so he imagined. Her dark hair fell loosely to the middle of her back. He wondered how she kept it shiny and clean.

"Mason, this is an acquaintance, Mr. Price. This is Mason Highbourne. Mason was attending divinity school when he was picked up. It appears the First Amendment no longer applies if you write or speak about the Lincoln government unfavorably."

Mason gave him a slender, faintly damp hand. "I regret your imprisonment if you only spoke your mind, Mr. Highbourne. But I don't write War Department policy. It's a lovely day, Margaret. Are you allowed outside?"

"Yes, they don't deny us that. Excuse us, Mason?"

The young man muttered something, sat down, and began to deal a hand of patience.

Quite a few prisoners were taking the air in the compound under a brilliant sky filled with fat cumulus clouds. Sounds came over the walls from nearby streets: hoofbeats of cavalry, distant band music, the rattle of caissons and limbers bound for the wharves. The sun was baking the mud, as it would bake and harden the lanes and roads in Virginia. The earth smelled of springtime.

Margaret took his arm. Lon felt the roundness of her breast against his sleeve. The physical reaction was immediate. She said, "You're dressed differently."

"I came to say good-bye. I'm leaving the city. It may be the first and last campaign of the war."

"I wouldn't count on the South being beaten so easily." The breeze tossed her dark hair around her shoulders. He saw her rippling image reflected in a puddle.

"Before I go, I have to ask a question. You may think it impertinent, but to me it couldn't be more important." She waited, her head tilted toward him. "How strong is your attachment to McKee?"

A shoeless contraband walked by, mud squeezing up between his brown toes. Not old, as Lon first thought, but a young man, stooped and prematurely gray from slavery and perhaps the prospect of a life in the North that didn't want him.

Margaret touched the little golden palmetto tree hanging on her breast. "I promised to marry him. My father taught me that you don't break promises."

"Well, I respect that. I wish things could have worked out differently."

Her hand moved to his arm, closing gently. "There are moments when I feel the same."

"In spite of the work I do?"

"I've tried hard to hate you. I can't."

He didn't know which was stronger, his regret or his longing. "I hold you in the highest esteem, Margaret. The first day I saw you, I fell in love with—"

"Don't." Cool fingers against his lips stopped the rest. "You only rouse feelings that I can't permit."

"You mean in other circumstances . . . ?" Overcome, he didn't dare finish. Tears brimmed in her dark eyes. She dashed them away.

"Yes."

Heedless of other prisoners in the yard, she flung her arms around his neck. "Yes, yes! Now go. And for God's sake take care of yourself."

He felt her warm tears. She pressed a kiss on his cheek before she broke the embrace and ran away toward the prison entrance. In a window on the second floor, he saw someone dart back; someone who'd been watching. He thought it was the divinity student.

At the doorway Margaret raised a hand. A little wave, then she plunged into shadow, gone.

*   *   *

Lon left the prison by a guarded gate in the plank wall of the compound. Five minutes later, Mason Highbourne tapped at the warden's door on the first floor and slipped inside.

26

March 1862

The following day Margaret had a less welcome visitor.

She had been upstairs, visiting with Rose in the room she shared with her daughter. The furnishings consisted of a narrow bed, a broken chair, a pallet for little Rose, a piece of looking glass hung from a nail, and Rose's sewing machine. A sprig of jasmine drooped in a fruit jar on the table. The room had no windows, but the door could be closed for privacy. Sympathizers who visited Old Capitol brought stories of Rose's fame in Richmond. The Wild Rose was a Confederate heroine.

Rose asked if Margaret had been crying.

"Yes. I'm ashamed to admit it, but this place wears me down." She could hardly say otherwise; her cheeks and nose were red. She'd wept silently and fitfully all night, churning with fear that Lon Price would be killed, longing for intimate physical contact with him, guilty over her father's unpunished death, confused about her future with Donal.

They discussed Hanna Siegel. She hadn't visited either of them in prison. Margaret regretted it, but took it as another consequence of the war.

Back in Room 16, she fell into conversation with Dr. Whyville. He had been arrested and jailed two days after her arrest. She mused on the ironies. "We're both here because of an innocent bookmark."

"Not so innocent, my dear. Each little flower represented ten artillery pieces of a particular kind. The red flowers signified six-pound guns, yellow the old twelve-pound howitzers, white the twelve-pound 1857 Napolcons. Rose shouldn't have written the key in a book." Rose's arrogant confidence, her carelessness in keeping too many secret names and records where they could be discovered, was a subject much discussed by those thrown in jail because of it. Rose had been a dedicated spy, but not a prudent one.

"I believe that gentleman is looking for you," the doctor said, gathering up his playing cards. The court cards were famous Indian chiefs.

The man walked up to them. He lifted his gray bowler respectfully. "Hello, Miss Miller. Remember me? Colonel Baker?"

Margaret's temples started to hurt. A middle-aged woman sitting in her bunk vomited into a pail. The stench carried; Baker fanned himself with his hat.

"I was advised that you were here, but duties at the War Department have kept me from calling until now. Would it be more pleasant to stroll in the compound?"

"No. And you needn't waste your time. I've said all I'm going to say."

"Which so far amounts to precisely nothing. I've discussed your case, your silence, with Warden Wood. However, I'm not here to pry, only to inquire about your comfort."

"Really? Isn't that a bit ridiculous? Look around." The old woman retching in the bucket had half the inmates retreating from her, and the other half looking on with disgust.

"You needn't endure this, you know. You could have a room to yourself. Better food. It can be arranged."

"By paying these venal jailers? No thank you."

"Someone else could pay them. A benefactor. A special friend." Baker's eye slid along the curve of her bosom. "You're an extremely handsome woman."

She remembered the pursuit up and down Sixteenth Avenue in the hot sun; she'd seen the same glint in his eye then. Her smile was full of sweet venom as she said, "Mr. Baker, whoever you are, whatever you do, I want nothing from you. I don't traffic with Yankee trash."

Baker's cheeks bloomed with deep, rougelike color. Holding his bowler, his knuckles were white.

"The opposite of friendship is enmity, Miss Miller. Not a wise choice in these times."

"Get out of my sight."

"Certainly, after I remind you that enemies of the government can be kept in prison for years, without cause, without recourse to the legal system, or any hope of pardon. I'm afraid you have just guaranteed that fate for yourself, Miss Miller. Good afternoon."

Part Three

RETRIBUTION

27

April 1862

"Godamighty, what's 'at?"

"Professor Lowe's balloon boat," Lon said. "Never been anything like it. I told you about it."

Sledge's lapse was forgivable. There was too much to absorb in the display of martial might encircling them like a great sunlit cyclorama. Below the bluff in the York River, a steam tug towed a Navy coal barge fitted with a flat deck, deckhouses forward and balloon inflation equipment aft. Secured above the deck by mooring lines, one of Lowe's India silk balloons floated. Fifty feet high, it was handsomely painted with stars and a fierce Federal eagle.

That was only part of the spectacle of the Army of the Potomac debarking at Fort Monroe, at the tip of the peninsula where the York and James rivers joined. A garrison of ten thousand under elderly General Wool had held the fort since the outbreak of hostilities. Side-wheelers and barges unloaded men, materiel, wagons, ambulances, and artillery, including giant seacoast mortars that were moved inches at a time by teams of a hundred horses. Off the barges onto the piers came huge reels of telegraph wire to link McClellan with his field generals, and his headquarters with Washington. What a great, modern world they lived in!

"Is Lowe really a professor someplace?" Sledge asked.

"Don't think so. Mostly he gives public lectures. He's a scientist, and scientists are always called professor."

Behind the two men stretched a white ocean of tents, their own submerged in it somewhere. The air resounded with axles grinding, whips cracking, noncoms shouting cadence, pigs squealing and cattle lowing in hastily built slaughter pens. In the past fifteen days 125,000 men had moved down the Potomac—companies with their regiments, regiments with their divisions, divisions with their brigades, brigades with their corps. The boss said Little Mac was on his way to Fort Monroe by steamer right now. Three miles south across the water, the rebel base at Norfolk hid in haze; the enemy presence seemed unreal, no threat at all.

"Godamighty," Sledge said again. "Lon, did you ever see such an army? Bet we bust into Richmond before the first of May. Then we can all go home."

It was a bright, hopeful moment, this hot April Fools' morning. Lon remembered it because they were so full of anticipation and confidence, and because, after that, everything went wrong.

* * *

McClellan counted on a force of more than 150,000 for the campaign. Lincoln and the War Department seemed intent on denying it to him. On March 31, Blenker's ten-thousand-man division was ordered to Harpers Ferry to reinforce Frémont's new command. General Wool's garrison had to remain at Fort Monroe to guard against raids by *Virginia*. McClellan counted on a trump card, McDowell's I Corps, waiting outside Washington for orders to march. April 3, the day after the general's arrival on the Peninsula, Washington signaled that I Corps would be held back to defend the city.

"Before God, it's unconscionable," Pinkerton said to his men. "I have never seen the general so angry and bitter. If there was ever a doubt of the intent of the Washington cabal, it's gone."

Still, numbers favored the Federals; confidence remained high. The Army advanced on the old colonial village of Yorktown twelve miles up the Peninsula, where Cornwallis had surrendered to end the Revolution. Heintzelman's III Corps took the main road; Keyes's IV Corps marched in the same direction closer to the James. The soldiers sang a new "Battle Hymn," words set to the old tune of "John Brown's Body." The day was gloriously sunny.

The second day, the skies opened. Torrential rain turned the roads to glue. McClellan's staff had been told the roads were passable in all weather. Old General Wool had issued faulty maps showing the Warwick River running parallel to the James. Actually it cut across the Peninsula, flowing toward Yorktown. The rebels were dug in behind it. McClellan's great juggernaut ground to a stop. Weather kept Professor Lowe's observation balloons grounded.

Lon and his colleagues were bedeviled and bitten by sand fleas, deer flies, gnats, and mosquitoes. They slept in mud and damp. In a matter of hours Lon's clothes were stiff and rank. They wouldn't be washed until and unless he did it himself. All the Army laundresses had been left behind.

At least they ate decently. Pinkerton had found an Italian cook whom he paid out of his own pocket. Spaldini's English consisted mostly of profanity. He relied on his hands, waving them about when he wasn't chopping or slicing ingredients or stirring the stew kettle. Pinkerton relaxed his stand on alcohol and allowed small glasses of port to be served at the evening mess. He ate and drank nothing. Since arriving, he'd been sick with dysentery.

Yorktown lay behind enormous fortifications, some left over from the Revolution. These were protected by deep outer ditches, and bombproof dugouts to nullify artillery. A second Confederate bastion at Gloucester Point, across the York, menaced both the Federal Army and its gunboats in the river.

Camp talk said the Federals could easily storm the Yorktown fortifications and overcome the estimated fifteen or twenty thousand defenders. McClellan preferred a slower, safer method, a siege. Commencing April 6, earthworks were dug by night, and guns brought up during succeeding days. The fortifications were masterpieces of engineering, great ramparts of earth held firm by gabions, dirt-filled baskets, topped by sandbags. Impatient for action, Lon wasn't impressed by such niceties of military science.

Pinkerton tottered through the days gray-faced and weak. He was burdened with all sorts of new work from the War Department: orders to pursue bounty jumpers, requests from politicians who wanted some favor from the general, summonses to sit in court-martial hearings, complaints against crooked contractors. Some of the complaints fell to Lon to investigate. He became an unwilling expert on biscuits infested with worms and on the purple shine of rotten beef. He wrote reports and more reports.

His beard had grown thick and long; a majority of the men in the Army looked like biblical patriarchs. Wherever he went, Lon kept his loaded pistol in one coat pocket and the Brady photograph in another. He longed for a picture of Margaret Miller.

The telegraph brought word of a big battle at a place called Shiloh Church in faraway Tennessee. A general nicknamed Unconditional Surrender Grant was praised. The rebs had lost one of their best, General Albert Sidney Johnston.

A few deserters made their way through Union lines. Lon interrogated one from the Ninth Alabama. The wall-eyed corporal was eager to cooperate. "They's a new man advisin' Jeff Davis. General Bob Lee. Seen him as we passed through Richmond."

Lon wrote it down, though he'd heard it before. "How many men in your regiment?"

The corporal wriggled on his stool, scratched at unwelcome visitors in his crotch. "You mean on the rolls or ready to scrap?"

"There's a difference?" A suspicion about that had nagged him for days.

"Shit, yes, johnny. How many men you think we got?"

"We estimate seven or eight hundred to a regiment."

"On the rolls, mebbe. That don't mean fit for duty. They's always a bunch sick, or put in irons. Then they's the cooks and drummer boys and some too yella to shoot a musket. Six or six-fifty might be more like it, though I ain't never counted heads."

Lon wrote it down. Pinkerton always wanted the larger number, the aggregate present, which he then inflated by the usual ten percent. Lon wondered why they were accumulating reams of misleading information. He was angry that no one faced the issue.

*　　*　　*

An annoyingly brash Confederate general, "Prince John" Magruder, continued to balk the Union Army along the ten-mile Warwick River line. Between its five mill dams, the flooded river created a series of ponds too wide and deep for an assault by infantry or cavalry. The narrow dams were the only way across, and the rebs had them blanketed by sharpshooters hidden in the woods and behind fortifications.

Magruder's artillery blasted anything that moved. His men demonstrated regularly in view of the Federals. His bands played all night long to interrupt sleep. Lowe's balloons went aloft every day to observe. Sometimes Lowe rode in the basket with one or more observers; sometimes he sent one of his aeronaut-navigators. Members of Pinkerton's little cadre went up occasionally, studying terrain and making sketch maps. Lon's turn came toward the end of April.

Sledge was supposed to go up with him, but he was suffering from the same latrine quickstep that had plagued the boss. Zach Chisolm had lingered on the edge of the group for weeks, barely tolerated, never invited to sit at the regular mess table. He asked to take Sledge's place. Pinkerton grudgingly agreed. "The balloon navigator has the final say."

Lowe's balloons regularly ascended before dawn, when enemy campfires could be seen. Changes in their location often revealed troop movements. At half past three in the morning, Lon and Zach set out to walk several miles to one of Lowe's ground stations, a clearing behind the lines out of artillery range.

Calcium lights with silvered reflectors bathed the clearing in a white glare. The lights were set at a safe distance from the gas generators, two bulky wagons that were basically acid-proof retorts on wheels. Iron filings went in a hatch on top. Sulfuric acid was poured through a vertical tube to create hydrogen gas. Canvas-covered piping ran from each tank to a square wooden apparatus with a single, larger pipe coming from the other side. This pipe inflated a balloon in less than two hours.

Thaddeus Lowe's entire complement of fifty men appeared to be working tonight. Although the Balloon Corps reported to the Army topographical engineers, Lowe and his crew were civilians. Lon spotted the husky six-foot professor studying a map with a smaller man who had a pug face and soup-strainer mustache.

"Hello, my boy," Lowe said as Lon approached. Thaddeus

Sobieski Constantine Lowe wasn't even thirty, but everyone
noticeably younger was "my boy." He was a big, showy man
with glossy black hair and powerful shoulders. He wore a long
black coat, high boots, and a fatigue cap bearing a balloon-
shaped metal badge stamped with the letters *BC.* Lon imagined he was a commanding presence on the lecture platform.
"You're Mr. Price?"

"I am."

"Mr. Harper's your navigator this morning." Lon held out
his hand. The pug-faced young man ignored it and stared at
Zach.

"Who's this?"

"Zach Chisolm. He's attached to our unit."

Harper rolled up the map. "Didn't bargain on no niggers."

Lowe cautioned him with a stern glance. Harper tramped
away to the balloon. By its painted stars and stripes, Lon recognized it as *Liberty.*

The single hose from the wooden apparatus snaked over
the ground to mate with the balloon envelope where it ta-
pered to a filler port. The balloon's beige walls were slowly
expanding, contained inside a web of linen cords. The cords
ran down to a thick wooden ring surrounding the filler port;
each cord was tied off on the ring. Below the ring hung a blue
wicker basket painted with white stars. Men were attaching
sandbags to the basket for ballast. The balloon was sixty feet
high, strangely beautiful swaying there on its manila mooring
lines.

"We have no fog and a favorable breeze," Lowe said.
"Harper is instructed to go across the river. Our balloons are
always shot at. Are you prepared for that?" Lowe's blue eyes
were fixed on Zach. Zach looked resentful at the implication
of weakness.

"We'll take the same risks as your aeronaut," Lon said. A
horseman trotted out of the woods. Lon recognized the be-
spectacled civilian who jumped down from the lathered animal.

"Stein, what the devil are you doing here?"

"Finding my way back to Major Allen." Elvin Stein was a
small, fidgety man. The calcium lights reflected from the little
circles of his spectacles. In his shabby velvet-collared coat and

muted yellow waistcoat he could have passed for an insurance agent or a schoolteacher. He certainly didn't look like a spy.

Stein dippered water from a bucket, drank some, and poured the rest over his grimy forehead. His trousers were torn in two places, as though he'd ridden through brambles.

"The game's blown in Richmond. I barely got out. A skiff brought me down the James. I stole this horse back there a ways."

"What went wrong in Richmond?"

"Lewis and Scully found Tim Webster laid up with arthritis, all right. Hattie was nursing him. You remember Senator Jackson Morton of Florida?"

"The boss had Morton and his family under house arrest in Washington for a while."

"And Lewis and Scully guarded them. Two of Morton's sons are in Richmond. They recognized and identified Pryce and John. General Winder, the provost marshal, has a list of all our operatives, damned if I know how."

"Rose Greenhow might be responsible. What else?"

"The rebs tossed Pryce and John in the Henrico County jail. Pryce and some others managed to escape, but Pryce was caught. He and John were shoved in Castle Godwin. Used to be the old jail for coloreds. Now it's a hellhole for war prisoners. They were worked over by the provost's detectives. Nasty bunch. Both our lads held fast, denied everything, though I heard Scully almost broke. They went on trial. The verdict was quick. Guilty. No exchange, no parole. The sentence was hanging."

"My God," Lon said.

"Haven't told you the worst. Scully couldn't take the thought of dying. He said if they pardoned him, he'd confess. He ratted out Pryce, and Tim and Hattie too. Pryce is an Englishman. The acting British consul's interceding to get his sentence commuted, but Tim and Hattie don't have an escape hatch. Where exactly do I find the boss?"

Lon gave directions. Stein hooked his foot in the stirrup and swung up. "This was a fine gentleman's game to start with. It isn't anymore." He rode away into the dark woods.

In the white glare, Lowe supervised the closing of the gas bag. Harper bellowed, "Hey, detective. If you're going aloft, get over here, you and your coon."

A muscle stood out in Zach's forehead. Lon said, "Maybe you should stay behind. I have a feeling he's a mean son of a bitch."

"He don't scare me none."

"All right, but don't let him provoke you. We're all supposed to be on the same side."

"Oh, sure," Zach said, making a face. As they walked toward the balloon, Lon heard Stein's ominous words. *This was a fine gentleman's game to start with. It isn't anymore.*

Harper was already in the balloon basket. Lon threw his leg over and climbed in, then Zach. Distantly, Prince John Magruder's artillery boomed to salute the dawn.

28

April 1862

The pear-shaped balloon rose slowly toward the tree line as the ground crew paid out its mooring ropes through pulley blocks. The balloon was a pretty sight, its coats of varnish shining ever more brightly as it lifted from the treetops into the light. The basket tended to sway, which Lon found a not unpleasant sensation. Zach looked bilious.

Lon noticed a rifle wedged between the basket and a pile of extra sandbags. One of the new Spencers, seven-shot, with lever action. It was the only thing about Harper that he envied.

Daylight bathed the flat, wooded Peninsula slowly revealing itself as they ascended. Lon asked about the two loops of rope hanging down through the wooden ring just above them. Harper said one controlled a valve that vented gas from the top of the balloon, for a slow descent. The other opened something called a rip panel, in the balloon's upper quadrant, allowing for quick collapse of the envelope in an emergency.

Zach said, "How high might we be goin', sir?" Harper didn't

answer. From an instrument box lashed to the outside of the basket he took naval field glasses, useful for scanning a wide area when magnification wasn't critical.

"Harper," Lon said. "Did you hear his question?"

"Three to five hundred feet's usual for observation. You can see twelve, fifteen miles on a good day. Today we'll stay fairly low." Harper spoke without lowering the field glasses.

A scene of spectacular beauty and clarity spread before them. They were floating toward the near side of the Warwick River, wide and placid as a moat in the breaking light. Lon asked Harper to identify a narrow dam.

"Lee's Mill."

Rifle pits were dug on the river's far bank, on land cleared of brush and small trees. Lon detected movement in the rifle pits, and in the woods behind. Out of the trees came a puff of smoke followed by the bang of an artillery piece. "Spotted us," Harper said. "Giving us the usual hello and good morning."

Lon guessed they might be three thousand yards from the concealed gun. The shell burst harmlessly at less than half that distance.

"They got twelve-pounders in there," Harper said. "Smooth bores, in four-gun batteries. Nothing to fret over. Range is too long and twelves can't fire at a high angle. Mostly they scratch on your nerves."

Fervently Zach said, "They sure scratch on mine." Harper's response was a patronizing stare.

He replaced the field glasses in the instrument box; they had told him what he should examine more closely. He uncapped a lacquered telescope tube, pulled the segments apart, and squinted through the eyepiece.

To their right, Lon could see all the way to Yorktown—the quaint rooftops, Joe Johnston's fortifications swarming with men, the equally busy Union earthworks facing them. Gloucester Point was visible across the narrow river channel. Straight ahead, a mile or so beyond the Lee's Mill dam, the rebs had built an abatis, a wide rampart of felled trees with ax-sharpened branches pointing outward to hinder an enemy advance. Some distance behind the abatis lay an enormous earthwork. Tree stumps in front of it had been cut to provide a wide field of fire. Lon tapped Harper, pointed to the earth-work.

Harper said, "Fort Magruder. Second defense line in case the first fails. Don't seem like much has changed around here since yesterday. Let's float on over for a closer look." He leaned out of the basket and exchanged hand signals with tiny figures on the ground. The crewmen paid out the lines and the balloon drifted to the river. Its shadow appeared on the smooth water.

The morning was still. Lon heard birdsong, a hound bark-ing somewhere. Smoke in the woods identified campsites coming alive. A sudden air current from the east struck the balloon and drove it down. When the gust died, Harper untied a sandbag and dropped it to help the balloon recover altitude. Lon thought the navigator looked anxious.

He borrowed Harper's telescope and watched artillery lim-bers racing down a distant dirt road, then a cavalry troop in a column of fours advancing at a walk, over toward the old colonial capital of Williamsburg. A couple of eager boys in butternut homespun climbed out of a rifle pit and banged off futile shots at the balloon. Another downdraft pushed the bal-loon toward the ground, but it recovered and rose quickly. Lon's pulse beat a little faster.

"Amazing, how much you can see from here," he said to Harper.

"At first the shoulder straps laughed at the professor's no-tion of scouting from the air. But a bunch of 'em—Fitz-John Porter, Stoneman, Heintzelman, Little Mac too—they all took rides. Now they believe."

As they floated above the placid river, Lon felt the wind, harder than before. The gusts tended to make the balloon plunge suddenly. Each drop of ten or twenty feet drove Lon's stomach up to his windpipe, or so it felt. More rifles banged away in hopes of a hit. "Damn wind's movin' us too close," Harper said. "Got to go higher. Make yourself useful, nigger. Throw out four or five sandbags."

"Look, Harper, don't use that word with Mr. Chisolm. He's a free man, good as you."

"Fuck he is." Harper turned his back. Wind pushed them downward again. The bottom of the basket exploded in a shower of splinters. Harper leaped back. A marksman had hit the basket from directly underneath.

"Jesus. Almost got me. Grab me that rifle, nigger."

Lon yanked the Spencer from behind the sandbags and fairly slammed it into Harper's hands. "I told you to shut up with—" Harper swung the Spencer butt first into Lon's mouth.

Lon's lip split open. Blood ran down his chin. He was more outraged than hurt. As the balloon sailed toward the woods, he brought his fists up. Harper raised the rifle, shielding his face. "You want to have it out or you want to get away? We're too low, goddam it. You"—Zach—"drop all the sandbags. Price, yank that tether line. Three sharp tugs, wait, then three more."

Zach untied and dropped the sandbags. Lon gave three tugs on the manila line, then another three. Two sharp tugs answered. Shouts, oaths, and a stutter of rifle fire protested the falling sandbags. One of the batteries in the woods boomed. Harper yelled, "Keep your head down. This low, they can hit us. They's seventy or eighty lead balls in every—" A timed-fuse shell detonated in midair.

Lon and Zach ducked. Lon held the top of his head. Lead balls whistled through the rigging. One knocked a triangular chunk from the wooden ring. Two net lines broke. Harper shouted at Lon, "When you pulled the tether did they answer?"

"Think so. I felt two tugs."

Bullets from the rifle pits chipped the sides of the basket. "Why'n hell don't they reel us in? Got to lighten more." The navigator had a crazed look. He levered a round in the chamber, cocked the Spencer, and aimed at Zach.

"Do your countrymen a service, nigger. Jump."

Zach's mouth dropped open. Enraged, Lon tore the Colt out of his pocket. A boom warned of another shell on the way. Lon launched himself across the basket at Harper.

The navigator swung the Spencer to club him. The artillery shell detonated close to the balloon. Not two feet from Lon, a lead ball drove into Harper's right eye. Harper's hands flew in the air. His wrist tangled in the rip panel rope and dragged on it as he fell, crying a woman's name. With a crack, the rip

panel opened above them. Gas vented noisily. They plum-
meted.

A third shell burst. Lead balls tore through the gas bag. Lon
only had time to snatch the fallen Spencer and shout, "Hang
on, Zach," before they crashed.

Harper shrieked. Lon bit through his lower lip, starting a
fresh flow of blood. He had a nightmare glimpse of Harper's
lolling head, one eye a bloody cavity, the other dead white, the
iris rolled up out of sight.

Lon shoved Zach out of the basket and tumbled after him,
a moment before the balloon and its net of ropes collapsed on
the basket and all the yelling men in a rifle pit on which they'd
landed.

Lon scrambled up with the Spencer. Not far away, the river
shone like a mirror of pink glass, bisected by the narrow dam.
"Run for it, Zach. Follow me across."

Rebel soldiers piled out of the rifle pits, whooping about a
Yankee turkey shoot. Lon bent over and ran with all his
strength. He didn't look behind, trusting to his ears to tell him
Zach was there, running just as hard.

Rifles cracked. A bullet ripped Lon's pant leg. He stumbled, almost fell headfirst into the river, but righted himself.
He skidded onto the narrow wooden cap of the dam, ran a
quarter of the way across. Bullets plopped and plucked at the
water around him.

Halfway across . . .

Three-quarters . . .

The ground ahead was sparsely treed, poor cover. At the
end of the dam he tripped on a buried stone and fell sideways
to the sloping bank. Landing in the mud, he slid downward on
his belly. His brogues went into the water. He slammed the
Spencer's butt into the bank and gripped it like a pole to arrest the slide. With all his weight on the barrel he pulled himself out of the water. The Spencer's stock split and broke,
hurling him to the bank face first. The impact left him gasping
and spitting mud.

"Get up, Lonzo." Zach knelt. His long, tapering fingers slid
under Lon's arms to lift him. He was crouched that way when
the first reb in a file of six crossing the dam fired his musket.
Zach yelled. The bullet threw him down across his fallen friend.

*   *   *

We shall meet, but we shall miss him.
There will be one vacant chair . . .

Margaret laid a red four-spot on a black five and listened to
the singer. She didn't know his name, but he had a lovely
tenor. The words of his ballad affected her even though it was
a Yankee song, written after Ball's Bluff.

We shall linger to caress him
While we breathe our evening prayer.

She stared at the patience layout, the fiftieth or five hun-
dredth she'd dealt in the days and weeks that blurred together
with a dreadful sameness. Prisoners left, others arrived,
dragged in by Stanton's private police. Dr. Whyville was ailing
again. General McClellan was advancing on Richmond. Was
Cicero safe? She fought against worry and despair that pulled
her down a little more every day. She hated herself for suc-
cumbing, yet seemed helpless to reverse the descent.

She thought often of Lon Price. Was he in danger? Why did
he prey on her mind? She knew very well. She was in love
with him; a hopeless, wrongful, aching love. She told no one.
Lon was the enemy.

Well, it was over. It had never started, really. Doubtless
she'd never see him again.

The sad song ended. She laid a black trey on the four. Her
hair was stringy and dull. She had no soap to wash it properly,
and only half a bucket of water once a week. Under her clothing, red insect bites itched on her legs, her neck, between her
breasts.

Warden Wood, the pious little monster, let her use the
walled sinks. "That's all I can do, you've made your bed. I'd be
your friend but I'm not permitted. You were seen embracing
a Pinkerton detective in an effort to seduce him."

Margaret laughed at the absurdity.

Wood blathered on, "You offended Colonel Baker, offended him deeply. He's a very influential man. Very close to
Mr. Stanton. It's out of my hands. I'm so sorry."

Someone approached her table. She glanced up with a flinty look. "Hello, Mason." She no longer believed Mason Highbourne was a divinity student. She didn't know what he was, other than a spy.

"How is Rose dealing with her celebrity, has she confided?"

"No, Mason." Margaret played another card. "Why don't you ask your friend the warden? Perhaps he knows." Somehow Rose had smuggled a letter across the lines to Thomas Jordan-Rayford in Virginia, full of purple language describing the "outrages" of Pinkerton's "ruffians" when they had invaded her home and searched her person. The sensational letter was printed in the *Richmond Whig*, then throughout the North, and in England.

Some of Rose's partisans kept vigil outside the Old Capitol every day, hoping to glimpse her at a window. Flowers were left on the prison steps with memorial cards praising her devotion to the South. Kindly visitors bringing in food baskets also smuggled clippings from Southern papers that lauded Rose as a frontline soldier, or a saint. The whole Confederacy knew that when she was officially interrogated in March, she treated General Dix and Judge Pierrepont with disdain, denying all the charges assembled by "the Jew detective," and vilifying Lincoln in front of the crowded hearing room.

"Why do you constantly accuse me of being the warden's friend?" Highbourne said, petulant.

"Why? Because your cheeks are shaven. Your coat's brushed, your linen's clean. Someone's feeding you well. Who would do all those favors when you claim you're too poor to offer bribes? Everyone knows you're in the warden's quarters nearly every day. Does that answer you, Mason? If so, please take yourself out of my sight."

Highbourne drew his shoulders up and pulled his head down. She thought of him as an offended turtle, assuming turtles could be offended. "Arrogant bitch," he said, and stalked off.

Margaret wanted to laugh. Instead, her eyes filled with tears. They were wearing her down. Prison was wearing her down. With a little cry—half in anger, half in despair—she swept the patience layout off the table. Prisoners looked up from their sewing or their reading, then looked away.

She thought of Donal McKee. He'd gone back to New York. Donal's presence would have helped. She didn't love him, but his visits were moments of relief and rest. She longed for him to come again, soon.

29

April–May 1862

Zach was on his knees, his right hand braced against the ground. His left arm hung like the broken wing of a bird. An armband of blood wrapped his homespun shirt above the elbow. Lon saw all this in the seconds it took to sit up and lever a round into the chamber of the broken Spencer.

The first reb reached the end of the dam. Lon shot at him and missed. The soldiers, all young and green, collided with one another like circus clowns. Lon chambered and fired a second round. The last three men in the file retreated. The second and third reb jumped or fell into the river. Only the redheaded youngster who'd come over first held his ground, hastily reloading his musket. Lon levered the Spencer again and came up with an empty chamber. Harper had kept only two rounds in the piece.

Lon pushed Zach flat to the ground an instant before the redhead shot at them. The reb's aim was no better than Lon's. The ball buzzed overhead and landed in a patch of dead brush near the trees. Lon rolled on his stomach and fired the pocket Colt twice. The redhead faced about to run, slipped, and took a header in the water with his musket.

Lon helped Zach stand. "You hadn't taken that bullet, it'd got me."

" 'S all right. You my friend. Han't had many in my life. Can we fly out of here 'fore those rebs finish their swim?" In the river there was noisy splashing, a cry of "Charlie, I cain't swim!"

"Can you run?" Lon said.

"It's my arm, not my leg. Sometimes I wonder how you white folks got enough brains to run the world like you do."

Lon laughed, waved his friend forward. "Go through there." They ran to the patch of dead brush. In his pocket Lon found the waterproof tube of matches. He struck one, tossed it into the brush. They left a rampart of blue-gray smoke behind them as they limped away toward the ground station. Gradually the yelps of the rebs faded.

Lon reported to Lowe that both *Liberty* and Harper were lost, driven over the river into enemy range by freak winds. He said nothing about Harper's meanness and cowardice. What was the point? The man was dead, and all his bad traits with him.

* * *

The surgeons dug a flattened musket ball out of Zach's arm, patched him up, and pronounced him lucky to have no bone damage. He recuperated in the pup tent he occupied by himself. Lon looked in when he could; brought Zach extra hardtack and a canteen holding a mix of water and sutler's whiskey. Sledge was scornful of so much fuss over a colored man. Lon reminded him of Zach's act of bravery.

McClellan's siege guns were nearly all in place by the end of April. George Bangs said the bombardment of Yorktown would begin soon. On May Day, right after breakfast mess, Pinkerton called his men together in his tent in the headquarters compound. The boss's tent always stood within sight of the general's. A fierce wind battered the canvas walls. Pinkerton looked frail and haggard.

"Gentlemen, it's my duty to convey unhappy news. The rebellion has taken a new and sinister turn. On the twenty-ninth, last Tuesday, despite every humanitarian appeal that I could make, we lost a valued colleague and friend. Timothy Webster."

Silence. Men shuffled their feet.

"Tim was a dedicated and nerveless agent. A complete professional who repeatedly risked himself by entering Richmond to gather information. His reports were models of thoroughness and detail. He missed nothing, from shortages of hay or Army overcoats, to the number and equipment of

Richmond's defense batteries. Through misfortune and betrayal by a drunken coward, John Scully, Tim and Hattie Lawton fell into the hands of the Confederate provost marshal. General Winder incarcerated them and placed them on trial. The verdict against Hattie was relatively humane, a one-year sentence with no restrictions on parole or exchange. Tim wasn't so lucky. The tribunal sentenced him to hang."

The wind snapped the tent canvas with sharp gunshot sounds.

"Under a flag of truce arranged by General Wool, I personally crossed the lines to deliver a written appeal to the Davis government." Pinkerton found a paper on his field desk. "This is part of what I said. 'The course pursued by the Federal government toward spies has heretofore been forbearing. In many cases such persons have been released after a short confinement, and in no case has anyone charged with spying been sentenced to death.' "

Pinkerton laid the paper aside. "The effort was fruitless. Tim met his maker with a brave heart, but it was an ignominious death. A shameful public carnival, held at the city fairgrounds. Hawkers sold souvenirs. Respectable ladies of the town came out in fine carriages to observe the demise of a Yankee. When at last the noose was dropped around Tim's neck and the trap sprung, through some ungodly circumstance the rope unraveled. Tim fell to the ground, alive. He was compelled to climb the steps again, take the rope again—a double death."

An operative raised his hand. "Sir, how do we know all this?"

"Mrs. Lawton. Hattie wrote a full, heartbreaking report. We have friends buried deep in Richmond society with the means to smuggle out messages."

Pinkerton shut his eyes a moment. "Tim Webster's death opens a new and ugly chapter in our struggle. Our enemy has revealed his true face. We must always be vigilant, but henceforth, whenever it becomes necessary, we must be ruthless."

A sharp sense of being watched made Lon look around. Sledge was staring at him, as if to say he knew it would come to this. He'd warned Lon, only to be met by foolish denial.

Well, no more. Lon left the tent with the others. No one spoke.

*　　*　　*

On Saturday, May 3, two days before McClellan's guns were
to open the siege, Joe Johnston's artillery took the initiative.
Shot and shell thundered into the Union lines commencing
late in the day. The guns boomed long after darkness fell. In
the morning, scouts broke down the Yorktown sally port and
found that under cover of the barrage, Johnston had with-
drawn his men. He'd slipped away west, toward Richmond,
leaving the town to the Federals.

On Sunday, Spaldini rushed into Yorktown in search of
fresh vegetables for the Pinkerton mess. The street blew up
beneath him. The rebs had buried columbiad shells rigged
with fulminate of mercury detonators. The infernal devices
went off under the weight of a man or a horse. Lon heard of
it late Sunday night and searched the hospital tents until he
found Spaldini.

Awake but delirious with pain and opiates, the bright-eyed
man lay on a pallet under a smoking lantern. In his fractured
English he repeated something that sounded like "How I
cook now?" Stained bandages covered the stumps of his
wrists. The torpedo had blown his hands off. Somehow the
surgeons had kept him alive.

"Better if it killed me. Better."

Lon couldn't find a single word of comfort to offer. It didn't
matter. He was sure Spaldini didn't recognize him. He left the
tent. In the morning George Bangs told him Spaldini had died
at four a.m.

*   *   *

While Sledge snored and hard rain beat on the tent, Lon read
his Bible by candlelight.

He read Exodus. *Thou shalt not kill.* He read Isaiah. *They
shall beat their swords into plowshares, and their spears into
pruning hooks. Nation shall not lift up sword against nation,
neither shall they learn war anymore.* He read St. Matthew.
*Blessed are the peacemakers, for they shall be called the chil-
dren of God.*

How often Mathias Price had quoted or preached from
those texts. Lon believed in their meaning and their worth.
Yet they no longer seemed relevant to the morass of hatred
and killing in which he found himself.

He blew out the candle. The mournful rain poured down, sluicing off the tent walls and seeping underneath. He lay listening to bugling and drumming, the slosh of boots in the mud, the rattle of chains and creak of wheels that went on all night. He was still awake, shivering in the damp, when bugles blew reveille and the rest of the Army moved out to pursue Joe Johnston.

30

May 1862

Dr. Whyville succumbed. Apparently he had but one relative, a cousin. She traveled from Fairfax Court House to claim the body. She was a mousy little person, completely in black even to the lace handkerchief for her weeping eyes. She watched the jailers removing the body in a cheap pine box. Halfway down the staircase she began to scream. "Murderers. Murderers."

Everyone in Room 16 stopped whatever he or she was doing. Margaret sat numbly, unable to make sense of the card layout on the table. The scream echoed through the building until the woman left with her burden.

On May 5, Monday, the prison was aflutter with rumors that its most famous inmate would leave next day, paroled to Richmond because her powerful presence in Washington was a continuing irritant and embarrassment.

Rose and little Rose said good-bye to their favorites among the prisoners. Rose looked splendid. Her color was high, her eyes lively and as defiant as Margaret had ever seen them.

"Do what you can to get out of this filthy place," Rose said after they embraced. "You don't deserve the treatment Baker and Wood have given you."

Margaret replied with a resigned shrug. "Will you do something for me in Richmond?"

"If it's in my power, of course."

"Try to find out if my brother Cicero's all right."

"I will, and I'll get word to you, depend on that."

Little Rose tugged her hand. "Mama, the coach is waiting."

A crowd had gathered outside to see them off. Like a queen taking leave of her subjects, Rose waved and called good-bye as she swept grandly away from the filth and gloom of Room 16. Margaret joined the applause. The sound of well-wishers chanting *"Rose! Rose!"* reached all the way from the street. Margaret heard little Rose on the stairs:

"We showed these damned old Republicans, didn't we, Mama?"

* * *

Three days later, Washington reveled in news of a sharp engagement at Williamsburg on the Peninsula. Two Union brigadiers, Kearny and Hancock, had distinguished themselves. That day, Hanna surprised Margaret with a visit.

Hanna wore a suit of dark gray cloth, a buttoned waistcoat, a flowing silk tie. Trousers cut off at mid-calf showed gray stockings with vertical black stripes. Margaret didn't know whether the suit was tailored for a woman or whether a boy's suit had been altered. Either way, Hanna was flatbosomed and unfeminine. Her face was pale, free of paint or powder.

Greeting Margaret, Hanna was reserved and hesitant. After she presented a small Edam cheese wrapped in a checked napkin, Margaret hugged her and the mood warmed. Hanna pulled up a stool and whispered like a conspirator. "You'll never imagine where I've been."

"I'm sure I won't. Tell me."

"Virginia. Falmouth. General McDowell's corps is camped there, waiting for orders to reinforce McClellan. I wore a uniform and mixed with the soldiers as though I belonged."

"Really! You talked about doing that, but I never thought you would."

"I got leave from the Canterbury, packed up my kit and bedroll, and marched."

"What did the major say?"

"Oh, he objected strenuously. But he had no time to stop me. Mr. Stanton keeps his employees too busy."

Hanna gazed around the room that had become Margaret's universe. "I'm sorry you're in this place. I asked Papa if he could do anything. He said you were Colonel Lafayette Baker's prisoner and he was the only one who could write a release order. Papa warned me not to visit you because you're a dangerous spy. I told him I'd come even if it were true."

"Well, let's not worry about whether it is. Here I am, and here that fine Colonel Baker intends for me to stay. Tell me more about your adventure. Isn't it terribly dangerous to be a woman in disguise?"

"I wish it were. You have to avoid only two things: undressing in front of men, and using the latrines. I roamed around the camps for a whole twenty-four hours, even slept awhile, with no mishaps. Hundreds of men are separated from their commands. A lot are stragglers who couldn't keep up."

"What if someone asked you to identify yourself?"

"Oh, they did. But I'm an actress, don't forget. I pitched my voice low and identified myself as Private Siegel, from a fictitious Ohio regiment." In a music hall accent she said, "*Mit* a liddle bit of *Deutsch* to trow dem off." She giggled. "If they asked why I didn't have a musket, only a haversack and bedroll, I said someone stole it. The officers are too busy and frankly too green to worry about every last man."

Amused, Margaret said, "If it's that easy, you might as well join up."

"I could. Most volunteers never take off their clothes for their examination. A doctor checks their height, their hands, and especially their feet. That's all."

"Well, you've had your taste of it, so you needn't keep taking chances."

"Oh, yes, I'll go back. My first time was a dreadful disappointment. I saw nothing but country roads, campfires, and a lot of callow boys sitting around wailing sentimental ballads or reading lewd books or gambling. I have to see the elephant."

"Beg pardon?"

"Go into battle. Hear a real musket ball whizzing by. I'll bide my time until there's more fighting near Washington."

"You think there will be?"

"I have little doubt of it. Papa says most in the War Department believe McClellan is an incompetent egotist, and overly fearful. Mr. Stanton believes he'll fail." Hanna looked at the dismal surroundings. "Is there really no way you can get out of here?"

"Oh, yes. I could be a turncoat. Betray some of my fellow prisoners to the warden." *Or give in to Baker.* Margaret brushed a straggle of hair from her forehead. "You know I could never do such a thing."

Hanna squeezed her hand. "I do. I am so sorry the war's driven us apart. We'll patch things up when it's over."

"I'm sure of it." An aching doubt lurked behind Margaret's smile.

She watched her friend walk to the stairway. Margaret took much of the blame for the breach in their friendship. But how could it be helped, given their different loyalties?

*   *   *

Just when it seemed that her personal horizon could grow no darker, there was an unexpected ray of light. She came back from a noontime visit to the walled sink, and there, standing in the middle of Room 16 with his mauve gloves and lacquered stick—there was Donal.

His curly hair gleamed with barber's oil. His black eyes warmed when he spied her. Prisoners smiled as Margaret ran to him, her tangled hair flying. She threw herself in his arms, buried her face in his neck. "I've worried so. No letter, no word at all."

"I'm sorry, darling. I was detained two weeks in Nassau. The damned anaconda that Scott's wrapped around the South is playing hell with trade. The South's eager to exchange cotton for cash, but the blockade has restricted the supply. Never mind, I'm here to see about you."

He stepped back, studied her face. "What are they doing to you? You look simply terrible. I intend to remedy that."

Uncontrollable tears welled in her eyes. At that moment, seeing Donal so confident and concerned, she almost loved him.

31

May 1862

In the muggy warmth of springtime, Captain Frederick Scott Dasher, First Virginia Cavalry, rode north on a wooded road in Spotsylvania County. By Fred's reckoning they were some fifteen miles below Fredericksburg, where McDowell's Army corps was encamped.

The reconnaissance detachment of thirty-five men was half the squadron normally led by Captain Calder, who must have known someone influential in Richmond, because he didn't know a damn thing about horses. Calder's black stallion had collapsed and died when he overfed and overwatered him after a hot march from Williamsburg covering Joe Johnston's retreat. Calder was presently away in search of a remount. That each trooper had to supply his own horse was one of the idiocies of the Confederate government Fred served with a mixture of pride and guilt. He'd have no problem with remounts so long as the family horse farm near Front Royal remained in Confederate territory. His horse, Baron, came from there. Baron was a huge and intelligent gelding with flanks as shiny as coal; the kind of animal that terrified the Union soldiers at the battle of Manassas, sent them running from the "black horse cavalry."

Fred's commander was Brigadier General James Ewell Brown Stuart, whom he'd known and admired back at the Military Academy. Fred had enlisted with Stuart at Manassas, before Joe Johnston pulled back to the Rappahannock. Without making anything special of it, Fred understood that Stuart liked him personally and trusted him professionally. For that reason Stuart had sent him north of the Pamunkey River, to look for signs of a McDowell advance.

Fred rode beside Jonas Eberhart at the head of the column

of twos. Eberhart was one of Calder's second lieutenants. He was earnest but untrained. His experience consisted of occasional work at his uncle's livery stable. Not your typical, bred-to-horse Confederate cavalryman.

Butterflies swooped in bars of sunlight between the trees. Mockingbirds and jays sang and scolded. Fred had three scouts well ahead of the column, and eight men riding single file on each flank. The whole detachment could swing right or left quickly in case of attack.

The column advanced in silence except for the jingle of bits and the clop-clop of hooves. Yellow dust sifted upward as the riders passed, coating flanks and faces. Each man carried rations in his saddlebags but no bedroll. Fred didn't plan to stop for a night's sleep.

A Richmond-built copy of a Sharps breechloader hung from his shoulder sling. A pair of new LeMat .40-caliber over-and-under revolvers from Belgium jutted from his saddle holsters. The LeMat's upper barrel fired from a nine-shot cylinder; the lower was smoothbore for shotgun pellets. So far he'd only fired the weapons twice, in a skirmish at Dranesville, and while covering the retreat from Williamsburg.

Sweat gathered in his curly red hair and trickled from under his forage cap with its bright yellow crown. His two-day growth of beard itched. He craved a swig from his canteen. He knew he was drinking too much. His consumption had increased after he left Washington.

A horseman trotted up. It was the courier, John Mosby. Private Mosby was a slight, stooped young man with strange, disturbing eyes that never seemed to stay still. A lawyer by training and a former adjutant to the irascible Grumble Jones, Mosby resented discipline and displayed a recklessness that ran counter to Fred's careful professionalism. For some unfathomable reason, Jeb Stuart liked Mosby and was seeking a commission for him.

Fred studied the sun. About an hour until noon, he judged. They'd been advancing at an alternate trot and walk since daybreak. Time soon to unsaddle the horses and cool their backs. Make sure saddle cloths were smooth when they resumed the—

The sound of a rider broke his thoughts. He raised his hand

to halt the column and trotted forward, past Private Mosby slouching in his saddle. One of the scouts came charging through a sunlit dust cloud.

"Captain, sir." The breathless private saluted as he reined in. "Yank infantry column about four miles up the road. We saw a second column five or six miles east."

"McDowell?"

"I'd say almost surely, sir."

"Good work. Go back and keep watch but retreat ahead of them. We don't want to be seen."

The scout galloped away. If they had indeed bumped into the vanguard of McDowell's corps moving south, Stuart and the high command wanted to know. Undoubtedly the Yankees were marching to link up with McClellan for the assault on Richmond. Fred trotted back to Lieutenant Eberhart.

"There's Yankee infantry coming down this road. We'll divide the column. Take half the men west, keep the enemy under observation, but stay hidden. I'll take the other half east. No firing unless you're discovered. Do you have a watch?"

"Right here, sir."

"Stay abreast of the Yanks until five o'clock. If they're still marching, leave them. You remember where we watered horses last night?"

"The creek east of the Snell crossroads."

"We'll rendezvous there. If either party doesn't show up within thirty minutes after sunset, the other goes on and reports to General Stuart. Get going."

The column split. Unlike some of his aristocratic brethren in the cavalry, Fred didn't consider the average Yankee to be stupid. The foot soldiers would see and understand the meaning of hoofprints and horse apples on the road. It couldn't be helped. He doubted they'd break formation and search the woods if their orders said to join up with McClellan with all due speed.

He led his men off the dusty road, picked up his flankers, and headed into the forest. After a half mile, with the road still in sight, he ordered the men to dismount. He cautioned them to keep their horses under control. Most of the animals in the First were well trained, but not all. Sometimes green mounts reared and nipped and behaved like circus horses.

"If you have to piss, do it quickly and quietly." That said, Fred untied his canteen from a saddle ring and walked off. He batted insects as he uncorked the canteen with his teeth. He took a generous swallow of the popskull. Awful stuff. God knew what the sutler put in it.

He corked the canteen and returned to the line, feeling better. Private Mosby leaned against a tree, chewing on a twig. Mosby watched Fred as though he knew Fred's secret.

Forty minutes later they glimpsed the column, videttes riding well out in front. Blue-coated boys and their mounted officers advanced at a walk. Mosby stroked his beard. "Sir, hadn't we ought to burn them down?"

"Take on a few hundred infantry? I don't think so, Private. Our objective's to observe and report."

"Yes, sir. Is that West Point strategy, sir?"

"No. Orders." They stared at each other. Mosby looked away first.

A harmless green snake slithered underneath a corporal's horse. The horse shied and whinnied. Other horses snorted and stamped. The frantic corporal soothed his mount with a combination of whispering and stroking. On the road a few heads turned. The horse quieted. The Yanks kept marching.

Fred and his men followed the infantry column at a safe distance. A little after four, Fred turned them southeast. They lost sight of the road. Ten minutes later he ordered the troopers forward at a trot.

They reached the rendezvous point on the creek as a molten sunset burned through the western trees. Lieutenant Eberhart arrived soon after, flushed and happy that he'd come through without incident. They rode south at full gallop, covering eight miles in a half hour, then relaxed to a slow trot, doing three miles in the next thirty minutes. Fred ordered a walk and gave permission for the men to sleep in the saddle.

He couldn't, though he hooked his knee over the pommel, dropped the bridle, and folded his arms on his chest. His nerves were wound up tight. More than once, he saw Private Mosby's sardonic eyes glinting in the moonlight. Mosby struck Fred as unreliable; potentially violent, if not deranged.

Baron walked steadily and dependably. Fred's thoughts turned back to the wellspring of his guilt, the Military Academy.

He remembered vivid scenes and moments, starting with his first long climb from the Hudson steamer pier to the heights of the Plain. He remembered beast barracks that summer, the upperclassmen screaming that he wasn't a human being, he wasn't even a plebe, he was a low, vile, scrofulous, abominable *thing*. One of the most joyfully abusive of the upperclassmen was Jeb Stuart of Virginia, class of '54. Every cadet had a nickname, bestowed by others. Stuart's was Beauty, precisely because he was far from that.

Fred recalled long nights of study by lantern light, and even longer ones standing guard in bitter weather to work off demerits. He remembered friends, two of the best being a young Pennsylvania cadet, Billy Hazard, and another from South Carolina, Charles Main. Relatives of both had gone through the Academy and fought in the Mexican War. Charlie Main gave Fred his nickname, Carrots, in honor of his hair. Maybe he'd bump into Charlie in one of Stuart's six regiments of horse. He supposed Billy served the Union.

One of the clearest and most painful memories took him back to a chapel at which the new Academy superintendent, Colonel Robert E. Lee, addressed the cadet corps and faculty. Lee quoted *Henry V* and called the cadets a band of brothers. He said they owed their loyalty not to any state or region, but to the nation which had educated them; the nation they swore to serve loyally after graduation.

Like the nation, the band of brothers was broken. And what of the brothers themselves? Were some of them broken? Fred shook his head, angry over the morose and unmanly thought. He had many of those lately.

They reached Stuart's headquarters on the Pamunkey after daylight. The twenty-nine-year-old general, spruce as ever in his polished thigh boots, gold-tasseled sash, and marvelous full beard, was eating breakfast with Colonel Fitzhugh Lee and the burly Heros von Borcke, who'd landed at Charleston on leave from his Prussian dragoon regiment. Stuart had taken a fancy to von Borcke's outlandish pink and white riding costume and added him to the staff.

Fitz Lee was West Point '56, a year ahead of Fred. His beard was as splendid as Stuart's and helped conceal his youth. A genial hell-raiser at the Academy, Fitz had nearly been dismissed by the superintendent, his uncle. Men respected Fitz because he'd campaigned with the regular Army in the West and been wounded. There was another Lee serving with Stuart, Robert's son Rooney. Though a competent horse soldier, he was a Harvard man, hence not part of the West Point circle.

Stuart waved Fred to a camp chair. Fred reported on what they'd seen. Stuart was pleased. "We'll dispatch a courier to General Johnston at once."

Fred knew he shouldn't bring up Mosby, but he did. "I don't know what to make of the man. I don't think he's Army material."

Stuart's teeth gleamed in the middle of his russet-brown beard. He was a short, powerfully built man who exuded both good cheer and absolute authority. "I admit he's an odd bird, but I have a hunch he's a devil of a fighter. The challenge is to find the right place for him to fight."

Fitz Lee and von Borcke asked permission to leave. Stuart signaled his orderly to refill Fred's tin cup with hot coffee. "Permit me an observation, Captain. You're not looking too chipper. Did you encounter problems other than Private Mosby?"

"Not really, sir. It's just that, all last night, I kept remembering the Academy."

Not unkindly the general said, "It's a problem for you, isn't it?"

"Sometimes, yes."

"You're not alone in having regrets, and a measure of guilt. We all left the Army we loved. I saw my wife's father choose to stay with the other side"—Stuart smiled—"which he will have cause to regret continuously. Fitz was a tactical officer at the Academy when the war started. I should imagine many others have divided feelings—General Longstreet, General Johnston, certainly President Davis. But once you stand at a fork in the road, and you choose the way, it's senseless and dangerous to look back constantly."

"I tell myself that. The guilt comes anyway."

"Because you're a decent man who took an oath and hated to break it. We have no time for guilt. We have one duty—to carry out every mission zealously, despite what it costs, despite who gets in the way. Now to matters at hand. I have three

other detachments scouting near Fredericksburg, but I want
yours there too. We don't dare lose sight of McDowell for one
moment. You don't mind being absent from the staff?"

"Truthfully, sir, I prefer being in the field."

"How do you get on with Calder's men?"

"Some of them lack experience, but they follow orders and
learn quickly. They're a good lot."

"Except Private Mosby."

"I didn't mean to raise—"

"Never mind, I've heard the complaint from others. We'll
find the proper slot for him. Catch what rest you can, and remember what I said." The general leaned forward, his brilliant
blue gaze unwavering. "Once you stand at the fork and
choose the road, you can't afford a backward glance. You
might miss an enemy waiting to ambush you."

"Yes, sir."

Fred stood, saluted, about-faced. As he left, Stuart summoned his orderly. "Find Mosby. He's to carry a signal to
General Johnston."

Fred tramped along the riverbank. How he wished it were
easy to follow the general's advice, forgive yourself for a decision that carried elements of doubt, a haunting sense of a
trust betrayed. When he was a boy, his mother had taught him
the meaning of honor, the importance of a promise. Sometimes he'd resented her righteousness, as he resented all the
preachers and schoolteachers who hammered rhetorical nails
into his conscience to make it stronger. His canteen held the
only reliable medicine for the pain and doubt. He'd only
drunk half of it on the scouting expedition. Before noon, in
the privacy of his tent, he helped himself to the rest.

*   *   *

Thirty-six hours later, on the afternoon of May 27, Fred's detachment discovered Union troops on the march again—
north, toward Fredericksburg. Fred and his men scouted to
determine that it wasn't an isolated retreat, but a movement
of the entire corps. For whatever reason, McClellan would not
be reinforced by McDowell. Fred led his troopers back to Stuart at full gallop with the news.

32

May 1862

Visitors regularly brought war news to the Old Capitol. Confederate sympathizers gleefully reported the repulse of five Federal gunboats on the James. Confederate artillery at Drewry's Bluff had turned them back eight miles below Richmond. The city was temporarily safe from a river attack.

The outlook on land was less sanguine. McClellan's mighty army was poised for what would surely be the biggest battle since Manassas. Southern partisans hoped Joe Johnston would launch a ferocious offensive to drive the enemy off the Peninsula.

At the start of the third week of May, Margaret was surprised to be visited by an elderly Episcopal priest she didn't know. Warden Wood had moved her to the relative privacy of Rose's old room, where she received the caller. He sat so that his back blocked the view of anyone looking in. As he chattered about the sins of the Lincoln government, he slipped his hand under his black rabat and gave her a letter. She wasn't surprised by the priest's opinions; Washington's Episcopal congregations were notorious for harboring Southern loyalists.

At the end of the visit she thanked the priest and saw him to the door. A guard loitered outside, a man relatively new to the prison. His name was Hodges. He was not merely old—sixty, sixty-five—but repellently so, with a sagging paunch and false teeth that gleamed like china when he grinned, which was every time he encountered Margaret. He made her flesh crawl.

She closed the door partway and tore the envelope open. She recognized Rose's handwriting. Rose was in Richmond.

Little Rose and I received a tumultuous welcome, far beyond my expectations. The city is in a perfect state of terror, with McClellan's mongrel horde of Germans and Irish and God knows what else no more than twenty miles away as I write. Mrs. Davis and the President's four children have fled to Raleigh. The government will ship its treasury to South Carolina if it appears the city will fall. Our nigger houseman has laid in pouches of tobacco to use as currency with an occupying Army. I have even heard that Davis will burn Richmond before letting it be conquered.

Here is happier news for my dear friend. Though I have not seen your brother, Cicero, I have reliable word that he is alive, and attached to the provost marshal's department, though in what capacity I do not know.

Margaret sobbed with relief. She heard noises outside, stepped to the door, and immediately stepped back at the sight of Hodges's china grin.

"Anything wrong, miss?"

She slammed the door on him.

*   *   *

Lon lost weight. He let his beard grow longer. It gave him a coarse, rustic look that might be useful if Pinkerton ever sent him behind enemy lines. McClellan's Army camped along the lower Pamunkey, between White House, a sprawling plantation owned by the Lee family, and Cumberland Landing farther south. Lon interrogated prisoners, deserters, and contrabands and daily grew more disturbed by the discrepancy between figures he turned in and those reported to the general.

Little Mac used Pinkerton's estimates to delay his advance on grounds that he needed reinforcements. Phil Kearny, the one-armed brigadier who'd distinguished himself at Williamsburg, snidely referred to McClellan as the Virginia Creeper. A drinking companion of Sledge's, a civilian operator in the Army telegraph service, said he'd decoded a War Department message in which the President bluntly told McClellan that he must move on Richmond or give up the job and return to defend Washington.

"They'd hang my pal if they knew he passed such stuff,"

Sledge said. " 'Course, he was drunk when he told me. Do you 'spose the general's got a yellow streak?"

"I imagine he's careful because he doesn't want to lose men needlessly."

"Or maybe lose his reputation? I hear he may run for president as a Democrat in two years. I think he'd beat Lincoln easy."

Lon confessed his own doubts about the general, particularly McClellan's well-known and frequent protests that Stanton and Lincoln were undermining him by withholding troops.

"We keep hearing we're outnumbered. I add up numbers from the men I question, I make some educated guesses, and I just don't believe it, Sledge. I reckon we have a hundred thousand effectives, but Johnston can only muster three fourths of that. Elvin Stein agrees, and he's been in Richmond."

"D'you say anything to the boss?"

"He's sick again. Cross as hell."

With another of his cynic's shrugs, Sledge said, "If you don't mind getting your ass scorched, talk to him. Maybe you'll catch him in a listening mood."

"Easy for you to say."

Sledge grinned. "Sure. I'm not like you. I got no conscience over these things."

*   *   *

In the heat and stench of the windowless room, Margaret woke. A streak of lantern light showed where the door stood ajar. She'd closed it before blowing out her lamp.

A floorboard creaked. Still sleepy, she put her hands underneath her to push and sit up. She smelled the liquor on the intruder's rancid breath.

Although his face was in shadow, she recognized him by the shape of his head. He touched her leg through her sweaty cotton gown. "Come on, sweet, you must be aching for it by now." Fingers moved spiderlike up her thigh.

She struck with her right hand. Her nails, ragged from lack of care, raked the man's cheek, making him yell. He called her a name, pushed her down, jammed his hand beneath her gown, and rubbed her privates. She hit him with the butt of her palm. He sprawled. She screamed for help. He jumped up and ran out, slamming the door.

Gasping, she pushed hair out of her eyes. A guard with a lamp kicked the door open without knocking. Margaret jerked the hem of her gown over her knees.

"What's going on, woman? Why'd you yell?"

"Hodges was here. He tried to hurt me."

"Couldn't be. Hodges ain't got night duty."

"I tell you it was Hodges. Call the warden."

"Shut your clapper. The warden don't come in till seven a.m."

He left. Margaret wrapped her arms around her knees and rocked on the cot. She slept little the rest of the night, and when she did, she woke with a scream rising in her throat, feeling that rough hand between her legs.

Warden Wood came to see her at eight o'clock. He claimed to believe her story. His hand-wringing and eye-rolling would have done credit to an actor in melodrama.

"Oh, Lord, I'm sorry, Miss Miller. I'll put Hodges on a detail outside the building, you won't be bothered again. These things happen. Men have appetites. I don't care for Hodges, but I take what I'm given, what else can I do? If you weren't an enemy of the state, I could fix a lock on your door." Wood scratched at a nostril. "This could have been avoided. You might consider being nicer to Colonel Baker if he calls again."

As he surely would; she knew it with sudden certainty. Had Baker put Hodges up to it to break her spirit? If so, he was succeeding.

* * *

In the evening damp, after Lon had questioned his last prisoner, penned his last report, darned his socks, or trimmed his beard with scissors and a scrap of mirror borrowed from Sledge, he liked to walk along the winding river, smoking and reflecting.

The night resounded with challenges from sentries and passwords called in reply. Owls hooted; insects buzzed. Heat haze on the water diffused the lights of anchored gunboats. Somewhere a bugler practiced an evening call that was new to the army. George Bangs said a brigadier on the Peninsula had composed "Taps" during the campaign. The melancholy notes brought thoughts of Margaret. War or not, he couldn't give her up. When he saw her again, he'd declare his feelings and gamble that they would matter to her.

On one of his nocturnal rambles, he decided he could no longer keep silent about the numbers. "May I speak to you, sir?" he said next morning in Pinkerton's tent at White House plantation.

The boss's sunken eyes held no friendliness. "I'm extremely busy." It was evident. Pinkerton's field desk was all but hidden by piles of documents. Papers were stacked on the ground near his stool. Dried ink splotched his hands and shirt cuffs.

"I'll be brief, sir. It's about our reports to General McClellan. I just wonder if the figures create a false picture. Lead to the wrong conclusions."

Pinkerton's blue-gray eyes were glacial. "Go on."

"At Yorktown we thought we were outnumbered, but every assessment we've made since then says Joe Johnston had about fifty thousand effectives, and we had at least seventy-five. If that's true, we could have overwhelmed their defenses. Instead the general ordered a siege."

"You're overstepping, Alonzo. You didn't attend West Point. You're not a strategist."

"I can read reports and add, sir." He'd wanted to speak reasonably, persuasively to the boss. He realized the atmosphere was too highly charged, given Pinkerton's blind loyalty to his patron. Yet conscience made him press on.

"I'm only saying what's common knowledge. The siege gave Johnston nearly a month to reinforce his army. Some men say Yorktown was really a defeat for us."

"What men? Give me their names."

"I don't know their names. I wouldn't implicate them if I did. They were only expressing opinions, which I happen to agree wi—"

"These men you refer to are insubordinate. You are tending that way."

Lon exclaimed, "Sir, I protest. You said yourself that we inflate the figures at least ten percent, but the raw figures are flawed to begin with. We estimate the aggregate number of

men present as best we can determine it, but that number in-
cludes sick and wounded. We may even be counting men
who've deserted. We should estimate only the number fit for
duty. Otherwise it's a false picture."

"Alonzo, you are here to follow orders, not interpret or crit-
icize them. I will send you to Washington with some reports
too lengthy for the telegraph. Perhaps a week or two at a desk
in the capital will restore your perspective. We continue to
bolster our forces by every available means because the general is constantly undermined by the secretary and the President. The Washington cabal—"

Lon's temper let go. "Do we have any evidence that a cabal
really exists? If so, I'd like to see it. Then I could say I'm sorry
for doubting, but until then—"

"Enough! Requisition a horse and report to Mr. Bangs at
six a.m. tomorrow. He will give you the material for Washington and the passes you'll require. I am frankly disappointed in
you. I thought you had the makings of an outstanding intelligence analyst. I was misled. Good morning."

* * *

Toward the end of the third week of May, Donal McKee visited Old Capitol again. Donal had been in the city for a week,
though for what purpose, he didn't say. He and Margaret
spoke privately in Margaret's room.

"I have been cultivating the British ambassador, Lord
Lyons." Whiskey on Donal's breath couldn't mask a subtler,
sweeter perfume. It wasn't a scent a man would wear.

"You know I carry a British passport. His lordship therefore pays attention. Further, he knows I control one of the
largest supplies of raw cotton on the continent, and that I
can hire men and ships to get some or all of it through the
blockade to English mills that will shut down if supply is cut
off."

Donal laid his stick and top hat on the table. He was more
ebullient than Margaret had seen him for a long time. "His
lordship and I met on three occasions, the last being a delicious champagne supper."

With young ladies from a "boardinghouse" for dessert?
She was instantly ashamed of the thought. She knew Donal

and his predilections. Not only was he a man of strong appetites, he was a man of wealth. Women were attracted.

He took her hand and spoke earnestly. "Lord Lyons and I reached a happy agreement. As a result, I can make a proposal that will unlock the gates of this unspeakable place."

Margaret was almost dizzy with excitement. Donal was pleased; she read it in his confident smile. He held her hand more tightly.

"If you look favorably on the scheme, I can get you out of here in a matter of days. And no one, not that villain Baker, nor Stanton, Lincoln, nor even God Himself can prevent it."

33

May–June 1862

Zach had his arms deep in a wooden tub of suds. When he wasn't fetching and carrying for Pinkerton, he washed dishes and cleaned up the mess, not without complaint. "You're an errand boy, I'm washin' tin cups," he said to Lon. "Where's this important secret service we're 'sposed to do? I might as well wait on the white folks at Willard's."

"My fault." Lon picked a biscuit crumb out of his beard. "I'm not the boss's favorite right now."

Zach draped his scrub rag over the edge of the tub. "You be careful up there in Washington city. You're the only friend I got. There's a whole lot of meanness swirling in the air round here."

"Something more than usual?"

"I'd say so. Couldn't sleep last night, so I went walkin' where I'm not allowed but no one saw me. Boss's tent was lit up like always. He had a visitor. The big general, carryin' on like a crazy man. Something about soldiers pulled back to Washington."

"McDowell's reinforcements?"

"Must be. The big general called Mr. Stanton nasty names. Called him Judas Iscariot."

"Good God."

"You better come back, 'fore things get worse."

* * *

Bad thoughts followed Lon on his ride to Fort Monroe and his steamer trip upriver. The trip took a day and a half. Pinkerton did it often, rushing to testify at some court-martial or contractor hearing, then rushing back without sleep, which helped account for his haggard looks and foul temper.

When Lon reached Washington, he learned that McDowell had indeed been ordered back from Fredericksburg, to protect the city against Stonewall Jackson. Was there something to McClellan's claim of a cabal after all?

He found the city excited by the nearness of Jackson, and by action on the last day of May at Seven Pines station on the York River railroad. Bulletins at newspaper offices proclaimed a Union victory, with the Confederate commander, Johnston, twice wounded. At Pinkerton headquarters the perspective was different. Kate Warne, deskbound with paperwork, told Lon, "We had a telegraph about it. McClellan lost something like six thousand killed and wounded. He's never taken that kind of licking before. Heaven knows what it will do to him. They say he's losing his grip, and Lincoln's out of patience."

"If Johnston's wounded, who replaces him?"

"Bobby Lee. Davis announced it."

"How did we find out?"

"Our people in Richmond."

With McClellan failing, how strong was Pinkerton's position? Lon remembered Lafayette Baker's warning at Old Capitol: *Don't back the wrong horse.* It no longer seemed foolish or self-serving.

Uneasy, he delivered sealed dispatch pouches to the War Department in President's Park. There, Secretary Stanton received petitioners every morning, standing behind a podium desk and bellowing questions and orders like the worst martinet. Dozens of petitioners jammed the hall benches, waiting to be abused in similar fashion.

The second-floor library held the telegraph office. Stanton had seized the instruments and removed them from Army of the Potomac headquarters. Lon heard the receivers clicking and clattering as he headed out of the building. At the entrance he bumped into the President. Lincoln tipped his old stovepipe hat and apologized; he didn't recognize Lon. He squeezed past petitioners who scarcely noticed him and hurried upstairs.

Lon's next delivery, to the quartermaster general's office, consisted of several bundles of ledgers seized from a contractor caught selling weevily biscuits to the Peninsula Army. Sledge had impounded the books using brass knuckles. He boasted that the contractor was laid up with a severe case of broken bones and black eyes, giving him ample time to contemplate his malfeasance.

Nervously, Lon prepared for the personal part of his visit. A barber trimmed his hair and beard. At Shillington's bookshop he conferred with a clerk over a gift. The prissy clerk recommended a relatively new translation of *The Rubáiyát*, poems of Omar Khayyám that Lon had never read. The clerk assured him they had much to do with romance, and fate, though with an elegiac tone appropriate to wartime.

"Wrap it in fancy paper," Lon said. "It's for a lady."

"She will appreciate your tender spirit."

Old Capitol was the same dismal place he remembered, though it looked even bleaker and sadder on a warm afternoon with thunderheads gathering in the western sky, like a warning of Stonewall's presence below the horizon. He got no argument from the jailers when he showed his credentials, but he got a surprise. Margaret had a room of her own; the one formerly belonging to Rose Greenhow.

He took the stairs two at a time. He was determined to lay out his case, reveal his feelings, ask if she could feel the same about him once the war ended. He scanned Room 16's dispirited population of readers, writers, sleepers, and card players. She wasn't among them. He went quickly to Rose's room, knocked. Margaret opened the door.

"Yes, what is it?" She wore a dress of dark tartan cloth, black and green, that hugged her hips and breasts. She peered at him, trying to see the face behind the long beard.

"Good Lord. It's you."

"Hello, Margaret." Flushed and warm, he offered the wrapped book. "I know they only permit gifts of food, but no one stopped me." Her face was thinner, colorless. The pallor made the black rings around her eyes all the more stark. She examined the package with a bemused smile.

"Thank you so much. Won't you come in?"

The room depressed him. A dim lamp sent a thread of smoke toward the water-stained ceiling. Someone had put bullet holes in the floor and outer wall; guards, he presumed. Margaret insisted he take the only chair.

"This is a distinct surprise. I assume you've been in Virginia?"

"Yes, with General McClellan."

"He's doing poorly, and against inferior numbers." She said it with a touch of defiance, a suggestion of pleasure. What was there about this woman that fascinated and excited him? He didn't know. He just knew he loved her.

She sat on the bed, tucking her plaid skirt around her long legs. "Have you been safe?"

"Oh, yes. Most of the time we work behind the lines, well out of danger." Never mind about the balloon expedition. The need to confess his feelings was building like steam pressure in a machine. She began to unwrap the book.

"I know why you didn't have trouble with this. The guards are more lenient because I'm leaving."

"Leaving? When?"

"Warden Wood's to sign the papers next week, as soon as my fiancé returns from Bermuda. You remember Donal. We'll be married the day I'm released."

If she'd beaten his forehead with a hammer, he couldn't have been more stunned or hurt. Every hope, every declaration he'd rehearsed, was blown out of his head. She rested her hands on the book in her lap as she explained.

"Baker's dedicated to keeping me here forever, you see. Marriage is the only way around him. Donal has lived in America since he was a child, but he's kept his British citizenship. Evidently it's helpful with circumventing some export laws. He lodged an official protest about me with Lord Lyons, the ambassador. Relations with Britain are sensitive.

The damned black Republicans are afraid Her Majesty's government may recognize the Confederacy, so they're cautious. They won't detain the wife of a British subject."

"That's the only reason you're marrying him? To get out?"

"We've been engaged for quite some time. I'm very fond of Donal, he's a man of substance and—"

Lon pulled her to her feet. The book tumbled to the floor. "Do you know why I came here? To plead with you to wait, endure this war, so that when it's over, I could ask for your hand."

"I hope—dear God, I hope I haven't led you on."

He held her shoulders and gazed into her brown eyes. "No. In spite of all the differences between us, I've seen the looks you gave me. I thought they said you could care for me. Or I could make you care, given time."

She fell against his shoulder. Her long dark hair tangled with his beard. He felt the fullness of her body. "I wouldn't have dreamed of it the day we met." She drew back with a searching look. "But—yes. You could."

He brought his mouth to hers, clasping her waist. The hell with decorum, all was lost anyway.

She was stiff in his arms for a moment. Then he felt a change, an urgency as she threw her arms around his neck and returned the kiss ardently. Her mouth was wet and sweet. She ground her hips against him. When she pulled away, she looked as young and wide-eyed as a doe surprised in the forest.

"I can't do this, Lon. This damnable war doesn't allow—"

"The war will be over in a year or two."

"I can't spend a year in this filthy place, let alone two. I won't spend another month! You don't know all that's happened." She spun away, hiding her face. He reached out to touch her, saw her shoulders trembling, withdrew his hand. When she turned back to him, tears gleamed on her cheeks.

"I told you before, Yankees killed my father. Men who work for the same man who employs you. I don't know whether I could ever get over that. I promised to make someone pay for Father's death. So far I've done a lamentable job, but when I'm free, I'll have a second chance." She hesitated. "There is one more obstacle."

"You don't care for me."

"Heaven help me, I do. But I faced Donal in this room and promised to marry him. I don't break promises."

"Not even if it means throwing your life away?"

"I think you had better go."

"Margaret—"

"No, please. Go!" The last word was strident. Again she turned away, leaving him to gaze at her tangled hair, and at the book of poems he'd dated on the flyleaf, with the inscription *Affection always, L. Price.*

What a witless, hopeless, adolescent gesture. He clapped his hat on his head and walked out.

Long afterward, he reflected that Margaret's rebuff was the moment, the encounter, that killed the last of his romantic feelings about the war, transforming it to a brutish task that had to be finished quickly, using whatever harsh means were necessary. He could almost hear Sledge laughing and congratulating him on his new sagacity.

He walked through Washington wrapped in a feverish daze. In the west the black clouds piled up and thunder crumped, like the cannon of Jackson's army advancing.

34

June 1862

Madness was Fred's term for Stuart's plan. Behind their hands, some officers whispered, "Suicide." Fred preferred madness—divine, heroic, whatever you wanted to call it, but madness.

It began June 12. After choosing men from the Fourth and Ninth Regiments and the Jeff Davis Legion, Stuart ordered them to saddle and ride at two a.m. They moved north from Richmond in the moonlight, twelve hundred troopers including detachments led by Fitz and Rooney Lee. Lieutenant

Breathed of the Horse Artillery commanded a rifle gun and a twelve-pound howitzer. Von Borcke rode with them, and the general's banjo player, Sam Sweeny, a minstrel man stranded in the capital when war broke out. That damned Mosby was with them.

Since they were headed toward Louisa Court House, they assumed they would reinforce Jackson in the Valley. They bivouacked for a short time at farm near Taylorsville, close by the South Anna River. Scouts returned before daybreak. Stuart ordered signal rockets fired, but no bugling for reveille. They mounted and rode east, toward Hanover Court House, and then Stuart revealed their real mission: a secret expedition behind enemy lines, ordered by Johnston's replacement, Bob Lee. Many officers distrusted Lee because of his dismal record of defeat and retreat in western Virginia last year. Lee was a fastidiously moral man; austere, almost unapproachable. You could give Little Joe Johnston a friendly pat on his bald head and he wouldn't take it amiss. No one tried that with Granny Lee.

Gone was the convivial jocularity of the pre-dawn hours. They were heading for McClellan's right flank, to discover where it was; how well protected. They soon found out. No Yankee trenches could be seen along Totopotomy Creek, though they should have been there to protect Porter's position on the Union right.

Rooney Lee encountered the enemy first, Stoneman's cavalry, a hundred strong. Rooney Lee drew his saber and ordered a charge. His men galloped at the enemy shouting the new rebel war cry, an ululating yell that froze the blood of enemies. The Federals broke and scattered. Fred and the rest came up, chased the Yankees for nearly two miles, and collected a few frightened prisoners.

The Federals regrouped and drew some of Stuart's men into a sharp fight. Fred fought with his saber in his right hand, a LeMat in his left. He took a sword cut on his cheek. Another Yankee saber nicked Baron's ear. The gelding didn't buck or falter; Fred had time to fire into the face of the Yankee captain.

He saw the scatter-shot shred the captain's face, saw him sink from his saddle. Though he'd never taken a human life before, he was unmoved. In the smoky confusion, horses neighing, blades clanging, small arms crackling, he marveled at the ease of killing someone if that someone meant to kill you first.

In the abandoned Federal camp at Old Church they plundered stores they could carry, burned the remainder, and rested while Stuart plotted his next move. Could they cross the rain-swollen Pamunkey? No, they had no pontoons. Could they go back? No, the rear guard reported Federal horse and infantry in pursuit. What, then? Go forward, southeast. Cross the Chick-ahominy at Forge Bridge, beyond the Union left flank, reach the James at Charles City, and return to Richmond—riding entirely around McClellan! It appealed to Stuart's bravado and his oft-repeated warrior's credo: "Die game."

With the plan afloat, Fred heard "suicide" whispered for the first time. It really was madness, made all the madder by the season. June was the month children burst out of school-house prisons, young women became brides, farmers dug rough hands in black soil, thanked God for good growing weather but prayed for rain. No such spirit prevailed as they took the road for Enon and Haw's Shop. After two days and nights in the saddle, little or no sleep, haversacks empty, numbness and fear set in.

Even the general showed signs of it. The plume on his fancy hat seemed to droop. The red rose pinned to the lapel of his short jacket wilted. Sam Sweeny no longer sang "Camptown Races" or "Kathleen Mavourneen," nor was he asked. They were beyond McClellan's right wing, scarcely five miles from his great base at White House. They'd be lucky to get out with their lives. Fred drank furtively from his canteen, a precious sip at a time.

On June 14, Saturday afternoon, they bore down on Tunstall's Station, a depot on the York River railroad linking White House with the Union front. Stuart called Fred to a conference in the saddle.

"Take Captain Knight's squadron along that branch road. Garlick's Landing isn't far. Destroy whatever Union stores you find and ride to Tunstall's Station." Garlick's Landing was a hamlet on the river; scouts had reported a small garrison, and two river steamers tied up.

"Will you stop at Tunstall's, General?"

"Long enough to rip up the rails, tear down the telegraph, and see what other mischief we can do. Good luck." He rode away before Fred could salute properly.

Fred relieved himself in a pine grove, a useful opportunity to revisit the canteen. Soon he was moving at the head of his column of twos down a lane of great elms and sycamores the sun lit like a green cathedral. Farm families rushed to the roadside to wave and call encouragement. A cry of "Shoot a few bluebirds for us, boys" made Fred laugh.

When the column emerged from the dense woods, he saw a scattering of rude buildings about a mile ahead. Tiny blue figures scurried among parked wagons. He screwed his telescope to his eye, observed a few civilians as well as soldiers, but no fortifications. He raised his hand.

"Form column of fours. Draw sabers"—the metallic slither of many swords always sent a chill down his spine—"trot." The last word was roughly articulated; he'd taken the reins between his teeth.

He hugged Baron with his knees, pulled his LeMat from its saddle holster with his left hand and rode with saber raised. Hot air fanned his face. Behind the unpainted cottages and storehouses, masts of a small steamer could be seen.

A Union bluebird spied them and ran to spread the alarm. An iron bell clanged. The rebel horses made a rising thunder on the sunlit road. Men gave voice to the savage yell. Fred called for the charge. They roared into Garlick's Landing in the face of scattered return fire. Behind him, Fred heard a trooper cry out as he pitched from his mount. The trooper's horse veered and dragged him away through undergrowth; his boot was still caught in the stirrup.

A blond sergeant darted from behind a wagon, aiming his rifle at Fred. Fred wheeled Baron past him and cut the Yank's neck open with a violent downward saber stroke. The man's eyes opened wide with surprise. His gushing blood splattered Baron's flank and Fred's boot. Fred fired into the man's chest for insurance.

Outnumbered Yankees were already throwing down their arms. A two-story building with a sagging roof stood at the head of the main pier. Some kind of hostelry, Fred judged from the water troughs and benches and faded signboard. Upper shutters flew open. An old woman in a mobcap waved a white pillowcase. A trooper rode up beside the Union flag hanging over the main door and tore it down. A Yankee ran out of the place and shot the trooper at close range, blowing him backward off his horse.

Fred spurred ahead, saber sheathed in favor of a second revolver in his right hand. Three more Yankees ran out of the tavern, knelt to fire. Behind him he heard bluebirds chirping for mercy, but the three in front of him wouldn't give up so easily. He rode at them from the right and put two rounds into the nearest. The man seemed to leap from the ground and fly against the building, dying in the air. Fred galloped past, turned Baron a hundred eighty degrees, and without hesitating fired both revolvers.

The Yankee on the right had already fallen on his face, wounded by someone else. Fred's left-hand revolver took out the third man, throwing him sideways. At the same moment, a girl of nine or ten wearing a patched dress ran out the door waving a small bright flag bearing the cross of St. Andrew. Fred's shot from the right hand, intended for the soldier already down, struck her instead. A blood flower bloomed on her flat bosom while she was smiling radiantly to greet the liberators.

"Oh, Jesus! Oh, Jesus Christ."

He jumped from the saddle, hat falling off. He ran forward, knelt in the dust. She focused on his face. Her eyes were a lovely cornflower blue. Her hand sought and closed on his. "Grandma? Grandma, it hurts." Her head rolled sideways, raising a puff of dust.

The old woman ran from the dark doorway into the sunshine. "Why did you shoot her? We're loyal to Jeff Davis, she kept his picture under her pillow."

"Ma'am, she appeared suddenly, I didn't mean—"

"You butcher! You murdering bastard! Oh, damn you, she's my only grandchild." She fell onto a bench and tore at her breasts. An elderly man stepped from the tavern to comfort her, saw the child's corpse, lurched back inside, sick.

The LeMat in Fred's left hand was heavy and hot. Blinking, he gained his feet, confronted Captain Knight on horseback.

"It happened accidentally. She ran out. I didn't see her in time."

The captain cocked his head toward pillars of smoke rising south of them. "Looks like the general's taking care of Tunstall's."

Fred fairly screamed, "Goddammit, Captain, I didn't do this on purpose. Do you think I'd shoot a child?"

"No, sir. Not intentionally." Knight's eyes flickered with pity or contempt. "We've taken about twenty-five prisoners, sir. What shall we burn?"

With the white iron of guilt searing his gut, Fred gave orders he couldn't remember afterward. They set fire to covered wagons laden with sacks of grain and coffee. Soon Garlick's Landing smelled strongly of roasting beans. Sentries on the two Yankee steamers gave up quickly. The rebs swarmed aboard, torching supply wagons waiting to be off-loaded.

Fred's detachment had lost two men in the skirmish; a third suffered a thigh wound. They rounded up the Yankees, mounted them on mules from a pole corral. The prisoners caused no trouble. Fred moved like one of those mechanical wonders you saw at dime museums, lifelike figures that nodded and played cards and imitated living creatures. Hiding behind Baron, he swallowed whiskey, emptying the canteen. He threw it on the ground in a burst of rage.

Leaping flames and floating sparks greeted them in the twilight as they approached Tunstall's. The little depot was a pile of black rubble. Telegraph poles had been axed and thrown across the rails. Fred reported to General Stuart, who commended him and Captain Knight.

"There was an accident, sir. A little girl rushed out of a building some Yankees were defending. My ball hit her instead of them." The words were like gall. "I killed her."

Jeb Stuart's blue eyes had a curious glacial quality. He no longer looked spruce, but bedraggled, mud on his boots, dirt streaking the back of his red-lined cape.

"It's unfortunate, Captain. In wartime such things happen. I'm sorry. We must press on to the Chickahominy before the men collapse entirely." Stuart rode off, a black figure against the flames of burning wagons.

At Tallysville they came upon a Federal field hospital. Stuart ordered the patients and surgeons left alone. Some abandoned sutlers' wagons yielded beef tongue, pickles, layer cakes, ketchup, and other edibles, along with champagne and wine. The starved cavalrymen ate and drank everything. Fred sampled the champagne and then put away a half bottle of claret.

They found the Chickahominy in flood. Rooney Lee nearly drowned when he dove in to test the river's depth. Stuart's ordnance officer scouted downstream to Forge Bridge. The bridge itself was washed away, but stone abutments remained, as well as an abandoned warehouse stocked with lumber. Troopers crossed the river on an improvised plank bridge, leading their horses in the water below them. After the two fieldpieces crossed, and the prisoners and the captured animals, a rear guard torched the makeshift bridge.

On the morning of June 15, Brigadier General Jeb Stuart rode into Richmond well ahead of his troops. He could report to Lee that McClellan's right wing hung in the air, without significant protection. Tumultuous mobs cheered the return of the exhausted riders straggling in from the Charles City road. They arrived with 165 captured Yankees and nearly twice as many horses and mules. Fred Dasher arrived with a wound that would never heal.

Stuart recommended a number of men for promotion, among them John Mosby. One more reason Fred sought a tavern and drank himself into a stupor.

35

July–August 1862

The clouds of glory that trailed George Brinton McClellan for months blew away in a storm of fighting at the gates of Richmond. The storm lasted seven days. It saved the city, ended the Peninsula campaign, and blotted McClellan's reputation, for which he blamed others.

After engagements at Oak Grove and Mechanicsville, a major battle at Gaines' Mill on June 27 produced a costly Confederate victory. News walkers, soldiers who roamed the camps like living newspapers, told what little they knew as night came down. Artillery boomed fitfully in the distance. Near midnight, Allan Pinkerton called his anxious operatives together over the mess tables at White House. Lon saw an eerie resemblance to John Brown as Pinkerton addressed them.

"Today the rebs whipped us at an unknown cost of many thousands. We lose battles because our force is too small. General McClellan places responsibility squarely on the President and his clique, and will so inform Mr. Lincoln by letter. Starting tomorrow, this base will be abandoned. We move down to Harrison's Landing on the James. The general will forgo the assault on Richmond to save his Army, and when he does save it, as he will, it will be no thanks to anyone in Washington. Only the cabal, not the Confederacy, can defeat the nation's finest soldier."

Men hardly dared look up, so wild and terrible was the accusation. Pinkerton's burning eye swept the tent as if to discover anyone who would dispute him. The most skeptical face was Zach's. He stood behind Lon, arms folded, luckily in shadow where the lantern's dim glow didn't reach.

When Pinkerton walked out, there was a communal sigh. Next morning the first long wagon train moved south over rain-rutted roads, followed by a lowing herd of Army beef.

With Savage Station, Frayser's Farm, and Malvern Hill on the first of July, the seven days ended. Richmond was redeemed, though casualty estimates pouring across the Pinkerton desks suggested that Lee had won the city's reprieve at a cost of something like a quarter of his Army.

The Army of the Potomac celebrated Independence Day behind secure fortifications at Harrison's Landing. Bands played, artillery saluted the holiday, and McClellan issued another proclamation, commending the Army for performing nobly. There was no mention of victory. Even so, the troops were heartened. Sledge was in fine spirits next day, when he found Lon washing socks and drawers in a tub of grimy water already used by a dozen others. Both men gamely tried to ignore the screams and the grind of saws amputating limbs in nearby hospital tents.

"I hear Lincoln's coming down tomorrow," Sledge began.

"I'm sure it isn't to see me."

The unexpected sourness made Sledge frown. He wore what he'd worn for weeks, a loose white shirt with a patched elbow Lon had mended for him, but he'd spruced up by tying his black string tie in a bow and combing his hair with water. Lon commented on his neatness.

"Just saw the boss. He said Richmond will stand a while longer, so we're starting over."

"Meaning what?"

"He's sending me in to spy on fortifications."

Lon's reaction was disappointment, and envy. "Dangerous duty, Sledge."

"Sure, but we've sat on our bums long enough."

Lon twisted his underwear to wring water into the tub. Sledge chewed his gold-plated toothpick. "He wants to send two men. I asked for you."

Lon laid the wet garment aside and wiped his bare chest with his palm. It got rid of some sweat but didn't cool him. The summer heat was fierce, the sky unclouded, the sun pitiless. Steam rose from the muddy ground. Lon's nose and shoulders were red and ready to blister.

"What did the boss say to that?"

"He said all right. Can't say he was kicking up his heels, though. What did you do, spit in his face?"

"I imagine he thinks so. I questioned the figures we developed for the general these past months. I didn't believe them."

"Guess old Stanton didn't either. Not my burden," Sledge said with one of those shrugs that amounted to the entire Greenglass philosophy.

"When do we go?"

"After things settle down. A week or two. Are you game?"

"Of course." After months of dull duty relieved only by the excitement of the balloon flight, Lon couldn't wait.

"What about Zach?"

"I expect he should go back to Willard's. He won't be happy."

"Who the hell's really happy in this camp? We failed, bub. Davis and Lee sit in Richmond thumbing their noses, Little

Mac's in the shit house, and if the boss can't hang on, he'll sink with him. We're better off behind enemy lines."

Given the risks, Lon doubted it, but he didn't argue. Sledge went off whistling. Lon picked up his laundry and trudged toward his tent, wincing as another victim of the saws screamed.

He was depressed at the thought of McClellan dragging Pinkerton down. The boss had failings, as they all did, but Lon still admired him, not only for his hatred of slavery, but because he stood by his men. For months he'd fought the War Department over the issue of pay. Stanton's bureaucrats claimed they couldn't honor Pinkerton's payroll vouchers because each consisted of a total sum due, with no explanation. The department wanted a list of operatives. Pinkerton consistently refused on grounds that it could endanger his agents, should some clerk with reb sympathies get hold of such a list. During Lon's time in Washington he'd met a captain who had witnessed an argument between Pinkerton and a loud-mouthed European at the War Department, a man named Siegel. The boss was so exercised and vehement, the captain expected him to attack Siegel or have a seizure.

Pinkerton lost the battle. The department continued to send a portion of the payroll, never the whole amount. And it was always late. How could one man deal with so many responsibilities without buckling?

Pinkerton's problems raised other questions for Lon. What if the boss fell along with his patron? Could Lon switch his loyalty and work for Lafayette Baker? Could his need to do anything he could to hasten a victory overcome his loathing for the man who had imprisoned Margaret Miller?

The image of Baker's face dissolved to another, grimly erotic. Margaret lay naked in the marriage bed. Lon's spirits slumped. General McClellan wasn't the only one suffering defeat this summer.

*   *   *

Lincoln didn't rid himself of McClellan, but instead called him back to rebuild the Army of the Potomac for the defense of Washington. The President did it despite another discourteous letter the general sent from Harrison's Landing. The grapevine said Little Mac not only lectured Lincoln on strategy, but also on politics, especially the slavery issue. He said it should play no part in military decisions.

Washington ordered McClellan to abandon the Peninsula and move the Army to Aqua Landing and Alexandria. He protested but he obeyed. To command the new field Army, the Army of Virginia, Lincoln summoned General John Pope, the hero of Island No. 10 in the Western theater. The capital received Pope with the same optimistic fanfare McClellan had enjoyed when he came to town.

*   *   *

Hanna impatiently awaited her chance to go back to the battlefield. Margaret was suddenly, mysteriously gone from the Old Capitol, leaving a letter that Hanna read with amazement.

> *By the time you peruse this, dear friend, I will be a married woman. Donal and I were wed in the prison and immediately after, I was set free. Such is the magic of diplomacy. I hope the despicable Baker will foam and growl like the mad dog he is.*
>
> *Donal wishes to live in New York, but first we will make an overland journey to Richmond, for a reunion with my brother. Donal will obtain diplomatic papers to pass us through both Yankee and Confederate lines without interference. There is some risk, of course, as battle lines seem to shift suddenly. He is willing to bear the risk for my sake, and also because he can make important business contacts in Richmond. The government is eager to ship as much cotton abroad as it can, to pay for goods it can no longer buy from the North. I trust we shall come out of the whole adventure unharmed.*

The letter closed with a wish for Hanna's happiness and safety, and a promise of mended friendship *when the clouds rise and the skies clear again.*

Nowhere in the letter did Margaret say that as a newly married woman, she was happy.

*   *   *

The retreat from the Peninsula began in August. After days of waiting, Lon and Sledge prepared for their mission. George Bangs gave each of them a closely written list of passwords and countersigns and instructed them on contacting the one agent of the Richmond spy ring whose name they were permitted to know. Siegfried Retz, a recent immigrant and opponent of slavery, ran a butcher shop.

"You won't get to him immediately," Bangs said. "If events proceed typically, you'll be locked up until you're deemed ready to be put in a work brigade. At worst, you'll be handed a uniform and sent to the front lines, but the later it is in the year, the less likely that becomes. Should it happen, you'll simply desert again."

"Oh, sure, easy," Sledge said, rolling his eyes.

They chose new names. Lon was Private Albion Rogers, Sledge was Private Sam Snowdon. They outfitted themselves with blue kersey trousers, belts with brass buckles, and dark blue sack coats on which they pinned red cloth badges, diamond-shaped. Phil Kearny had introduced corps badges during the campaign and the idea had caught on.

On the night they left, Pinkerton sought them out and shook hands with both of them. He had no reproaches for Lon. It gratified him.

They made their way toward Richmond through the shell-blasted countryside, keeping away from main roads. A cool wave of northern air brought the first whisper of autumn. They saw only three Confederate patrols the first day and easily avoided them. By late on the second day they came within hearing of the city's church bells. Then, on a dirt track snaking through the forest, bad luck showed up in the form of three armed Confederates who suddenly rose in front of them, having marched up the inside of a shell crater. Irregulars, Lon judged; two of them were no more than fourteen. He and Sledge raised their hands without being told.

The bearded leader had the look of a backwoods cretin. Half his front teeth were missing. He wore an old felt hat pierced by bullet holes and a comic-opera uniform: emerald green coat, baggy mauve trousers. In his red sash he carried a bowie knife and an oversized .45-caliber Allen pepperbox. He mocked them with his salute.

"Colonel Jeffa Mars, Henrico County Defenders. Where abouts you boys headed?"

Sledge groveled appropriately by kneading his forage cap in his hands. "To Richmond, we hope. Had a bellyful of fighting for the wrong side."

Colonel Mars looked them up and down. "What's your names?"

"Private Sam Snowdon, Heintzelman's Third Corps, First Division." Sledge touched the red diamond badge.

"Private Albion Rogers, same," Lon said. "Let me reach under my shirt, I'll show you something to prove we mean what we say."

"Go ahead, but slow."

Lon unbuttoned his sack coat and produced the Brady photograph. "Here we are, both of us. Had this taken in Washington City. I'd never have signed up except for my girl back home in Albany, New York. She wouldn't go to the hayloft with me unless I said I'd serve. I did, and she did."

Colonel Mars busily scratched his genitals. "Well, sir, that's a hell of a price to pay for a little piece of cunny. Old cock's got a way of knocking good sense out of a man, don't he? Say hello to Captain Seamus Tipper and Captain Bellephon Forney, two of the bravest lads ever fought for Southern rights." Captains Tipper and Forney were malnourished adolescents equipped with rusty trade muskets that could have been thirty years old.

"We're gettin' a lot of you bluecoats lately," Mars said. "If you two boys want to serve the side of the righteous, if you truly hate niggers and all who bow down to kiss their asses, then I say welcome. If on the other hand you're lying about it, if you're yella cowards or spies or anything like that, we got hangmen who can always handle one more."

The self-appointed colonel might be a backwoods ignoramus, but he had a certain deadly shrewdness. The cool air of early evening was suddenly chilling. The late-summer sun cast long shadows. Through the treetops Lon saw a vee of waterbirds winging south. He wished they might fly away as easily.

Colonel Mars vigorously massaged his crotch again. " 'Fore we march off to town, let's see what you got in your pockets. Turn 'em out."

Nothing to do but obey; like Sledge, Lon was unarmed. He'd stored his pocket Colt and other personal effects in a small box that Zach had promised to carry back to Washington. Sledge showed the only item he was carrying besides tobacco, his gold-plated toothpick. Colonel Mars's eyes popped.

"Say, let's see that thing." Visibly upset, Sledge laid the toothpick in Mars's filthy palm. Mars held it up so it caught the sun. He raised it to his lips, licked it lovingly. "Gold, is it? Mighty good." Captains Tipper and Forney sniggered and elbowed each other. "Think I'll just hang onto this." Mars slipped it in his coat pocket.

"My pa gave me that pick," Sledge said.

Jovially Colonel Mars replied, "So what's that got to do with me?"

"It's mine. Give it back or I'll take it back."

"Hey, here's a brave one," Colonel Mars said to his companions. The boy captains leveled their muskets. Lon flashed warning looks, but Sledge ignored them or didn't see. "Take it away from me if you can, Yank."

Sledge had a moment to reconsider but he didn't. He stepped forward, raising his big fists. Colonel Mars pulled the pepperbox from his red sash and shot him in the forehead.

Sledge rolled on the ground and lay still. His bowels let go. Lon trembled with shock, struck dumb by the sudden, senseless killing. Colonel Mars squinted at him.

"How about you? Want to die for a toothpick?"

Church bells rang in Richmond, the notes sweetly floating over the summer countryside. A hare peeked from a wild raspberry bush and retreated. Philo Greenglass lay dead with a hole in his skull and a mask of blood around his eyes. Lon remembered the mission, numbly shook his head. Colonel Mars smiled, showing his rotted teeth.

"All right, then. March."

36

July–August 1862

The final days of the Peninsula campaign took Stuart's men behind enemy lines again. On June 25 the general led two thousand riders out of Richmond to rendezvous with Jackson's infantry marching swiftly and secretly from the Valley. Stuart's force included elements of Fitz Lee's First Virginia, Rooney Lee's Ninth, Wickham's Fourth, the Jeff Davis and Wade Hampton Legions, and Pelham's artillery. It was among Hampton's South Carolinians that Fred Dasher spied Charlie Main. They hailed one another, brought their horses together.

"My God, Charlie, you look grand. Not a day older, and brown as mahogany."

Charles Main, a lean and ruggedly handsome young man, touched his cheek. "Still carrying this leather face from two years ago, when I quit the Second Cav down in Texas."

"You think we can win this war?"

"Hell, Carrots, I don't know. Sometimes I think we're fighting for all the wrong reasons. Let's meet and talk soon as McClellan's whipped. Adios."

*   *   *

Stuart guided Jackson's foot cavalry to McClellan's unprotected right flank. Jackson was a pale, cadaverous man, not yet forty. Instead of a regulation uniform he wore a soiled, worn-out uniform and, pulled down over one eye, a shabby cap from Virginia Military Institute, where he'd taught. Fred first saw him sitting on a rock consulting a map. He could scarcely believe this mundane person was the famous Stonewall.

Fighting soon engulfed them. With shells coming in hot and fast, shattering trees, blowing up the earth, lifting men and horses in the air and dismembering them as they died, Fred rode in a charge that routed seven hundred Union lancers whose quaint weapons proved useless. His detachment demonstrated in front of McClellan's White House base. The show of force was so effective, the Yanks torched the plantation house and its outbuildings and sped their infantry to safety by boat. To ruin captured Yankee locomotives, Pelham's artillery blew holes in the boilers from a range of fifty yards.

The troopers foraged in the ashes and blackened beams of the lovely old house. They found crates of unspoiled delicacies, and whiskey. Fred drank his share, temporarily soothing a bad case of war nerves. The land between the Chickahominy and the James was like nothing he'd ever seen, a horrific wasteland of burned forest, fallen trees, fields littered with maggoty corpses, streams fouled with rotting mules and horses. Smelling the air, many a soldier couldn't keep food down.

After seven days of fighting, McClellan fell back, Richmond rejoiced, and the cavalry rested.

* * *

Jeb Stuart reported to Lee and returned with a major general's commission. He recommended many in his command for promotions, including Fred. Fred wasn't cheered. He felt the war, or his part of it, was on a downward path.

Exhausted in soul and body, he was unwilling to forgo the dangerous medicine he took for relief. He feared he was becoming a sot. He dreamed awful dreams, brightly colored, full of noise. In them, the little girl at Garlick's Landing died, then died again, endlessly.

He arranged a meeting with Charlie at cavalry headquarters, a farm near Atlee's Station north of Richmond. They relaxed and visited in the warm shade of a huge oak. On the farmhouse lawn, General Stuart romped with his children while his handsome wife, Flora, rested in a rope swing hung from a hickory limb. A summer breeze carried the chuff-chuff of a military train on the Virginia Central line.

Fred and Charlie laughed and reminisced about the Military Academy. Legs stretched out, a little cigar clenched in his teeth, Charlie observed that the cavalry had become the eyes and ears of the Army, so he and Fred were in effect spies in the saddle. Then he confessed that he was, as he put it, entangled with a woman. She lived in Spotsylvania County.

"Tell you the truth, Fred, it's because of her that I'm beginning to hate the damn war. Fellow might be killed any day of the week, bang, no warning, and I don't think it's right to fall in love with that hanging over you. Trouble is, I did. Don't know where it will lead."

"What's her name?"

"Augusta Barclay. Widow woman. God, she's handsome, and sweet. How about you? Anyone special?"

Fred shook his head. Much of his life had been devoted to the old Army, and his few brief love affairs hardly deserved the name. Usually he relied on red-light houses. Of late he'd felt a great need for a woman. He envied Charlie.

Along the sunlit railway, a train of flatcars passed with soldiers hollooing and waving hats. Fred decided they were new recruits who hadn't seen the elephant. The whistle sounded, long and mournful. Fred and Charlie brushed themselves off and prepared to say good-bye.

They embraced like brothers. Charlie said, "We'll talk again when, as, and if we're all done with this fuss." He set his battered slouch hat on his head. "You sure you're all right, Carrots? You look pale as the inside of a flour sack."

Fred saw Garlick's Landing. He saw the girl die. He hadn't spoken of it. He itched for a shot of whiskey.

"I'm fine. You take care. Regards to your lady."

"Thank you. Godspeed, Major, sir." Fred had revealed his coming promotion. Smiling, he returned Charlie's mock salute. He watched his handsome brown-faced friend go jauntily in search of his horse. He stood in the hot shade, silent and sad.

*　　*　　*

He spent the rest of July and the early part of August at a training camp at Hanover Court House, drilling new men. He was secretly pleased to hear that John Mosby, foolishly endangering himself on a scouting mission, had been captured by Yankee cavalry. In August he heard that Mosby was free in a prisoner exchange.

McClellan was moving his Peninsula Army up the Potomac as possible reinforcement for John Pope's new Army of Virginia. Pope advanced to an exposed position somewhere between the Rapidan and Rappahannock rivers. Lee decided on a preemptive strategy, a move against Pope before the two armies united.

After observing Pope's Army from a hilltop called Clark's Mountain, Lee sent Stuart and a small escort to probe enemy positions. Fred was part of the group, along with Mosby. They made camp at a farm outside Verdiersville just before midnight on August 17. The men stretched out to sleep on the fragrant lawn while Stuart settled on the farmhouse porch.

In the silence of the starlit night, Fred woke to the sound of horses approaching on a nearby road. He kicked free of his blanket. On the porch, Mosby roused Stuart. "Yankee cavalry, sir. Be here any minute."

They ran for their horses. Stuart vaulted onto Skylark so vigorously his plumed hat fell off. Stuart and Fred and the others galloped away from the farm in a hail of gunfire and narrowly escaped the pursuers. Stuart was incensed over the loss of his hat.

A day later, Pope inexplicably began to retreat north to the Rappahannock. Lee sent Stuart's men to spy on the enemy Army, harass its lines of communication, and impede the withdrawal. This time Stuart took fifteen hundred riders and two fieldpieces. Inordinately jolly after escaping capture, he shouted as they rode out, "Boys, we're going after my hat!"

Their first objective in the enemy's rear was a railroad bridge over Cedar Run at Catlett's Station, on the Orange and Alexandria line. To reach it they circled wide to Warrenton, northwest of Catlett's. At a tavern where they paused to rest at dusk, a lieutenant brought a lanky white-haired Negro to Stuart. "Pickets caught him outside of town, General."

"Didn't take a whole lot of catching," the black man said. "My name is Simon Biggs. I'm a teamster, and a free man. Blasted Yankees impressed me like Englishmen used to shanghai sailors. Been driving their blasted freight wagons six months now. I got too much 'nigger, do this, nigger do that,' so I ran off." Sitting at a plank table near Stuart, a tin cup of stale beer in hand, Fred reflected that neither side in this war had a monopoly on meanness.

"And where exactly did you come from, Mr. Biggs?" Stuart asked.

Simon Biggs understood that he commanded the situation, no matter how many pistols and sabers surrounded him. He stretched the moment, fastidiously straightening the frayed collar of his old gray work shirt. He squinted at Stuart and smiled in a foxy way.

"Why, General, I come from the headquarters camp of another general, John Pope."

In the stillness Fred heard a fly buzzing. Mosby, ever eager to draw attention to himself, jumped off his bench and strode to Stuart's table, the better to listen. Watching, Fred drank from the tin cup, looking like he'd swallowed poison.

"Is the camp near?" Stuart's voice held a suppressed tension.

"Close by Catlett's Station."

"Is Pope himself there?"

"Not sure. He was a while ago. All his baggage is piled up, though. I can show you."

Stuart shook hands. "Thank you, Mr. Biggs, delighted to have your cooperation." To the assembled officers Stuart said, "In the saddle in two minutes."

On the dusty pike leading to Catlett's, a strong breeze buffeted the riders. Clouds sailed underneath the stars and hid them. White fire flickered in the clouds. Leaves peeled from trees as the wind rose. Fred felt raindrops pecking at his cheek.

The wind reached gale force for a few minutes but dropped off as the rain fell harder. The steady fall became a cloudburst. They advanced at a walk while thunder rolled continuouly. Lightning brought an eerie version of daylight. Astride a mule at Stuart's side, Simon Biggs pointed to faint lights ahead. "Yonder's the camp, other side of the stream. Stream's shallow."

"Then we'd better cross before it floods. Forward, column of twos."

Close behind Stuart, Fred pulled a bandanna out of his collar and hooked it over his nose to soak up rain. He tugged his hat brim down to shield his eyes. Baron balked and whinnied. A touch of Fred's hand calmed the horse.

They waded the rushing stream and spread right and left on the muddy bank, still a quarter mile from the tents and wagons somewhat more clearly defined by dozens of lighted lanterns. Fred braced himself with whiskey from his canteen. Thunder crashed. Stuart was bareheaded, water streaming from his beard, homage to this journey to reclaim his hat.

Lightning burst as Fred drew his saber. The blade shimmered like Arthur's Excalibur. He'd always loved the gallantry of the Arthurian legends. Reality was different.

"Private Freed, sound the charge."

Rain slashed Fred's face as Baron leaped forward and they came down upon the Union camp. Lanterns in the tents silhouetted men inside. They seemed to be relaxing, eating and drinking, safe from the rain. Fred raised his voice in a long wailing yell that joined hundreds of others.

He rode with the reins in his teeth and his LeMats in his hands. A boyish sentry stepped in his path, vainly trying to fire his musket. Fred shot him in the chest. Thunder crashed.

Troopers slashed guy ropes so tents collapsed. Caught underneath, men struggled to escape and were shot like fish in a net. Confused sentries ran about, shot or sabered if they didn't instantly throw down their weapons. Stuart's men sheltered torches under their ponchos to light them, then tossed the lit torches into supply wagons. Another sentry lunged in front of Baron, hands raised. "I quit, I surrender." Fred put a bullet in the man's chest.

As Fred swung down a lane between tents, he heard a chilling scream from one of them. Either some recruit's voice hadn't changed or someone was harboring a woman. He holstered one revolver, protected the other inside his coat, and jumped off Baron. He splashed through standing water and at the tent entrance pulled the LeMat from under his coat.

37

August 1862

After the failed Peninsula campaign, boatloads of wounded arrived at the Potomac piers. Many of the wounded died in hospitals, and secondhand shops soon filled up with discarded uniforms. Hanna sorted through the melancholy merchandise, bargained, and made purchases. A stiff-sided backpack of the kind carried in European Armies. A pair of sky-blue kersey trousers, a dark blue four-button sack coat. A chasseur cap with only a tiny spot of blood on the crown. A pair of mud-scows, the cheap square-toed Army shoes supplied by contractors. Somehow the shoes were more grisly than the clothes. Who was the poor boy who died wearing them?

If a shopkeeper wondered aloud about a woman buying such things, Hanna said she collected war souvenirs. Why not? Washington was a crazy place that summer. Work crews added to the bedlam on Pennsylvania Avenue by tearing it up for a new street railway. Secesh ladies came across the Potomac bridges with no trouble, to shop or to visit like-minded friends. Odd new paper money circulated: greenbacks from Mr. Chase's Treasury, and shinplasters, notes of all sizes and designs issued by Northern cities.

Lincoln called for more men and inspired a new anthem: "We are coming, Father Abraham, three hundred thousand strong." Trainloads of recruits arrived. Major Siegel worked until ten or eleven each night, complaining constantly of the long hours and low pay. Yet he seemed to revel in his insider's position, carrying home tales of the new and unpopular general-in-chief, Halleck, or the widespread uncertainty about the boastful commander of the new Army of Virginia, Pope, whose drunken troops roistered in the Manassas camps. The Union now had two armies in northern Virginia, Pope's and McClellan's. The latter was slowly being hammered back into shape at Alexandria by its chastened, almost disgraced general.

Hanna hid her purchases in an old armoire in the little house near the Navy Yard. When Pope moved into the field in August, she decided she'd better not delay.

Unfortunately, Derek Fowley had cast her as Juliet in an autumn production just starting rehearsals. When she told Derek she'd be away for a bit, he said he was sick of dealing with "inconsiderate artists." Hanna laughed, a fatal response. Derek stuck his face two inches from hers and shouted that Zephira Comfort would replace her. Hanna giggled uncontrollably; there was enough of tubby Zephira for two Juliets. She realized the curtain had fallen on her career with Derek.

At one o'clock next morning, the major came home smelling of schnapps. Hanna repeated what she'd told Derek. Siegel flung himself into a chair and yelled, "Where you going? I got a right to know."

"I'm going to see the camps."

"You already did it once."

"I want to go again."

"What for? You got no business with the soldiers"—the major's pink lips curled into a smirk—"unless you're making money off them like some women do."

"Papa, that's a nasty joke."

"I don't care, I don't know what you are anymore, Hanna. You're not a man, but you're a queer sort of woman. You want to take these chances with yourself, I wash my hands." He knocked the chair over as he weaved to his feet. "I got to sleep. Stanton's called a meeting at seven o'clock."

Hanna stared after the squat, shuffling figure, wanting to shout as loudly as he had. *You don't know what I am? I'm your daughter trying to be a person you'll care about.* She wondered if the major could ever care about anything but himself, his personal advancement, and how she disappointed him merely by existing.

*   *   *

She chopped her straw blonde hair so it was short again. She stuffed corks in her pocket to char and rub on her face, to darken her fair skin and suggest a beard. With her hard-sided

European backpack and her blue eyes, she could pass for one
of the thousands of slavery-hating German immigrants who'd
signed up to fight for Father Abraham.

Her plan for working her way south toward Pope's Army
was beautifully simple. She only spoke her native language,
German.

Two things made the scheme viable. One was the great
number of Germans already in Pope's Army, led by General
Franz Sigel. Sigel came from Missouri and, before that, the
failed European revolutions of 1848. He commanded one of
Pope's three divisions. Hanna had seen him in a Washington
parade, a slight, bearded man with a morose expression.
Whenever she was stopped and questioned, she answered
with a phrase many a German soldier used if he understood
no English. "I fights mit Sigel."

Asked about her unit, she answered, *"Schimmelfennig,
Brigade Erste."* Colonel Alexander Schimmelfennig was another 1848 exile from Germany. If other questions were put to
her, she mimed helplessness.

Some who stopped her wanted to know what she was doing
traveling alone. *"Ich bin krank.* Sick." Everyone knew of the
Union's huge invalid corps in Washington. Hanna was waved
on, often with a compliment. Deserters didn't walk boldly, as
she did. They skulked, and they never went south.

Pope's Army lay somewhere below the Rappahannock. A
Friday evening near the end of August found Hanna short of
her goal, caught in a violent thunderstorm. She limped into a
large camp on the Orange and Alexandria railway. A sergeant
of the guard intercepted her, shouting above the roar of the
rain, "Name and unit?"

"Hugo Rauch. I fights mit Sigel. *Schimmelfennig, Brigade
Erste. Ich bin krank.* Sick." She pointed and pantomimed
being lost. "Schimmelfennig where?"

"Damn 'f I know. This here's General Pope's headquarters
camp." Which, to a casual glance, looked lightly guarded. The
sergeant indicated a large walled tent, brightly illuminated.
"That's his baggage yonder. General himself, he ain't here."

For a camp in a war zone the place seemed curiously relaxed. Hanna smelled coffee and bacon. Her stomach
growled. She'd eaten her last biscuit at noon.

The sergeant took her to a second lieutenant lounging in one of the tents. He said they were shorthanded. Before continuing in search of his unit, Private Rauch could earn a meal by making himself useful. They found an old oilcloth poncho and a musket. At half past nine Hanna was standing guard in the wagon park, huddled in the lee of a big freighter.

She congratulated herself on getting this far. Despite her hunger and wet clothes, she was in good spirits, planning how she'd steal away and dry her uniform when the sun shone again.

Between thunderclaps she heard horsemen, and bugling. Then came pistol fire, and a chilling cry that had to be the rebel yell she'd heard about. It roared from hundreds of throats. Her stomach heaved, an unexpected reaction to seeing the elephant.

A ball struck the wagon behind her, tearing out splinters that stung her cheek. She fumbled with the musket as riders crossed her line of sight. Bursts of lightning revealed bearded faces, wet horses, uniforms of rain-soaked gray. Some of the riders wore hats with black plumes. Confederate cavalry, operating behind enemy lines.

An officer ran out of a tent with his dinner napkin tucked in his collar. A reb shot him and the napkin turned red as he tumbled into the mud. Tents were set afire. Men shouted that they'd found cases of food and wine. Fighting her fear, Hanna crept away. A reb on foot charged out of the dark, showing his saber in the lightning flash. The reb grabbed her musket, then her arm. Hanna raked his face with her short, broken nails.

Spitting mad, he stuck his saber in the mud and bearhugged her, trying to break her spine. As they danced grotesquely in the rain, he exploded with a stupefied, "Huh?" His hand groped the front of her sack coat, hurting her bound breasts.

"Mary and Joseph! Lieutenant Buford? Sir, wait'll you see the bird I caught!"

Moments later Hanna was shoved into a tent where a lantern burned on the ridgepole. The man who'd caught her, a youthful Confederate trooper with yellow hair, knocked her cap off.

"Who are you?"

"I fights mit Sigel."

"Sigel recruiting girls these days?" The lieutenant came in. "We got us a female tricked up as a foot soldier, Lieutenant Buford."

"Well, I heard of cases of that," the lieutenant drawled. He was tall, with a black-plumed hat and a coarse, jowly face. Hanna crossed her arms on her chest. "Hold her." The trooper yanked her arms behind her. Buford seized her collar and ripped the sack coat open, popping buttons.

He reached under, squeezed her breasts. A smile spread over his damp face. "You caught a rare and tender bird indeed, Sergeant. Should we have a little feast?"

The trooper's eyes gleamed as he caught on. "Is it safe?"

"If we're quick. I'll go first. Put out the lantern and keep watch."

Hanna threw herself at the canvas wall, intending to tear it or burrow under it. Lieutenant Buford hooked her leg with his boot. She sprawled, landing hard. The lieutenant's feet straddled her hips. When she tried to crawl away, he stamped on her calf. The pain made her gasp.

The sergeant blew out the lamp hung from the ridgepole with baling wire. The last things Hanna saw were the lieutenant's smug smile and his red member growing from the gap in his trousers.

38

August 1862

Fred stepped into the tent, saw two men. One, an ugly lieutenant, knelt between the legs of a soldier who lay on his back. Fred had a swift impression of yellow hair, a boyish face smeared with dirt. "What the hell's this?" Fred waved his revolver. "Stand up."

The lieutenant struggled to his feet, his erection shriveling.

Fred dug in his pocket for the tin matchbox in the shape of a knapsack. He tossed the box to the lieutenant.

"Give us some light."

The lieutenant poked a lighted match into the black tin lantern painted with a white *U.S.* He lit the candle and shut the isinglass door. He returned the matchbox, saying, "Major, please let me explain something." He had a thick redneck accent, offensive to a Virginian.

"Never mind. You're going on report for molesting a fellow soldier."

"Sir, look again. It's a her."

One glance corrected Fred's mistake. He was a she, all right, blue-eyed, and shaking like a frightened child. Under her sack coat, cloth strips bound her small breasts.

Fred felt a brush of air—the sergeant, starting to leave. Fred pivoted and jabbed the revolver under the man's chin.

"Not one more step." To the lieutenant Fred said, "Identify yourself."

The lieutenant stuffed himself back in his pants and saluted. "Lieutenant Henry Buford, sir. Jeff Davis Legion."

"Mississippi troops?"

"Yes, sir. Caught this piece of Yankee trash sneaking around and—"

"Shut up. You're a fucking disgrace." Fred gigged the sergeant. "You?" The reply was a gargling sound. Fred cocked the weapon. "Don't be shy."

"S-s-sergeant Cleatus Voss. S-sir." Another cracker.

Fred took the LeMat from the noncom's neck. Burning tents and wagons threw firelight patterns on the canvas walls. An occasional shot resounded, but the fighting had given way to boisterous revelry as the troopers ripped through the booty of Pope's camp. All the saddle weariness Fred had forgotten during the last few minutes returned: the sore tailbone, the ache under his balls, the raw skin on the inside of his thighs. "Both of you are going on report to Colonel Martin. Now crawl out of here."

Lieutenant Buford buttoned his pants, slid by Fred, lifted his knee to kick the noncom's rear, as though he were responsible for their predicament. The men disappeared into the drizzle.

"Get up. Fix your clothes."

The girl sat up, then stood. She was unsteady. Fred grabbed her sleeve. Her straw blonde hair was damp. Her eyes had the vivid color of a spring sky. She was a pretty thing, with delicate features that would allow her to pass for a young man. Swallowing, he let go of her.

"How'd you get here? Where are you from?"

"Washington. I wanted to see some fighting."

"Well, you've seen it. Go back home. This is no fancy ball, miss. Men die out here."

What should he do with her? He decided to shirk the responsibility and let the commanding officer decide. Of course they had to let her go. If she stayed a prisoner, he could imagine how many times she'd be raped by captured Yanks and randy rebs alike.

"What's your name?"

"Hanna Siegel."

"German?"

"The next thing to it. Austrian. You don't sound Southern."

"Virginia. Spent a long time in the North. I've got to see the general about you."

"Which general?"

"James E. B. Stuart, of Stuart's cavalry. My name's Frederick Dasher."

"I'm very grateful to you for what you did, Major Dasher."

"Fine," Fred said, close to losing himself in the blue depths of those eyes. He hadn't been with a woman since he rode out of Richmond weeks ago. This pixie with her sooty cheeks and ragtag uniform touched him somehow. She was no taller than his shoulder; she had to turn her face up to speak to him. It made her seem vulnerable; induced emotions in him that were unexpected, and dangerous.

"Take the laces out of your shoes," he said.

"Why?"

"Because I can't trust you and I have to see the general. Sit down on the cot." He grasped her arm again, as if to steady her. It was really because he wanted to touch her.

Hanna pulled the rawhide laces from her muddy shoes. Fred shoved the revolver in his pants, tied the two thongs into one, wrapped the rawhide around and around her wrists, behind her back.

"Not so tight."

"Sorry." He finished the knot. "You're on your honor to stay here until I'm back."

"I couldn't run twenty steps right now."

The inside of his mouth was dry as ashes. *You'll run like hell if they toss you in with men who haven't been close to women for a while,* he thought.

"You can sit if you like."

"Thank you." As he lifted the tent flap, she said, "Do you own slaves, Major?"

"I own a horse farm near Front Royal. Six Negroes work for me. About four years ago I signed manumission papers for all of them."

"So you don't think the Confederacy's war is moral?"

"I didn't say that. I left the U.S. Army for the same reason General Lee did, to fight for Virginia. I'll be back."

In the lane, faithful Baron waited, head down, without a tether. Fred patted the black, muttering about this complication in their lives. He took his canteen off the saddle, shook it. Some whiskey left. He drank it.

He found Stuart in a quadrangle of large headquarters tents. Three were ablaze but the fourth was untouched. Fitz Lee was parading in front of it in a plumed chapeau and a blue officer's overcoat with the black sleeve braid of a general, to the delight of Stuart, von Borcke, and some others.

"Look here at this, Fred," Stuart exclaimed as Fred came up and saluted. "General Pope's finest coat. I'll take it in exchange for my hat. That's not all we found. We have field orders, cipher books—what is it? What's wrong?"

"I took a prisoner a few minutes ago, sir."

"Congratulations. No cause for a glum face, is it?"

"This prisoner—sir, it's a woman." With hands on his hips, Fitz Lee stopped parading and fixed his attention on Fred, as did the others. "A young woman from Washington who dressed up like a man to see some fighting. I need to know what—"

A captain ran out of the dark, breathless. "General, we can't burn the railroad bridge. Timbers are too wet. We don't have enough axes to chop them down."

"I'll have a look." Stuart started away, pausing at the firelight's perimeter to say to Fred, "Treat the woman like any other captive. If she's man enough to wear a uniform, she's man enough to go to prison."

A couple of the officers smirked. Fred started to object but Stuart was already gone in the direction of rain-flooded Cedar Run.

He couldn't believe the general meant it. A Virginia gentleman didn't consign a girl of nineteen or twenty to a prison full of rats and rapists. Shaking his head, he hurried back to the tent. Hanna raised an expectant face as he walked in.

"General Stuart wants you treated like any other prisoner of war. Imprisoned until you're exchanged." She reacted as if he'd hit her. She whispered a German word, perhaps *Himmel*.

"The general isn't himself. We're in a tight place, miles behind the Union lines. We can't be burdened with a lot of prisoners, he'll wake up to that. On your feet."

Puzzled, Hanna let him swing her around. He worked at the knot in the rawhide and broke two fingernails before undoing it.

"I'm going to lead you out of here. Keep your hands behind you, as though you're still tied. We'll walk to the nearest cover, the woods, and then you run like the devil. All the way back to Washington. And don't try such a damn fool stunt again."

"No, no, I won't. Why are you doing this?"

"I just don't believe in throwing women into the kind of prisons they have in Richmond. They aren't fit for dogs, let alone humans."

"Will you get in trouble?"

"I'll handle it." Though he didn't know exactly how. "When we go outside, look scared."

With a brave smile she said, "I've performed in plays but I don't have to act this part."

Perhaps it was the whiskey or the rain or the lost feeling that had plagued him ever since he'd killed the little girl. Whatever it was, it drove him to clasp her fragile shoulders in his big hands, bend down, and kiss her.

She went rigid. Then her mouth responded. The touch of her lips was cool, though he felt them warming before he stepped back. His head whirled. Something had happened.

"Your name's Hanna."

"Yes."

"I won't forget."

"Nor I."

"Hands behind your back."

They went out into the rainy dark.

*   *   *

Stuart's cavalry retraced the route to Warrenton. They had prisoners, and General Pope's dispatch books, though by happenstance the general himself had been away during the raid. The Confederate treasury was richer by $350,000, the contents of Pope's money chest.

Young ladies of Warrenton turned out at dawn to wave hankies and cheer the exhausted troopers. Stuart ordered a halt to rest the horses. He summoned Fred to the porch of a house belonging to a family named Lucas and there asked about the female prisoner.

Fred saw no point in dissembling. He admitted he'd let her go. Stuart reacted with predictable anger. "You realize you disobeyed a direct order."

"The order was given very casually, sir. I thought I might have some latitude."

"You did not. I can't let this pass." Stuart jerked Fred's sleeve to distance them from listeners. "Blast you, why are throwing yourself away? What's happened? You needn't bother to answer, soldiers gossip. You're drinking yourself to death. Now this."

Weary and savagely thirsty, Fred wanted to shout, *I drink to forget who I killed in this damned misbegotten war.* He remained stiffly silent.

"Do you have anything to say?"

"I did what I thought was right and humane, General. I'm sure the young woman was no older than twenty. She must have stumbled into Pope's camp by accident."

"No excuse. I gave you a direct order. I won't court-martial you, we can't afford to lose a good soldier. But you are reduced in rank to private. I'll sign the papers personally."

Rays of the misty morning sun spread over cottage rooftops. Trees dripped last night's rain. Somewhere a mockingbird sang. Young ladies mingled with the grimy troopers, praising them and offering dippers of water and slices of bread. Stuart spied someone in the crowd. He watched a moment, then wheeled back to Fred.

"To deter you from making another mistake and doing real harm, I will also transfer you. John Mosby is after me to set up a small force of partisan rangers to raid behind the enemy's lines. I'm inclined to agree to it, because I think the task and the man are suited to each other. I'll assign you to Mosby. Henceforth you'll take orders from him."

39

August–September 1862

The headlight of a southbound train lit up the rails of the Orange and Alexandria line. Hanna dove off the embankment, huddled on wet ground until the train passed. A few minutes later, distant gunfire said the train crew was getting a hot reception from the rebs.

She climbed back to the track and trudged on through intermittent rain that lasted most of the night. By morning she'd caught a chill. About midday she holed up in a thick copse, sick with fever and the quickstep. She lay there until dark, when she felt strong enough to struggle on.

She decided the pain in her middle was emptiness, not sickness, so she stopped at an isolated farm and begged a slice of bread from the woman of the house. The woman was lank as a string, with large moles on her lined face. She raised her oil lamp to study Hanna.

"What's a girl doing in that uniform?"

Hanna tried the first story that came to mind. "I'm a nurse. Lost my unit."

"Didn't know Billy Yank had nurses with him. You can sleep in the barn, it's warm. I'll bring you a plate and fill a sack with some food in the morning." Hanna's backpack had been stripped from her by her captors. "Wait, I'll find a blanket."

Hanna leaned on the doorframe and closed her eyes. The war hadn't squeezed the humanity out of everyone, as she sometimes feared. She ought to know that, remembering the major. She saw his face bending toward her. Gray-green eyes with a strange, sad intensity—

"Here you are."

"Thank you, ma'am. You're very kind."

"I have a husband and a son fighting for Lee. If you came across either one sorely wounded, I would hope you'd tend him regardless."

"Yes, ma'am. I would."

"You struck me as that sort. This way."

*   *   *

Hanna left the farm Sunday morning, trekking north. She moved away from the railroad when she saw Confederate horsemen strung along the horizon to the west. Nearing Bristoe Station, she heard small-arms fire and turned east awhile. As she walked through woods and fields, she frequently saw large masses of infantry on the march, though too far away for her to identify them.

By midweek she was near Manassas Junction. Black smoke rose from the Union supply depot there. On the road to Washington she joined a great river of refugees, white families in wagons, blacks on foot, all hurrying away from the destruction. A burly black man wearing bib overalls named the culprit. "Stonewall Jackson. He's burnin' ever'thing he can't carry." Hanna saw blood on the black man's bare feet.

She wasn't much better off. The broad soles of her mudscows had worn through. Some greedy contractor in Maine or Massachusetts was enjoying cognac and cigars from the sale of the shoddy goods.

Sentries guarding the Long Bridge made no effort to stop the refugees. If they had, they might have been trampled or torn apart. The city streets swarmed with frightened people. Hanna heard one well-dressed matron screaming at her children, "Lee's coming with a hundred fifty thousand men!" Off in Virginia, a growl of cannon fire suggested it might not be an idle warning.

Footsore and filthy, she limped into the little cottage near the Navy Yard on Friday morning. She raided the larder for some sausages and a loaf of stale bread. She scraped mold off the crust before she fried slices of bread with the sausage.

She pumped water from the backyard well, heated it, and poured it into the zinc tub. She sank into the tub naked and drowsed in its soothing warmth. The gray-green eyes of the reb officer, Dasher, shimmered inside her eyelids. As she reached down to scrub herself, she wondered why the memory of him was so affecting.

She slept most of the afternoon and early evening. The major came home at half past ten, disheveled and ink-stained. He greeted her without affection or great surprise, saying, "I thought you might be killed."

"No, Papa, I'm fine."

"You don't look fine. You look sickly. Where did you go?"

"Virginia. As far as a place called Catlett's Station."

"My God. That's where they raided Pope's camp."

"I must have been there beforehand. I know nothing about it." She wouldn't alarm him with the tale of her capture.

The major flung off his coat and stamped to the stove; she'd cooked a pot of lamb stew. Changes in her father were apparent. Little of his clerkship salary came home; he spent most of it dining with his superiors at the better hotels. As a consequence his middle had puffed up, losing its military trimness. His reddened eyes spoke of hours of close reading. A month ago he'd visited an optician for his first pair of spectacles. It sent him into a rage for days.

He ladled stew into a cracked bowl. "What you did was stupid, Hanna. How am I going to stop you from doing stupid things?"

She sat at the deal table, folded hands resting on the scarred wood. "Don't worry, I had quite enough. I did see some fighting. From a distance," she added quickly.

He studied her silently for a moment. In a surprisingly mild voice he said, "Took some nerve." It was the nearest thing to a compliment she'd heard for many years. She smiled.

"I'm glad to be here with you, Papa."

"Well, you may not be so glad tomorrow or the next day." He sat and began to tug off his polished knee boots. "There's more fighting at Bull Run. A big engagement. Pope trying to catch Jackson—smash him head-on, with McDowell attacking from the Gainesville flank. Nobody knows how it will come out. The President's camping in the telegraph room. This morning Stanton issued orders for all of us to collect papers and pack them up."

"Why?"

"In case rebs come over the bridges." The August night was warm, yet Hanna felt a faint chill.

"If that's not bad enough"—he sucked stew out of his spoon, licked his lips but left a gob on his chin—"guess what else Stanton did. He loves the colored, that man. He's ordered the Department of the South—it's headquartered on some pissy little island off South Carolina—he's ordered them to recruit five thousand niggers and train them for guard and patrol duty. What's coming next? A corps of apes? Wouldn't happen in the old country."

Next day, Saturday, was sultry and oppressive. Hanna went to the Canterbury to ask about her job. She'd been replaced. Oddly, it didn't seem to matter, not with the whole city trembling in fear of invasion. In the streets she heard more than one drunken soldier goddamming John Pope and the entire high command.

In the afternoon she stood in a large crowd as bulletins were hung up outside the Treasury. GREAT UNION VICTORY AT BULL RUN! The cheers and applause stopped when the crowd saw the next long paper. TEN THOUSAND FEARED DEAD, WOUNDED. Subheads announced a call for surgeons and male nurses to gather at the Treasury at five o'clock.

A mob of sightseers—congressmen, families with children—streamed toward the Long Bridge as the day waned. Hanna stood awhile at the Washington end of the bridge, watching new refugees making their way against the exodus. She was struck by how easy it would be for traitors to enter or leave Washington this night.

On her long walk home, she saw a squad of cavalrymen surround a public hack. The corporal in charge ordered the driver down at pistol point and turned the two passengers into the street with six pieces of luggage.

"But we're just arrived from Dayton," the gentleman protested as his wife sniffled. "I have business with the quartermaster corps."

"This rig's needed for wounded. Ride shank's mare. Brewster!" A private jumped on the box of the hack and drove off.

Hanna encountered similar scenes farther on: horses herded from a livery barn while the owner vainly objected; a gold-trimmed barouche commandeered at a fine residence by infantrymen. Every home and business was being searched for a wagon, a sulky, a dogcart, anything with wheels.

Major Siegel didn't turn up until half past one in the morning. He was pop-eyed with fatigue.

"It's terrible, Hanna. We didn't whip them, the Army's in retreat. Sigel's corps broke, McDowell's too. Heintzelman and Porter are smashed. That yellow dog McClellan held his troops back so Pope couldn't win. Tonight the secretary signed a petition to the President. He and Chase worked it up. They want McClellan dismissed. Stanton said Chase wants him shot."

"My God, Papa. Things are falling apart."

"The bottom's out of the tub, all right. Go to bed. By Monday we may have to pack and run."

It certainly seemed so on Sunday, with soldiers pouring across the Potomac along with terrified Virginians, white and black. All testified to the defeat. The beaten Army was taking up positions in the city fortifications. The major came home that night with more bad news.

"Two days, we had twelve, fourteen thousand casualties. Pope's finished. But Lincoln wants McClellan to take the Army again, can you believe it? He wants to put a failure in charge! He thinks the troops still have confidence in McClellan. The secretary ranted for an hour when he heard. It would be comical if it wasn't so disgusting. Pack a bag."

"Tonight?"

"Yes. By tomorrow we may evacuate the department. If it goes, we go." Undoing his cravat, he took closer notice of her. Hanna continued to sit in the parlor rocker, her body in repose, her smile pensive.

"What's the matter with you?"

"What do you mean, Papa?"

"Ever since you came back from that lunatic trip, you been

acting peculiar. I don't know how to say it exactly—not yourself? Dreamy? Did you tell me everything? Did some roughneck soldier get hold of you and—and . . . ?"

"No, Papa. Nothing like that. I'm happy to be home with you, that's all. I was terribly scared most of the time in Virginia. I realized I'd made a mistake."

His face said he doubted the explanation. He took the parlor candle, leaving Hanna to sit in the steamy dark and rock, head back, eyes shut. She hadn't told the major anything close to the truth. What had happened to her was the encounter with the Confederate major. There was something gallant but sad about him. As though he were with her in the room, she smelled his wet wool uniform, the rain on his skin, his sweat, and whiskey.

She imagined his gray-green eyes. She saw his face come down to hers. She felt and tasted his kiss. *That* was what had happened.

* * *

Monday, September 1, the city again listened to the crash of artillery in Virginia. Hacks and dogcarts and omnibuses and hay wagons and rockaways rumbled in across the Long Bridge with their freight of sobbing and screaming wounded. Drunken deserters brawled in the middle of the Avenue with no one to stop them. Late in the day a torrential rainstorm broke the heat and drove people indoors. By midweek, when it became apparent that the Army had survived, the city was again defended, McClellan again in charge, the crisis passed. But not the air of defeat and despair that infected everyone, soldier and civilian, except those who saw second Bull Run as a triumph for their side.

Hanna thought continually of her gallant officer. She prayed he was alive and safe. She longed to see him again.

40

October 1862

Lon started down Franklin Street at Capitol Square, where a mammoth George Washington, now "the Father of the Confederacy," heroically bestrode his bronze horse. He walked with his head up, confidently, trying not to draw attention to himself. Under his arm he carried a half-pound tin of English tea for which he'd paid five dollars of Lieutenant Turner's money. The prison commandant had a taste for terrapin, fresh oysters, and other delicacies not offered by the Confederate commissary department. A grocer sold the tea out the back door, for an inflated price, telling his regular customers that tea from London was no longer available due to the blockade.

The October air was bracing, the hilly street busy with pedestrians and conveyances of all sorts. Lon found the butcher shop of Siegfried Retz five blocks east of the square. From the shop's doorway he scanned the sunlit sidewalks. He saw no one suspicious. He pulled the frayed cuff of his cadet gray shirt to the base of his left thumb, covering the single two-inch manacle on his left wrist.

"Gentleman Lon" no longer existed. Lon's beard had grown to the second button below his collar. His skin fit his bones like a drumhead; all the fat had been starved off him in the weeks since Colonel Mars had delivered him to his jailers. The charming old city of hills and waterways had plenty of jails for war prisoners, along with plenty of crippled veterans begging in Capitol Square, plenty of speculators, cardsharps, and pickpockets at the hotels, plenty of lonely soldiers' wives glancing at strangers on the street. Above all, Richmond had plenty of hatred for any of "Lincoln's hirelings."

The shop smelled of meat and sawdust. A handsome colored boy in a clean white shirt and trousers sat on a box by the open display case, waving a whisk over a few sad cuts of gray meat afloat in puddles of melted ice. Startled by Lon's appearance, the butcher dropped his cleaver on the block. He was perhaps thirty, wiry, with mournful brown eyes and a russet mustache with waxed points.

"Siegfried Retz?"

"Yah, sure, that's me." He spoke English with a heavy accent.

"Do you have cutlets for sale?"

Retz squinted at his visitor. "Pork cutlets or veal cutlets?"

"The lady of the house hates pork."

"Veal's all we got anyway." With the exchange of recognition phrases out of the way, Retz tapped the boy. "Hiram, take a stroll. Buy an apple if you can find one." He gave the boy a coin. The boy left, skipping. "I wondered when somebody would show up."

"I've been here since August. Major Allen sent two of us, posing as deserters."

"I hope you're luckier than the one they hanged, Webster."

"We didn't start out with very good luck. A reb caught us and killed my partner. He took me to what he called the depot prison."

"Libby. It's an old chandler's warehouse."

"It's a hellhole."

"There's worse. What's your name?"

"Lon Price."

"Sig Retz. That's a little joke in English, huh?" He pantomimed a few puffs. He had an abrupt, breathless way of speaking. Lon liked him.

"Come on in back. I got no customers, as you can see. When I stepped off the boat in Boston five years ago, I thought I'd make my fortune in America. I picked the wrong town."

Retz lifted a curtain so Lon could pass. The back room, lit by gas, contained a single bed, a chair and cushion, a stove, a small desk piled with ledgers, a lacquered ice cabinet, a tall stack of newspapers. For all its poverty, the room was immaculate.

Greedy for news, Lon scanned an *Enquirer* from the top of the stack. The largest article inveighed against Lincoln's proclamation of emancipation of slaves in "all states in rebellion," to take effect January 1. He'd heard rumors of such a plan for months. Evidently the titanic battle in Maryland in September had given Lincoln the confidence to announce it. McClellan had partially redeemed himself at Antietam by turning back Lee's invasion of the north. The *Enquirer* piece brimmed with purple wrath: phrases like *egalitarian madness* and *mongrelization of the pure blood of our forefathers*.

"What do you think of that, huh?" Retz asked.

"The proclamation? I'm for it."

"Yah, sure, just don't say it too loud around here, they'll hang you from a lamppost." Retz wiped his hands on his stained apron. "You got anything for me?"

Lon took a folded paper from under his shirt. "For Major Allen. I believe he's back in Washington now."

Retz nodded, studying the penciled foolscap sheets. Lon had spent days gathering information, stealing a little extra time from each errand for the prison commandant. His several hundred words spoke of everything from the miserable state of the Confederate economy to the number and size of cannon defending the riverfront. He'd encoded the message using the Vigenère tableau and the keyword *preacher*. The first line read "EIMCGYIGDIX"; deciphered, it said "Price Report."

"How will this get to Washington?"

"I pass it up the line. You don't need to know any more." Retz folded the sheets and hid them in a slit in the chair cushion. He tapped Lon's manacle. "The warden give you the prison jewelry?"

"Right, Lieutenant Turner. Mean bastard."

"Not half so mean as the one they shoved out last fall. Captain Todd. Half brother of Lincoln's wife. A drunken hound and torture specialist. Papers said the Congress wanted to investigate him. Instead they transferred him. You want some beer?"

"Thanks. I haven't tasted beer in months."

Retz took a tin growler from the ice cabinet, filled a small stein. Lon savored the smell and taste of the brew, tepid though it was. "I like to hear about that bracelet."

"It's a long story."

"I got no more ice. I got no good meat to sell. You see how many customers are storming my door. Time, now—that I got plenty of."

*   *   *

Colonel Mars had delivered Lon to the authorities on a sweltering August afternoon. For his trouble he would receive a bounty of one Confederate dollar. His greater reward came from parading Lon along Main Street. Lon's uniform attracted a crowd of urchins, invalid soldiers, and well-dressed civilians. A one-legged veteran on a crutch threw stones. One gashed Lon's forehead.

The language of the crowd was amazingly foul. "Blue-belly prick!" "Lincoln whoreson!" The women were as obscene as the men. Mars let them have their way until they wearied of it and Lon's face was dripping with their spit. Ever since Sledge's murder, rage had built up in him, with no outlet. The gauntlet of hate turned the screw tighter.

Their destination was Richmond's receiving prison, situated in a district of warehouses, shanties, stables, and vacant lots. Three floors overlooked Cary Street, one block from Main. Nineteenth Street sloped downward from Cary to Canal Street; the Canal side had an additional floor. It was a fine old brick building, with LIBBY PRISON painted large on the outside.

They passed a street corner sentry box and entered through a heavily barred door. Armed guards patrolled the hall. Lon looked into a communal kitchen with several stoves. A frail bald man came out of the commandant's office a few steps farther on. "Thank you for your time, sir. If you suspect any prisoner of being more than he seems, turn him over to us."

The man put on a brown felt bowler. His left leg was crippled, making him tilt as he walked. A thick-soled shoe scraped the floor. The man stared at Lon as he passed by.

The commandant, Lieutenant Turner, was a severe young soldier of twenty or twenty-one. Clean-shaven, he wore his hair short. "Name and rank?" he said in a rumbling bass voice.

"Private Albion Rogers." Lon gave the numbers of his regiment, division, and corps. Turner's clerk wrote them in a large book.

"We'll process you as soon as we can. Yankee deserters are sent to Palmer's Factory at Castle Thunder. The prisoners named the place. Something about the wrath of the gods falling on every man there. They're right; compared to Castle Thunder, this is a ladies' academy. We have one paramount rule at Libby. Stay three feet from windows at all times or you'll be shot. Our capacity is four hundred prisoners. We are warehousing three times that. If you die, you do us a favor. Orderly!"

A stripling in uniform sauntered in. "Hand this man over to the sergeant of the second floor." Turner said to Lon, "He isn't really a sergeant. We call him that because we put him in charge."

"Second floor, yes, sir." The orderly whacked Lon's elbow with his truncheon. "Step lively, Mr. Abolitionist."

Lon balked. "Look here, Lieutenant. I had to swallow their damn oath when I enlisted, but I deserted because I sure God don't want to fight so niggers can strut around pretending they're good as white men. When do I get a chance to serve the right side?"

"In the future. Perhaps. Take him out."

On the way to the stairs the orderly jabbed Lon with his truncheon. Then again. And a third time. Lon wheeled around, red-faced.

"Something griping you, blue belly?" The orderly hit Lon's ear with his truncheon. Lon reeled to the stairs, grappling for a hold on the sticky rail. "You piece of Yankee shit. Will you stand up or do I knock your head off right here?"

Lon stood up.

*　　*　　*

According to Mathias Price and his fellow clergymen, Satan's domain lay somewhere below the surface of the earth. Lon found hell a different way that day; he ascended to it.

The staircase wall was a tapestry of squashed insects, scribbled oaths, obscene drawings of sex organs. Starting upstairs, the smell of human excrement was noticeable. At the first landing it was strong. Going farther up, it was sickening.

A crowd of prisoners waited on the second floor, whistling and shouting, "Fresh fish, fresh fish!" The prisoners were cadavers; filthy, shrunken shells of men. They poked and squeezed Lon. One whispered, "Got any money? You can have me for a dime."

"Shut your fucking traps, ladies," said someone at the rear. The inmates fell back like the Red Sea, revealing a stout soldier. On his blue blouse he wore a medal cut out of tin. A red bandanna tied around his forehead gave him a piratical air. His right eye had a disconcerting tendency to wander toward his ear. Lon was nearly sick from the smell of an inner room where prisoners had relieved themselves on the floor. He saw a soldier lying with his head in some of it. The stout man pointed this out to the orderly.

"Sonny died last night. Most likely the nostalgia got him. Been staring at the ceiling and crying for near a week."

"Form a detail and move him downstairs," the orderly said. He poked Lon. "This here's your floor sergeant, Private Griff."

The orderly went down the stairs. Lon and Griff stared at one another. The other prisoners looked on. Griff's eye wandered again. He extended his hand, twitching his fingers.

"Shoes. Take 'em off and hand 'em over. Think of it as paying your second-floor membership dues."

Lon had an urge to attack the bastard. He didn't want to be put in irons his first day, so he sat on the steps and pulled off his broken shoes. Mars had warned him that most personal property was confiscated, either stolen by guards or by inmates. Once he knew the ropes, Mars said, he could steal what he needed from others.

"Swell. Now turn out your pockets."

"I don't have anything but this." Lon showed his ivory-handled jackknife, which Mars had allowed him to keep, calling it "the prisoner's essential."

Griff said, "Fine, I'll take it."

"The man who captured me said prisoners always keep their knives."

"I don't give a rat's tit what he told you, mister. I can trade a nice blade like that."

Lon shook his head. "Sorry, no."

Griff sighed as if dealing with a witless child. "Now listen, fish." He stepped in close. He raised his knee up suddenly, ramming Lon's privates. Lon doubled over.

Griff yanked him up by the hair. "I said let me have—" Lon closed his fist around the jackknife and swung a roundhouse right at Griff's head.

Griff windmilled into the wall. The other prisoners scrambled away. One yelled, "Hot damn, Paddy, here's a donnybrook."

Griff lumbered at Lon like a maddened bear. Lon was half blind with sweat and rage. He remembered leaping in with both fists up, but he remembered nothing else until he came out of a fog, hearing applause and whistling. Guards hauled him up by his shoulders. Griff lay on the landing, his crotch stained, his nose flattened, blood bubbling on his lips. His right leg was bent beneath his left. Lon looked wonderingly at his own bleeding knuckles.

A guard held him against the wall at pistol point. Another tried to straighten Griff's bent leg. Griff screamed. Lieutenant Turner ran up the stairs to investigate the commotion. The astonished reb kneeling over Griff said, "I think his leg's broke, sir. I think this one did it with his bare hands."

Lon's eyes glared from the thicket of his hairy face. "Son of a bitch tried to take my jackknife."

* * *

To Retz he said, "I thought I was a goner. The commandant threw me in a detention cell in the basement, dark as a cave. No food or water for three days, not even a bucket to pee in. Then they sent me back to the second floor and I found Turner had elected me sergeant of the floor in absentia. I behaved myself. I organized the details that bring food from the kitchen twice a day, I stopped fights, I wrote letters for some who couldn't. Presently Turner called me in and said he needed another orderly, someone who wasn't a fool or a crazy bully. If I was trustworthy, if I wanted to serve the Confederacy the way I said, I'd be released for short errands, then longer ones. Turner set one condition."

Lon showed his left wrist. The iron manacle gleamed in the gaslight.

"Anyone who sees this knows I'm a fish. Trusted a little more than some, but a fish. I had to take a loyalty oath. I didn't like it, but my boss sent me to do a job, so I went along. They fitted me out in gray so I wouldn't get knocked in the head every time the lieutenant sent me somewhere. A couple of weeks ago I felt it was safe to start gathering information. That's the story."

"Yah, sure, quite a tale," Retz said, his admiration evident. "You spies are smart fellas."

"Only by accident. There's nothing smart about this war, Sig. It's a bunch of wild animals tearing at each other. My dead partner taught me that."

"You going to keep bringing me messages?"

"As often as I can."

"You want more beer before you go?"

"No, thanks, but I would like to sit a few minutes with those newspapers. Prisoners aren't allowed any, except for a little handwritten sheet they publish themselves."

Sig Retz gestured. "Be comfortable, stay as long as you like. I got to see what's become of Hiram. I might get a customer. Pigs might fall out of the sky too."

Lon dropped into Retz's cushioned chair. It amused him to sit on a coded report that could get him executed.

On page two of a *Richmond Dispatch*, next to a jeremiad about food shortages and outrageous prices, he spied an item that hit him harder than any fist. At a reception hosted by Britain's consular representative, J. Cridland, Esq., the guests included another citizen of that country, businessman Donal McKee, Esq., of New York City. *Mr. McKee, who has substantial commercial interests in the Confederacy, is temporarily in residence in rented quarters on Church Hill, together with his wife.*

41

November 1862

At the foot of the stairs Margaret said, "Has Mr. McKee come down yet, Eudora?"

"Came down, ate, and left." Eudora whisked her feather duster over an ornate Chinese jar decorating the foyer. She was a full-bosomed black woman in her early thirties. Her beige complexion suggested a white forebear or two. Eudora cooked and cleaned; her brother, Morris Thompson, did the other chores. Both were slaves. They belonged to the fine ten-room house on Twenty-fourth Street, Church Hill. The house belonged to the estate of a bachelor attorney who had died the previous December. Donal had leased the house for six months. It was a dusty old place, unnecessarily large, though it had a lovely garden planted with cherry and apple trees, and trellises heavy with sweet Carolina jasmine.

"Did my husband say where he was going?"

"Exchange Hotel, for a meeting." More likely another marathon card game. Sometimes they ran on all night. When the sun rose, Donal and his new friends would go home, bathe, and freshen their linen before resuming play.

Margaret found it hard to believe that four months ago, a giant Union army had stood six miles from Richmond; so close, people said, the watch fires of the enemy were visible from the city's hills. The Yankees were turned back, the war moved north again, and an elite class of Southern gentlemen carried on with business and pleasure as though other men were not fighting and dying for them. If you chanced to drive too near Chimborazo or Winder hospitals, the screams and lamentations of the injured reminded you of the fact.

"Is there any real coffee?"

"No'm, only the mix with parched corn. I'll bring it to the dining room. You brother be here again?"

"We have breakfast every Wednesday, Eudora, you know that." Finding Cicero safe and well in the Confederate capital was one of the few good things about this enforced stay. "He should arrive by nine. Please be ready to serve him."

"All right, ma'am." Eudora's lovely brown eyes reflected the dislike the two women felt for each other. From the first night, all of Eudora's smiles and pleasantries had been lavished on Donal. She was plainly taken with him, and jealous of Margaret or anyone else with a claim on him.

Which perhaps explained why, in late September, Eudora had whispered to Margaret about a trip she'd made downtown in search of food. Leaving a grocery that had nothing to sell, she saw Margaret's husband drive by in an open carriage with an attractive white woman Eudora knew to be a widow.

Jealousy distorted Eudora's pretty face as she passed the tidbit to Margaret, who promptly reprimanded her. Ever since, Eudora had been not merely her rival but her enemy.

Margaret hoisted the skirt of her beautiful morning dress of amber silk and walked to the dining room. The dress was part of the Paris wardrobe Donal had bought her before they came South.

Although the coffee was partly substitute, it took away some of the lingering torpor of sleep. Outside the window, crimson maple leaves drifted down. A woman passed with a market basket on her arm. Miss Van Lew was a well-off spinster of the neighborhood, an odd little creature with ringlets and an unlovely big nose. Eudora cheekily dismissed Miss Van Lew by saying, "Folks call her Crazy Bet."

The whole city was a bit crazy in Margaret's opinion. Its masses of wounded and crippled depressed her, as did its empty shelves and indifferent storekeepers and resentful housewives. With an air of desperate gaiety, young ladies continued to attend hops at the better hotels, or visited Camp Lee, the old fairgrounds, toasting marshmallows at campfires and singing "The Bonnie Blue Flag" or "Lorena" in the purple dusk. Jefferson Davis's wife, Varina, a gracious, olive-skinned woman whom Margaret liked, openly said she found Richmond a standoffish place, lacking the friendliness of the Mississippi frontier where she'd grown up. Margaret hoped it wouldn't be too long before they embarked from Wilmington or Charleston on a risky run through the blockade squadron.

Still, she preferred a beleaguered Confederate city to New York, in Yankee territory. Wherever they were, Donal would find pliant women; she was resigned to it.

Happily for Margaret, Rose Greenhow and her daughter were in residence at the Ballard House. Rose was writing a memoir of her imprisonment. She had a certain weary gauntness now, was less ebullient than Margaret remembered. Her hair showed a great deal of gray. Little Rose was growing and developing and taking an interest in boys.

Rose said Jefferson Davis had personally paid her $2,500 for services in Washington, claiming that but for her, the first battle of Manassas would not have been a victory. Mary Chesnut, the sharp-tongued wife of a Confederate congressman, spread a story that Seward or Stanton had sent Rose to Richmond to spy. Margaret heard it from Varina Davis, who laughed. "Of course Mary thinks ill of nearly everyone. She keeps a diary, you know. I pray I'm not in it."

Certainly Varina's husband would be. There was a large anti-Davis faction in town, led by the editorialists of the *Examiner*. They said that because of his West Point training and Mexican War service, Davis believed he could dictate to his military commanders. Varina said the torrent of criticism caused Mr. Davis severe dyspepsia.

Twice a week Margaret met with Rose and a circle of ladies to knit socks and gloves for soldiers. On other days, she walked, trying to wear away her unhappiness by tiring herself. On the streets she saw painted women openly soliciting trade. She saw recruiting parades, usually with a Negro or two marching in the impromptu band. She found it ironic that a black drummer or fife player helped to find men to preserve the system that enslaved him. As often as not, the band played "La Marseillaise" instead of "Dixie."

Several times she saw a procession of poor Negroes from the country, led or driven by a white man, on the way to one of the so-called slave jails. The slave trade was still brisk, with frequent auctions. Once, taking a wrong turn into a narrow alley near the canal, she was transfixed by the sight of a black youth naked on an auction block. As white gentlemen surrounded her and urged her to leave, her gaze locked with the tormented eyes of the human merchandise. He seemed to cry out silently for succor, or at least recognition that what was happening was sinful. She slept badly for nights afterward. In Baltimore she'd seen nothing so harrowing, though perhaps she'd consciously avoided such sights.

Cicero arrived on the dot. He roomed at the Spotswood Hotel, deeming it easier than looking after a house. She'd found him by placing a small advertisement in the *Enquirer*, among the many ads offering a high price for an army substitute. Cicero worked for the military Signal Service, in a civilian capacity. That's all he would say, though he assured her that he was doing important work.

"It hurts the Yankees, and I quite like it," he remarked once. "Every few days I take another pound of Yankee flesh for Father. I've taken plenty for you too, Margaret." His smile was warm and benign, disturbingly so.

"Sister dear, good morning," he said as he limped into the dining room. He bent to kiss her forehead. His eyes sparkled. His brown suit of checked wool, his bottle green waistcoat, and the matching scarf knotted around his collar testified to a salary that kept him well above the poverty level.

"You seem quite cheerful," she said.

"We've caught a Union journalist posing as a patent-medicine salesman. He was brazenly passing out business cards at the Spotswood bar. I expect he's a spy. We'll find out. We have some methods I wouldn't dare mention on such a beautiful day. Hello, Eudora."

"Day, sir," Eudora said as she placed a small portion of scrambled country eggs in front of him, together with two slabs of fatty bacon whose price Margaret didn't want to guess. Eudora then served a basket of coarse bread baked in the kitchen. She had a smile for Cicero, but none for Margaret. He tucked his napkin into his shirt and briskly attacked the food.

"I thought Donal might be joining us."

"He's gone off to another of his infernal card games. He says it's a way to meet important businessmen. I hope that's all he's doing. I really have no way of knowing."

"Do I hear the faintest hint of wifely jealousy? You're barely a new bride, Margaret."

"Perhaps I have cause for suspicion. You know Donal's reputation."

"You alluded to it a few times before I left Baltimore, that's all. You aren't suggesting he's seeing another woman?"

"I know he went buggy-riding with one. Some cotton planter's maiden aunt, no doubt."

Cicero said, "Ow," and ducked, as though avoiding a bullet. He covered her hand with his. "I hope you're imagining these things. Donal's a splendid catch. He helped you out of a hellish situation."

"Yes, he is, and he did," she agreed. "May we talk of something else?"

She wouldn't admit to Cicero that her relationship with Donal had deteriorated subtly but quickly since the honeymoon in Washington. Donal had grown less attentive as the weeks went by, although he remained a tender and considerate lover. When he chose to visit her room at night, he could arouse her to a state beyond anything she'd ever imagined. Shamefully, when they made love, she sometimes imagined the Yankee detective in her arms.

She and her brother gossiped and speculated about the new Union commander, Burnside, who had replaced McClellan. Cicero left shortly before ten, dragging his thick-soled shoe down the mansion's marble steps with excruciating slowness. At the window Margaret watched his progress along the brick sidewalk. What did he do that gave him such pleasure? If he was taking revenge for their father's murder, why did it trouble her?

In the afternoon she again took tea with Varina Davis and several cabinet wives in the pillared mansion on Clay Street that everyone called the Confederate White House. The President looked in at one point, greeting the ladies with Southern courtesy, bowing to kiss each hand and tickling Margaret's with his chin whiskers. Like the cushions and draperies and everything else in the mansion, he smelled of cigars. She thought he looked tired and worried.

She chose to walk home. The day had grown bleak. Factory smoke stained the slate-colored sky. Leaves scurried at her feet. Eudora greeted her the moment she stepped in the house.

"Man brung this a while ago. Axe me to give it to you right away." She put a folded sheet of wallpaper into Margaret's gloved hand. A dab of maroon wax sealed the note.

"Who was he? What did he look like?"

"Like somebody what ought to come to the back door, which he done. Not so old, but weary-looking. Beard down to here"—she touched her bosom—"thick enough for a bird's nest. Had on old gray things, like soldier castoffs. Oh, and he was white."

"Thank you, Eudora. You may go." Eudora had no choice but to leave with the mysterious note unread.

Margaret carried the note into the parlor. She sat on a horsehair sofa and drew off her gloves. Distant cannon fire rattled windowpanes. Only the local artillery practicing, she hoped.

She broke the wax seal. The inside of the wallpaper was unprinted. The message was inscribed crudely by a blunt pencil.

will you meet me friday 4pm shockoe hill
burying ground?
i hope this request does not carry too high
a Price.

Why only one word capitalized? Who . . . ?
"Oh, God." It was him; she had no doubt of it.

42

November 1862

Stone angels and seraphs and crosses surrounded him in the Shockoe Hill burying ground. Libby inmates said Tim Webster lay up here in an unmarked grave. When Lon arrived at half past three, he walked the pauper's section for ten minutes, a necessary gesture of respect to a brave operative.

Gravediggers had interred someone earlier in the day; he passed the new grave on his way to the southwest side of the cemetery. There he laid the bundle wrapped in butcher paper on the ledge of a monument. Before collecting the commandant's laundry he'd delivered a pouch of reports to the provost marshal's office. Under citywide martial law enforced by General Winder, he had to be off the streets by dark, even with a proper pass.

His vantage point allowed him to watch traffic coming up both Second and Third streets. A mist had settled; the James and the canal hid in a low cloud of it. Lamps burned like hundreds of cat's eyes. His gray sack coat with all but one button missing was none too warm.

Church bells rang four. The deep notes reverberated in the mist. He rubbed the cold metal of the manacle with his right thumb, back and forth, back and forth. What if she didn't come? Didn't understand the message he handed to the black servant?

A stray cat wandered among the tombstones, meowing at him. He told it to scat. When he glanced down the hill again, he saw a buggy climbing Second Street. The driver was a woman, alone. Although a gray veil on her black hat blurred her features, he knew it was Margaret.

He stepped from behind a monument crowned by a marble Christ with outstretched hands. He waved. The buggy careened around the corner. How fine she looked in her black riding habit and yellow gloves!

He ran to tie the horse to one of the iron posts along the curb. He helped her down, excited by the rich heaviness of her figure, the almost shy smile he saw when she raised her veil. Her wide mouth was a deep cherry red.

"I knew you sent the note, but when I saw you, I thought I'd made an awful mistake. I thought you were someone else." She touched his beard.

"Makes me look like a hundred other soldiers. That's why I grew it."

She saw the manacle. "What's this? Are you a prisoner?"

"Libby. I'll explain. Let's move away from the road."

She slipped her arm through his. The touch of her breast aroused him. He led her deeper into the cemetery. Mausoleums designed as small Greek temples screened them from the streets.

"Do you still hate me because of who I work for, Margaret?"

"If I did, would I be doing this? It's risky for a woman to be seen here alone."

"Then why did you come?"

"Don't you know? I couldn't help myself. I had to see you again."

He smiled. "Are you happy?"

"Don't ask that question."

Gently he stroked her cheek with his thumb; felt dampness. "I have to know. You broke my heart when you said you were going to marry McKee."

"I was desperate. I was at the bottom of the well. Baker would have kept me in the Old Capitol forever. Donal was able to get me out of jail and out of Washington. There was no other way."

"But are you happy?"

"Oh, Lon. Who is allowed to be happy in these times? I made an arrangement. Donal's fond of me. He likes the way I look and dress. I'm useful. He is, shall we say, friendly with a great many women. But he couldn't introduce most of them as a hostess in his home. An arrangement." She rested her hand on the front of his old coat. "Don't press the matter. I wish you'd hold me."

He wrapped her in his arms, pulling her tight to his chest and kissing her throat above the black collar of her riding habit. Behind them, unseen in the mist, gravediggers hailed one another; the voices were moving away, no threat.

He kissed her mouth. The kiss was long, deep, as painful as it was blissful.

"How did you know I was in Richmond?" she said. He told her of seeing the news item. "I want to hear all about you. How you got here. Is it secret work for the Yankees?"

"It was." He drew her to a monument with a wide base where they could sit, hidden from the road. He rested his manacled hand on her knee as he told the story of the capture, Sledge's death, besting Griff, then the slow process of earning the trust of Lieutenant Turner.

"Is there a possibility you'll be exchanged?"

"I suppose. I've reported my whereabouts to Washington."

"How?"

"I have a contact in town. I shouldn't say any more. How long will you be in Richmond?"

"I don't know."

"Will you go back to New York?"

"I think so. I loathe the idea. I don't suppose it matters. Wherever we are, Donal can always find willing ladies."

"You've been married what—four months? Are you saying he's already deceiving you?"

"I knew Donal's nature when I accepted his proposal. I didn't want to rot for years in that damned prison."

"Well, it's a hell of a situation." They were silent a moment. "Margaret." She turned to him. "I love you."

"Oh, please don't say—"

"I love you."

Her dark eyes glistened with tears. "And I love you."

She pressed her gloved hands to his damp cheeks, caressing him with her mouth and her tongue and her trembling body. When she pulled back, she dabbed her eyes, then lowered her veil.

"You mustn't think of me anymore. You'll forget me if you just try."

"Forget you? You're part of my existence, part of myself. You've been in every prospect I've ever seen since we met. To the last hour of my life, you remain part of my character."

Her eyes grew round as she realized what he was paraphrasing. "That's Pip, isn't it? When Estella wants him to forget her."

"I memorized it. Occasionally we're allowed books in prison. Good-hearted local people bring them. Prisoner's aid, it's called. I reread *Great Expectations* last month. What Pip feels for Estella when she marries Drummle is the way I feel about you. Dickens said it perfectly. We can go apart, but you'll never leave me. Never."

She gripped his hands with such ferocity, his fingers hurt. They heard horses.

He sprang up. She pressed against his shoulder, straining to see the black carriage coming up Third Street carrying two men. A third, a civilian, followed on horseback. The carriage's standing top hid the driver and the passenger in shadow. Mist wrapped the brass side lamps in spectral halos. The carriage looked evil, like some devil's equipage driving up from hell.

Margaret whispered, "That's Donal's phaeton." She saw Lon's expression. "Oh, God, you don't think that I . . . ?"

"No, no," he said, guilty and ashamed; he'd thought exactly that. "Did anyone else see the note?"

"Only our house girl, Eudora. The sealing wax was intact when she gave it to me."

"Wax can be melted and sealed up again, with no trace of a break."

"Then she must have read it. The girl dislikes me. She told Donal for spite."

The phaeton wheeled around the corner, rocking to a halt behind the buggy. The horseman, a burly man in a frock coat and broad-brimmed planter's hat, dismounted to confer with the other two men. He raised his arm to point. Lon and Margaret had been spotted.

Margaret pushed him. "Run."

"What will you—?"

"I'll work my way out of it, don't worry. Sweetheart—*run!*"

He spun and dashed into the misty graveyard. He should have known he stood little chance on foot, but he wanted to draw the men away from her. He heard a horse galloping. The booted and spurred rider pursued him through the tombstones as though chasing quarry in a foxhunt.

He ran faster, arms pumping, breath hissing through his teeth. The rider caught him easily, pulling a revolver from a holster tied to his leg. "Stop or I'll put a bullet in your back."

Lon skidded into an oak tree, scraping his nose on the bark.

"Turn. Raise your hands." The man's face was florid; a gold front tooth gleamed. "Now walk ahead of me, to Mr. McKee and Mr. Cridge."

"Who are you?"

"Parsons is the name. My partner Humboldt Cridge and I are agents of General John Winder, Provost Marshal of Richmond."

The man who ran the prisons—and dealt with spies.

*   *   *

Lon followed the trail of torn sod left by the horse. Parsons walked his mount, resting his revolver on his thigh. Lon passed Margaret where he'd left her. Thank God he couldn't see her terror or confusion behind the veil; it would have destroyed him.

Donal McKee waited with his phaeton, his thumbs in the pockets of his embroidered waistcoat. His passenger was examining the laundry bundle. He was a bland sort, about forty, with a round, ruddy face appropriate to a schoolteacher, a choirmaster, a kindly relative in a Victorian novel. When he lifted his hand to adjust his derby, he revealed a hideous scar that ran from the base of his thumb all the way to his cuff.

McKee called out to his wife. "Please wait there until we're finished." He was so controlled, it was impossible to gauge the depth of his anger. The man in the derby looked Lon up and down.

"Hummy Cridge, sir. Provost marshal's office." His voice was soft, even soothing. Behind little round spectacles, his tawny eyes looked older, colder, than the rest of him. "Do you have a pass to roam about the city?"

Lon produced it. Cridge studied it. "The signature is General Winder's. The pass is issued to Albion Rogers. You are Rogers?"

"Yes, Private Albion Rogers, Heintzelman's Third Corps, First Div—" Cridge's arm lashed forward like a striking snake. His fist snapped Lon's head to one side.

"Now, sir, that's not true at all, is it?"

McKee said, "I told you, his name's Price. My wife said that much after we met him in Washington. He signed the name Price to the note."

"Yes, sir, I saw that," Cridge agreed. "You're positive it's the same person?"

"No doubt of it. He was on police duty at Lincoln's inauguration. At least I think so. He made regular circuits in the crowd. Kept track of people. I saw him confer with another man who did the same thing. I'm sure he's here under false colors."

Cridge looked sad. " 'They that plow iniquity and sow wickedness reap the same.' Job, fifth chapter."

Lon said, "It's the fourth chapter. Eighth verse."

"Well, what have we here, a biblical scholar?" Cridge said cheerfully. He struck Lon again, rocking him on his heels. "A man who knows his Bible will hang as easily and speedily as the heathen. 'Bloody and deceitful men shall not live out half their days.' Do you know which psalm that's from?"

"Up your ass, you reb bastard."

Cridge's face turned the color of plums. He signaled Parsons, who stepped forward, reversed his revolver, and hammered the butt on Lon's skull. Lon dropped to his knees. Margaret cried out. McKee smiled.

Cridge pinched Lon's chin in his fingers. "I want to know why you're wearing Confederate gray and a prison manacle. I want to know whose laundry that is. I want to know if there's a Union spy ring in Richmond. My superiors and I have all the time we need to find out those things, and we will. Stand up."

43

November 1862

The Confederate White House at Twelfth and Clay was a pillared stucco mansion more gray than white. Lon was held for half an hour in a windowless upstairs room. Parsons guarded him with no overt animosity, saying only, "I wish you'd sit down," when Lon paced. He agonized about Margaret. Would McKee punish her? If he hadn't been rash about writing the note—

A military aide opened the door. "The President is ready to see you."

Lon and Parsons followed him to a modest office overlooking the lamplit city. A ticking shelf clock showed half-past six. In a visitor's chair in front of the President's desk, a handsome and burly officer of sixty or so regarded the prisoner with a hostile eye. From an engraving he'd seen, Lon recognized the provost marshal, Brigadier General John Winder, another West Point man who'd changed sides. On the Peninsula, soldiers had gossiped about Winder's son, an Army captain who'd arrived in Washington after the war began. Pinkerton wanted him to sign a loyalty oath. McClellan chose to send him back to duty in California.

The general's thick white hair swept down to his ears in elegantly combed waves. Even his own officers, Turner included, thought him harsh and inflexible. Whenever his name came up, someone usually recalled that his father had commanded troops that ran from the British in 1814, leaving Washington unprotected, to be sacked and burned.

Jefferson Davis pointed to an empty chair. "Please be seated, sir." His reputation for courtesy was deserved.

"Thank you." Lon eased into the chair. Davis's left eye had a cloudy film on it. His sour breath was apparent across the desk. He covered his mouth and belched softly as he studied a paper. Parsons lounged by tall bookcases. Cridge stood next to him with his derby pressed against his vest in a way that struck Lon as servile. He noticed a third civilian standing in a dark corner, arms folded. It was the bald man from the hallway at Libby.

Davis said, "You insist your name is Rogers, sir?"

"Private Albion Rogers, that's correct, sir." Lon spoke up, trying not to appear frightened.

"A gentleman of excellent reputation has provided a different name. General Winder's detectives have a note which you delivered to the gentleman's house, signed with the same last name. You still deny a dual identity?"

"Yes, sir."

"I admire your courage, though you'll find it misspent. I suspect you're an operative of General McClellan's chief of secret service, Pinkerton."

Harshly Winder said, "That won't do you a penny's worth of good if you're entertaining thoughts of rescue by means of exchange. General McClellan has been relieved."

"Yes, sir, I've heard that."

The bald man spoke from the shadows. "When a failure departs, so do his favorites. Week before last, we intercepted a letter sent across the lines with some exchange protocols and rosters. Your employer, Pinkerton, wrote to Pryce Lewis in Castle Thunder to say he was resigning his duties and returning to what he called his old stand in Chicago. We delivered the letter after reading it. Lewis will confirm its contents."

Davis clasped veined hands on the desk. "It's futile to continue with your deception, Mr. Price. Two of your colleagues are presently confined in Castle Thunder, Mr. Lewis, and Mr. Scully. If you were sent among us by Mr. Pinkerton, those men will identify you. Make it easy on yourself. Give us a list of your contacts in Richmond, agents of the Union government, and we may be inclined toward leniency."

Hummy Cridge coughed and immediately launched a fulsome apology, which Davis waved silent.

Lon said, "I can't do that, sir. I don't know what you mean

by contacts. I deserted from the Union Army because I don't believe in their cause. I came to Richmond to stand with the Confederacy. That's my story."

Davis looked pained. "Your side will lose, you know. Lincoln has no truly capable generals, only incompetents, or egotists such as McClellan. I know, I served with many of them in Mexico. We have the Military Academy's finest on our side, starting with General Lee. Our cause is just. We seek independence from the domination of Northern industrialists. Freedom to pursue our own way of life without interference from race-mixing hypocrites who will never permit freed Negroes to set foot in their parlors unless forced or bribed to do so."

Lon didn't reply. What could he say? Davis was utterly wrong about slavery, though perhaps close to the mark on the issue of Northern hypocrisy. As for the generals, it seemed depressingly true. McClellan had been turned back by inferior numbers when Richmond was within in his grasp. It all seemed muddled, and of no importance compared to Margaret's plight, and his own culpability.

The clock ticked. Cridge started to cough again. Winder bristled. Davis's clear right eye picked up tiny reflections of the gaslight. He spread his hands over the desk. "Gentlemen, I'm afraid this is pointless. Mr. Price, you will regret you refusal to cooperate. Castle Thunder isn't the most comfortable of accommodations. Mr. Miller, please take him away." He reached for a folio of papers, signaling the end of the interview.

Lon's ears rang. *Miller?*

The bald man limped across the carpet, seized Lon's arm, pulled him out of the chair. Five minutes later they were in a closed carriage rattling away from Capitol Square.

*   *   *

In her bedroom on Church Hill, Margaret watched the rain. It rivered off the roof and dispelled the mist. She was barefoot, wearing only her black dressing gown ornamented with flying cranes, in the Japanese style.

The terrible scene at the graveyard had ended when

Winder's detectives took Lon away in the phaeton. Donal drove her home in the buggy. He said not a single word. As they arrived on Church Hill, he handed her a black umbrella. After she alighted, he drove off. Undoubtedly she'd hear from him later. It was an awareness, not fear. Her fear was for Lon out there in the dark with Winder's thugs.

At her dressing table she took a brush to her long dark hair. Usually the routine pleased her; tonight it was mechanical. Her dressing gown fell open; the mirror reflected the high round tops of her breasts.

Footsteps in the hall alerted her to Donal's arrival. He entered without knocking. His English dressing gown, burnt orange silk with a quilted collar and tasseled belt, fit him perfectly; no surprise, given what he paid for clothes. He smelled of talc and some oily preparation glistening in his curly hair.

Donal sat on the end of the bed. She started to speak. He raised his hand.

"Let me be clear with you, Margaret. I don't care about the nature of that Yankee chap's work, or who his employer may be. I do care about whether you've dallied with him."

"If you mean has he taken me to bed, no."

"Not that you wouldn't like it, do you mean?"

"I care for him, Donal."

"More than you care for your husband."

She looked at him without flinching. She didn't need to answer.

Thoughtfully he said, "The event that occurred today embarrassed me severely. It will continue to do so as long as we're in Richmond. A man can't tolerate something like that. Accounts must be balanced. One misdemeanor, one punishment. Do you understand?"

"Are you saying that if I don't do it again, you won't punish me again?"

"You're a bright girl. How a bright girl could make such a dreadful mistake eludes me. I suppose we're all victims of our humanity from time to time."

"You certainly are, Donal."

He didn't like that. He picked up her yellow-dyed gloves

from the corner of the dressing table. "Charming. I believe they'd fit me." He snugged one on, then the other. Her heart raced. The sense of threat was sharp.

"I don't want to do this, Margaret. I regret it."

"Then why—"

The last thing she saw was his yellow fist flying toward her eyes. When she woke, naked on the bed with one eye swollen shut and her face and breasts hurting, he was straddling her. His face contorted as he thrust into her and brutally completed the punishment.

*   *   *

Their destination was Eighteenth and Cary, a block from Libby. The lights of shops and hotels along the way flashed over the faces of Hummy Cridge and the bald man seated opposite Lon. Rain pelted the carriage and puddled in the street. Despite the chill, Lon was sweating.

He speculated about his captors. Cridge he assessed as lower class, with pretensions. The man relished brutality and could no doubt always dredge up some biblical phrase or patriotic cant to justify it. The other man, Miller, struck him as brighter, more calculating, therefore more dangerous. Miller sat awkwardly, his crippled leg stretched across the width of the coach. Lon thought of Miller as the staff general, Cridge one of his field officers. They were a pair to fear.

Miller studied his buffed nails. "Don't imagine you'll get out of this, Price. I'm certain you work for Pinkerton, or did. His ruffians killed my father in Baltimore." Lon sat very still.

"Pinkerton also imprisoned my sister, the lady with whom you're apparently acquainted. Since your side locked her up, abused her, and made her suffer, we'll reciprocate, though with a slight difference. Margaret got out of prison. You'll rot there. Eh, Cridge?"

" 'Deed he will, Mr. Miller. 'Let the wickedness of the wicked come to an end.' "

"Every Sunday Mr. Cridge teaches in an evangelical church school," Miller said. "Ah, here we are."

Through the carriage window Lon saw the lights of three brick buildings comprising the notorious prison.

"Do you want a moment for a last look around?" Miller asked. "You won't be seeing Richmond again. Castle Thunder will likely be your last residence on earth."

Part Four

INSURRECTION

44

December 1862

When Margaret was growing up in Virginia, she played with a favorite doll, made of cloth filled with straw. The smiling mammy doll had a crazy-quilt apron whose array of colors and patterns she found fascinating. For days after Donal punished her, the mirror reflected the same kind of patchwork coloration on Margaret's battered and swollen face.

Sometime during that dreadful night, Eudora had slipped out of the house with her belongings, evidently preferring the wrath of soldiers enforcing the curfew to a confrontation with Margaret. Eudora's brother, Morris, denied knowing anything but the obvious. "She run off, nothin' more to say." Regardless of how many questions Margaret asked, the answers were essentially the same. "She run off. I don' know where. We never was close." During these exchanges Morris didn't raise his eyes to look at Margaret. She soon gave up.

Donal again treated her courteously. He said nothing about her bruised face or the reason for it. He absented himself frequently from Church Hill, often staying away all night. He no longer came to her room, for which she was thankful.

Margaret didn't dwell on the state of her marriage. To do so was to insure another long bout of weeping, a pointless indulgence since it always led to the same truth: She had accepted Donal's proposal willingly. Only she was to blame for what had resulted.

She tried to suppress thoughts of Lon Price but found it impossible. She bought some books, wrapped them, and drove the buggy to Libby Prison one stormy afternoon, presuming Lon was still locked up inside. She handed the books to the ill-mannered guard at the entrance with small hope that Lon would receive them. With sleet flying in her face and stinging her eyes, she drove away up Canal Street, turning uphill at Eighteenth past Castle Thunder, another prison with an even worse reputation. She hardly glanced at the grimy brick buildings, old tobacco factories, now enclosed by a high board fence.

It snowed heavily and often in early December. The fluffy whiteness, so pretty as it drifted down, quickly turned to ugly brown slush. People were depressed, sullen. Enthusiasm for Christmas was dampened by shortages, and by the prospect of Lincoln's emancipation edict taking effect on January 1. Nat Turner's slave uprising was very much on the public mind. Editorialists whipped up the fear with denunciations of "this hateful call for the insurrection of four millions of slaves, and inauguration of a reign of hell on earth."

With Eudora gone, and no other help readily available, shopping fell to Margaret. She bought little; she cooked for one and ate by herself. Her forays into the stores showed her the terrible pressure the war was exerting on the civilian population. Prices were outrageous. A bar of yellow soap had gone from a dime to more than a dollar. Newspapers complained that family grocery bills had gone up ten times too.

Donal didn't gloss over the difficulties of the Confederacy. "The newspapers won't print the truth, but you hear it nonetheless. There's a shortage of firewood for the Army, so wherever they happen to be, they tear down the homes of loyal citizens. Soldiers are trapping barn rats and roasting them because there aren't enough rations. I'm happy to make money from these people, but I find them a pack of bunglers. The South can't win. I'd bank everything I own on that." Bitterly, Margaret wondered if her name was on the list of things he owned.

As if to contradict Donal's negative opinion of the Confederacy, in mid-December Richmond thrilled to news of a huge battle up at Fredericksburg. On December 13, the Army of the Potomac under its new general, Burnside, hurled itself at the rebels and was in turn hurled back, at huge cost. An assault on Longstreet's troops defending a place called Marye's Heights brought the day's bloodiest action. Burnside turned tail.

The victory should have set church bells ringing in celebration. Instead, the papers denounced "Granny" Lee for failing to press his advantage with a counterattack, thereby destroying Burnside's wounded Army. It was two days after the equivocal victory that Donal said he'd finished his business in Richmond. They would be leaving to spend Christmas visiting the company office in Savannah.

"It's warmer down there. At least it should be this time of year. Leaving Richmond strikes me as a wise idea. Your friend is still locked up here. 'Lead us not into temptation,'" he murmured with a taunting smile. Margaret knew the marriage was finished every way except legally.

She paid a farewell visit to Rose Greenhow. Rose wanted to go to England. If Her Majesty's government recognized the Confederacy, as the Davis government desperately hoped, London would welcome Southerners. Margaret wished Rose success with completing her memoir and kissed her good-bye. She refused to kiss little Rose, now growing into young womanhood and more impudent than ever.

Two days before they were to leave for Georgia, Margaret dined with Cicero at Madam Zetelle's popular restaurant on Main Street. Cicero was talkative, cheerful, peppering his conversation with references to "making the Yankees squeal." When she asked how he did that, his answer was a coy smile.

"Do you have anything to do with prisoners of war?" she asked.

"Occasionally."

"Are you acquainted with a prisoner named Alonzo Price? I believe he's in Libby."

"Price." A pause. "No. Why do you ask?"

"He was a friend of someone I knew in Washington."

"If he deserves some special attention, I'll be delighted to arrange it."

"You don't mean special attention to make him comfortable."

"No, quite the opposite."

Margaret shivered. Her brother's good humor had a cruel underpinning. Cicero liked hurting people, and now, evidently, he could do it without being held to account. Sometimes he no longer seemed like her flesh and blood. She promised to write and wondered if she would.

On a dark and blustery morning, Morris drove them to the depot. She and Donal boarded the southbound cars of the Petersburg Railroad. The train bore them through snowy fields, a desolate landscape devoid of color and, for Margaret, any sign of happiness or a normal life.

Gradually they left the snow behind. Watery December sun shone on cotton fields beside the railroad tracks. Leaving North Carolina, the sense of an enemy presence virtually disappeared, even though Yankees occupied one of the South Carolina sea islands, an insignificant place called Hilton Head, not far from Savannah. It was principally a coaling station for the Federal blockade squadron, Donal said; no threat to the mainland thus far.

The graceful old city of Savannah basked in mild winter sunshine. Breezes from the nearby ocean stirred the palms and rattled the palmettos planted around its handsome squares. Ships filled the river and crowded the wharves. An air of prosperity prevailed. The war seemed far away.

They boarded in separate rooms rented from a Mrs. Wilkes and took their meals downstairs at her boardinghouse table. Margaret's face had healed. The last bruise was barely noticeable. While Donal occupied himself at the company office, Margaret unenthusiastically shopped for Christmas gifts. The stores overflowed with luxury goods—fine cigars from Havana, French champagne and cognac and perfume, and most anything else you could think of, from corset stays and bolts of satin to liver pills and hideous caricatures of Abe Lincoln hand-tinted to make him even more repulsive. Margaret bought Donal a fine pair of leather gaiters and a case of Spanish port.

On Christmas Eve he insisted that they stroll down to the riverfront. A concertina in a crowded tavern carried the tune of "Good King Wenceslas" while rough-voiced sailors bellowed the words. Donal led her along the cobblestone quay to a long, narrow cargo vessel painted a misty gray. Her two funnels were shorter than any Margaret had ever seen. Even at this hour, black stevedores were carrying bales of cotton aboard, lashing them on the open deck and covering them with tarpaulins.

"What do you think of her, my dear?"

"I don't know much about ships, but she's unusual, I'll say that."

"In many ways," he agreed. "Very shallow draft. She can do at least eighteen knots. Her bunkers are full of the most expensive coal, anthracite. It produces no smoke. The cotton that you see is worth about nine cents a pound here, but across the pond, ten times that. It's a McKee cargo."

"The ship's a blockade runner?"

"Aye, built in Glasgow and owned by a syndicate recently formed on the Isle of Wight. She steamed up the river last night, after a three-day run from St. George's, Bermuda. An uneventful run, I might add." A boyish enthusiasm bubbled in his voice. "The profit potential of this ship is enormous. More than two-thirds of the runners incoming and outgoing make it through the Yankee squadron. The master, Captain Ayers, formerly sailed with the Royal Navy. On each trip he can clear five or six thousand pounds from private cargoes he's permitted to carry. Compared to that, however, the profit of the owners can be astronomical."

The lap of the river, the tang of the salt breeze blowing across the Low Country marshes, the sight of sweating blacks loading cotton while white men sang carols, made it the strangest Christmas Eve she could remember.

"Does the ship have a name?" None was painted on the transom.

"I wondered if you'd ask. She's the *Lady Margaret*. Your Christmas gift."

"A ship for a present? I've never heard of such a thing."

"Now you have. She was financed with money from McKee, Withers. I am principal shareholder in the syndicate. On this run she's bound for the Bahamas. You and I will spend New Year's in the sun while I visit the Nassau office. Then we'll sail to New York. The business climate up there is splendid. The mayor, Fernando Wood, still wants to secede from the Union and establish the city as a separate state trading with both governments. I shall support him wholeheartedly."

Not a little upset, she said. "Donal, I really prefer the South, even Richmond, over New York. It's Yankee country, and I'm not a Yankee. Must we live there?" She could imagine the isolation, the discomfort, even the ostracism, she'd experience.

He took her hand. "Yes. It's a matter of business."

"And a spouse has nothing to say about it?"

His smile faded. "If you insist I answer that, no. Please don't spoil the evening, darling. Wouldn't you like to step aboard and meet our captain?"

She followed him up the gangway. Stars twinkled in the royal blue sky above the river. The Bible said this was a night when a star of hope shone for the world. If it was there, she couldn't find it.

45

January 1863

In her bedroom in the little house near the Navy Yard, Hanna dipped a cloth in her china washbowl and pressed it to her face. Warm water soothed her cheeks and eyelids. When she took the cloth away, she fancied she saw a face on the surface of the water. The face of the gallant Confederate officer, Frederick. She saw him often in dreams, and every day, more than once, she relived the unexpectedly sweet and moving moment of their kiss. She prayed his compassion went undiscovered and unpunished.

Cold sunshine streamed through the windows of the cramped parlor where she found her father at his writing desk with a stack of documents. It was New Year's, the day the Emancipation Proclamation became law. The District had already freed its slaves last April, much to Major Siegel's displeasure. He boasted of supporting the Unconditional Union Party, the wing of the Democrats endorsing the war and loyal to the administration, but his professed allegiance was a sham, intended to curry favor with Stanton. Of course he endorsed the war, because of the opportunities it afforded. On issues such as punishing the South and freeing the Negroes, he more properly belonged with the Union Democrats, the wing of the party pledged to bringing a prompt peace without social upheaval. After today, Hanna felt sure, there would be upheaval in plenty.

She leaned over the major's shoulder to see his work. He appeared to be copying a list of prices charged the War Department for items of military equipment. In a flowing hand, at the top, someone had written *Confidential—Do Not Circulate*.

"Is this extra work from the department, Papa?"

"It's extra work for me. Certain gentlemen will pay a nice sum to know what contractors are charging. That's how they slip in a lower bid."

Hanna wasn't greatly surprised by his scheming. Washington had become a town of speculators and trimmers feeding or hoping to feed at the government trough.

"Should papers like that be coming home?"

Annoyed, he said, "I return them and no one's the wiser. Don't worry about it. Just enjoy the rewards."

She could remind him that the rewards he referred to weren't cascading down on her. Her portion was a mere trickle—an extra dollar or so every month for groceries. The major had recently bought a new saddle horse, a gray gelding appropriately named Foxy.

He squared the papers into a neat stack. "Will you go with me to the mansion later?" The President and the First Lady traditionally received mobs of well-wishers at the residence on New Year's afternoon.

"No, I have duty at the hospital. Then I'm going to the National Hotel to catch a glimpse of Mr. Booth."

"Who?"

"The Shakespearean actor. Edwin Booth's younger brother, John. He's in town negotiating with Leonard Grover for an engagement. He's never played Washington, though he's a sensation everywhere else. In the evening he greets admirers in the lobby of the National. I read it in the *Star*."

Siegel polished his monocle. "That sort of thing don't interest me."

That too was no surprise. Though Hanna and her father shared the same house, increasingly they lived and moved in separate worlds. She didn't care to know too much about his, for fear her disappointment would turn to disgust.

Protected by a fur hat and mittens, she set out before noon for the Armory Square Hospital near the Smithsonian. She worked there several days a week, helping in the wards from a sense of patriotic duty. She no longer had a regular job. The hospital represented a change in her life, and despite the pain and suffering she saw, it was a good one.

Much had changed in Washington for everyone. At Fredericksburg, General Burnside had destroyed his reputation. "Didn't want to be called scared, like McClellan," the major said, "so he sent ten thousand men up that hill, one damn assault after another. Reb artillery and six ranks of infantry cut them down. Not one man reached the stone wall on the heights. Charge of the Light Brigade all over again. Officers on Burnside's staff say he went insane for a while." Burnside had been replaced by General Joseph Hooker. "Fighting Joe" had the task of reshaping the Army for the spring campaign.

Hanna hadn't stepped on a stage since her last appearance with Derek Fowley's little company. Derek had quit his job selling shoes and had volunteered as an ambulance driver, probably to avoid more dangerous duty at the front. The Quartermaster Corps, not the Medical Corps, supervised the ambulance teamsters, but not very effectively. Hanna cringed at the rough handling of the wounded brought from the Potomac piers. She heard stories of casualties having their valuables stolen while they lay awake and helpless.

She'd run into Derek at the hospital once when he was off duty. A new prosperity was evident in his fine wardrobe. He told her Zephira Comfort had fallen in love with a married officer from Michigan and run off to follow him as an Army laundress. "No loss," he said with airy condescension. "There are charming ladies available on every street corner. All of them weigh less than that cow."

Hanna made her way to the hospital on foot, crossing streets no better than lakes of mud. A few dirty snowbanks were melting in the pale sunshine. Rounding a corner, she saw a colored man being stoned by a trio of soldiers. They chased the black man into an alley. A moment later Hanna heard screams.

She ran to the alley but it was empty. A gate in a board fence banged shut. The soldiers had taken their victim somewhere to continue their sport. Emancipation might be the law of the land, but enforcement in human hearts would be a long time coming.

A lone cloud passing over the Smithsonian spires caught her eye with its blazing whiteness. She saw Frederick's face on the cloud, as though on a canvas.

The journey into Virginia had burned something out of Hanna. She'd proved whatever it was that she needed to prove to herself; she no longer wanted to traipse off to battlefields dressed as a man. She didn't want to fight the rebels, either. Most especially not Frederick.

* * *

Her hospital shift ended at seven. She went directly to the National Hotel at Sixth Street and the Avenue. Under the gaslights in the marble lobby, young Booth was holding court for a mixed crowd of scruffy journalists and respectable ladies and gentlemen. Hanna recognized the handsome Leonard Grover from Baltimore, who now ran his own theater on E Street.

She whispered to a stout lady at the rear of the crowd, "Is there any word of a local engagement?"

"Oh, yes. Mr. Booth announced that he'll be playing Grover's in the spring. Have you ever seen someone so unconscionably handsome?"

She hadn't. The scion of the Junius Brutus Booth family of Maryland was a slender, superbly built young man in his twenties, with silky dark hair and mustache. His vibrant eyes had a slight exotic uptilt. He was reputed to be athletic, improvising all sorts of hazardous stunts and leaps and furious duels in his performances. Hanna noted a bandage wrapped around one hand.

"What do I think of it, sir?" Booth was saying in a deep, commanding voice. He addressed a journalist writing in a small notebook. "It's a disgrace. An abomination. It will not be tolerated by decent white men and women who have an ounce of patriotism in their souls."

"Does he mean the Proclamation?" Hanna asked her informant.

"Yes."

"Who's that with him?" A blonde woman, petite except for her sizable breasts, sat close to Booth on the round velvet sofa. She gazed at the actor worshipfully.

"His mistress, Ella Turner. Sister keeps a parlor house on Ohio Street. I expect he can have any women he wants. He can have me." She giggled; people shushed her. Booth threw a hot glance her way before continuing.

"The President of the so-called Union is a vulgarian. No better than a farmer, with a farmer's taste in filthy barnyard humor. Alas, his performance is no longer mere comicality. 'That foul defacer of God's handiwork, that excellent grand tyrant of the earth,' as the Bard says, is determined to bring down the whole of society, North and South, with his damnable doctrine of nigger equality. We must turn him out, and you may quote me, sir."

Across the lobby, someone hissed. The actor dropped the blond's hand, leaped to his feet. "Who made that cowardly noise? Speak up. I'll gladly defend my opinions with your choice of pistol, rapier, or bare knuckles." A clerk behind the marble counter drooped his head over the guest ledger. A dough-faced man slunk toward the staircase. Another guest hid behind his newspaper.

Booth took his seat. One of the reporters raised his hand. "You said turn the tyrant out, Mr. Booth. Do you mean by electing General McClellan a year from November?"

"Far too slow, though I applaud the general's tolerant position on slavery. It accords with the views of Southerners, with whom I've always felt myself most at home."

"Well, if you wouldn't remove Lincoln at the polls, how would you do it?"

The dark wells of Booth's eyes seemed to expand. A look came into them that set Hanna on edge. "I leave that to others, along with Macbeth's reminder that 'twere well if it were done quickly."

"Good God, he's talking treason," a man said, his words overlapped by Booth's announcing that he and Miss Turner desired a rest and would retire. The reporter persisted, "Aren't you afraid of making such inflammatory statements, sir?"

"I am not, sir. Our forefathers enjoined us to love liberty and justice and, if necessary, to overturn oppressors to gain those civic blessings. Abraham Lincoln is just such an oppressor."

"Secretary Stanton's detectives arrest people for that kind of talk."

"I should like to see them try to arrest me. They are welcome to attempt it, though I encourage them to come armed."

Scattered applause identified a few secesh in the crowd. Though Hanna didn't like Booth's remarks, she'd come here for a purpose. She pressed forward along with others, a small leather-covered book in hand. Booth flourished his pencil as he signed autographs, his smile amiable and winning.

"Hello, my dear," he said when Hanna reached him. "What's your name?"

"Hanna Siegel. I'm an actress."

"And a mighty pretty one." His dark eyes were hypnotic; they could have seduced a virgin cast in bronze. "Are you local?" She said she was. "We usually gather a supporting cast from the town where we appear. The engagement at Grover's will occur in late April. Apply to Mr. Grover if you're interested."

"Thank you, Mr. Booth. I appreciate that."

"Charmed," he said with a regal bow and a look that spoke unmistakably of bedrooms, assignations, free love. He passed on to the next adoring fan, and Hanna slipped away, the book clasped in her hand like a precious jewel.

Though he'd offered her a marvelous opportunity, she didn't know whether she could take advantage of it. Booth's hatred of the President disturbed her. Besides, handsome as he was, Johnny Booth was no rival for the gallant officer Frederick, whom she thought about all the way home.

46

January 1863

Castle Thunder consisted of three brick buildings. The largest, the original tobacco factory, faced Cary Street. Two smaller buildings formed a quadrangle closed off by high wooden fences and in the rear by a brick wall with sentry booths on the corners. The prison housed Confederate officers awaiting court-martial, civilians suspected of disloyalty, Union deserters, and accused spies. It had gaslight, running water, and the same abysmal stink of human waste as Libby just up the street.

Lon missed Christmas because he was receiving special attention from four men he came to think of as the four horsemen of the sixth chapter of Revelation: the riders on a white horse, a red horse, a black horse, and a pale horse, death. The first one, and the one who spoke with greatest authority, was the bald man he'd encountered first on the night of his arrest. Cicero Miller was his name, Margaret's brother. What his position in the government was, Lon couldn't say. He didn't suppose Miller would allow a prisoner to question him. That such an icy, calculating man could be related to the woman he loved utterly confounded him.

Miller received him in a small office, together with the prison's bizarre warden, George Alexander. Captain Alexander wore black hose, black knee breeches with buckles, and a loose black shirt. His beard was long, and black. Nero, the huge boar hound that padded after him wherever he went, likewise was black.

Lon stood with his hands manacled behind him. The bald man rested his thick-soled shoe on a stool. It was freezing outside, and chilly in the office.

"That rogue who brought you in, Mars, failed to interrogate

you for useful information. But I'm sure you have things to tell us, Private Rogers. You *are* continuing the game of calling yourself Rogers?"

"Albion Rogers is my name."

Miller sighed. "Oh, yes, certainly. Now tell me, what ciphers have you memorized?"

Lon said he didn't know any ciphers. The bald man repeated the question five times, and Lon returned the same answer each time. "Warden," Miller said, "show him the inner room."

Captain Alexander chattered about himself as he escorted Lon down the hall. He was a native of Georgia. He'd served in the Federal Navy thirteen years. His dog Nero had fought three full-grown bears and killed them. If Lon had been wearing even of a scrap of a blue uniform, Nero would have torn his throat out. Altogether a fountain of cheer, the warden.

The so-called inner room had gaslight but no windows, a slimy floor, and a sickening stench. Ball and chain for twelve prisoners hung from the sweating walls. At the moment only one man was confined, a skeletal creature Lon recognized. "Scully!"

John Scully looked up, then quickly turned his watery eyes away. Alexander said, "Drink has rotted his mind. That and a disease he picked up from one of the women we keep here occasionally. We go this way."

The door opened into the yard behind the building. Alexander led him to the brick wall, pointed out bullet holes. "The unlucky are executed on this spot. You may be one of them. Meanwhile you can rest in what we call a condemned cell."

A black box, off the inner room, with no light, no air; nothing but dreadful silence after Alexander slammed the door.

* * *

When Cicero Miller questioned him again, Lon met the third horseman, a tall, stooping fellow who constantly spat tobacco juice that dribbled into his gray beard. "Mr. Caphart was formerly a police detective in Norfolk," Miller said. "The prisoners call him the Antichrist." Caphart smirked. "Give us the names of your contacts in Richmond."

"I don't have any. I don't know what you mean." Lon was

starved, exhausted, fighting depression after three days and
nights in the condemned cell.

The questioning went on for fifteen minutes. Then the bald
man gave up. "He's yours, John."

Caphart marched Lon to one of the smaller buildings, a
room with a dirt floor and a post about seven feet high in the
center. Two sets of handcuffs dangled from the top. Caphart
ordered Lon to remove his shirt, then stretch on his toes so his
wrists fit into one set of cuffs. Caphart locked the cuffs and
opened a toolbox, producing a leather strap. He laid a stroke
on Lon's back, plainly enjoying himself. Lon clenched his
teeth.

Caphart laid on nine more, each cutting deeper, bringing
more blood. Lon hugged the post and jammed his cheek
against it to keep from crying out.

"That's enough. For now." Caphart wiped the bloody strap
with a rag. He left Lon hanging on the post, his back and
shoulders afire with pain.

*   *   *

At the end of twenty-four hours they took him down. A guard
dressed his back with a stinging salve and returned his shirt.
Groggy, Lon stumbled through a downpour to the office in
the main building. There he met the fourth horseman, a man
he'd seen before.

"Yes, sir, good morning, sir," Hummy Cridge said. "I hope
you're enjoying our hospitality?" Lon told him to go to hell.
Cridge slapped him.

"Now, now, we have business," Miller said. Outside the
barred window, a freak winter storm raged, rain and lightning
instead of snow. "Let's discuss another issue, Mr. Price. Yes, I
said Price. Never mind how I know your name. Who sent you
to Richmond? Who do you work for?"

Weaving on his feet, Lon said, "No one. I belonged to
Heintzelman's—" Cridge slapped him.

"Again, please," Miller said. "Who do you work for?"

The repetitious exchange of question and denial continued
for a while. Finally Miller said, "Take him out to the cage. The
weather may restore his reason if nothing else will." Lon had
a renewed sense of the evil of the man. His three henchmen

were thugs with sadistic tendencies they might exercise indiscriminately. Miller's cruelty was measured, calculated. He was the pale horse.

Cridge donned a slicker. He and a guard marched Lon to the open yard, pushed him into a rusty iron cage in one corner. Cridge raised his eyes to the storm. " 'For they have sown the wind and they shall reap the whirlwind. So persecute them with thy tempest, and make them afraid with thy storm.' "

The guard locked the cage. The black sky lit with blinding whiteness. Cridge's merry face streamed with rain, then disappeared. Lon sank to his knees in mud, holding the bars and trying at the same time to hold on to what was left of his courage.

* * *

They kept him in the cage two days and nights. A sweep of polar air followed the storm. When they lifted him from the ground where he lay shivering and mumbling, snowflakes were whitening his hair.

Fever burned and froze him for a week. He survived by willing it; by saying over and over to himself that the fiery sweats and convulsive chills would pass if only he refused to surrender to them. When he came back to a semblance of life, he was a bearded skeleton. He had a new homespun shirt, straw for a bed on the floor, and a block of wood for a pillow. His jackknife had long ago been confiscated.

He was quartered in what was called the citizens' room, at one end of a long hall on the second floor of the main building. Three others shared the room, a fat man named Rampling, who sat staring at his hands for hours; John Scully; and Lon's colleague Pryce Lewis, a bitter ghost of his old self.

"That fucking devil Pinkerton abandoned us in here. I've suffered the torments of hell and I hold him responsible. When I get back to Washington—"

"You won't find him," Lon said. "He's in Chicago. He quit when McClellan did."

"Then who's in charge?"

"I don't know."

As January passed, Lon's pain lessened a little each day. He slowly regained his strength. The bald man didn't reappear, so

Lon assumed he'd temporarily shifted his attention to other matters.

They were allowed the run of the second floor, which included the so-called prison parlor, a whitewashed room with barred windows at the other end of the hall. Here prisoners met and filled the hours with conversation. They speculated on their food. "Notice how we always have a lot more meat after a cavalry engagement?" There was endless talk of escape, of digging tunnels and other schemes. "Lad I know over in Palmer's Factory, he used a red-hot needle on his face. Jesus, it must have hurt. They thought it was smallpox and threw him in the prison hospital. He climbed out the window at night. Nobody's pulled that off a second time."

From the embittered Pryce Lewis, Lon learned that Hattie Lawton had been exchanged after Webster's hanging. Lon said nothing about his own work. He didn't know Lewis's strength, whether he might suddenly bargain for his freedom by betraying others.

A small, frail, middle-aged woman with a hooked nose and a basket on her arm visited the prison regularly. She distributed hard candy, blankets, playing cards, pencils, and used books. "That's Miss Van Lew," Caphart informed him. "Crazy Bet. Old bitch loves the Union and everybody knows it, but she's a friend of Winder. He thinks she's harmless. Give her to me, I'd flay the skin off her back." Caphart regularly performed that service for prisoners chosen at random. They were hauled off to the other building and returned in a bloody heap. One had died minutes after Caphart threw him on the parlor floor. A bored prisoner shouted, "Man in here just got his discharge." Guards came for the corpse several hours later.

A January thaw set in. Sunshine flooded the rooms and brought small crowds to the streets to gawk. Castle Thunder had no rule about prisoners staying away from windows; Warden Alexander liked subjecting his prisoners to the abuse of the public. Lon was sitting by a window in the citizens' room one sunny morning when a piping voice said, "Beg pardon, sir, I don't believe I've had the pleasure." There stood the hooknosed lady, her head tilted to one side like a curious bird's. Matted curls that might once have been blonde were faded to yellow-gray. A threadbare cotton dress enhanced her shabby appearance. Her hand was dry as paper when he shook it.

"Elizabeth Van Lew, sir. Your name?"

"Private Albion Rogers."

"Oh, yes; oh, yes, Rogers." She smiled in a vacant way and rummaged in her basket. "I have one comb left. I have some stomach pills. Oh, and this book. I'm afraid it isn't quite suitable for adult gentlemen, but there are some pretty illustrations. Won't you please take it to pass the time?"

Keeping her back to the room, she thrust the book at him. Her blue eyes were so clear and intense, it changed his impression of her instantly. The worn book, faded gold letters on a brown cover, was a Mother Goose. As soon as he took it, she exclaimed, "La-la, off I go," and tripped away down the hall, singing to herself.

Seated again, he turned the faded pages. He stopped at the page with the verse about Mistress Mary. In the line asking how Mary's garden grew, the word *your* was lightly underlined in pencil. A few pages on, "Hi-ho, what can the matter be?" he found a second underline in "tie up my pretty brown *hair*."

On the illustrated page for "Rub-A-Dub-Dub," *baker* was underlined, and a circle drawn around the bulbous nose of the baker afloat in the tub.

He found no other marks. He laid the book down and covered it with straw. Was the underlining random, or did it mean something? Because of that moment in which Miss Van Lew had tried to communicate something with her eyes, he decided it could be the latter.

Your. Hair. Baker. Nose. Baker, nose, hair, your.

He caught his breath. *Baker,* capital B. His mind raced, sorting the words.

Baker, nose, your, hair.

Baker knows you're here.

47

February–March 1863

In February, Miss Van Lew visited Castle Thunder twice a week. Lon only glimpsed her; she didn't approach him. Her behavior left him confused and frustrated. Had he invented the message in the book out of desperation and misguided hope?

The last day of the month, a Saturday, was bright and mild. Lon joined a dozen prisoners for a half hour's freedom in the walled yard. It was no great boon; the overflowing latrine pits steamed in the sun.

Miss Van Lew, typically unkempt, appeared with a basket of flowers. She looked at the prisoners apathetically shuffling around the yard, spied Lon, and came toward him with mincing steps and a foolish grin.

"Care for a posy, sir? Brighten your day."

The flowers were poor, ugly things, wire and wallpaper scraps to which watercolors had been applied. He chose one. "Thank you." He wished she'd brought bread. The prison was observing one of Jefferson Davis's fast days, decreed by the President to conserve food and test the loyalty of all good rebels. Stores and markets closed for the day.

She linked arms with him. "Care to walk with me, sir?" After a few steps she hissed through her teeth, "Don't look at me. Frown or laugh, as though I'm talking nonsense. I can't say how long they'll permit us to talk. That swine Alexander wants to stop me from speaking to inmates. Turner wants to revoke my prison pass altogether. Thank God for my friend Johnny Winder." They turned away from the reeking sinks. "Colonel Baker wants you out."

"How does he know I'm here?"

"Through me."

"Do you work for him?"

"No. We don't have time for lengthy explanations. I'm to help you escape."

"How?"

"I have a man here, inside."

Lon stabbed a hand into his beard, caught an unwelcome visitor, and disposed of it. "You're not a bit crazy, Miss Van Lew."

"I hope not. But they must keep thinking I am, all these jailers and their sadistic detectives."

"There are a couple of them I want to meet on neutral ground someday."

"Listen, please. It's arranged for next Friday, two hours after dark. Do you have a timepiece?"

"No. They took everything."

"Then you'll have to gauge the hour as best you can. The Cary Street door will be open. The guard will be elsewhere. Go straight down to Canal, don't stop for anyone or anything. One of my couriers will be waiting with a wagon. Probably Mr. Rowley of Charles City. He's a farmer who supplies food to the prisons. He can travel freely at night."

"What happens after I—?" She pulled away suddenly. Warden Alexander had emerged into the sunshine, Nero at his heels. Miss Van Lew plucked a paper flower from her basket and waved it.

"Dear Captain! Here's a blossom just for you." She went skipping across the yard, waving the flower above her head. The boar hound growled. She kicked dirt in the dog's face. The captain laughed at that, disarmed

Lon twirled the paper flower. What a strange creature. Could she possibly be clever enough to run a spy ring that included farmers and butchers and God knew who else? Did he dare trust her promise of a door standing open next Friday?

He decided he must. Pinkerton was gone, but the odious Colonel Baker offered him a chance for revenge against these bastards; revenge for Sledge, and for himself. His life was worth nothing in Castle Thunder. He might as well gamble it on Crazy Bet.

*   *   *

Wednesday, when Lon's anticipation was mounting, Miller reappeared.

"My duties required me to be in Baltimore and New York," he said as a guard prodded Lon toward the prison parlor, which had been cleared of loungers. "Take a seat on the stool, please."

The March afternoon was cloudy, the light dreary. Hummy Cridge stood behind Lon, slapping a bulging sock in his palm. He informed Lon that the sock contained minié balls. Warden Alexander waited at the open doorway to bar intruders.

Miller's left shoe scraped as he took a position in front of Lon. "Now, Mr. Price, tell me how you know my sister."

"I don't."

Miller glanced at Cridge. The detective said, " 'The Lord hateth a lying tongue.' " He smashed the loaded sock on Lon's shoulder. Exquisite pain danced down his arm and into his neck.

"Margaret Miller was her name before marriage. Margaret Miller of Washington and Baltimore."

"I'm from upstate New York."

Cridge hit him. Lon almost fell off the stool. Miller was angry. What frightened Lon was the lunatic gleam in his eye. Miller, not Miss Van Lew, was the crazy one.

"The hell you say, Price. You're lying. You're a filthy, conniving liar. My sister knows you."

"It must be a mistake."

Cridge hit him.

The questions went on, and the beating. Lon's head lolled. Blood drooled from the corner of his mouth. A piece of tooth lay at his feet. At the end of a half hour Miller was apoplectic.

"I am accustomed to getting the information I want. I can't make a career out of interrogating you. I have many more important duties. But I will break you down, Mr. Price. I will succeed, because I place no restrictions on the methods I'm willing to use. I will come back, and I will succeed, and you will crawl and tell me everything."

Miller jammed his derby on his head. "Put this piece of dung where he belongs." Cridge threw the bloody sock on the floor and yanked Lon up by his left arm. Lon couldn't suppress a strident cry.

He stumbled past cowed prisoners who had watched the interrogation from the hallway. At the door of the citizens' room, Cridge kicked him in the small of the back. Lon toppled forward on his face. Rampling and John Scully and Pryce Lewis stared at him but didn't move to help him. Lon lay with his right cheek in the blood running from his nose.

* * *

On Thursday he could barely stand. He was a mass of misery, from his purpling legs to his bruised chest to his aching arms and shoulders. In a little more than twenty-four hours he had to attempt to escape. If anyone stopped him, he wouldn't have strength to fight. He hardly slept that night, turning on one side, then the other, then back again, finding no relief from the anxiety or the pain.

Miller didn't return on Friday, which was a blessing. A second blessing was the weather, stormy again. Black clouds sailed over the city. Gale winds rattled the prison windows. Every few minutes there was a cloudburst.

At nightfall the storm was undiminished. Lon lay rigid in the straw, trying to guess how much time had passed. Finally, hopelessly unsure, he dragged himself to his feet. Pryce Lewis woke from a doze. "Where are you going?"

"Latrine. Sick."

Lon shuffled into the hall. His left leg trembled and almost gave out. He leaned on the wall to prevent a noisy fall. After a minute he limped to the staircase. Thunder shook the building, muffling other sounds.

He knew that just one guard patrolled the lower hall during the nighttime hours. He prayed it was the guard loyal to Miss Van Lew. On the lower floor, all the gas mantles but one were shut off, and the remaining one was trimmed low. He moved toward the entrance one slow, arduous step at a time. He passed under the glowing gas fixture. His bent shadow leaped ahead of him on the wall.

Thunder rolled. The floor vibrated. Ten steps left.

Now nine.

Six . . .

Sudden confidence warmed him like whiskey. Sometimes in life, a whole string of bad things happened one after another, with no rational cause. But sometimes too, the dice rolled the right way; the cards came up all aces. Two more steps and he was out the door into the pelting rain.

The rain felt wonderful, cool and cleansing. It fell so heavily, he couldn't see lights along the canal, or in the windows of Libby a block away. He slipped and slid down the cobbled slope of Eighteenth Street to Canal. Sure enough, huddled in a poncho and a black sombrero, a man sat on the seat of a wagon with a two-mule hitch. Man, mules, and wagon glistened with a silvery radiance, then vanished as lightning flickered out.

Lon came on the wagon from behind. "Rowley?"

The round eye of a gun barrel poked from under the poncho. "Price?"

"Where do I hide?"

"Under the straw, and be quick."

Climbing the wagon wheel felt like climbing a mountain. He groaned as he hauled himself over and flopped on the wet straw. Lying on his back, he piled straw on his legs, his torso. The wagon was already in motion, bumping over rough paving. One of Lon's hands touched something that moved.

He lay with his face exposed to the rain. The farmer would get him out of the city, he would rest a little to renew his strength, then go on to Washington and—

He heard a horse approaching. "It's the watch. Cover yourself." Lon rolled onto his belly, flung handfuls of soggy straw over his head. He could barely breathe. His face was hard against the wooden wagon bed. Something squeaked.

"Hold up there. Who are you? What's your business?"

"Hugh Rowley of Charles City. I'm a victualer for the prisons. I come this way twice a week."

"Devil of a night for it. Show me your pass."

"Bring your lantern and lean over here, I don't want the ink to run." The squeak sounded again, close to Lon's ear.

After a minute the watchman said, "It's in order, you may pass on." A tiny spot of cold touched Lon's cheek. He almost screamed. A second rat sank its teeth into his hand. He thrashed uncontrollably. "What the fire is that?"

"Barn rats," Rowley said. "I try to clean them out, but a few always manage to ride along."

"Well, I have the cure for that."

Alarm in Rowley's voice: "What are you doing?"

The rat bit Lon's hand again. He heard layers of sound: the roaring rain, the watchman's horse moving up beside the wagon, the cock of a pistol. Lightning struck close by. The watchman leaned over the side of the wagon and emptied his pistol into the straw.

One shot hit Lon. The last thing he heard before consciousness faded was the watchman saying, "That'll take care of your rats."

48

March 1863

Splinters of light. Sensation returning. Right leg heavy and stiff; the slightest motion painful.

He rubbed his eyelids. Saw a room, a patchwork quilt, a crude footboard someone had carved and finished by hand. A sunlit muslin curtain danced at an open window, a grape arbor beyond. He said, "Oh," remembering.

"There you are," a man said. "My wife's cooking some beef soup. Reckon you must be starved."

Lon saw his benefactor at the bedside, his big hands on his hips. "Where are we?"

"Rowley's farm. Charles City County. Got here night before last."

Memory poured into him: the escape, the storm, the rats, the gunshots. Rowley continued, "I feared you were dead but I couldn't look at you till I got away from the watchman. When I stopped, I saw he'd plugged your leg. I tied it off best I could and drove on."

Lon fingered his beard lying outside the quilt. "I don't remember any of that."

"The Lord was on our side. He kept the rain and thunder

going strong. The guards at the city limit waved me right through. We got here at sunrise, about the time the storm quit. Our pastor studied medicine before he heard the call. He dug the ball out and dressed your leg. Regular doctors in the neighborhood are secesh."

Lon moved his leg again; grimaced. "Feels like I'll be wrecked forever."

"Don't think so, but you'll hobble awhile. My son Ike's carving you a walking stick. Ah, here's Miz Rachel with the soup." A buxom woman brought a wooden tray into the room.

The soup was hot and delicious. Lon was clumsy with it, twice spilling some into his beard. Two slices of white bread slathered with country butter accompanied the soup. He ate half a slice. Rowley's wife pointed to the beef bone on the tray. "Suck the marrow, it'll give you strength."

He had just enough strength to do as she asked. Soon, with the warm breeze blowing over him, he was asleep.

* * *

Days passed. He rested, ate, talked with Rowley when the farmer came in from his fields in the evening. War news was scanty. Lon asked about Elizabeth Van Lew, whom he called a most unlikely spy.

" 'Cause she's a lady, and acts so daft," Rowley agreed. "She's Union to the core. Schooled up in Philadelphia as I recall. Her family freed their slaves when she was nine or ten. Not everyone in Virginia is part of the slavocracy. I never owned a human being, black, white, or green, nor will I."

"This Richmond ring. How extensive is it? How many people?"

"Don't know. She keeps that secret, for everyone's protection. I know there's a superintendent of one of the railroads, and a German butcher—"

"Retz. I met him."

"—but that's all I know. This farm's one of her depots."

"What do you mean, depot?"

"Place where scouts pick up cipher messages. Miss Van Lew sends two or three a week. They send back requests for certain kinds of information. Couriers like me deliver them to her."

"Who sends requests? Who does she work for?"

"Why, the Union Army, I reckon. The scouts are spies, but they're Army. You'll meet one presently."

"It wasn't the Army that arranged my escape, it was Colonel Ba—someone else. How did the Army get in on it?"

"General Hooker. He set up some kind of spy branch the end of last year."

"Have you heard of a man named Pinkerton? He ran a secret service for General McClellan on the Peninsula." Rowley shook his head. "Or Major E. J. Allen?"

"Him neither. I'd better go see to my laying hens. In the morning Ike will help you try the walking stick." Rowley dimmed the bedside lamp, leaving Lon to ponder the reshuffling of the cards that had occurred since his imprisonment. Was the Army's new spy bureau connected in any way with Lafayette Baker? He wouldn't know till he was in Washington. That was his goal, Washington. He kept it in his thoughts as he drowsed off with the lamp still burning.

Margaret passed through his dreams, and her brother, Cicero, and Hummy Cridge. They were torturing her. He woke in a sweat of terror. Moonlight whitened the footboard and quilt. Someone had blown out the lamp. He was awake for an hour, shaken by the bad dreams.

*   *   *

Next day he took his first steps with the aid of Rowley's husky son, and the stick, a hardwood limb shaped roughly and finished with a clear lacquer. After ten steps his right knee buckled, but Ike was there, catching him with ham-sized hands. "You'll make it, sir. You're doing just fine."

Sometimes at night Lon heard a horseman arrive or leave. One sunny morning Rowley brought in a skinny, long-jawed man wearing farmer's clothes. Not much more than twenty-five, Lon guessed, but his face was lined and darkened by weather. A long mandarin mustache gave him a sinister look.

"Leonidas Whittaker," he said as they shook hands. "My job's to get you to the Potomac. We'll start tomorrow if you're up to it."

"I'm up to it," Lon said, though his leg hurt like the devil. He had to reach Washington to find a way to strike back at

Miller and Cridge and their ilk. When he'd done that, he'd sort
out the situation with Margaret. Plainly her marriage was a
mistake and would eventually end. How Margaret's brother
fit in was something he couldn't deal with rationally; not yet.
It remained a huge problem.

The journey with Whittaker required four days. The scout
had a big roan; Lon bounced along on a mule. They hid by day
and traveled at night, progressing slowly through fields and
woodlands, avoiding roads and Confederate patrols. Whittaker was a cautious man who spoke only when he deemed it
necessary, but Lon was an aggressive questioner. He soon
drew out the story of what had changed in his absence.

Plagued by the amateurish mistakes of the first two years of
the war, the new commanding general, Hooker, had concluded that the gathering of intelligence should be the
purview of the Army. His provost marshal, General Marsena
Patrick, created the Bureau of Military Information and put
in charge one Colonel George Sharpe, a Yale lawyer and former commander of the 120th New York. Sharpe ran the string
of scouts who picked up messages at the depots round about
Richmond.

"Are you acquainted with a Colonel Baker?" Lon asked.

Whittaker chewed a blade of grass and regarded a sulphur
butterfly hovering over his outstretched boot. They were resting in a glade beside a purling creek, waiting for sunset.

"Yes, we all know Baker. He works directly for Stanton.
Calls himself chief of the National Detective Police. They run
a secret operation. General Patrick don't like it, but Baker's
wormed himself in pretty deep, so we have orders to steer
clear of him and his men."

At twilight, a couple of elderly home guardsmen hailed
them across a cornfield. Some hard riding got them away, pursued only by a few rounds of musket fire. The two-mile gallop
on muleback pounded Lon's leg and lit the fires of pain again.

They passed by the hamlet of Weedonville in the dark. Near
the Potomac below Aquia Creek, Whittaker brought them to
a cabin belonging to a solidly built black man whose name
was Eakins; first or last, Lon never found out. Eakins's clothes
were poor but his determination formidable. He showed Lon
a pirogue hidden in reeds on the riverbank. He'd felled the

tree, charred it, and hollowed it out himself. He made two or three runs across the Potomac weekly, carrying messages or passengers.

"Ten year ago, master sold me off," Eakins explained. "Sold my wife, Clytie, and my son, Eakins Junior, to another man, from down North Carolina way. Only good thing, my new master freed me 'fore he joined up with the rebs. I could've run North, but I stayed here to fight best way I could. They took my wife and my boy. They broke up a family. God's my witness, I'll find Clytie and Eakins Junior, after I see Linkum bring the jubilee an' hang Jeff Davis."

The first night with Eakins was too clear for a crossing. The next night brought fog; they poled and paddled to Maryland under cover of the murk. Eakins helped Lon out of the pirogue. "You on freedom's ground now. You safe. Tell Father Abraham that Eakins is one more good soldier on his side."

"I will." Eakins's handclasp was like a vise.

Eakins jumped in the pirogue and paddled away. Lon buttoned the old denim jacket Mrs. Rachel Rowley had given him, fished a pebble out of his shoe, and set off for Washington City.

*   *   *

Lon's Irish landlady in K Street shrieked when he appeared at her door. She'd already let his room, assuming he was dead down there on the Peninsula. But she had a smaller room, a refurbished garret. His things were stored in her cellar. She hadn't had the heart to sell them.

"I don't have a room for Mr. Greenglass," she said.

"Mr. Greenglass won't be coming back, Mrs. Phelan."

"He . . . ? Oh, dear Lord." She crossed herself.

Lon cleaned up and prevailed on the landlady to trim his beard to a respectable length. He brushed his black suit, rolled up for so long that the wrinkles looked permanent. He tied a black boot lace into a bow knot at the collar of his white shirt and trudged to the War Department.

"I am here to see Colonel Lafayette Baker."

The guard at the entrance stuck out his chin. "Provost Marshal Baker don't see anyone without an appointment."

"He'll see me. Give him my name. Alonzo Price."

"I'm not authorized to—"

"Give him my name," Lon said, a baleful glint in his eye. Only two or three years separated them, but the guard was a soft-cheeked innocent. Lon had the look of a man who'd walked through fire. The guard left him on a bench, ignored by civilians and high-ranking officers who bustled in and out with great self-importance. The guard returned at double time.

"Take the stairs to the basement. Room at the end of the hall." As Lon went down the steps, he heard a stentorian voice he took to be Stanton's, rejecting someone's plea at his morning audience.

The gaslit lower hall was gloomy, without windows, and smelled of the eternal Washington dews and damps. Baker waited in the doorway, like a figure in a picture frame. He shook Lon's hand in a comradely way.

"We pulled you out. By heaven, I'm pleased."

"I'm grateful to you, Colonel Baker."

"I arranged for your removal from Virginia because I respect your abilities, Mr. Price. Come in, close the door. We have a great deal to talk about."

He seemed less arrogant than Lon remembered. His wintry gray eyes were less hostile, or perhaps Lon only hoped so. A fancy gold frame on his desk held a miniature oil portrait of a woman. Baker noticed Lon's curiosity. "My wife." Lon didn't know Baker had a wife.

They talked for an hour. Lon related all that had happened to him since Allan Pinkerton had sent him to Richmond with Sledge.

"You understand that Pinkerton's completely out of the picture," Baker said.

"So I was told. Do you know the man I described, Cicero Miller? Slightly crippled, left leg shorter than the right?"

"I know him by reputation. He's high up in their Signal Service. Considered to be one of their smartest agents. Some say he's not quite right in the head. Based on what you told me about Castle Thunder, you must have similar suspicions."

Lon nodded. "How did you learn that I was imprisoned?"

"Miss Van Lew isn't one of my operatives, but occasionally I have access to her information, through channels we won't discuss. Years ago, she sent a free colored girl to Philadelphia to be educated at her expense. The girl remained in the North, but when the war started, Miss Van Lew asked her to return to Richmond. I don't know how it was pulled off, but this young woman secured a position in the residence of none other than Jeff Davis. Waiting on his table. Serving his food."

"Remarkable," Lon said, though knowing Miss Van Lew, he wasn't altogether surprised.

"One evening when Cicero Miller dined with Davis, they discussed your case. The colored girl was in and out of the dining room many times. Miss Van Lew reported what the girl overheard."

Baker held out a cigar case, silver, obviously expensive. Lon declined. "I can't offer you a drink, I'm a temperance man," Baker said rather piously. "Permit me to ask about your prospects and intentions."

"I want to see the secesh whipped, Colonel. I want to see the worst of them dead."

"I applaud your determination. We have not exactly enjoyed a cordial relationship in the past, but it isn't necessary to be friendly in order to work together. If, as you declare, your goal is to punish the rebs, I can guarantee you many excellent opportunities. You can utilize your experience by working for me, or you can throw it away and join the Army. You don't impress me as a man who enjoys regimentation."

"No."

"Then what do you say?"

Lon suspected it was a pact with the devil. He didn't care.

"Yes, sir, I'll sign on."

"Splendid." Baker came around the desk and gave him a brotherly slap on the shoulder. "Mr. Peter Watson, the assistant secretary, will handle the papers and discuss salary and allowance. We're paid well in this department. I suppose you should submit a formal resignation to Mr. Pinkerton in Chicago."

"I will. He owes me back pay."

"I doubt you'll get it. Salaries for his people were badly in arrears when he left. We run a much more efficient operation." Baker held out his hand. "Welcome to the National Detective Police, sir. We'll see Jeff Davis roasting in hell before we're done."

49

June–July 1863

In the sticky heat of summer, Washington seemed engaged in a wild pursuit of pleasure. Business was fine at the hotels, the theaters, the National Race Course where hordes of soldiers and civilians watched trotters compete for handsome purses. Army officers displayed themselves with their bawds; past indiscretions were evident in the numbers of women lugging infants around town—"Peninsula bastards," they were called. Certain well-to-do former residents of the District were quietly returning from Richmond, disenchanted with the Confederacy and fearful of its coming defeat.

The war continued to rumble below the horizon. Since mid-June the War Department had received reports of Lee's Army on the move from Fredericksburg to Culpeper, possibly presaging a second invasion of the North. On June 9, ten thousand of Stuart's cavalry fought a ten-hour battle with an equal number of Union horse at Brandy Station. For once the Federal cavalry acquitted itself well.

In the West, Ulysses Grant tightened a noose around Vicksburg on the Mississippi. Despite gossip about alleged drunkenness, Grant was gaining favor with the administration. He seemed just about the only winning general on the Union side.

The enemies Lon dealt with were closer at hand.

In his garret, he lit a candle and propped the small window open with a stick. No air was stirring. He swatted a mosquito buzzing at his ear and opened the dossier of the latest suspect.

Mr. Chauncey Hull, a Yale graduate, taught young ladies at a local academy. He also wrote literate and forceful letters to newspapers. Mr. Hull's letters accused the government of suppressing dissent and illegally infringing the rights of citizens by means of the Enrollment and Conscription Act, passed and signed in March. Though not yet in operation, the new draft had already incited riots and disturbances in Wisconsin, Indiana, and Pennsylvania. Mr. Hull called the draft an evil law created by despots. His seditious views brought him to Baker's attention. Lon would take Mr. Hull into custody tomorrow morning, accompanied by another agent.

They met outside Hull's apartment house. Eugene Sandstrom was new to Baker's organization. Eugene was thin, with a bland, pleasant face and a ready smile. He'd been training for the local police force when Baker recruited him. Eugene reminded Lon of himself in the early months in the war: pumped full of worthless idealism.

Lon and Eugene were two of some forty to fifty men in Baker's private police department. No one knew the exact number except Baker himself, and presumably Mr. Stanton. Lon found it amusing that the gnomelike secretary with his fishbowl spectacles and asthmatic voice had become the most feared man in Washington. He saw something of Cicero Miller in Stanton. A zealot who expected absolute obedience, Stanton ordered the arrest and detention of anyone with the slightest whiff of disloyalty on him, or her. Journalists, clerics, proponents of a negotiated peace, disaffected Army officers— Baker caught them all in his net.

"Third floor back," Lon said as they stepped into the dark lower hall. He led the way up creaky stairs past closed doors that breathed out odors of stale cooking. A grime-encrusted skylight over the stairwell dimmed the sunshine to a twilight haze. Lon's plaid suit was uncomfortably hot. Sweat soaked his collar.

"What's this fellow done?" Eugene said as they climbed

"Inflammatory letters to the papers. Men shouldn't obey the draft, England should recognize the Confederacy, that sort of rot."

"So you can't express an opinion anymore?"

"Not in this town." Lon slipped the Colt .31 from his jacket. Zach had returned it to Mrs. Phelan for safekeeping, as he'd promised. Zach was working in Willard's dining room again, not happily.

On the third floor, a door next to the stairs opened. A mousy woman stepped out. Lon said, "Go back inside and stay there." The frightened creature saw his gun and nearly fell down in her haste to obey.

At the door of the back flat, Lon glanced inquiringly at Eugene, who had a four-shot Sharps pocket pistol in hand. Eugene replied with a nervous nod. Lon knocked.

Seconds went by. He heard someone breathing on the other side of the door. He knocked again, loudly.

"Who's there?"

"Police."

Then a woman's voice. "Who is it, Chauncey?"

"I don't know, love. They say they're police. I'm sure it's a mistake." A key rattled; the door swung in.

"Your name is Chauncey Hull?"

"That's correct, sir." Hull was fifty or so, gone to fat. He had a round, rosy face and muttonchop whiskers. He brought Micawber to mind. "Do you have identification?" Lon showed his tin badge, a star within a circle, with the words NATIONAL DETECTIVE POLICE stamped in a bar running across the middle. Less aggressively, Hull said, "Am I under arrest?"

"That's the size of it. Get your coat."

"What's the charge?"

"You'll be told when someone wants to tell you."

"Show me your warrant."

"We don't need one."

"Habeas corpus—"

"Doesn't exist. Eugene, go with him so he doesn't pull anything." Eugene slid past his partner, diverting Lon's attention a moment. Hull bolted between them into the hall. The woman screamed, "Oh, don't."

Lon pivoted, caught Hull's collar, pulled him back. He pounded the gun butt against Hull's right ear. Hull collapsed, breaking his fall by grabbing the stair post. Lon hauled him up, jabbed the gun barrel in his cheek.

"More?" Lon shook the trembling teacher. "You want some more?"

"N-no, I'll go peaceably. Let me stand up. Tell Hortense I'll be all right." Eugene walked to the woman hysterically weeping in the apartment.

Hull stumbled several times on the way out. He was cowed. "Are you taking me to Old Capitol?"

"Carroll annex. They've reserved a cozy apartment for you in solitary." Eugene regarded Lon with dismay. Lon stared him down until he looked away. The boy had a lot to learn about waging war.

* * *

That same week, Corporal Fred Dasher of the 43rd Partisan Ranger Battalion rode into Richmond driving a wagonload of prisoners. The Yanks had been captured by Mosby's men the week before, up in Loudoun County. Two other mounted partisans with rifles rode guarding the wagon's flanks.

Escorting prisoners was the lowest duty a man could be given. Fred had done it a dozen times over the past months. He was resigned. He couldn't expect much better from a commander who had made his feelings plain when Fred reported. Fred remembered the iciness of Mosby's eyes that day. Curiously, he also remembered the finely bound book on Mosby's field desk. *Plutarch's Lives.*

"We have a mutual dislike of one another, Mr. Dasher. But we have a mutual duty, so we'll forgo personal animosity. Stay sober, obey orders, all will be well. Step over the line in any respect and no excuses will serve. You'll be dealt with summarily."

Fred needed no elaboration. At the headquarters camp in Fauquier, a Yankee deserter serving with Mosby had forced himself on the adolescent daughter of a householder with whom the soldier was billeted. Mosby passed sentence personally. A sergeant marched the offender away at pistol point. The man was never seen again.

John Mosby's rangers were a raffish lot of Union deserters, Confederate veterans recovered from wounds, disaffected Marylanders who swam the Potomac to locate the guerilla captain at his headquarters in Fauquier County. Mosby called his men "conglomerates." Fred associated with them only when necessary. They didn't know how to drill or put up a tent like proper soldiers. When they weren't raiding, they slept in quarters provided by the populace and had their meals cooked and served to them. Most had enlisted for plunder. Recently some of them had split $30,000 after selling Yankee goods in Charlottesville. Mosby admitted that greed motivated most of his men. He allowed them to do what they liked between raids so long as no crimes were committed against civilians.

The conglomerates were fine marksmen; they practiced endlessly. As a unit, they had stuck a lot of burrs under enemy saddles. They harried the Orange and Alexandria railroad, derailing locomotives, burning bridges, tearing up crossties and setting them afire with turpentine. The conflagrations melted iron rails nicely. The exploits of Mosby's partisans had spread his name across the Confederacy and earned him promotion to captain, then major.

Fred looked slightly more presentable than most in the battalion. He'd foraged a decent light gray sack coat and sewn on his two stripes when Mosby awarded them as a sop to his former rank. He wore spurs on his knee boots, and a brace of Union Army Colt .44s taken off a dead Yankee during a raid.

He drove the wagon across a guarded bridge to Belle Isle, the small island in the James used intermittently as a prison since the start of the war. At the moment Belle Isle held five or six thousand men, in conical Sibley tents crowded on six acres behind earthworks that served as a deadline. Originally it was thought that Belle Isle's open air would be healthful, but summer heat and winter cold proved that false. Conditions were primitive. Prisoners bathed and drew drinking water from the river, which they also used as a latrine. Belle Isle's young commandant, Lieutenant Bossieux, was a martinet.

Fred concluded his business with Bossieux as quickly as he could, left his subordinate to fend for himself, and retired to a Richmond alehouse. There, he rested his aching left leg on a wooden bench. It was a strange life, he reflected. He served the cause by serving a man he disliked, though he was professional enough to overcome West Point snobbery and recognize Mosby's military skills. He drank when he could and was staying reasonably sober. He paid for a woman's favors when opportunity arose. He scratched his crotch and decided it was time to pay for such favors again, before he rode out of Richmond at sunrise.

Something profound had happened to him in those moments with Hanna Siegel, the strange and pretty girl who had wanted to be a soldier until she discovered the realities of

war. He supposed he'd never see her again, at least not until
the war ended. If he searched for her, he'd probably find her
married or gone from Washington leaving no trace.

He no longer believed the South could win, no matter how
many Mosbys, Stuarts, or Lees it mustered. The North's resources in men and materiel were too overwhelming. And he
understood that all the dangerous dashing about, galloping
through pine forests, jumping creeks and fallen trees while
Yankee bullets whined, could easily result in one of those bullets catching him fatally. It no longer mattered. Feelings were
burned out of him, except guilt, and his yearning for the girl
he had impulsively kissed that rainy night.

"Bring me another," he shouted at the landlord. By the
time Fred finished his fourth tankard he was too tired to hunt
for a whore. He passed the night on the bench, head lolling,
his dreams full of mingled images of Hanna and the young girl
he had murdered.

*   *   *

Margaret found New York no less lonely that she'd imagined,
but far less hostile. Many of the Yankees she met on her excursions to Lord and Taylor's or the A. T. Stewart Marble Dry
Goods Palace were not ogres, but in fact quite agreeable. Further, anti-war sentiment in the city was strong. Editorial gas-
conades in the *Daily News* and *Journal of Commerce*, while
not openly supportive of the Confederacy, flirted so auda-
ciously with that position that she assumed the editors would
face arrest were they in Washington.

If possessions and real estate were the foundations of happiness, Donal's town house on Gramercy Park North was
everything a married woman could want. The town house offered Margaret a spacious bedroom of her own, a sewing
room, library, music room—three entire floors with a servant's floor beneath. A black woman cooked for them, two
other black women, sisters, worked as parlor maids, and an
aging Irishman named Phineas Farley ran the household. All
of them went home at night.

Margaret inhabited the town house like a quiet ghost. Familiar activities palled. Mr. Trollope didn't amuse, and Mr.
Hugo's new doorstop of a novel about a poor man pursued

all his life for stealing bread was simply too big to hold comfortably for long. She resurrected what she remembered of piano lessons and played ballads on the spinet—"Aura Lee," and "Lorena," written in Chicago but long ago adopted as a Southern song. Thoughts of Lon Price in prison were often with her, most intensely when she played the sad songs.

On Independence Day, curiosity took her to lower Broadway to watch the annual parade. It wasn't much of one, she decided, observing from the scanty shade of her parasol. There were a couple of marching bands, several ragtag units of cavalry, and the perennial trio of elderly men portraying the Spirit of '76. New York troops were noticeably missing. Twelve regiments had been rushed to Pennsylvania to join a titanic battle. To judge by the headlines, the outcome did not look favorable for Margaret's side: REBEL ARMY FAILING! THE GREAT PIRATE CONFEDERACY CAVING IN! GENERAL MEADE APPEARS TRIUMPHANT!

She'd never heard of General Meade until late June, when he'd replaced Hooker as the Army of the Potomac's sixth commander. Hooker was banished to Tennessee after failing against Lee at Chancellorsville. That battle cost Lee the services of the mighty Jackson, who died of pneumonia May 10, a consequence of gunshot wounds and amputation. The Union could take no credit; Jackson had been shot accidentally by Confederate pickets.

Donal's connections had secured a pass for her to the Academy of Music on Fourteenth Street, where the governor would address the New York Democratic Association at two o'clock. People stared as Margaret slipped into her seat. A woman alone was assumed to be contemptuous of convention, if not a harlot prowling for customers.

Horatio Seymour, an unimpressive man in his fifties, was serving his second term in Albany. He reiterated his opposition to the Enrollment and Conscription Act. It was unconstitutional, its quotas unfair. He denounced the Republicans and vowed to press the fight against the draft by sending a personal representative to plead with Mr. Stanton for its repeal. This touched off a final, four-minute ovation.

Afterward, it took Margaret ten minutes to flag down a

hansom. Several responded to her signal, but each time, a boorish New Yorker jumped in front of her and leaped inside. The last person who tried was a stout matron. Margaret poked the woman's thigh with her parasol and captured the cab.

Lower Broadway was a clangorous tangle of omnibuses, carriages, carts, livestock, and desperate pedestrians risking their lives to cross from one curb to the other. Walking to your destination was usually faster. In the cab she reread a long letter from Rose in Richmond. An unfamiliar man had brought it to the servant's entrance just before she left for the parade.

The letter was dated May 14, thus had been a long time in some illicit pipeline. Rose had found a London publisher and would soon leave for England to promote her memoir, as well as sympathy for the Confederate cause. Good for her.

Presently the cab delivered Margaret to the green and pleasant enclave of Gramercy Park. As she paid the driver, she saw a slender man alighting from another cab on the park's south side. It was Edwin Booth. Donal had squired her to a performance of Booth's *Hamlet* last month, one of the rare occasions when he took her somewhere in the evening. Donal pleaded a continual press of business at the McKee, Withers offices on Fulton Street. She suspected he spent an equal amount of time in the taverns and music halls and, no doubt, a bordello or two.

Margaret no longer felt guilty about such thoughts. The marriage was a shell, a mistake from which she longed to extricate herself. But on what grounds? She had no evidence of adultery, only suspicion that Donal betrayed her regularly and without remorse. If she did free herself, she'd carry the stigma of divorce forever. What would she gain, other than a soiled reputation and a different kind of loneliness?

Penelope, one of the black maids, greeted her with a conspiratorial whisper. "Gentleman waiting for you in the library, Miz McKee."

"I'm not expecting visitors. Who is it?"

"Said you'd know him. Said he wanted to surprise you."

Hot and perspiring after her long outing, Margaret wanted a bath. She was piqued at the stranger's impertinence. She flung the library doors open and gasped at the sight of dusty black shoes resting on a fine marble table. "Cicero!"

"Hello, sister dear." He removed his feet from the table, laid aside a *Tribune* he'd been scanning, and rose to kiss her cheek. "You're pink as a lobster."

"I've been out in the sun all day. I never expected to see you anywhere near New York. What are you doing here?"

Cicero peered into the hall, closed the doors. "Hoping to have supper with you and Donal, if you'll invite me."

"I doubt Donal will be home. He's away most evenings." Margaret kept her marital problems to herself.

"Pity," Cicero said. "Perhaps next week, then."

"He's sailing for Nassau on Monday. How long do you plan to stay?"

"I'm not certain. I'm visiting a few acquaintances to, shall we say, take the pulse of the city."

She sat beside him, arranged her skirts. "Isn't that terribly risky?"

"Less than you might think. I've visited Chicago, Baltimore, even Toronto, with no difficulty. I travel as a copperhead lawyer from Kentucky."

"Copperhead. I've heard that word a lot lately."

"Copperheads are men in sympathy with us, mostly in the Middle West, but there are some here as well. I understand they wear a copper penny as a badge." He picked up the discarded *Tribune*. Its boldest headline announced THE ENEMY REPULSED AT ALL POINTS! "Does Donal read this rag?"

"Yes, and several others that favor the Republicans. He says to be informed, we needn't agree with the informant."

Cicero's bald pate glistened in the heat, like Margaret's cheeks. Beyond the tall windows, the green of the pocket park faded in the scorching light of late afternoon.

"I passed by the *Tribune* building this morning," he said. "By chance I saw Greeley himself arguing with someone at the entrance. The old poltroon was wearing that white coat you read about. He's one Yankee I'd like to send to the gallows."

Cicero's eyes had a peculiar blankness; almost reptilian, she thought. "You really must tell me why you're here. This is enemy territory after all."

"Strictly speaking, of course it is. But you must be aware of the city's fierce opposition to the war. Governor Seymour barely squeaked through the spring election, but he carried New York and Brooklyn by huge margins. Working folk are in turmoil, especially the Irish. They hate the rich, they hate the Republicans, and most of all they hate the niggers, whom they blame for the draft. It's a volatile situation. It could be exploited."

"Exploited? How?"

He limped to the window. With his back turned he said, "I'm sure I don't know. I was only speculating." His tone had changed; a wall had arisen.

"Cicero." He faced her. "Are you and these acquaintances, as you call them, planning to stir up trouble?" She was more fearful than disapproving. He laughed and pressed his palm to his scarlet waistcoat, feigning shock.

"I? Your gentle brother? How could you think that?"

"May I ask where you're staying?"

"You may, but I won't tell you. Safer for both of us."

His reticence discouraged her from probing further. She diverted the talk to the subject of Lee's desperate gamble to carry the war into the North. Evidently he'd been hurled back in two days of bloody fighting around the little town of Gettysburg, Pennsylvania.

They dined on an excellent light supper of potted chicken and spring vegetables, with a pale rosé wine. Queer and secretive as Cicero was, Margaret enjoyed his company after a long separation. At half-past seven he kissed her decorously, limped down the stone steps, and turned toward Lexington Avenue. His shadow stretched ahead of him, jerking from side to side as he limped out of sight.

Phineas Farley, the houseman, met her in the foyer. "Would it be agreeable if I went home a bit early, ma'am? I don't like to leave my Eileen by herself these nights."

"Certainly, Phineas. Is there trouble in your neighborhood?"

"Gatherings in the street, ma'am. Lots of drinking and rough talk. It's the draft. A gentleman of means will be able to buy a substitute for three hundred dollars, but not the poor. The boyos in the volunteer fire companies are particularly hot about the idea of fighting for the ni—for Africans. I fear worse trouble when the first numbers are drawn next month."

A volatile situation. It could be exploited . . .

"You may be right. By all means, go home."

Upstairs, she undressed and bathed. Fireworks showered the night sky with red, white, and blue lights. The sticky air brought distant music of a brass band. She closed the shutters and settled in bed to struggle on with Victor Hugo. Donal returned sometime after midnight, when she was asleep.

50

July 1863

On Monday after the Fourth, Baker called him in. "Read this."

A DECLARATION OF WAR AGAINST USURPATION AND TYRANNY! The crudely printed handbill damned the draft act and called for *punishment of thieves, Pharisees and despots who defile the temple of our liberty.*

"Where did this come from, Colonel?"

"New York. I have a man inside police headquarters there. The handbills appeared Friday, before the holiday. Enrollment clerks canvassing for names of able-bodied men have been threatened, even beaten and stoned. We suspect a man named John Andrews is fomenting mob action when the names are drawn. Others may be sent from Richmond either to direct him or assist him."

"Who is Andrews?"

"A no-account lawyer from Virginia. He's been in New York four years. I want you to take the train up there. Should violence occur, leave the mobs to the police and find those inciting them. Apprehend them or remove them. Think of it as killing enemy soldiers. You won't be questioned or criticized."

Baker's cold gray gaze, the calm way he authorized murder, shook Lon, not an easy thing to do anymore. "I understand.

By the way, I wrote Mr. Pinkerton and received a reply. He sent half my back pay."

"I'm surprised you got that much."

"He said all the delays and disputes originated in this department."

Baker froze. "I know nothing of that. In New York, you can call on our informant on the force for guidance. However, don't for a moment think of asking for police cooperation. Half the patrolmen are crooks, but they all have to obey rules. You do not."

*   *   *

A hog rooted in the alley behind Willard's Hotel. Noise dinned through the closed kitchen door. Lon stood near the door, smoking. A black man in rags lurched toward them, his eyes glazed by sickness. He held out his hand.

Zach said, "We can't help you. Go to a hospital." The man shambled on. "Got the smallpox, don't he?"

"He has the look. Too many people are sick and wandering like that."

Zach shied a stone at the hog, then wiped his hands on his apron. Lon explained the assignment. "Two pairs of eyes are better than one. You might be able to go places I can't. It's been a long time since you chased rebs."

"Not since the Peninsula. Going to be rebs in New York, you think?"

"I have a feeling. They won't be in uniform but they'll be enemies all the same."

"Like to catch me one or two. 'Course, if I was white, I could fight proper."

"You're a bitter man, Zachariah."

"You be bitter too if you lived in this country in a black skin."

"Would you be happier joining one of the new black regiments?"

"Oh, I know how that works. Colored men don't get the enlistment bounty they pay to white sojers. Get ten dollars less in every pay envelope too. Plus the black man's got to buy his own uniforms and kit. No thanks. I'll go with you. Headwaiter won't like it. Short notice."

"If he objects too strongly, I can arrange for him to think it over in Old Capitol."

Zach shook his head. "Lord, Lord. Where'd you get so fierce all at once?"

"Where do you think? Richmond."

* * *

They arrived by train early Thursday morning, July 9. Even in a city of eight hundred thousand it was hard to find a hotel that would rent a room to a colored man. Finally they were successful at a sailors' rest on Water Street, a block from the South Street piers crowded with coasters and oceangoing steamships. Not far away, in a fine Greek Revival building on Fulton, Margaret's husband had offices. Lon had established that by using a city directory in Washington.

Baker's paid informant, Detective Sean Ruddy, met them in an alley on Murray Street, just west of City Hall Park. Ruddy was an avuncular Irishman with curly white hair and a watermelon-sized belly. His first words to Lon were, "Who's this?"

"Zachariah Chisolm. He works with me."

"Jesus, what next?"

Ruddy gave them a description of John Andrews: six feet tall, red beard, ruby ring on his right hand. Lon wrote the address of the lawyer's office in a notebook.

"Washington suspects other Confederate agents are in town."

"Superintendent Kennedy has the same feeling. We don't know who they are, or where."

"Do the rebs have a hangout? A place where they congregate?"

"I think I told you all I'm going to tell you. The money I'm getting ain't grand. So long."

Lon grabbed Ruddy's wrist, spun him, and twisted his arm at the small of his back. Ruddy's jaw jammed against the brick wall.

"Do you want to rethink that? The alternative is finding yourself on Mr. Stanton's list. People on the list tend to disappear suddenly."

"Ow! Jesus Christ, let me go. I'll tell you." Lon stepped

away. "Try the Roost, corner of Bond Street and the Bowery. They oughta call it rebels' roost." As Ruddy left, he shouted, "You let that dinge wander in an Irish neighborhood, you won't see him again."

* * *

The second-floor office of John Andrews, on Elk Street a block above City Hall, was locked tight. Lon examined a layer of dust at the foot of the door. "No one's been here in a while."

The rest of the day and all of Friday reminded him of the legend of Orpheus descending into hell, only they were searching for spies, not Eurydice. At Sportsmen's Hall on Water Street, a screaming crowd surrounded a walled pit where four huge Norway rats fought a bulldog blind in one eye. They watched the bulldog die. No one knew Andrews.

In nearby bordellos, whores invited them to partake of the wares, even Zach. Some of the ugliest wore the gaudiest clothes, including black net stockings and scarlet boots with little bells attached. One fat girl thought she'd been with a man resembling Andrews but remembered no details.

They trudged on to the gambling dens of Park Row and Vesey Streets, where poor men who could ill afford it squandered their money away on faro and dice. No one knew Andrews.

In the triangular plaza called Paradise Square, streets intersected to form the Five Points, the heart of the city's most vicious slum. A dozen filthy children surrounded Lon and Zach, tugging at their hands, pleading for money. They reminded Lon of Fagin's gang. He emptied his pockets of coins; the children fell on them like the rats on the bulldog. Lon didn't bother to ask about Andrews.

The run-down Bowery, once a fashionable street, was lined with pawnshops and gun shops and concert saloons. The Roost was a shabby workingman's tavern. "White man's place," Zach said. "You go in by yourself."

A Union Jack and a lithographed portrait of George III hung on the stained wall of the tavern, along with a French tricolor and an engraving of Madame Defarge knitting by the guillotine, a Confederate battle flag, and a newspaper artist's heroic rendering of Stonewall Jackson. Rebels' roost indeed. Neither the barkeep nor the few patrons drinking whiskey at eleven in the morning knew John Andrews. Or so they said.

At the Bull's Head, a cattle drovers' hotel on Forty-third Street near Lexington, Lon wanted to buy two buckets of lager beer. He was turned away at the taproom door because of Zach. Lon's sunburned face reddened. Zach calmed him with a hand on his sleeve.

Strolling around in back, near the crowded cattle pens, they saw a man unloading wooden crates from a wagon. He had a furtive air. The boxes held metal cans. Lon whispered, "We'll come back." An hour later, after being jeered by volunteer firemen in black shirts lounging outside a firehouse on West Forty-eighth—"Hey, nigger, sing us a coon song"—they returned to the Bull's Head. Lon used a pick to open the padlocked door at the rear of a storage building. The drayman had delivered four of the wooden boxes. Lon pulled out an unmarked can, pried the lid off with his knife. He held the can out for Zach to sniff.

"Turpentine?"

"Turpentine," Lon said. "Enough to set a hell of a lot of fires."

* * *

Rough men. Sweated shirts, overalls, hobnailed boots. A few women, foulmouthed as the men. Ugly stares at Zach. Under the blazing sun, Third Avenue steamed. Lon estimated the crowd at two hundred.

Nine o'clock by his pocket watch. By standing on the wheel spoke of a dray, he could see into the draft office in a row of four-story brick-and-frame tenements on the east side of Third at Forty-sixth. It was the only draft office ready for business Saturday morning. Three nervous members of the Invalid Corps guarded the doorway. A couple of strong girls could overwhelm them.

One of the provost marshal's men stepped outside. "In accordance with the national conscription law enacted by the Congress, the draft for this Ninth Enrollment District, Twenty-first Ward, shall now commence."

The crowd muttered. A clerk turned the crank of a lottery

drum. Another, blindfolded, reached into the drum for one of the folded slips. He handed it to the man at the door.

"First draftee is William Jones, Twenty-second District, Forty-sixth Street, corner of Tenth. Is he present?"

He wasn't. The crowd responded with catcalls. The marshal retired. The drum revolved. More names were drawn but not announced. A northbound horsecar clanged its bell, unable to move until the spectators grudgingly moved.

Lon was better dressed than most around him. He wore a tan linen suit, yellow bandanna knotted at his open collar, yellow straw hat with a striped silk band. He might have been a prosperous merchant or country doctor and would have gone largely unnoticed but for Zach. Clearly he'd made an error in recruiting his friend. At the appropriate moment he would suggest that Zach catch a train for Washington. He expected Zach would refuse.

About ten o'clock, a slim young man Lon hadn't noticed before started to harangue the crowd. "It's the nigger-worshiping black Republicans brought us to this." The young man wore dark trousers, a soiled white jacket, a smoking hat with an embroidered band. A small round pin with the glint of copper ornamented his lapel.

"What do we do, you're such a smart bastard?" said a toothless woman.

"Organize a protest. Elect leaders. Formulate a plan."

"Form-you-what?" a man shouted. People laughed. The young man smiled to show he was with them.

"Take action. You don't need guns. I've seen pitchforks in stables, pieces of lumber at construction sites, broken paving stones right there in the gutter. Use those." The young man noticed Lon watching him.

Lon nudged a workman who must have bathed in his own sweat. "Who is he?"

"Never seen him before, but ain't he right?"

Lon moved on. No one knew the young man in the smoking hat. Lon observed him for a half hour. Then a remark from Zach distracted him and when he looked again, the young man was gone. Lon had memorized his face.

At noon the marshal in charge announced, "We have our

quota for today. Office closed." He slammed the door. The surly crowd began to disperse.

Lon untied his bandanna and wiped his face. The city faced a long, hot weekend. The groggeries would be open at all hours. He'd keep searching for Andrews, and now the slim young man, until the draft resumed Monday morning.

Zach fell in step beside him, warily glancing to the right and left. Because of Zach's color they were enemies here, and they both knew it.

*   *   *

The sun sat over the rooftops like a yellow boil. The poor left their tenements hoping for a breath of cooler air, but there wasn't any. Lon and Zach continued to hear angry talk. In the late afternoon they split up, Zach heading for the Negro slums while Lon drifted into the Tenth Ward.

His nerves tightened up when he stepped into a saloon on Allen Street. A red-bearded man with a ruby ring on the little finger of his right hand stood on a chair, surrounded by listeners swilling beer.

"There would be no draft but for the war. There'd be no war but for slavery. So who's responsible? Niggers. Every man, woman, and child with a black hide."

One of the listeners said, "Kill them."

John Andrews smiled. "It's a thought. I'll buy a round, gentlemen. Let's talk about Monday."

Lon moved as close as he dared. The men surrounding Andrews kept their voices low. Presently Andrews said, "All right, boys, we'll give them something to remember, won't we?" His cohorts agreed and Andrews sauntered out. Lon counted to ten and followed.

A boy urinating on a wall cursed Lon loudly when he ran by and bumped him. Andrews looked back, spied Lon, plunged into a passage between tenements. Lon ran after him.

The passage was dark as a cavern. It sloped downward, past a tiny backyard where a man in a butcher's apron stirred a steaming kettle of greasy brown soup. Farther along, a family of five crouched in the dirt, using their hands to eat from a bucket. Lon kept running, between buildings so close together that they blocked out all sunlight.

He lost Andrews in the mazy slum. When Lon regained the open streets, the sun was fat and red in the west. He trudged to City Hall Park. There he found Zach walking back and forth, not daring to sit on the benches.

"I had Andrews but he got away. He's stirring up a fight."

"Don't seem to be much going on with the colored except the usual Saturday things. They're skittish, though. Talked to one lady at her washtub, she said all hell's gonna pop Monday and colored folk better beware."

"There's something I've got to do now, Zach."

"I know." Lon had shared his plans on the trip north.

"I'll see you at the hotel. Watch yourself."

"Oh, sure," Zach sighed, as if he knew caution wouldn't do much good if he chanced to take the wrong street and meet the wrong white men. A patrolman in a frock coat sauntered toward him, swinging the famous weapon of the Metropolitan Police, a locustwood club. Zach moved on, a lonely figure casting a long shadow in the red twilight. Lon was on his way to Gramercy Park.

51

July 1863

He knocked four times; waited nearly five minutes on the stone stoop. At last a firefly glimmer appeared in the fanlight. A bolt rattled. The door opened partway. Margaret raised a lamp to see him, a pepperbox pistol steady in her other hand. The dark cascade of her hair shimmered in the light. He whipped off his straw hat so she could see his face.

"Oh my God."

"Hello, Margaret. Please let me in." A patrolman had appeared on Lexington. He gazed around the park, bull's-eye lantern swinging. She stepped back. She wore a sand-colored dressing gown, silk or some other thin material. The lace hem of an undergarment touched her bare ankles. Lon pushed the door shut behind him.

The lamp held them in a caul of yellow. Margaret managed a nervous smile. "I don't ordinarily receive gentlemen callers at night."

"I should imagine not."

"Donal's in Nassau for ten days."

"I know. I made sure."

"How? Oh, but it's rude of me to keep you standing. Put your hat on the table. Come this way."

In the parlor she set the lamp down and closed the draperies on the windows overlooking the park. She seemed less nervous, but wouldn't look at him directly. Lon perched on a divan, devastated by her beauty, and his feelings for her, a passion suppressed for months. She sat on the other end of the divan with a good distance between them.

"How did you find out Donal was away?"

"I'm a detective. A lot of detective work is just common sense and plodding. I looked up the McKee, Withers office in a city directory. I also found this address listed with Donal's name. I shadowed your houseman on his way home this evening. He stopped at a tavern. I bought him a whiskey. After two, he was talkative. I never expected you'd be here by yourself. I only wanted to know if you were safe down in Richmond."

"We left Richmond in December. We spent Christmas in Savannah."

"I escaped in March."

"I couldn't have known."

"Not even if you'd been there," he agreed. "They don't advertise escapes unless they're so sensational they can't be hushed up. I literally walked out of Castle Thunder. Well, stumbled. I had help I can't tell you about."

"Yes, we're still on opposite sides, aren't we?"

"It won't last much longer. Not after Gettysburg." He clasped her hands between his. Her skin was chilly. Her hair seemed to breathe out a scent of vanilla. "Are you all right, Margaret? Are you happy?"

"Happy? I've never been more wretched. I made a mistake marrying Donal. In so many ways. I think he wanted me"—

hesitation—"physically for a while, but the moment he got what he wanted, he began to lose interest. Now I'm a fixture, like a kitchen stove. That's Donal's idea of a wife. He feels no obligation to be faithful, I might add. I suspected most of that before I married him. I have no one but myself to blame, unless it's that damned Baker, who kept me in prison."

The stillness of the dark house wrapped them in a compelling intimacy. He felt heat in his face as he said, "If you feel that way about Donal, leave him."

"God, yes, I would, but for one thing. I took vows. It would be dishonorable to break them."

He slid close to her. Their knees touched. Under the silk gown her nipples were visible. "McKee's no proper husband. You just said so. I love you. I've been in love with you forever."

"Lon, please."

"It's true. Nothing will change that."

"The war—"

"Forget the war."

"How can we? There's such a huge gulf. So much hatred on both sides."

"Not between us."

"Do you really think we could overcome who we are, and what's happened to us?"

"It may not be easy but we can do it. Come away with me, as soon as we can arrange it."

"How long will you be in New York? Are you on a case?"

"Yes. One draft office started drawing names today. They'll all be open on Monday. Washington's afraid there may be disturbances, perhaps stirred up by Confederates. I was sent here to do whatever I could to stop it."

"So we're still fighting the war. Except that I've done a pathetic job of avenging my father."

"Maybe you were never cut out for that. Maybe you should leave it to someone else." On the verge of mentioning her brother, he pulled back. He couldn't tell her what Miller had done to him in prison. Instead, he said, "Back in Ohio, my father was a minister. He preached that an eye for an eye leaves two people blind." Lon realized it was a lesson he'd chosen to overlook of late.

She sighed. "Perhaps you're right. Sometimes I think I don't know myself, or where I'm going in this world."

"You're going with me. You're going to pack and leave this house and let me take you to Washington. Do you still have your place there?"

"Oh, yes. I've thought of selling it but things have moved too fast. I've had no time."

"When we get to Washington, we'll decide what to do next. The first step is to leave your husband."

"I wish I had the courage."

"You do, I know it." He took hold of her shoulders. Her eyes were huge, dark, a little frightened. He leaned toward her. She didn't withdraw or resist. He kissed her. For a moment she didn't respond. Then, suddenly, her arms flew around his neck.

He caressed her breasts. She murmured, "Oh God, oh God." His hand rested on her knee. He lifted the silk gown and the garment beneath. She opened her lips.

Finally the embrace ended with both of them laughing as they gulped air. Margaret leaned back, her hair disarrayed, her cheeks reddened. She loosened the satin strings that tied the collar of her gown. She opened the gown and let it fall away from deep cleavage. Her undergarment didn't reach above the waist.

"Here?" he said.

"The bed would be better."

She left the lamp burning in the parlor and led him upward through the dark. They struggled out of their clothes, he taking longer, sitting beside her on the bed. They kissed and caressed as he dropped his shoes, his trousers, his shirt. The closed-up house was hot as a furnace.

Their arms and legs tangled. She kissed with wild ardor, stroking his hair, his naked shoulders, whispering, "I've wanted this so long. You don't know how much." Then they were together, her legs clasping him, her back arching under him, her nipples crushing up beneath him, hard as little stones. It hardly seemed a moment until something in both of them released in one great, long convulsion. Margaret cried out, fell back, gasping.

"I love you, Lon. Oh, heaven, I do. It's sinful, it's against all reason, but I can't help it."

"I love you, Margaret. Now and always."

"Hold me. Kiss me. I want you again."

Damp hair hung on his forehead. A trickle of sweat tickled his nose. "In a little while," he said, and kissed her with consuming tenderness.

*   *   *

Much later, three in the morning, after they'd enjoyed each other a second time, they lay in each other's arms listening to a distant bell. She murmured, "What's that?"

"Fire bell. It's a long way off." But it reminded him of Monday morning.

After a silence she said, "I must tell you something. My brother's in the city."

"Your brother Cicero?"

"Yes, from Richmond. He doesn't know you, I asked him once." *Lying bastard,* he thought.

"You spoke of Confederate agents," Margaret went on. "He may be one of them."

Castle Thunder rose up in his imagination. Cridge, Miller, the beatings. How could he tell her? Someday perhaps he could, but not now. Still, he had his job. "Where is he? A hotel?"

"He wouldn't say."

"Then why tell me?"

"Because if everything's going to be open between us—if we're going to be close—I can't have secrets."

He believed her. It relieved him, yet it made things more difficult, because he had secrets of his own. In a level voice he said, "Well, since we don't know where he is, we can't worry about him. If there's no serious trouble on Monday, I'll come for you Monday night, about the same time. If something keeps me away, I'll be here Tuesday night. But I promise I'll come."

"I'll be waiting." She kissed him.

He left in turmoil. He wished she hadn't said what she had about her brother. Now he had to search for Miller; apprehend him if possible.

Ridiculous idea. With eight hundred thousand people to hide him, he'd never be found.

But Miller was identifiable; he stood out. Suppose Lon did catch him. Could he hold back from doing what he swore to do to Miller after Richmond? It would be hard to keep from venting his rage.

He would do it somehow. He would discharge his duty, turn Miller over to his superiors unharmed, and at the same time take Margaret away to a new life.

Somehow.

52

July 1863

Lon never cut himself shaving or trimming his beard. Sunday morning his hand slipped and the razor gashed his cheek. He bled heavily. He wondered if it was a sign.

He asked Zach to leave the city.

"No, sir. I've seen the bad looks, but I can't run off like some whipped hound. I got to strike a blow."

In the pitiless heat the two roamed the east and west sides, finding widespread unrest, but nothing immediately threatening. They drifted back to the Bowery about four. Zach stayed outside the Roost while Lon went in.

A drunk lay in the sawdust and his own vomit. A sad-eyed boy with a huge cranium listlessly dabbed at the mess with a slops rag. At the bar Lon paid for a whiskey. A new barkeep was on duty. Lon laid three more fifty-cent shinplasters on the scarred wood. The barkeep raised an eyebrow. Lon told him what he wanted. The shinplasters disappeared.

"Yeah, he come by here. Noon or so. Bald as an egg. Tilts to port when he walks, ain't that him?"

"It is. Did he give his name?" The barkeep shook his head. "Is he staying around here?"

"Couldn't say. He spoke awhile to some of my regulars. Fired 'em up pretty good. They went off to plan things for tomorrow."

"Plan what?"

The barkeep eyed the spot where the shinplasters had been. Lon laid out three more.

"Said there'd be a coon hunt. They'd catch coons and roast 'em."

"What else?"

"I had to wait on trade, y'unnerstand. I didn't hear everything. They talked about Thoid Avenue. I heard the word *armory* a few times, and something about steam."

The New York State Armory, Second Avenue at Twenty-first. The Union Steam Works nearby. Guns. Manufactured and stored in both locations. Baker had given him a list. He handed a coin to the poor idiot boy and walked out.

* * *

Hell boiled over in New York that hot, overcast Monday.

Lon asked Zach to cover the black slums, looking for rebs they'd already identified—Andrews, and the slim young man. Lon mentioned Cicero Miller again, on the remote chance that Zach might happen on to him. "Meet me in City Hall Park around six o'clock."

At half-past eight, pistol in his pocket, Lon stationed himself on the corner of Forty-sixth and Third, across from the draft office. It opened at nine, but the provost's men didn't immediately draw names, as if they expected trouble. About ten-thirty, minutes after the first name was pulled from the drum, Lon heard a low roar, like an ocean surge. Behind the shimmers of heat to the north, men and women ran into Third Avenue from Forty-seventh. Lon estimated a hundred. They kept coming; he estimated three or four hundred. They filled the street. Far too many people to have gathered spontaneously.

They waved placards: NO DRAFT! They brandished sticks, chains, rocks, cleavers. Some shinnied up telegraph poles and cut the wires with axes. The telegraph connected Mulberry Street with thirty-two police precincts. A mob didn't attack communications without being prompted.

People swarmed around a stalled horsecar, dragged passengers off, punched and kicked them. Two rioters threw an older woman onto the horsecar steps. One held her while the other lifted her skirts and unbuttoned his fly.

Rioters piled up in front of the draft office. Others kept moving south. Lon recognized black shirts and leather fire helmets from the Forty-eighth Street firehouse. More and more people poured out of Forty-seventh; a thousand or more.

Women shouted obscenities. Men shouted, "Kill the rich!" The mob focused its rage on some sixty precinct police who came charging into them swinging locust clubs. The police clubbed men, women, youngsters, anyone who challenged them. It was a losing fight. If one rioter fell, four replaced him. Desperately outnumbered, some of the police fled. Those remaining hammered on the draft office door, and when it opened, rushed inside. Rioters followed, reappearing to shout, "They ran out the back, goddam cowards." The mob howled.

"*Torch it!*"

"*Kill the rich!*"

"*Hang the niggers!*"

"*No draft, no draft!*"

Lon saw metal cans and bottles passed forward into the office. He'd seen the cans before. Someone tossed a match. A fireball erupted from the doorway. A man standing too near caught fire and ran around like a decapitated chicken. People laughed and let him burn.

Two women attacked a lame soldier with iron pipes. The boy's head broke like a melon. Third Avenue was a heaving sea of humanity. Fifty Invalid Corps soldiers, armed, appeared in Forty-sixth Street. Some were tough and sturdy, others pallid, not yet recovered. Their lieutenant ordered the mob to retreat. Men and women charged him. The soldiers fired into the crowd, to the sound of hideous screaming. Rioters fell. Others trampled over them, attacking and scattering the soldiers. The black-shirted firemen flailed their belts like whips, splitting faces open, putting out eyes with the brass buckles.

A rioter shoved his fist in Lon's face. "Why aren't you fighting? Kill the rich!" Lon screamed back, "Kill them all!" and pumped his fist in the air. Satisfied, the rioter went on.

Flames ate through the walls of the enrollment office, and upward to tenement rooms. Floors gave way; walls collapsed in torrents of sparks. Fire bells clanged in the cross streets, but horses and equipment couldn't pass the human barrier, nor were the firemen especially game to try.

In the two hours that followed, the mob divided many times. Roving bands in the Forties and down into the Thirties tore up tracks of the New Haven railroad at Fourth Avenue, broke into stores, carried off anything useful or desirable and set fire to the rest. Lon guessed the liquid in the incendiary bottles to be one of several concoctions called Greek fire.

Heavy clouds appeared at noon, threatening rain. Smoke from burning buildings added a second cloud layer and dropped particles of soot in Lon's hair. He roamed with his gun in his pocket, appalled, angry, guilty because one man couldn't hope to stop the destruction. Nor was he supposed to try.

Every few minutes rumors flew through the crowd. "They killed John Kennedy."

"Dirty sod was coming up here by himself to stop us."

"Hurrah, Superintendent Kennedy's dead!"

The head of the police force killed? Disorder was becoming chaos.

About two o'clock, Lon walked through an aimless crowd on Third Avenue, amid wreckage of carriages, drays, carts, and overturned trolleys. Someone shouted, "The armory, the armory." Lon spotted the embroidered smoking cap of the slim young man he'd seen on Saturday. "Let's take the armory. Weapons for everybody!" Energized again, rioters surged into the cross streets, flowing toward Second Avenue.

Lon shouldered past the slower ones. When he couldn't force his way through, he showed the Colt. A burly man wearing an eyepatch stuck the point of a knife in Lon's throat; reached for the gun. "Mine." Lon shot him in the leg.

People screamed, backed away from the wounded man. Lon had a clear path into the avenue. The slim young man saw him, started to run. The tongue of a pushcart tripped him. He sprawled on the wooden sidewalk on the avenue's near side. Lon closed the gap.

The smoking cap fell off as the slim young man sat up, pulled a derringer from his coat. Lon fired one shot to the chest, the second in the forehead. The slim young man fell sideways, out of the game.

For blocks around, stores and tenements blazed. Smoke thickened beneath the storm clouds. Now and then a phalanx of police in frock coats appeared to make another charge. Each time a few rioters fell but the police always retreated.

The mob stormed south to Twenty-first, to a five-story wooden building with a signboard reading MARSTON & CO. Lon's list said Marston manufactured carbines on the two lower floors, stored them in a third-floor drill hall along with older muskets, bayonets, and ammunition. The list also said Mayor George Opdyke was a silent partner in Marston.

The mob broke down the doors and pushed inside as another hundred police attacked with clubs. A furious melee of brass knuckles, pitchforks, bricks, and bottles ensued. Rioters choked the armory door. Some reached the third floor, kicked out window lights, threw down carbines, muskets, and bayonets.

Then someone inside set the place afire. The old building burned like paper. Flames engulfed the stairs and reached the third floor in two minutes. Trapped rioters jumped screaming from the broken windows. Those on the first floor kicked and hit and stomped their comrades to escape. A double line of coppers waited outside, beating the rioters savagely, dropping them in bloody heaps. Lon was stupefied; this wasn't warfare, it was mass insanity.

He started south and immediately ran into a slum gang moving north. "Look out, look out, the Bowery B'hoys are comin'!" Before Lon could avoid it the gang rolled over him, throwing him to the ground, kicking him, pelting him with stones. Then they rushed on, chanting, "Bowery B'hoys rule, Bowery B'hoys rule." Lon struggled up, nauseous with pain. The reopened razor gash bled all over his tan linen suit, already a patchwork of rips and stains.

Slipping through alleys, hiding out or detouring to avoid other gangs, he traveled south through a wasteland of looted stores, broken glass, burning vehicles, wounded people sitting or lying on curbstones, others watching from rooftops, black carrion against the ominous sky. A hundred people marching north sang, "We'll hang old Greeley from a sour apple tree."

He saw evidence of mob violence all the way to City Hall Park, which he reached at five-thirty. For an hour he wandered past benches hacked into kindling, small cannon set up to defend City Hall, temporary barracks with smashed windows. The fine municipal fountain had been knocked to pieces. Water gushed from its central pipe and formed a small lake. Where was Zach?

As if summoned by Lon's fear, Zach's head rose up behind an overturned phaeton. In his belt he carried a dirk and a policeman's club.

"You awright, 'Lonzo? You a sight."

"You're not much better." Zach's sleeves were in tatters, his curly hair powdered with brick dust. His left eye was almost hidden by a swollen lid.

"Spot anyone we know?"

Zach shook his head. "Ran into some of them coon hunters. Got away, though. God's mercy, 'Lonzo, I never seen nothin' like this. Over by the East River they burned a bunch of colored shanties. And did you hear they burned a Negro orphan asylum uptown? Everyone got out but one tiny little girl, they killed her. I got that from a policeman. He said people almost killed the head man on the force."

"Superintendent Kennedy."

"He's in a hospital, Bell-something. Stab wounds all over him. What do we do now?"

"Keep looking for the men responsible. Remember the one in the smoking hat? He's dead."

"You do it?"

"Yes. Are you game to go back to that place on the Bowery?"

"Why not? Can't be more scared than I am a'ready."

A fiery haze spread over the city. Dusk came early because of the clouds and smoke. Moving cautiously, hands never far from their weapons, they passed through looted streets whose gas lamps had been shot to pieces. They turned a corner and saw an old Negro, fat and white-haired, hanging by his neck from a rope tied to a lamppost. Pinned to his trousers was a placard: NO DRAFT! Zach cursed.

The Bowery was relatively calm. Saloons were brightly lit and busy. Lon bought two roasted yams from a vendor brave enough to keep his cart on the street. Fire bells rang incessantly; guns racketed in the distance. Lon peered in the plate-glass window of the Roost. The saloon was packed, men drinking and laughing as if it were a holiday. A shiver ran down his spine. Sometimes the cards came up all aces.

"He's in there. Eating the free lunch and celebrating."

Puzzled, Zach cocked his head.

"Miller. This time we'll get him."

53

July 1863

Lon reloaded the Colt's empty chambers. He spoke briefly with Zach, who trotted off down Bond Street. When his watch told him three minutes had gone by, he curled his hand around the gun in his pocket and stepped to the closed door of the Roost. Its elaborate window, leaded glass, distorted the interior, splintering and duplicating images. Two smiling Cicero Millers raised two beer steins and drank with two mouths. Lon figured the crowd of men at forty to fifty.

He entered quickly and quietly, leaving footprints in the sawdust. He went unnoticed until he was at Miller's elbow. In the middle of a sentence, Miller felt himself pressed. He turned, scowling.

"Hello, Miller. Step over to one of those tables and we'll have a little talk."

Miller saw the bulge of the gun; Lon's position hid it from the others. One of them said, "Hey, pal, who's he?"

Miller's brow glistened with sweat. "An old friend." He dragged his foot through the sawdust, to an empty table. His smile was false and ugly. "How the hell did you find me? Did my sister—?"

"Your sister had no part in this. Wherever she is," he added, hoping to protect her. "We'll walk out of here together. If you so much as twitch, I'll put a bullet in you. I wouldn't mind." It was more bluff than certainty; he had no intention of killing Margaret's brother now.

"All right, all right," Miller said. "Let me put this beer down."

Lon nodded, aware of grumblings at the bar. In another moment the men might react. Miller whipped his arm up and threw the beer in Lon's face.

Lon sputtered, blinded. Miller kicked him in the crotch, twice. "This man's a damn police spy."

Half a dozen patrons rushed Lon. Miller darted behind them. Lon staggered against the table, in excruciating pain. As the first man reached him he yanked out the pistol and cocked it.

The gun cowed them long enough for him to slip past. Miller had fled to the back, through a dingy hall. The outside door slammed. Lon heard a shot. He tore the door open; saw Zach leaning against a board fence across the alley. Blood smeared Zach's left trouser leg above the knee. At the south end of the block Miller turned west, out of sight.

"Let me see." Lon squatted to look at the wound. The bloody hole in Zach's pants looked black in the red light from the sky. Fires were burning from the Hudson to the East River.

"Ain't bad, a scrape. Don't lose that man."

"He can't go fast. We've got to tie this up. God, Zach, I'm sorry."

Zach tore long strips from his ragged sleeve. He folded one into a pad, let Lon wrap the other around his leg and knot it on top of the pad. "That's plenty good enough. Don't let him get away."

Lon dashed to the end of the alley. Two blocks west on Bleecker Street, Miller scuttled along like a frightened crab, making fair speed in spite of his limp. Lon ran after him, Zach gamely following.

The armies of the night were marching. As Lon and Zach ran through intersections, they glimpsed Irish gangs hurling bricks through windows, setting bonfires in the gutters, chasing unlucky pedestrians. Gunfire crackled. The red sky created a kind of eerie daylight.

They crossed Broadway, another devastated street. An

abandoned horsecar smoldered, little more than a black skeleton. Broken glass lay everywhere, glittering like rubies. A black man pushing a wheelbarrow piled with household goods struggled past them, three black tots trailing along. "Hurry up, hurry up, we got to get to City Hall. Be safe there."

Zach hobbled as badly as their quarry, but he kept up. He pointed to Miller's retreating figure. "That man don't know where he's going. Those are colored streets, I was up and down 'em yesterday."

Running, Lon had fragmented impressions of pathetic shacks already trashed and looted, tiny gardens destroyed, clothes and cookware thrown in the dirt. A one-story colored grocery at Thompson and Bleecker was afire. A block ahead, a few steps past Sullivan, Miller threw another look backward. He checked his run and set himself in the middle of the street with his pistol. Lon shoved Zach aside needlessly; the bullet fell short. Miller ran another half block to MacDougal and into a corner tenement with smoke drifting from it. Zach said, "Why'n hell did he go in a building on fire?"

"Maybe he thinks the smoke will hide him. Maybe he's scared and not thinking at all."

Under a darkened gas lamp near the tenement, Lon assessed the situation. The three-story building looked deserted. Smoke billowed from first-floor windows; in one he saw a fitful glow of flame. "Same plan as before. I'll go in. You watch the back in case he tries to slip out."

"You be careful in there." Zach limped into a narrow passage between the tenement and a dilapidated cottage.

Lon's palms were slick with sweat. His chest ached from the pursuit. Pistol in hand, he crept into the building.

Bitter smoke stung his eyes and nose. In a room to his left, the wood floor smoldered. He stole toward a pitch-black stairway at the rear. A sound warned him; he slammed himself against the wall as Miller shot at him. He fired back, aiming low to wound, not kill.

Miller kicked and beat on a back door; swore a blistering oath. He couldn't open the door.

"Give it up, Miller. I've got you."

Irregular thumping on the stair said Miller was fleeing to

the second floor. Smoke thickened. The door of a room at the first-floor rear crumbled suddenly as fire ate through, illuminating scabrous walls and the stair with most of its balusters broken or missing. Why was the damn fool going up? To jump from a window?

As Lon climbed, the stair swayed and threatened to buckle. Miller fired again. Lon replied with two shots, then heard Miller's foot scraping, moving toward the front of the building.

The floor gave off ferocious heat. Fire gleamed between the ill-fitting boards. One snapped under Lon's weight. His leg went down through the hole. He caught the newel post of the stair to the third floor, pulled himself up and out. He slapped out embers burning holes in his trousers. The building was noisy with the roar and snap of the fire. Lon couldn't hear Miller moving any longer.

He edged forward. The hall grew lighter when another piece of the floor burned and fell. The glare revealed two closed doors at the front. Lon pushed the left one. Barred or blocked, it wouldn't move. He ran across the hall, tested the other door. Open.

He stepped back and kicked it. He jumped aside as Miller fired. In the black room Miller was a dim silhouette against an open window lit by the fiery sky.

Lon shot too late; Miller crouched down, hidden by the dark. Lon fired twice more. When he pulled the trigger again, the hammer fell on an empty chamber. He shoved his hand in his pocket, then remembered. No more ammunition.

He slid around the edge of the door. "You son of a bitch, where are you?"

Miller moved slightly; for a moment his skull shone like a billiard ball. His gun came up. Lon dropped to his knees and rolled sideways. Miller fired. As the reverberations died, he heard the same sound he'd heard from his own empty gun.

He stood up; wiped his hands on his jacket. His eyes were adjusting to the firelit darkness. "I see you in the corner. It's all over, Miller. I'll take you back to Washington and there'll be one less reb setting fires and stirring up—"

Miller threw his pistol. Lon dodged to the left. The floor broke under him. This time he found nothing to grab. He dropped into billowing smoke.

He landed on his side, dazed but able to roll away from the flames engulfing half the room. He glimpsed an open side window directly below the one Miller wanted to jump from. He crawled toward it, holding his breath under the smoke layer. Half of the floor above collapsed. Miller screamed as it broke away from the wall and tilted down beneath him. He fell into the flames. Lon reached the window and dove through.

His head thumped hard ground. He blinked and coughed violently as he struggled to his feet. A sheet of flame hid the room's interior. He thought he heard Miller scream again but couldn't be sure.

He backed away from the heat as flames licked from third-floor windows. Miller was gone, killed not by one of Lon's bullets but by his own panic. Could he ever explain it to Margaret? His chance with her might have survived Miller's incarceration, but how could it survive his death?

A section of burning wall buckled outward. Lon leaped away and caromed off the broken picket fence of the cottage next door. From MacDougal Street came a confusion of shouts:

"We got you, nigger."

"Where's the rope?"

"Yella bastards—" Something muffled the rest of Zach's outcry. Lon's heart pounded as he ran toward the commotion.

54

July 1863

Zach lay supine in the street. Five white men surrounded him. Ordinary men, plainly, even shabbily, dressed. One had a wall-eye, another a sagging paunch, a third a ragged white beard, a fourth a receding chin. Lon saw two open clasp knives, a pair of wooden clubs, and a slungshot, a New York street weapon consisting of a cord tied to a small leather bag of lead pellets.

Five men; not evil looking, or even very formidable, but transformed by the license of rioting into something bigger than themselves. Lon saw it in their faces. They'd torn off Zach's leg bandage and reopened his wound. He'd taken a blow on the forehead; blood ran down the right side of his face. He looked dazed.

The weak-chinned man, no more than twenty, grinned at Lon. "Join in, friend. We caught this buck in the alley back there."

"Bunce is huntin' for rope," said the man with the slung-shot, Walleye; he was the oldest of the five. "Seen a hardware with some goods left in it a few blocks back."

The first man said, "Me brother soldiered in the Eighty-eighth New York, the Irish Brigade. Climbed up Marye's Heights at Fredericksburg. Wouldn't be dead wasn't for the goddamned niggers."

Walleye said, "Soon as Bunce gets back, we'll show this boy how we treat upstart colored."

A line of sweat ran down Lon's cheek. He pulled out the revolver. "I don't think so."

"What are you, a copper?" the paunchy man said.

"Just somebody who doesn't want to see this kind of thing."

The men eyed one another. They were five, Lon only one. They had the numbers but he had a pistol. Aware of something happening, Zach hoisted himself on his elbow. The bearded man kicked dirt in his face. Lon drew the hammer back.

"Don't do that again. Stand away from him."

Walleye said, "Lad, be reasonable. You're a white man, we're white men, what do you care about some coon who's out to take a white man's job and rape his sister?"

Behind Lon, to the north, a new voice called out, "I've got the rope, boys." One of the men threw his wooden club suddenly. Lon ducked; the club sailed by.

Walleye stuck his fists on his hips. "Tyrone, you took a hell of a chance doing that. He could have plugged you. He didn't, though, did he? Want to know what I think? I think that pistol's empty. He's bluffing us with a goddam empty gun."

Smirking and nudging one another, they shuffled toward Lon, Walleye in the lead. Walleye swung the shot-loaded bag against his leg, *bump* and *bump*. The scene was brilliantly lit; the tenement had crumbled into a huge bed of embers. Lon saw a police wagon passing on Broadway, tiny as a Christmas toy. No help there.

"Take him," Walleye growled. The unseen Bunce ran up behind Lon and held him so Walleye's slungshot cracked on Lon's skull, nearly knocking him out. The others swarmed over him. Lon smacked a forehead with the pistol before they pulled it from his hand. He kicked testicles as Miller had, enraging the man he injured. "You nigger lover!" A splinter of honed steel flashed red in front of his eyes. The man drove the clasp knife into Lon's left leg, jerked it out.

Someone else's knife slashed his coat and shirt and scraped the ribs beneath. Lon's legs dissolved to water. The fiery night darkened as he fell. The bearded man booted his side where the knife had cut; Lon felt warm blood.

"Don't knock him out." That was Walleye. Lon heard him through a rushing noise in his head. "Tyrone, you and Miles roll him on his front. Pull his head up. Slap him if you got to. I want him to see this. Bunce, fix the noose."

"Oughtn't we kill him? He's a witness," the paunchy one said.

Walleye pulled a pint of whiskey from his pants, uncorked it, and took a swallow. He passed the bottle. "Witness to what? Police won't never come after us for killing niggers. Bunce, for Jesus' sake hurry up, tie that rope." Forked lightning split the sky. A heavy thunderclap followed.

Someone sat on Lon's back, yanked his ears to raise his head. Waves of sickness, weakness, surged through him. The white men lifted Zach, smacked the back of his head till he bent forward to receive the noose. They walked him to the lamppost, tossed the rope over, missed twice, and succeeded on the third try. The five gathered around the rope while the extra man kept Lon's head up.

"Is he lookin', Felix?"

"He's lookin'," said the man on Lon's back.

"Then here we go, boys, on my count of three. All together, one, two, three—*heave. Heave.*"

They raised Zach six inches. He made choking sounds. His feet kicked the air as they hoisted him another three inches. The bearded man tied the rope around the post and they stepped away to dust off their hands and admire their work: one free Negro, dangling in the noose like a skinny doll.

"He's dead, boys, I heard his neck crack," Walleye said with an air of good cheer. "One less dinge to befoul our fair city." After the next burst of lightning, the wind picked up sharply. Fat raindrops pattered the street.

The bearded man said, "Riley, you'll have to go see the priest, you've a lot to confess now."

Walleye laughed. "Hell I do. 'Tain't any sin to kill vermin. Come on, let's look for more."

The man got off Lon's back. Lon's head fell nose-first into the dirt. Arm in arm, the six strolled away, harmonizing a song about the dear old sod of Ireland. Zach's body turned in the hot wind.

The sky opened, releasing a deluge. In a minute, rivers of rain washed mud against Lon's face. A lightning flash whitened the world. The earth rocked. He hurt fiercely. *I'm going to die here like Zach,* he thought, sinking into darkness.

*   *   *

The ferocious thunderstorm blew itself out in an hour and didn't extinguish that many fires. The air turned hot and humid again. On Gramercy Park North, Margaret waited until half past two and then climbed the stairs to her bedroom.

She couldn't fall asleep with all the fire bells ringing, and the sky red. Thoughts of Lon chased through her head. He'd come tomorrow night. Tomorrow night he'd be there. A single portmanteau held the things she wanted to take with her: a few favorite possessions and items of clothing from before her marriage. Donal could have the rest, everything he'd bought her. He could sell them, burn them, or consign them to hell for all she cared.

Next morning, the two black sisters failed to appear, as did the cook. Phineas Farley arrived late, stricken and shaken. Although the thunderstorm had driven people inside and temporarily halted the rioting, scores were injured, an untold number were dead, and Negro men, women, and children feared for their lives. "Terrible, terrible," Phineas kept saying.

He had a copy of the *Tribune.* Margaret read Greeley's editorial.

*Foul forces have been at work to foment an uprising that
cannot be blamed on spontaneous public wrath. No
thinking person can doubt that the rioters have acted
under leaders who have carefully instructed them and
elaborated their plans for civic disorder, pillage, and
murder.*

Where was Cicero? What had happened to Lon? As the
day passed, her fears and anxieties worsened. By evening,
when Phineas bid her a reluctant good-bye to go home and
protect his Eileen, she was pacing the downstairs, sweaty in
her heavy traveling dress, unable to eat, unable to rest, unable
to keep away from the parlor windows where she saw
rooftops once again silhouetted against red skies.

A neighbor, an elderly gentleman retired from a brokerage
in Exchange Place downtown, looked in at half past seven to
be certain she was all right. He knew she was alone; would she
care to spend the night with him and his wife? They had extra
room. No, she said, she'd be fine, here in respectable
Gramercy Park she feared nothing. It was a pathetic lie.

"I wish you would reconsider, Mrs. McKee. Mobs have
been seen all over the precinct."

Margaret shook her head. "I'll stay. It's important that I
do."

The old gentleman briefly described some of the day's horrific events: a mob attack on the Union Steam Works where
four thousand carbines were stored; soldiers of the Eleventh
New York Volunteers confronting rioters on Thirty-fifth
Street with two small fieldpieces that fired grapeshot and canister into the crowd; barricades of wrecked wagons, carts,
fallen telegraph poles, tangled wire, in Ninth Avenue; Governor Seymour back in the city, speaking from the steps of the
Army's temporary headquarters, the St. Nicholas Hotel, declaring a state of insurrection, ordering rioters to cease and
desist, but still promising that the draft would end.

There was more. Soldiers fresh from the ordeal of Gettysburg were being rushed back to put down the rebellion. Hapless Negroes were being shot or hung from streetlamps
without cause. Ladies of the evening who happened to be colored were dragged from their establishments and stabbed to

death. The old gentleman didn't say, "Terrible, terrible," but his head shaking and hand wringing testified to a similar opinion. An hour after he left, a platoon of police marched in from Twentieth Street and stationed themselves around the park.

On a green marble table in the foyer, a sealed vellum envelope drew Margaret's eye more than once. Her farewell note to Donal; her statement that she was leaving him for another man.

At dawn, sleepless and still dressed, she carried the envelope to her writing desk. A smell of dampness and smoke soured the house. She felt a perfect fool for the hope and joy she'd allowed herself to experience since Saturday.

She opened the envelope, tore up the note. She wrote another while silent tears ran down her cheeks. She didn't know whether Lon was dead or alive, but she knew he wouldn't be coming for her. Not tonight. Nor ever.

Part Five

CONSPIRACY

55

November 1863–January 1864

For some weeks after she fled New York, Margaret had feared that Donal would be enraged by the note saying she'd no longer live with him and would pursue her. She felt a pang of disappointment when he didn't. Later she reflected that his disinterest confirmed the failure of the marriage.

She went first to Baltimore. She found the Miller town house dusty and abandoned. White cloths shrouded the furniture. A neighbor said Simms had left to cook for Union troops garrisoned in the city. She put the place in the hands of a real estate agent, withdrew money from three bank accounts, and traveled on to Washington.

The city's pursuit of pleasure was even more frenetic than she remembered. The darkening days of late autumn were filled with levees, private theatricals, hops at the large hotels, all described in detail by the papers. Dedicated ladies and gentlemen staged elaborate fairs to raise money for the Sanitary Commission, the organization that had virtually taken over the care and feeding of the Army. The Commission opened hospitals, operated huge warehouses, and sent wagon trains streaming to the camps with everything from dressings and medicines to onions and potatoes for prevention of scurvy.

The social season promised to have an exotic air. Hostesses were planning gala receptions for officers of the Russian fleet scheduled to anchor in the Potomac for the winter. Margaret had no personal knowledge of any of the events; she read about them. She left the town house on Franklin Square only when necessary.

She received no more letters from Rose. In the wake of the South's defeat at Gettysburg, Confederate envoys in England

and France had failed to win recognition of their government. The Northern papers said they never would. New names appeared in battlefield dispatches—Thomas, Sherman, praised for their leadership at Chickamauga Creek and Lookout Mountain in faraway Tennessee. Lincoln declared a national day of Thanksgiving in November, proof of the Union's resurgent confidence. Margaret ate alone, a modest meal prepared in silent protest. That night, at her mirror, she found strands of gray in her hair.

Stores overflowed with Christmas goods: wooden soldiers and popguns and clever mechanical dolls that sang; French perfumes and ladies' cloaks and gentlemen's cigar cases. She didn't know how or where to ship a present to her brother, having heard nothing from him after the riots. She had no one else to buy for except Lon, who was gone. Their night together, a thrilling memory, could still bring on depression if she dwelt on it too long. She accused herself of speaking too persuasively, too often, about the impossibility of their love in wartime. Lon must have decided she was right.

John T. Ford, the impresario from Baltimore, was enjoying success with his sparkling new "Temple of Thespis" on Tenth Street. For two weeks he engaged the popular John Wilkes Booth in his notable roles: Richard III, and Raphael, a sculptor, in an English version of a French drama, *The Marble Heart*.

Margaret saw Hanna's name in an advertisement for the latter play. She hired a carriage to take her to Ford's, where she bought a seventy-five-cent seat, best in the house.

Gaslight lent warmth to the handsome new playhouse. A bust of Shakespeare ornamented the proscenium arch. Every seat was filled. Hers was in the dress circle at stage right. She sensed an unusual excitement, prompted by patriotic bunting on a double box at the end of the dress circle stage left. From her seat she could look directly across to the box, but only those on her side of the dress circle had that advantage. The box couldn't be seen at all by the often noisy rabble who sat downstairs. As the houselights went down, an usher in the box pushed lace curtains aside, revealing several chairs and a large upholstered rocker. Abraham Lincoln loved the theater and was known to pay surprise visits to Ford's and Grover's.

An ovation greeted the first entrance of young Mr. Booth. Extraordinarily handsome, he rattled the rafters with his delivery. Unlike his brother, Edwin, whose acting was restrained and natural, he preferred the sweeping gesture, the bold stage move. Playing the poor sculptor in love with a woman who loved money more, he had competition for the attention of the audience. Those around Margaret watched the empty box.

Ten minutes after the curtain rose, there were exclamations on the other side of the dress circle, then applause. In the dark, Lincoln had made his way through a passage to the double box and seated himself in the rocking chair. His wife wasn't with him. A civilian guard stood behind him, in shadow.

Applause grew and spread to the orchestra and upper gallery. Lincoln stood to acknowledge the welcome, then with a gesture to the stage bade the players continue. Mr. Booth saluted the haggard President with an exaggerated bow. Margaret thought Booth looked annoyed. Lincoln and his guard left a minute before the last curtain.

She was unsure of the reception she'd get from Hanna, but nevertheless waited in the alley behind the theater. She was embarrassed to be in a crowd of giddy women eager to see the leading man. She was relieved when Hanna was among the first to come down the steps. "Hanna? Here I am!"

Hanna started when she recognized Margaret. She recovered quickly and ran to her. Hanna still wore stage makeup; her eyes were lined, her cheeks and lips vividly rouged.

"In heaven's name, what are you doing in Washington?"

"Donal and I separated. I saw your name and couldn't stay away. You were fine, Hanna."

"Thank you. It's a tiny part but I earn a salary, so finally I can call myself a professional. Isn't Johnny Booth marvelous?"

"He's very forceful. Do you have time for supper?"

"Oh, I'm sorry, Mr. Ford's giving a party for the cast. I'm heartbroken to hear about the separation. We must meet again, to catch up. Are you at home in Franklin Square? I'll send a note as soon as I'm free." Margaret wondered if she would; Hanna seemed stiff, reserved.

Her speculation was cut short by applause from the fifty or

so gathered at the stage entrance. Booth came out wearing a fur-collared overcoat and silk hat. He was showered with floral bouquets and two folded notes thrown by young women. Hanna squeezed Margaret's hand and whispered something that Margaret couldn't hear with all the noise. Booth's black eyes shone as he signed programs. Someone asked about performing for Lincoln.

"Infernal nuisance having him in the house. Throws everyone's timing off. Nor do I appreciate bowing before a damned tyrant." The crowd murmur stopped. Two men feebly applauded. Margaret slipped away without speaking to Hanna again.

In December, Margaret bought a set of tortoiseshell combs for Hanna. At New Year's she still hadn't heard from her friend. The gift in its floral paper remained in a drawer.

*　　*　　*

The black brougham with black window curtains swung into the mews between H and I Streets. Lon counted nine saddle horses tied to iron posts in front of a two-story house with draped windows. The horses whinnied and stamped as the brougham rolled up. Lon jumped out, followed by Eugene Sandstrom and two other Baker detectives. Piano music and laughter beat through the solid oak door. The breath of the four detectives clouded in the January air. The stars were icy and distant.

Lon unbuttoned his coat, loosened the six-shot Navy Colt .36 holstered under his arm. It was a simple, dependable weapon, turned out in vast numbers for the Union. He missed the old pocket piece, lost when Zach was hanged. This gun was larger. It had the virtue of being more intimidating.

Sandstrom blew on his hands. "What's the name of this crib?"

"The Blue Goose." To the driver Lon said, "Pull out and signal them to bring up the Black Maria." Baker's unit owned an old police wagon refitted with huge padlocks on the doors. The driver shook the reins. The brougham moved down the mews.

"How many on the list?" another detective asked. Lon pulled out a paper, tilted it to catch the light of a gas lamp above the front entrance.

"Six."

"The chief's throwing a hell of a big party."

"He aims to ship seventy to eighty whores down the Potomac. Every one of them secesh."

"Or accused of it by someone else," Sandstrom said.

Lon shot him a look. "Same thing." Eugene was exactly right, though. It was a rotten business, rounding up suspected traitors without real evidence. Lon especially hated harassing women. But he couldn't ignore three McClellan saddles among the tethered horses. Baker insisted that whores could get officers drunk and pry information out of them.

"Follow me."

He'd lain unconscious in the street after the white men killed Zach. A black barber discovered him, took him in, and sent his son for a policeman. Lon spent a week in a ward at Bellevue Hospital while units from Gettysburg arrived and quelled the rioting. Lon remembered only the last three days of that week.

Recovery had been long, difficult, and frustrating. His healed wounds hurt in the cold. Going up to the oak door, he felt every step.

He aimed the Navy Colt at the keyhole and blasted the mechanism apart with one shot. He kicked the door open and jumped into a melee of shouting and screaming, overturning furniture, shattering glass, obscene oaths. Hard to tell who had the foulest mouths, the male patrons or the ladies.

A captain with his blue blouse unbuttoned darted away down the long hall next to the staircase. Lon put a bullet in the floor at the soldier's heels. The man stopped instantly. Lon yelled, "The back door is blocked by my men. We're arresting some of the inmates of this house. Customers can leave. Just don't make trouble."

A motherly woman with high-piled gray hair stormed out of a side parlor. "You dirty fucking son of a bitch, who are you?"

Lon showed his badge. "Some of your ladies are going on a boat ride. They can work in Richmond, entertaining their own kind."

"God damn you, you pissy little runt, you can't tromp in here and act like you own—"

He cocked the single-action piece with his thumb. "If you're Madam Hanna, your name isn't on my list. I'll add it if you don't keep quiet."

Madam Hanna paled under her orange powder. She clutched her wattled neck and stepped back, making curious gobbling sounds. Lon consulted the list. "Here are the ones we want. Mary Ann Abelard. Dimity Baskin. Boots, also known as Helene Gunther. Eulalia Mimms. Says here she's black. Josie Stein and Annie Wheaton. Root 'em out, boys."

The detectives ran upstairs while the patrons gathered overcoats and hats and gloves and stole out. Lon heard the Black Maria clattering into the mews.

Soon the first girl came down, dragged by Eugene Sandstrom. She carried her cloak over her arm; her bosoms were practically falling out of her chemise. She called Sandstrom vile names until he shoved his pistol in her side. "Shut up and cover your tits." Lon smiled; Sandstrom was learning.

By midnight they had the six soiled doves cuffed and locked inside the black-painted wagon. Lon accompanied them to Old Capitol but rode outside, with the driver. Inside, they'd probably claw him to pieces.

The whole business was distasteful, but it was the game he'd chosen by coming back to work for Lafayette Baker after his recovery. The tactics of Baker and Stanton appalled him. Dozens were arrested every month—journalists, elected officials, government clerks, anyone caught opposing the war or suspected of it. Some were jailed for a day or two. Some were detained indefinitely in the overcrowded prisons. Lon knew he shouldn't work for a man he loathed. Nevertheless he stayed. Where else could he fight the war as Pinkerton had trained him to do?

He sopped his conscience by telling himself that every arrest was a payment for Zachariah Chisolm. He grieved for his friend. Zach died unhappy, believing himself cursed by his blackness, and by white hypocrisy. He saw no possibility of acceptance in the promised land of the North. It was a bitter fate, adding an extra measure of pain to a cruel death. Zach Chisolm had died thinking himself less than a man.

* * *

On a raw January afternoon when snowflakes swirled out of a dark sky, Lon stood on a Sixth Street pier, hands in his overcoat pockets, derby pulled down over his forehead. He and Lafayette Baker watched Eugene Sandstrom and three other detectives unload prostitutes from a line of hacks and patrol wagons. The women no longer swore or resisted. Prison had cowed them. They trudged up the plank of the little side-wheel steamer, struggling with small trunks or fat carpetbags. None of Baker's men offered help. One tiny redhead sobbed and petted a sickly looking parrot riding her shoulder.

Baker was pleased. "There go seventy-two disloyal females who won't trouble us further. A fine piece of work, Alonzo."

"Yes. Just fine."

His tone made Baker frown. Lon didn't care to watch the steamer leave with its cargo of secesh-minded whores. After all, women posed an enormous, a positively staggering threat to the Union, wasn't that right? All of Baker's good soldiers would agree it was.

Sunk in this sour thought, Lon said, "Excuse me," and walked off in the swirling snow.

56

May 1864

"Before our visitors present their proposal, let me review our situation."

Jefferson Davis spoke from the head of the conference table in the cabinet room. Tall windows framed a deluge of rain. It was almost as though the heavens mourned for the Confederacy, Cicero thought in his chair in the corner. The Davis government had lately suffered catastrophic reversals. That could only help him.

Davis, whom Cicero and many others considered incompetent, had his share of personal woes as well. Two weeks earlier, his beloved son Joseph had climbed on the rail of the residence balcony and fallen, splattering his brains on the bricks below. Joe Davis was four, the second child Davis had lost.

"Two weeks of fighting in the Wilderness and at Spotsylvania have cost General Lee eighteen thousand men," the President said. "In the equivalent time the enemy lost approximately thirty-six thousand. I know Sam Grant. He is a brutal and reckless soldier. He has no regard for human life."

Cicero's right hand crept over to scratch the hideously scarred back of his left. Burn scars covered his arm, shoulder, and neck, showing above his collar in ridges of gnarly red tissue. His left ear resembled a misshapen lump of wax that had melted and rehardened. He doubted even a whore would look at him naked unless she was drunk or desperate.

Secretary of War Seddon cleared his throat to ask for attention. He was a contemptible wreck of a man, emaciated and constantly sick. Davis had a strange affinity for men in ill health. Misery loved company, no doubt. Davis nodded to grant permission.

James Seddon spoke in a gentle Virginia accent. "The President is exactly right. Lincoln's new general-in-chief throws men away as if they were markers in a child's game. He enjoys Lincoln's full trust, so his policy will surely continue. He can lose thirty-six thousand or fifty thousand and replace them. Our losses cannot be made up so easily."

Cicero threw a look at his superior, Major William Norris. Cicero had known Norris in Baltimore. He'd always resented Norris's good looks, his success with women, the way he'd sailed through Yale. Norris was chief of the Signal Service.

He wasn't the only Yale lawyer present. Immediately to the left of Davis, Mr. Benjamin, the Jew secretary of state, sat like a little olive-skinned Buddha, reflectively caressing his trim beard. Judah Benjamin of St. Croix, New Haven, and New Orleans, was the President's most trusted colleague. His position at the table, and Seddon's at the other end, established their status.

Davis resumed. "Sherman is already into north Georgia. Ben Butler is on the Peninsula and could well threaten Petersburg. Sigel has only some eight thousand in the Valley, but look what that has cost us." He referred to Jeb Stuart, fatally wounded at Yellow Tavern five days ago, May 11.

"General Lee's troops are exhausted after two weeks of bloody combat. We cannot arm them, clothe them, or feed them properly. Our brave boys receive a field ration of a few ounces of flour, a bit of tainted bacon, and if God smiles, perhaps a spoonful of rice or molasses. That is for an entire day, gentlemen. Furthermore, the orders found on the body of Colonel Dahlgren in the wake of his failed raid prove that Lincoln will sink to the lowest levels of warfare."

Dahlgren had come knocking at the door with four thousand cavalry last March. His alleged mission was to free prisoners at Belle Isle and turn them loose to revenge themselves on Richmond's populace. The raid was foiled, Dahlgren killed in King and Queen County, but in his pocket, orders were found exhorting the freed prisoners to kill and burn "the hateful city," then assassinate Davis and members of his cabinet. Outraged, Lee dispatched copies of the orders to General Meade under a truce flag. Meade blandly called the orders false and swore they'd never been issued. Washington seconded the denial. Lincoln's hirelings were liars as well as killers.

Davis folded his pale hands on the table. The rain drummed the windows. Seddon muttered that they ought to light the gas. Davis said, "Shortly. Let us conclude our business first." Secretary Benjamin stroked his beard.

"Major Norris, the floor is yours."

"Thank you, Mr. President. Gentlemen." Norris rose, smiling slightly as if to acknowledge their common gentility. The major was in his forties, an elegant martial figure in gray and gold braid. Cicero scratched his scarred hand.

"I trust you all know Mr. Miller. He is one of my best civilian operatives, as well as one of the bravest. You have received reports of his accomplishments in New York last summer—gallant service unfortunately cut short by an enemy agent's brutality." Cicero had spun an elaborate story of fighting with Lon Price in a burning building. It had little relation to the truth. After Price had caught him in the Roost, Cicero had simply run, blind with terror. Confrontation had never been Cicero's style, except when all the strength was on his side.

He'd been so crazy with fear, he'd rushed into the tenement unthinkingly. He'd smelled the smoke, seen it curling from the broken windows, but his blood was up and his brain too dizzy for the meaning to penetrate. The same hysteria made him run upstairs to get away from Price. Fire engulfed the building, Price fell through the floor, and Cicero too.

His suit had caught fire on the left side. He managed to leap out a window. Rolling over and over, he might have been all right even then if pieces of the burning tenement wall hadn't fallen on him. Trailing flames from his clothes, he ran.

He blundered into someone's rain barrel filled by the recent storm. He plunged his head and shoulders in the water, then tipped the barrel to soak his lower body. His whole left side consisted of smoking rags. The real pain began then, made more sickening by the reek of his burned flesh.

He staggered on. Perhaps fear of death drove him. Somehow he reached the small lodging house in lower Manhattan run by a couple with known Confederate sympathies. Sobbing and raving, he lay in his bed until a doctor arrived to dope him with laudanum and end his agony. Until he woke again.

He screamed for a mirror and saw his bandages. They came off four weeks later but he already knew he was disfigured—crippled a second time.

Major Norris said, "Mr. Miller approached me with his idea three weeks ago. I will let him present it."

Norris took his seat. Cicero bowed and gave them a quick, perfunctory smile. He wanted to murder Lon Price. He wanted to bring a Confederate victory single-handed. He knew he could.

"Gentlemen, the kernel of my idea is not original with me. We have seen it propounded and discussed in the papers frequently. I refer to a negotiated peace, one which will let our Confederacy survive unhindered, as a separate nation."

Seddon frowned at the rain. Davis studied his pale hands. Secretary Benjamin, however, no longer stroked his beard.

"We also have another, more immediate problem. I refer to Grant's order last month halting prisoner exchanges, which is nothing short of an unprincipled attempt to reduce our manpower. We must force Grant to relent. At the same time we must strive to reach the larger objective, peace on our terms.

We cannot achieve either goal by conventional negotiation. We must have a bargaining chip. A trump card higher than anything the enemy holds."

"And what would that be, sir?" Benjamin asked.

"Abraham Lincoln, sir. Kidnaped and secured in our hands here in Richmond."

Softly but pointedly Mr. Benjamin said, "Lincoln has guards, military or civilian, depending on the circumstances."

"Not that many, Mr. Secretary, and not that often. He constantly upsets his staff by driving about town in his carriage without an escort, or stealing into a playhouse alone." Cicero paused for effect. "I have recently been in Washington to make sure."

That made them sit up. Norris smiled to himself. But Seddon scowled, a signal of trouble.

"Major Norris has acquainted me with the essentials of this plan, Mr. President. I oppose it on a number of grounds, not the least of which is the element of personal risk. Who in his right mind would attempt such a thing?"

Who in his right mind? Cicero wanted to leap on Seddon, batter his smug, sickly face until there was so much blood and gore no one would recognize—

They were staring at him. He'd blanked out for a moment. He fixed the sycophantic smile in place.

"I will, sir. As I stated, I have already worked secretly in Washington City."

"How in God's name did you get there?" Seddon's complaining tone said he knew he was losing.

"There is a great deal of illegal traffic back and forth across the Potomac. For twenty dollars gold, the local boatmen will risk the gunboats on patrol and the bluecoats on the Maryland shore."

Norris said, "As you know, Mr. Secretary, the Signal Service is more than flags and balloons and coded messages. We have resources in unusual areas. For example, documentation of a fictitious identity."

Cicero bowed to introduce his new persona. "Hiram Seth, publisher of a small newspaper in rural Maryland, at your service. Mr. Seth's visits were completely ignored by the authorities. As a result, I already have my eye on a couple of men capable of helping organize and carry out our plan. I'm sure I'll find more. The Yankee capital teems with people sick to death of the excesses of the Lincoln government. Further, we can supplement our manpower by calling on our partisan guerillas who operate along the Potomac."

He waited. The rain hammered windows and streamed down. The cabinet room had grown so gloomy, they might have been meeting in the lightless inner room of Castle Thunder. Mr. Benjamin thoughtfully delivered himself of an opinion:

"Your plan is enterprising. Your courage is unquestioned, particularly in view of the terrible personal injury you suffered last July. I will endorse the plan on two conditions. One, this administration will disassociate itself so it cannot be held accountable if the plan fails. My other condition is obvious. The final decision rests with the President."

Davis bowed his head, obviously troubled. "I was never taught to campaign this way. I do realize the hour is late and our situation fraught with danger. Major Norris, I authorize you to draft a memorandum of the plan for my review. If I approve it, you will put the plan in motion, understanding that, as Mr. Benjamin said, should failure occur before we have the, ah, captive in our hands, everything will be denied."

Norris couldn't help a boisterous enthusiasm. "Sir, thank you. Be assured, we won't disappoint you."

Davis turned his milky eye to Cicero. "You have it within your grasp to become a great hero of the Confederacy, Mr. Miller."

And something more important, Cicero thought. Much more important. His sober mien concealed his elation. He was no Bible-spouter like Cridge, but he knew an appropriate verse. *Vengeance is mine, I will repay, saith the Lord.*

57

June 1864

The partisan battalion now had two additional companies, B and C, with plans for more. New men arrived regularly, drawn by Mosby's name and celebrity.

A few months earlier, repeal of the Partisan Ranger Act by the Confederate Congress had nearly wiped out all independent commands. Brigadier Thomas Rosser had complained to Lee about the partisans, branding them "bands of thieves" and arguing that they put an evil stamp on the whole Army. Mosby galloped to Richmond, pleaded with Lee, and won exemption from the repeal. While Grant maneuvered and hammered unsuccessfully at Lee's Army at Spotsylvania and Cold Harbor during the spring and early summer, the partisans remained a presence in Loudoun and Fauquier counties—"Mosby's Confederacy," the press and populace called it.

Captain William Smith, a confidant of Mosby's, led B Company. Familiar with Fred's background, he requested him and promoted him to sergeant. "Despite your reputation as a man overly fond of the corn," Smith said with humorless candor.

Jeb Stuart's death at Yellow Tavern hit Fred hard. He could hardly thank the flamboyant cavalryman for banishing him to Mosby's unit, or ordering Hanna Siegel to some filthy Richmond prison. Yet neither could he dismiss Stuart's military genius and his importance to the Army. Stuart's death began a turnaround in Fred's life that was at first wholly unsuspected. An incident of low comedy brought it to the fore.

Mosby sent Fred with ten men on what was called corn patrol: the extraction of tribute from farmers suspected of Union sympathies. These were mostly Quakers; gentle people. It sickened Fred to ride into their farmyards and strip them of their remaining grain and livestock.

One man in Fred's detail aroused loathing of a kind he'd seldom felt in military service. The new recruit, tall and black-haired, hailed from Alabama. Fred guessed him to be anywhere from eighteen to twenty-one. He had the body of a Hercules and the brain of a rabbit. Having lost two brothers at Murfreesboro, he was poisoned with hate for the Yankees. He said he'd never wounded an enemy soldier. "When I shoot, I miss 'em or kill 'em." He made the boast often, with moronic glee.

The young man's proudest moment, which he described tediously to any who would listen, was meeting John Wilkes Booth during one of the actor's Southern tours. "Mighty fine show he gave. Went backstage afterwards. Mr. Booth shook my hand and poured me a whiskey in his dressing room. We talked about how we hated the son-of-a-bitching black Republicans. Booth said he'd like to murder a few. I said I would too. We shook hands on it."

No one knew where Lewis Powell had come from last winter. Desertion from some other unit seemed probable; he was experienced. He also seemed fearless, a quality Fred always equated with stupidity. Powell sensed Fred's dislike and made his own dislike evident with side glances and snickers, though he never disobeyed orders.

Another duty of corn patrols was destruction of stills discovered in remote areas. Mosby insisted that alcohol not only harmed a soldier, but robbed precious grain needed for food and fodder. Near the hamlet of Bluemont, within sight of the Blue Ridge, Fred's detail swooped down on a still operated by a toothless grandpa of eighty or more. They tore the coils apart and shot holes in the kettles. With Fred's permission, they helped themselves to some of the product.

Fred joined in, imbibing too generously. When the late-afternoon sun was spilling red light on the mountains, he ordered the detail back to the horses. He put his foot in Baron's stirrup and mounted so energetically, he fell off the other side. With all his men watching.

Most tried to choke back laughter, but not Lewis Powell. He whooped and pointed at Fred sitting dazed and drunk beside the black gelding.

At another time Fred might have shrugged it off; even

joked about it. In his depressed state he didn't find it funny. Sitting there on a smelly horse apple on which he'd landed, he had a sudden and painful sense of what he'd become.

The detail's return to camp coincided with a visit from one of the itinerant colporteurs who roamed the countryside supplying the troops with Bibles and religious literature. Christian revivals swept the Army periodically. During the latest, General Leonidas Polk, an Episcopal bishop before the war, had baptized Generals Hood, Hardee, and Johnston in widely publicized ceremonies.

The colporteur handed out tracts. To be courteous, Fred took one, intending to throw it away later. He stuck the the four-page leaflet in his pocket and forgot it until evening, when he discovered it again. He examined it by lantern light.

Its title was "Demon Drink." He remembered the shame of sitting in a horse turd, drunk and dizzy, and opened it. The tract's little homily posed a question. What was the point of a man fighting to throw off the yoke the Union wanted to place on the South if at the same time he willingly enslaved himself to spirits? The anonymous writer sprinkled his text with inspirational quotes. Lord Cornwallis: "A drunken night makes a cloudy morning." Saint Paul's letter to the Romans: "Let us walk honestly, as in the day, not in rioting and drunkenness." Words of the philosopher Seneca affected Fred like a dousing of icy water: "Drunkenness is nothing but voluntary madness."

He read the tract a second time. No radiant light descended on him from heaven. No choir of angels sang. Yet it was an epiphany, as profound and complete as it was quiet and personal. In the farmer's barn where he slept, Fred held his canteen in his hands a long time, staring at it while he contemplated the ruin he'd made of his life the past couple of years. He walked outside, uncorked the canteen, and poured the whiskey in the dirt. Bathed in the pure white brilliance of a full moon, he filled his canteen from water in the well.

*   *   *

Late in June, Captain Smith sent Fred to Lieutenant Colonel Mosby. The commander was living in a bedroom of a farmhouse and using its dining room for headquarters. Fred saluted. "Please have a chair, Sergeant. I'll be ready to talk momentarily." Fred was surprised by Mosby's cordiality. What was coming? A reprimand for the spectacle he had made falling off Baron? But that had happened weeks ago.

Mosby pushed his reading glasses higher on his nose and finished signing a series of orders. He laid the pen aside and fixed his pale eyes on Fred. "Captain Smith reports a remarkable change in your demeanor, Sergeant Dasher. Do you have anything to say about that?"

Fred cleared his throat. "Nothing special, sir. I've made mistakes in the past. I'm trying to correct them."

A male cardinal landed on the sill of the open window, tipping its head as if to look in. Finding nothing of interest, it flew away. Mosby said, "You reflect favorably on yourself with that admission. It was drinking, wasn't it?"

Fred grew almost as red as the vanished bird. "Yes, sir. Drinking. Too much drinking."

"You're sober now?"

"I haven't touched a drop for over a month."

"Is that a burden?"

About to deny it, Fred reconsidered. "Sir, it is. I've never gotten over something that happened on the Peninsula."

"The killing of the young girl. General Stuart described what happened. That would be a terrible burden for any man."

"Yes, sir. It's always with me. The whiskey makes—that is, it made it easier to forget. I finally saw what it was doing to me."

"Admirable," Mosby said. "In light of this change, I thought of you when Richmond asked us for a volunteer. We'll be cooperating with the Signal Service on a dangerous mission. The full details haven't been revealed to me as yet, but I know the mission involves putting a volunteer in considerable jeopardy, to gather information."

"Spy work, sir?"

"You could call it spy work. The Signal Service wants a man in Washington for a few weeks. General Stuart told me you'd spent time there, so you must know the city." Fred said yes, he did. "Then if you're willing to hazard yourself, I'll write the order."

Fred's mind raced. Was Hanna still in the capital? Could he find her? Mosby cleared his throat.

"Yes, sir, I'm more than willing. Will I go directly to Washington?"

"No, to Richmond first. There you'll become a Union war prisoner awaiting exchange. You'll have another name, another identity, provided by the Signal Service. Gather your gear. My orderly will deliver the papers to Captain Smith. You can leave before dark. That's all."

Fred leaped out of the chair so violently, Mosby's thin mouth twitched in a smile, something not customary for him. He astonished Fred by offering a handshake. "I'm proud that one of my men is willing to undertake this duty. I wish you the best of luck. I would ask that our past differences be forgotten if you can find that in your heart."

"I can, sir. Absolutely."

Though there was little room in his heart at the moment for anything but thoughts of Hanna Siegel.

58

June–July 1864

Margaret couldn't stay a hermit forever. In spite of emotional wreckage left by Donal and by Lon, her disposition compelled her to move back into the world, even the divided world of Washington. Twice a week she worked in the wards of the sprawling Armory Square Hospital near the Smithsonian. A newspaper appeal for volunteers drew her to it. She justified it on grounds that a percentage of the wounded were Confederate boys; war prisoners.

At the hospital she mingled with Yankees of every sort: pompous Army surgeons wearing green sashes; prim and efficient nurses, required to be spinsters by the first nursing superintendent, Dorothea Dix; male nurses with oddly gentle dispositions; quiet Negro orderlies; teamsters who delivered the wounded like so many pieces of cordwood, then just as indifferently hauled away the cheap pine boxes holding those the hospital couldn't save.

To her surprise, Margaret took the work in stride. The pus and blood, amputations and noxious smells, didn't bother her. When a young soldier begged for a dipper of water or a hand to hold, his allegiance no longer mattered. Blue or gray, he was simply an injured human being; another item on what the papers called the butcher's bill.

A letter arrived from Sparks & Spiderwell, Donal's New York attorneys. In prose both stilted and arcane, Mr. Spiderwell, Esq., stated what Margaret already suspected. She had no legal claim on any of Donal's property. He intended to divorce her, using the only available grounds, adultery. Since he didn't know about Lon, he'd have to invent evidence and buy witnesses, a common practice. She hoped the man who played her adulterous lover would be reasonably presentable.

Summer came on. Tulip trees and redbuds lost their blooms. Shad roe vanished from hotel menus. In Baltimore, Abraham Lincoln won renomination on a National Union ticket. The convention replaced his Vice President, Hamlin, with the military governor of Tennessee, Andrew Johnson, a man Margaret knew nothing about. Washington celebrated the nominations with a torchlight parade and illuminations at the Patent and Post Offices. The most radical Republicans, it was said, weren't eager to see Lincoln returned to office because he spoke of reunion with South, not punishment.

Militia drilled twice a week in Franklin Square. Residents took visitors to admire the statue of Armed Freedom standing atop the Capitol dome at last. The credulous consulted Washington's many spirit mediums, hoping to speak to relatives lost in battle. Hundreds of contrabands idled in the streets, jobless and hungry.

Margaret had a friend on Franklin Square; one she hadn't sought. Mrs. Fanny Fitch lived two doors away, cared for by nine servants. Early in the year, as a good neighbor, she brought Margaret a plate of apple tarts baked by her cook. Mrs. Fitch was a spry little lady with fiery red hair and a loquacious tongue. On her first visit, she informed Margaret that the late Mr. Fitch, of the Georgia Fitches, had made a fortune with a service that removed human waste from the city in a fleet of wagons. The rigors of the night-soil trade sent Mr. Fitch to an early grave but left his childless widow secure for life.

Fanny was a hundred percent secesh. When the resignation of Treasury Secretary Chase became public in late June, she crowed, "He knows the Union's bankrupt and ready to collapse!" Margaret was amused. Fanny's hopes were larger than her store of facts.

Early in July, a mixed Confederate force of cavalry and infantry invaded Maryland and captured Frederick, forty miles away. General Jubal Early demanded $200,000 or he'd burn the town. The burgers of Frederick capitulated and Early marched on Washington. Summer lassitude was immediately replaced by fear, though not among the secesh. Fanny took Margaret to her sewing room, which she unlocked with a conspiratorial flourish. On the worktable lay an unfinished Confederate battle flag.

"I'll hang it out when General Early marches into town. He was trained at West Point, you know. Class of '37."

"Surely Stanton will call for troops from Grant," Margaret said.

"Grant's busy trying to overrun Petersburg. Which of course he'll never do. Hasn't Bob Lee kept him chasing his tail for months? Besides, Grant is never sober long enough to win a battle."

Early's invasion created wild excitement in Washington. Margaret went out regularly to read bulletins posted at the *Star*. Saturday, July 9, the long sheets reported that Early had met a Union force under General Lew Wallace at the Monocacy River and defeated it. Old Jube now had a straight march to the capital.

A sorry mix of adolescent boys, elderly home guards, and Invalid Corps convalescents drilled in the square on Sunday. Late that day, the bulletins warned that Early had reached Rockville. Next morning the streets overflowed with refugees streaming in from the Rockville and Seventh Street roads. They brought clothes and valuables on their backs or in handcarts and told horrific tales of the rebels burning and looting farms. A cattle herd stampeded through Franklin Square, pursued by a farmer on horseback who shouted that Early would massacre everyone.

About one-thirty that afternoon, Margaret heard cannonading from the northern forts. Made nervous by the guns, she eagerly went to tea when Fanny sent her maid with an invitation. Fanny was so excited, her hand shook as she poured. "I'll be flying my flag this time tomorrow. The tide is turning at last."

Margaret said nothing. She'd heard that an entire Union Army Corps was coming up the Potomac to rescue the city. Later, a mulatto boy delivering groceries excitedly told her that units of General Horatio Wright's VI Corps were already piling off the boats at Sixth Street.

In the evening, Fanny's black coachman drove them out Seventh Street toward Fort Stevens. There, according to Fanny, President Lincoln had studied the enemy from a parapet and exposed his head to sharpshooters. "A missed opportunity," she lamented.

Progress up Seventh was slow. The driver fought a flood of Marylanders fleeing into town. In cottage yards, families loaded goods in burlap sacks and wheelbarrows. The moon rose behind a heat haze reddened by fires along the northern horizon. A half mile from Fort Stevens, the crowds of refugees stalled the carriage completely. Fanny ordered the driver to turn around.

Tuesday dawned hot again. Margaret dressed in her lightest lawn, took her parasol, and set out to see what had happened overnight. Two things struck her. The first was the remarkable state of the Washington populace. Children played in dooryards and alleys as though no threat existed. Shoppers thronged the stores as on any business day. If there was panic, she saw no evidence, except for the wandering cattle, and the refugees camping in weedy lots with their heaps of belongings.

On Seventh Street she watched companies of the VI Corps marching to relieve the forts. Although young, the soldiers had the hard-bitten eyes and sunbaked faces of men far older. No two uniforms matched. These were blooded veterans. And the North had thousands more. Fanny and those like her would one day burn their battle flags or hide them away in attics.

Coughing from the dust raised by so many tramping feet,

Margaret saw the companies pass, and when she walked homeward, she knew the war was lost.

* * *

By Wednesday, the crisis was over; Jubal Early was gone from the gates of Washington. Margaret returned to her hospital duties. On Friday night, she drove her buggy into the small stable behind the town house about half past seven. It had been a trying afternoon. Two boys in her ward, one from Mississippi, had succumbed to their wounds. The Mississippi soldier had died while Margaret sat with him, trying to finish a letter to his wife. His arm lolled suddenly and knocked the pencil from her hand. She cried.

The summer night was sticky and still. She let herself into the kitchen and pulled off her bonnet, eager to be out of her clothes and into a tepid bath. Her legs ached from standing.

Moving to the dark parlor, she struck a match. The light revealed her brother in a wing chair, a pair of white cotton gloves draped over his knee. Margaret shrieked softly and dropped the match.

"God above. How did you get in here?"

With a smile that was no more than a facial tic, he said, "I have keys that will open any door. I arrived about six. Actually it's my second visit. Oh, and kindly don't call me Cicero. For the moment I am Mr. Hiram Seth of Lower Marlboro, Maryland. Care to see my credentials?" His left hand shifted toward his lapel. Margaret's mouth and eyes rounded.

"What happened to your hand?"

He showed off the scars. "This isn't all." He hooked a finger under the old-fashioned white silk stock that he wore in place of a cravat. Pulling the stock away from his neck, he revealed more ugly red tissue.

"Modesty forbids me from showing the rest. The scars run down my whole left side. During the New York riots, I had the misfortune to be trapped in a burning building. I escaped, though occasionally I wish I hadn't."

"That's terrible. I'm so sorry. Are you here for more of your secret work?"

"Indeed I am."

"You're taking huge risks coming to Washington."

"In a good cause."

"You said you'd been here before. Was it early today?"

"Oh, no, it was during the winter. I didn't expect you were in residence at the time. I knocked on the front door merely to be sure. No one answered. A neighbor, a tiny red-haired lady, came along and told me you were indeed living here. Not with Donal, I gather."

"Donal and I separated. That is, I left him, right after I saw you last July. I made a dreadful mistake marrying him. He's divorcing me."

"Well, he was a splendid catch. Too bad it didn't work out." He sounded uninterested. "I'm afraid I can't offer you financial help, or even a great deal of brotherly support. I am evolving a scheme that has the government's highest priority. I can speak in confidence, can't I? I wouldn't want to think otherwise."

He licked his lips. "I am doing nothing less than trying to save the Confederacy before Davis drives it into the ground."

"Save the Confederacy? By yourself?" His staring eyes forestalled laughter.

"I can't reveal details, except to say that when the plan comes to fruition—when we strike—we will strike very high. So high, you will be astonished. That's why silence is mandatory."

What did he mean by striking high? Did he intend to attack someone in the Lincoln cabinet? Or Lincoln himself? It was lunacy, yet there he sat, blandly making his outrageous assertions.

The house creaked in the silence. She was exhausted, wanted to rest. She was wound too tight. "Do you honestly think I'd betray you, or anything you're doing? We've drifted apart, but not that far. Now, would you like something to eat? I cook for myself, I've no servants, but I can—"

"No, thank you, I have an appointment on H Street soon. Don't mention to anyone that I've been here. The Confederacy is in desperate straits. I'll permit no one to impede my plan. A breach would be punishable. Anyone can be sacrificed if necessary."

Though she'd worried about Cicero's mental state before, never had she been actively frightened of him. Now she was.

She pulled a stool up beside him to his knee and gently touched his disfigured hand.

"I want to hear more about this. Was it accidental?"

"No. Do you remember that detective you once asked about? Price? He was responsible."

Margaret's stomach wrenched.

"When I told you I didn't know him, I lied. I had him in prison in Richmond, but he escaped. Not before I had the pleasure of punishing him, however. I'd like to have ripped his eyes out of his head."

She whispered, "Cicero, what's happened to you?"

"Happened?" Again that curious ticlike smile. "The war happened. Nigger-loving abolitionists happened. Our father's murder happened. A murder you seem to have conveniently forgotten, Margaret." Her hand flew out, a stinging slap.

Instantly she regretted it. She began an apology but he interrupted. "Well, that tells me something. I'm not welcome here. I'll not call again." He snatched the cotton gloves and fitted his scarred hand into the left one.

"Please, Cicero, I didn't mean—"

"Oh, yes, you meant to chastise me. Somehow you've grown soft, Margaret. Soft and weak, at the very hour when courage is needed most." He lurched from his chair, stiff-backed as a military officer.

"I thought you'd support my work with enthusiasm. You don't. So let me repeat what I said before. Anyone who threatens us can be sacrificed. *Anyone*. Good evening."

His thick left shoe scraping, he dragged himself to the front door and went out into the night. Margaret put her face in her hands, shaking with fright.

59

July 1864

A fair-haired girl brought two steins and a pitcher of lager on a tray. She was about seventeen, and moon-eyed over the actor. "Mama doesn't approve of beer in the house but she makes an exception when you visit."

"Dear girl, thank you." Booth gave her a ravishing smile and patted her bottom. "May I present the landlady's daughter, Miss Anna Surratt? This is Mr. Hiram Seth, Anna."

"How do you do, sir?" Anna curtsyed. Cicero smiled as warmly as his temperament allowed. The high stock and cotton gloves hid his scars.

"What a sweet child you are," Booth said. "If you were a bit older, I'd propose." Anna giggled as she scurried out.

Booth checked the hall and rolled the door shut. Cicero peered out the second-floor window at the gray drizzle on H Street; the brick house stood at No. 541. Booth busied himself filling the steins.

"The landlady's a widow, from Maryland. She and her husband ran a little tavern, but it became a burden after he died. She's a harmless, pious creature, as you might judge from all the religious bric-a-brac. Her older son Isaac's in the Confederate army. John, the younger one, has an excellent record as a courier on the secret line to Richmond. Here, drink up."

Cicero reached for the stein. As he raised it, he confronted a set of false teeth floating in the beer. He dropped the stein. Booth whooped and caught the stein in midair. Only a little beer spilled.

Laughing, Booth said, "Forgive my little joke, won't you? I'm fond of them, as my friends know all too well." He fished the teeth from the beer and held them up. "Ivory, but a good

imitation. I have a spider and a worm too. Here, take mine."
They exchanged steins. Cicero was not amused.

"Please, be seated." Booth gestured gracefully, took a
chair, and crossed his legs. The actor shamed Cicero with
his elegant clothes: a royal blue frock coat, double-breasted
silk waistcoat with a yellow-and-blue check, fitted gray
trousers, square-toed ankle boots showing no dirt in spite
of the mud in H Street. He toasted Cicero. "Here's to success, then."

Cicero returned the salute. "You've started to recruit the
men?"

"Johnny Surratt's the first. There'll be more soon."

"Good. We'll shortly have someone in place in Washington,
to monitor the movements of the target. He will do it over a
period of several weeks, so we don't mistake some anomaly
for the daily routine."

"Who is this person?"

"A man from Colonel Mosby's partisan battalion. Chap
from West Point who knows the city. He was stationed here
before he came South. Dasher's his name, though I assume
he'll use a nom de guerre. I'm told he's reliable."

"He'd better be. This is a high-stakes game. How will I find
him?"

"He'll contact you, but only if it's necessary. He's coming in
as a released prisoner."

"Grant has stopped the exchange."

"The one-for-one exchanges, yes. Our prisons are so
crowded, we're releasing men unilaterally, from as far south as
Andersonville."

Booth gulped beer, then poured more. The actor had a reputation for drinking to excess. He could jeopardize the operation if he talked too freely in his cups. Cicero decided the risk
was acceptable.

Booth's black eyes sparkled as he paced the sitting room.
"This is a propitious moment, Mr. Seth. The tyrant should
have been brought down long ago."

"All the South agrees with that."

"Not only the South, sir. Some within Lincoln's own house
wouldn't be unhappy to see him removed."

Startled, Cicero said, "I'm not sure I take your meaning."

"Nothing so difficult about it. Don't you suppose Secretary Stanton resents being Lincoln's lapdog?"

"Are you suggesting—?"

"Not merely suggesting, sir. An actor meets a great many people. Hears a great many things. Don't you recall that the secretary once reviled Lincoln as 'the original gorilla'? As Byron wrote, 'Now hatred is by far the longest pleasure.' "

"Booth, are you honestly telling me there are persons in the Federal government as interested as we are in seeing this plan go forward?"

"I am."

"Will they help us?"

"Let it rest where it is for the present, Mr. Seth." Booth was annoyingly smug. Cicero suspected he'd learn nothing more unless and until the smug Mr. Booth chose to tell him. The man was a manipulator of the first order. It angered him, but it would be useful in recruiting men of lesser intelligence.

They talked a while longer. Booth refused to name those he might involve in the plan. Cicero also had another person to contact but kept that to himself. As the drizzle let up, he prepared to go. "Shall we meet again tomorrow evening?"

"My rooms. The National Hotel. Shall we say nine?"

"I'll be there. Here's to success."

"And the tyrant gone to hell where he belongs," Booth said with a smile that chilled even Cicero's dark heart.

*   *   *

Cicero loathed Washington for many reasons. Among the strongest was its large population of rootless colored people. Lincoln had turned the city into a veritable asylum of free niggers. At least they weren't permitted to ride the public cars, one of which Cicero boarded on Pennsylvania Avenue to travel to the heights of Georgetown next morning.

The rain had gone, leaving muggy air. His stand-up collar was damnably hot, but it concealed his scars, as did a pair of kid gloves. He wore a ridiculous and bulky cap of green tweed and carried a city guidebook with a red binding. Cap and book were prearranged signals.

The pleasant Georgetown campus had been abandoned

by its Southern students at the start of the war. Classes were still held, though some buildings had been converted to temporary hospitals. Cicero found a bench overlooking the Aqueduct Bridge and the fortifications across the Potomac. Presently a short, stocky man dressed like a peacock came marching along the path. Cicero presumed it was the right person. Short-cropped white hair and a dueling scar had been described to him. He pretended to study the red guidebook.

Bowing, the stranger said, "Is this place taken, sir?"

"No, sir." The man lifted the tails of his coat, seated himself, and refitted his monocle in his eye.

Cicero watched a barge move slowly downriver with its cargo of three giant mortars. "Siegel?"

"Yah, that's me. I'm usually addressed as major."

Cicero ignored the complaint. "My name is Hiram Seth."

"Good as any, I guess." Siegel's English was accented, his manner brusque.

"You're German?"

"Austrian. In the Army many years."

"And now working for Stanton's War Department. I've been told you might be open to an arrangement."

"Depends on the arrangement. Depends on what's wanted."

"That is not yet determined."

"Then I guess we got to talk about payment in advance. What do the shyster lawyers call it? Retainer."

The fish was on the hook.

"How much did you have in mind?"

*   *   *

On the third floor of the National Hotel, he found Booth disheveled and not a little drunk. The actor had a woman on his knee, a voluptuous little blonde, wearing thin cotton bloomers and a corset that barely contained her round breasts. Cicero could see part of the young lady's rosy nipples. He hardened almost painfully.

Booth waved his long cigar. "The lady's leaving. We were amusing ourselves until you arrived." The nature of the entertainment was evident from disarrayed bedclothes in the next room. "This is Ella Turner. Say hello to Mr. Seth, Ella." Cicero doffed his tweed cap.

"Ella stays at her sister's parlor house over on Ohio. She lives there, but she doesn't work there. Ella belongs to me." A mistress, then. In the papers Cicero had seen Booth's name coupled with that of the daughter of the eminently respectable Senator Hale of New Hampshire.

Ella said, "Pleased ter meet yer. What's wrong with yer hands?"

Cicero lost his erection. "A skin problem." Ella batted her eyes and skipped off to the bedroom to dress. After she kicked the door shut, Booth strolled to an open secretary. He showed his visitor a cut-glass decanter.

"Brandy? Very fine stuff." Cicero shook his head. "You don't mind if I do." Booth's thickened speech suggested that someone ought to mind; he was wobbling.

"So what do we have to talk about?" Booth tossed off a snifter of brandy as though it were well water. Some of the very fine stuff ran down his chin and stained his frilly shirt.

Speaking in a low voice, Cicero sketched his meeting with Major Siegel of the War Department. "The gentleman will help us if we need information from inside. I am paying him a fee." He didn't mention Siegel's name, or any particulars of their agreement.

Ella bounced out of the bedroom. "Kiss me, Johnny, I'm on my way." Cicero sat woodenly as they exchanged open-mouthed kisses. How he admired the actor. How he longed to be like him—sound of body, athletic, alluring to women. Cicero's envy was nearly hatred.

Ella tripped out of the room, leaving the heavy scent of her perfume as a reminder of her presence. Booth latched the door. Again Cicero declined brandy. Again Booth helped himself.

"Can you trust this fellow?"

"Only while he's earning money. He isn't a patriot like you, Mr. Booth. He's a mercenary. He may be a useful conduit of information, but as soon as he isn't, we'll sever our connection, probably by having him killed."

Booth tipped his head back and laughed. "I like you, Mr. Seth. You're so direct."

"Cards on the table. We have no room for error or misunderstanding."

After more brandy, Booth said, "I've been mulling the scheme ever since yesterday. I recommend that we kidnap him from Grover's or Ford's. He pollutes both places regularly. Also, I know people at both theaters. Ford's is my first choice. I stable a horse there and pick up my mail."

"Where we'll do it is yet to be decided."

"Since I'll be in charge, I think I'm the one to say—"

"It is yet to be decided."

On Sixth Street someone fired a pistol. Cicero stared. Booth stared.

Booth looked away first.

60

August 1864

The side-wheeler *Mohican Chief* idled in the Potomac, awaiting a berth at the crowded Sixth Street pier. A gray haze blurred the city panorama of trees and buildings. The Capitol dome rose above them, and the red Smithsonian towers, and a bit of the truncated shaft of the unfinished monument to the first president. A tangle of emotions bedeviled Fred. A certain nostalgic pleasure warred with a sharp sense of being among enemies.

He sat down in the shade, his back against the rail. He lit the stub of his last cigar. A shadow fell across his legs. Of the fifty Union prisoners who'd come up from City Point on the James, forty-nine must have asked him questions. Here came number fifty, a string bean with a wispy beard and missing teeth.

"Damn hot," the string bean said, crouching.

"Sure is. Always like this?"

"Don't know, never been here before." The string bean picked at a scab on his cheek. "That Sherman, he's pounding Atlanta."

"So they say."

"Atlanta falls, might be all over."

"Soon after, anyway."

"What prison was you in?"

"A new one. Millen, Georgia."

"Anybody else aboard from Millen?"

"No." And not likely to be. Camp Lawton, a Confederate stockade meant to hold overflow from Andersonville, wouldn't receive men until the fall. The Signal Service had advised him on creating a history for himself.

"Me and my friends, we was in Danville. Building number one, next to the bake house. Hot as hell's hinges this summer."

But surely no hotter than the parlor in the cheap hotel in the Rocketts section of Richmond. With gaslight hissing and heavy drapes shutting out the daylight, a Signal Service operative named Miller had rehearsed him the better part of a day:

"Name and rank?"

"Duane Sills. First lieutenant, General Eli Long's cavalry brigade, Army of the Cumberland."

"Where's your home?"

"New Zion, Kentucky. Little dot on the map close to Lexington. Horse country."

"When and where were you taken?"

"Chickamauga, second day. September twentieth."

"How'd you get out of the Millen stockade?"

"My father sat in the Kentucky legislature for two terms. He's a loyal Union man but his brother, my uncle, is high up in the Davis government."

They went over and over it. Fred didn't like the civilian. He was bald as an egg, with reddish purple scarring on his throat and left hand. He limped. He had a fanatical eye and a ready sneer. Compared to him, John Mosby could be considered benign . . .

The steamer tooted. Bells rang. *Mohican Chief* warped in to the long pier amid cheering and hat-waving from the newly freed soldiers. Fred joined in. They trooped up the pier in loose formation, weaving through stevedores rolling barrels and a company of replacements marching to their transport. The green soldiers cast envious eyes on the shaggy, unkempt men whose battles were very likely over.

A bull-voiced sergeant at the head of the pier waved them on. "Soldier's Rest that way. You'll have a meal and then be checked through."

Fred stepped out of line. "Where's the latrine, Sergeant?"

"Yonder, other side of the canvas. Don't take too long, sir," he said with deference to Fred's shoulder straps. Fred threw him a little salute by way of mockery and followed his nose to the reeking trench. It was screened from the pier head by a square enclosure of dirty canvas. A stevedore pissed loudly into the trench as Fred came in and unbuttoned.

The stevedore shook himself, nodded casually, left. Fred tore off his blue wool blouse and rolled it into a bundle. He tucked the bundle under his arm and walked out of the enclosure. He moved quickly toward a warren of small warehouses. He could feel his heart beating faster.

Out of sight of the pier head, he shoved the army blouse into a refuse barrel. The back of his gray cotton work shirt already showed big patches of sweat. A half mile from the pier, blending easily into foot and wagon traffic, he felt he was safe.

He peered into faces in the teeming streets. Where in all the confusion of the wartime city would he find her? How would he begin? He knew nothing but her name. He couldn't tramp from door to door: "Any Hanna Siegels here?" Nor did he have time. It tormented him.

In the scant shade of a fence outside a ropewalk, he stuck his hand under his shirt for the canvas belt they had given him before putting him with the other prisoners and marching all of them across Union lines at City Point under a truce flag. One compartment on the inside of the belt held money, another a forged Union Army pay card. From a third he took a limp paper bearing an address: 541 H Street.

* * *

Mary Surratt was a plain, dull-eyed woman, in contrast to the lurid religious objects decorating her sitting room. A plaster Jesus, pale and bleeding, hung on a wooden cross. On the wall opposite, a brightly painted Mary observed her son's suffering from her wall niche.

"Mr. Sills, we're so glad to see you," the landlady said with a nervous smile.

"Glad to be here, ma'am. I have important work to do."

"Oh, yes, we know. Some clothes were delivered day before yesterday. My son John should be home by suppertime. He's ever so anxious to meet you. I can't offer you fancy quarters. My regular rooms are taken. I've put my daughter, Anna, out of hers in the attic, you may have that."

"Thank you, ma'am. I'm sure it'll be adequate."

"Very hot, I'm sorry to say."

Fred smiled, resigned. "It's summer, ma'am."

"This way, then."

He could stand at full height in just half the attic; the roof pitched steeply. Mrs. Surratt's daughter had tacked personal things to the exposed rafters. Cards extolling love and friendship in verse. Faded ribbons. Souvenir photographs of General Longstreet, General Lee, the late and well-remembered Jeb Stuart with his prideful eyes, his huge beard, his plumed hat in his lap. Several cards bore photos of male and female theatricals. Fred recognized only one, Edwin Booth's handsome younger brother John.

He stripped off his shirt and washed with a basin of tepid water Mrs. Surratt brought up. In the dining room he met a soft and pudgy young man who introduced himself as Louie Weichmann.

"I have the room at third floor back. Johnny shares it when he's in town. We knew each other at St. Charles College." Weichmann clerked in the office of the Commissary General of War Prisoners. "We probably have your records somewhere."

"Probably." If the record included soldiers who didn't exist.

Mrs. Surratt served a plate of boiled beef and a bowl of red potatoes. A burly man with dusty hands waved as he went upstairs. When he came down, he introduced himself as John Holahan, a tombstone cutter. He plopped himself at the table and gathered his food with an expert boardinghouse reach.

Young John Surratt showed up shortly. Before five minutes passed, he let Fred know that he had a temporary job clerking at the Adams Express office and hated it. He was a slim, sandy-haired fellow who struck Fred as considerably brighter than his mother. After supper, sitting on the stoop away from eavesdroppers, Surratt offered Fred a cigarette, struck a match for him.

"You know what you're supposed to do, I guess."

"I do," Fred said. "I'll start tomorrow."

"You know Johnny Booth, the actor?"

"By reputation only."

"He'll want to meet you. He's running things in Washington."

"So I was told. Where is he?"

"He was up in New York till yesterday, raising money. Last night he rode down to Charles County. To hunt for real estate, so he can start a horse farm." John Surratt's smile told Fred it was just a story.

"I see."

"You travel a lot of country roads hunting for good property."

"You mean you travel a lot of escape routes."

Surratt chuckled. "That's true. Say, you want to stroll down to McFee's for a beer? Damn hot, and I'm thirsty."

"Sure." Fred dusted off his pants, squinted against the copper glare of the twilight sky. Reluctantly he added, "I suppose they have coffee. I gave up drinking."

* * *

Next day, as a first step, he went to the Executive Mansion in President's Park.

He shuffled through the public rooms with other visitors, rolling his eyes and volubly expressing horror at the damage done by souvenir hunters. Squares of cloth had been snipped from East Room draperies. Strips of wallpaper were missing. Upholstery in the Green Room had been crudely vandalized with knives or scissors.

In the afternoon he relaxed on the trampled grass between the White House and the three-story War Department, as many others citizens were doing. A straw hat shaded his face. This was the more pleasant side of the mansion, though it swarmed with mosquitoes and flies. The south side was a sprawl of stables and utility buildings, with squatter shanties visible on the flats beyond. Nothing could cut the foul stench drifting from the canal.

He opened a book from Shillington's secondhand bin. Poe's stories were full of thrills and rococo language, but he hardly paid attention. The book was a prop. He watched the mansion's north portico.

About four, a colored groom drove a handsome barouche to the portico. An elderly usher in knee breeches held the door as the President and his sour-faced wife came out, followed by a stout man in a dark frock coat and top hat. One of the Metropolitan Police assigned to guard Lincoln? Two officers worked the day shift, two others at night. Never in uniform, they carried concealed .38 revolvers. They reported to the District marshal, an old friend of Lincoln's who went heavily armed at all times. Miller had excellent information on security at the White House. Fred knew that Marshal Ward Lamon was unusually fearful of the President's safety, hence unusually protective.

In the shade near the bronze statue of Jefferson, Mrs. Lincoln hectored her husband about something. He nodded meekly as he helped her into the open carriage. Four uniformed cavalrymen riding black horses trotted up behind the carriage. Ohio light cavalrymen, quartered behind the mansion. They accompanied Lincoln on his jaunts about town.

The President took his seat and picked up the reins. A second groom brought up a roan for the unidentified civilian. Lincoln hawed to the team. The buggy rolled down a lane of well-wishers waving kerchiefs and shouting advice. The President tipped his tall hat to them.

The Ohio cavalrymen walked their horses behind the barouche. The man on the roan came last, scanning the crowd attentively. Lincoln drove out the iron gate and turned right on Pennsylvania Avenue with his bodyguards close behind. Could they be going out Seventh Street, to the presidential cottage at the Soldier's Home? Occupants of the mansion often summered there. Lincoln had, though lately he restricted himself to short excursions on warm evenings.

Fred noted the time, licked the tip of a pencil, and jotted an entry in a small notebook. He tucked Poe under his arm and strolled over to the elderly usher standing in the shade of the portico.

"Excuse me. That man who just left, the civilian on horseback. I think I know him. From the Metropolitan Police, isn't he?"

"No, sir, he's a special. Works for Colonel Baker. President Lincoln don't like all them soldiers traipsing after him. Tries to get shed of 'em sometimes. He's a whole lot fonder of Baker's men."

Affably, Fred tipped his straw hat. "Thanks, I guess I made a mistake."

Near the iron fence, he paused to jot another line in his little book. He walked through the gate without haste and disappeared in the crowds on the Avenue.

* * *

Two weeks later, in the middle of the night, he woke in Mrs. Surratt's attic and remembered something he'd forgotten. Plays. Hanna Siegel said she acted in plays.

He lay back in the dark, eyes open, smiling.

61

October 1864

Atlanta fell to Sherman in early September. The North took heart but the killing went on. In the midst of hundreds of thousands of family tragedies—fathers, sons, sweethearts, dead and maimed—the Siegels not only escaped tragedy but experienced good fortune. After Jubal Early's abortive raid, a few panicky owners in the suburbs put their homes on the market at sacrifice prices. The major snapped up a four-room cottage and barn on a lovely treed lot near the Rockville Road, beyond the city limits.

When he announced the purchase, Hanna said, "Where's the money coming from, Papa? How many times a week do you tell me your salary's too low?"

"It is! Can't fight the cheap sons of bitches I work for. I been making some investments. Military goods. Don't trouble your head."

"Because I'm a mere female?"

The sarcasm irked him. "That's the size of it. No more talk, I got to work on this plan. The whole department's working on it. Soldiers got to vote for the President in November. They vote in the field or we bring them home on leave. Stanton says if we don't—*kkkk*." His hand chopped like a guillotine.

"Some in Lincoln's own party want to do him in, you know. He isn't tough enough for them. I heard a rumor Stanton feels that way secretly, but I don't believe it. Washington's a nasty town for gossip."

* * *

Washington had become a thriving theatrical town thanks to Leonard Grover and John Ford. Grover liked Hanna's acting and put her on his list of reliable young women to engage when visiting stars needed to fill out a supporting cast. She worked with the nimble and funny Joe Jefferson when he brought his famed personation of Rip van Winkle to Grover's. Far less enjoyable were two weeks in repertory with the old lion of the American stage, Edwin Forrest. Hanna played Goneril five times in *King Lear*.

Forrest had kept his faithful audience over many years, though his reputation had never fully recovered from the Astor Place riots in 1849. Detractors still claimed he'd conspired with Bowery toughs and Know-Nothings to drive the English tragedian Macready off the New York stage by means of the riot. Hanna disliked Forrest, a bombastic man of fifty-eight who still had a lecher's eye.

In October, Grover cast her in a supporting role in *Uncle Waldo's Wisdom*, a weak example of a popular comedy genre: sophisticated city folk shown up by a canny New England rustic. Hanna hated the play but welcomed the salary.

After daytime rehearsals, she usually dined in a café frequented by theatricals. One evening Derek Fowley hobbled to her table, literally cap in hand. He was out of the ambulance service, shot in the foot by a drunken sutler.

Fawning shamelessly, Derek asked if she might put in a word for him with Grover. To get rid of him, she said she would.

"You've let your hair grow, Hanna. It's attractive."

"Thank you." Hanna's yellow tresses fell prettily on the

shoulders of her smart blue jacket. "Mr. Grover insists his actresses look feminine."

Derek couldn't resist a jab. "Not like soldiers?"

"That was a long time ago, Derek. I've gotten over it. So nice to see you. Good-bye."

*   *   *

John Wilkes Booth was seen frequently in the city, though not on the boards. Hanna encountered him holding court at the National again. She listened from the back of a crowd of admirers as he exclaimed, "A great, great loss. She was a true Southern patriot. She died more bravely than many a man would have done."

"Didn't she have a daughter?" someone asked.

"Safely placed in a convent school in Paris, thank the Lord." Hanna realized he was speaking about Rose Greenhow. Her death had been reported in the press a few days earlier. Rose had sailed from Greenock, Scotland, to Halifax, then on to Wilmington, North Carolina. A heavy sea pounded the steamer *Condor* as she ran through the blockade squadron to the Cape Fear River. Rose carried dispatches for Richmond and insisted on being rowed ashore at first light. Crashing waves capsized the open boat; Rose was drowned. The men accompanying her survived. Hanna wondered sadly what Margaret thought about it.

*   *   *

Hanna came out of Grover's stage door after a long, tiring rehearsal the next afternoon. Early autumn twilight had fallen. Martial music from the Avenue on the other side of the building signaled a parade in progress. Marchers from the Lincoln-Johnson clubs, she decided. The brass band played "We Are Coming, Father Abraham, Three Hundred Thousand More," not a selection heard at rallies for George McClellan. The Democrats were presenting the failed general as the nation's best chance for a swift armistice and a negotiated peace.

Hanna always stayed alert walking by herself. Thus she noticed a man in a drab suit lounging against the wall where the alley ran into Thirteenth Street. As she approached, he snatched off his cap, as though about to speak. She stepped wide of him, avoiding his eye.

"Miss Siegel?"

She gasped. "I don't believe it. Major Dasher?"

"Sills is the name at the moment. Duane Sills."

Gravely he shook her hand. He looked thinner; haggard.

Hanna waited until two men from the company passed on their way to supper. After she waved good-bye she whispered, "Did you desert the Army?"

"Oh, no, but I can't explain. I've looked for you."

"You have?" After more than two years, she couldn't gaze into his eyes without growing weak-kneed. She remembered how he had saved her, and kissed her, that dreadful night in Virginia.

"Diligently," he said. "I remembered you spoke about acting, so I've read every column about the playhouses. Every advertisement. I saw a piece listing the cast of this show and finally knew where to find you."

"That's very flattering, Maj—Mr. Sills. May I ask where you're staying?"

In the cool purple shadow of the alley his eyes had a guarded look. "A boardinghouse."

"I was on my way home to fix supper for my father. Would you care to join us?"

"Yes, Miss Siegel, indeed I would."

*   *   *

They rode the horsecar and walked the last few blocks to the house near the Navy Yard. They found the major donning gray gloves and a new top hat. Hanna introduced her friend Mr. Sills. The major shook hands, gave Fred a keen look to fix his face in mind, then said, "I can't stay to eat. Meeting someone at the Willard bar." The door banged, leaving them alone.

He sat with her while she cooked, saying little. Hanna served the stew with a loaf of bread she'd baked the day before, and a dusty bottle of Rhine wine. She apologized for not having claret. The major drank every drop that came into the house.

They ate by lamplight, in the kitchen, as easy with one another as though they'd known each other for years. Fred Dasher struck her as nervous, though; alert to the slightest sound from outside. He didn't talk about his business in Washington. She assumed from his reticence and the false name that it was clandestine military work. She didn't care. Of his recent Army experience he spoke only of the sad death of General Stuart, his former commander. She didn't ask whom he reported to now.

At the front door, he settled his cap on his head and said, "I'm not sure how long I'll be here. I'd like to take every opportunity to see you. I can pretty well arrange my time to suit myself."

"Then what about tomorrow? It's supposed to be a pleasant day, and I'm not rehearsing until evening. We have a dogcart and horse. I could show you the cottage my father bought out near Rockville. I'll pack a picnic lunch and call for you wherever you say."

He thought a moment. "All right. The boardinghouse is on H Street, number five forty-one. Noon?"

Hanna bubbled with anticipation. "I'm ever so glad to see you again, Dua—oh, I can't. You'll always be Frederick Dasher. I assure you I'll remember Sills when it's necessary. I'm a good actress."

"I've no doubt of that. I can't wait to see you onstage, if not this time, then when the fighting stops. It will end soon. Everyone on our side knows it, I think. Well, Miss Siegel—"

"Hanna."

"Yes. Hanna. Thank you." He leaned forward, as though about to kiss her. She raised herself on her toes. He drew back. "Noon tomorrow, then."

She hid her disappointment. "It will be just the two of us at the cottage. Papa works all day."

"Just the two of us. I'll look forward to it."

Their gazes held. She knew what would happen tomorrow, as surely as if they'd made a silent pact. He said good night and left. Hanna clapped her hands and whirled through the house, dancing and singing.

*   *   *

At five minutes before noon, she arrived at the brick boardinghouse on H Street. Fred Dasher waved and ran down the steps to the little dogcart. A horseman galloped by, swung around the corner of the house, and tied his fine bay to the post at the foot of an outside stair. He ran up to the second floor without a backward glance.

"That was John Booth, the actor!"

Fred tugged the brim of his straw hat lower. "Was it? I've never met him. I can't imagine he'd have business with Mrs. Surratt, or anyone living here."

They reached the cottage near the Rockville Road about one. Hanna carried the picnic hamper to the small kitchen. No furniture had been moved in yet. The rooms were empty, hollow, but immaculate, thanks to the former tenant. Slatted shutters laid bars of sunlight on the parlor's oak floor. Hanna ran to a closet where she'd stored a blanket, red and blue wool. Last Sunday she and the major had sat on the blanket, planning where they'd place their furniture. That is, she planned while the major complained. He wanted to buy all new pieces. "We got the money."

"Here, this will be more comfortable." She shook the blanket to unfold it. Fred helped her spread it. Only faint sounds penetrated from nearby lanes where Early's artillery had left deep craters.

They looked at each other with the blanket held taut between them. A kind of tormented sigh preceded his murmur of her name. "Hanna." He dropped the blanket and stepped on it as he seized her.

Excited but frightened, she put her arms around his neck and kissed him. Would he find her too slim, too boyish? *God, don't let it be so,* she thought as they knelt facing one another. They tore at each other's clothes like starving children suddenly shown a banquet table.

*   *   *

Afterward they lay naked on the hard floor with the blanket covering them. Hanna's yellow hair fanned across his shoulder. His arm was strong beneath her. Never had she felt anything like the ecstatic shudders that had run through her at the climax.

"I think I fell in love with you the moment I saw you," he said.

"I think I did too. I've never had many beaux."

"We don't know much about each other."

"Even less now that you can't talk about your work." He was silent. "Will you come back to Washington?"

"Don't know. I would guess not."

"When will I see you again?" She rolled over, her right breast pressing his side. She wished she weren't so small there. "I love you, Frederick. I can't bear to part."

He kissed her gently. "I love you. When the war's over, I'll show you my place near Front Royal, in the Shenandoah. A horse farm. Been in the family a long time. I suppose that damned Sheridan's stolen all the stock by now. Maybe razed the buildings too. But the land still belongs to me, and I'll rebuild. It's a beautiful spot."

"I'd love to see it." She caressed his face. "Has the war been awful for you?"

"No worse than for others. A terrible thing did happen to me at a place called Garlick's Landing, on the Peninsula. It threw me down for a good long time."

"Will you tell me about it?"

"Not yet. Someday."

"The war's so dangerous. So many chances for . . ." She couldn't say it.

"Nothing will happen to me. I won't allow it." He lifted her hand, kissed it. "I hadn't much to live for these past couple of years. Now I do."

Uncontrollably, tears came. "Oh, sweetheart, so do I. So do I."

62

October 1864

The closed carriage creaked down the Avenue in heavy traffic. Lon rode a sorrel mare, staying close to the door on the left side. It was the last Friday night in October; the evening of his first day on White House duty.

Assignment at the White House demonstrated Baker's confidence in Lon, but it couldn't give him the raw satisfaction of his regular job with the Detective Police. He was no longer tormented over arresting people with no warrant except his revolver. When he rounded up suspects without evidence, he told himself that if even half were guilty, it helped the Union. He took pleasure in knocking a suspect's teeth in if he resisted. He was still paying the secesh for Sledge, and for Zach Chisolm.

Tonight he felt like an undertaker. Everything he wore, his single-breasted black wool suit, waistcoat, cravat, and wide-brimmed felt hat, was black. In a sling under his left arm he carried a fine Deane & Adams .36-caliber, a five-shot, double-action piece less bulky than his Navy Colt. Baker insisted he buy it. "Ward Lamon is spitting nails over threats on the President's life, real or imaginary. He'd tie Lincoln to a chair to keep him out of theaters if he could." Lon remembered Lamon all too well. The man who had called Pinkerton an opportunist and self-promoter was marshal of the District of Columbia.

The thin and sickly-looking President had handed his stout wife into the carriage at the north portico. He didn't so much as glance at Lon. He was too busy ordering the four horsemen of the Union Light Guard to stay behind.

An electrical storm muttered in the west. Wind swirled dust clouds through the streets, together with debris and scraps of newspaper and the usual stew of city stenches. Seldom had Lon seen so many uniforms on the Avenue. Every train from the north and west disgorged hundreds of men furloughed to vote. The effort to save Lincoln's presidency pervaded the government. Baker said that for months, Stanton had routinely misfiled promotion orders for any officer suspected of favoring the Democratic candidate.

Lon heard music. He smelled the smoky torches before he saw the marchers. They spilled into the Avenue ten abreast, kept in cadence by a band. He tapped the carriage door. "We're running into an election parade, Mr. President. I suggest we turn off."

"Are they for me or against me?"

Lon squinted to read inscriptions on large boxy transparencies carried in the front ranks. "Definitely for. I see an

Elephant Club illumination, and a picture of General Mc-Clellan with a slogan, 'Enemy of freedom.' We can turn up Eleventh Street if you wish."

"All right, but stop around the corner so I can watch. I don't have all that many admirers in this town, you know."

Lon understood Lincoln's weary humor. Well before the nominating convention, some Republicans wanted him to step aside for a candidate deemed more acceptable. Grant, or Ben Butler. Lincoln's pocket veto of a Reconstruction bill infuriated its authors, Senator Wade of Ohio and Representative Davis of Maryland. In August they aired their grievances in Greeley's *Tribune*. The Wade-Davis manifesto accused Lincoln of usurping congressional powers; making laws instead of obeying and executing them.

Lon told the driver to park so those inside could see the parade. Few on Eleventh Street noticed the man leaning out the carriage window. Hundreds of torches, lanterns, and transparencies passed the intersection, followed by the band, then wagons carrying VETERANS FOR LINCOLN, another band, more marchers. Lon opened his pocket watch.

"Begging your pardon, sir, the curtain's already up."

"Yes, I'm sick of this. It's cold." That was Mary Lincoln, still as shrewish as Lon remembered from the terrible passage through Baltimore.

"All right, Mother, we'll go." A tap on the carriage roof started them forward. At the corner of Eleventh and F, a street boy yelled at passersby, "This way to Ford's, one block to Ford's, seats still available at Ford's."

The carriage turned right from F into Tenth, parking on the wrong side so Lincoln could alight on the curb. Gaslights shone on gaudy posters flanking the doors. Ford's was showing THE LAVISH REVIVAL OF THE HEARTRENDING DRAMA BY MR. DION BOUCICAULT—"STREETS OF NEW YORK." Lon dismounted. He handed the reins and a coin to a Negro boy.

"She be right here minute the show's over," the boy said.

"No, fifteen minutes before."

A sheet of lightning flamed across the dome of the sky but the thunder remained far away. The carriage door opened. Lincoln hit his silk hat on the door, grabbed it before it tumbled off. He laughed, and his eye fixed on Lon. "Say, I've seen you before. First time in Harrisburg, wasn't it?"

"You have a wonderful memory, Mr. President. Price is my name. I worked for Pinkerton's then."

"Yes, sir. Mr. Price. Welcome to the dullest job in town."

Lincoln helped his wife alight. She too remembered Lon. She wrinkled her nose in what amounted to a sneer. Life among the mighty had its penalties.

John Ford and an assistant manager ran out to greet the Lincolns and escort them up the carpeted stairs. Lon followed. They passed behind rows of turning heads in the darkened dress circle. Someone exclaimed, "There he is." People applauded. Lincoln waved his top hat, pulled along by his angry and impatient wife.

A passage led from the dress circle to the presidential box. Actually it was two boxes with a middle partition removed. The rich wallpaper was the color of red wine. Lincoln held a chair for his wife, then leaned over the rail to bow and acknowledge applause while the actors waited onstage. The President gathered up his coattails and sat in a rocking chair. He saw Lon step out to his assigned post in the passage. "No, no, Mr. Price, stay. Enjoy the play."

Lon thanked him, came back into the box, and stood with his back against the door. Mrs. Lincoln took a Japanese fan from her beaded bag, shook it open noisily. Her ostentatious fanning drew stares from the opposite side of the dress circle.

The evening's melodrama had a complicated plot involving a wronged man, one Captain Fairweather, a treacherous bank clerk named Badger, and a stalwart hero, Mark something-or-other. Lon paid little attention. He kept watch on sections of the theater visible to him.

Management lowered the curtain after the second of five acts. Lon asked if the President or his wife wanted to step out. Mary Lincoln snapped, "No." Across the dress circle, people rose, chatting and moving to the aisle. Lon saw Margaret Miller, seated by herself.

"May I go outside a moment, Mr. President?"

"Certainly, Price. Anything wrong?"

Lon lied. "No, sir."

He stood in the passageway, overwhelmed by guilt and renewed longing. Margaret's face shimmered in his thoughts like a lantern projection. He'd worked hard to purge her from his heart and mind after deciding in New York that he could do nothing else. Over the months the pain had eased, although it would never go away.

When he returned to the box, Margaret was studying the President and his wife. She saw him. She dropped her playbill and sat rigid, ignoring a gentleman trying to return to his seat. Her eyes seemed to burn like black opals. He couldn't look away.

The fire curtain rose; the gas mantles dimmed. Mr. Ford appeared from behind the proscenium. "Ladies and gentlemen, to honor our distinguished guests, the President and First Lady, we have arranged a special presentation. Mr. Sothern, whom you are enjoying in tonight's performance, will favor us with a recitation of the popular celebratory ballad by Mr. T. Buchanan Read, 'Sheridan's Ride.' "

"Well, it's election time," Lincoln whispered to Lon. "Can't hurt."

The audience whistled and cheered in response to the announcement. A week before, in the Shenandoah, General Philip Sheridan had galloped his great black horse, Rienzi, from Winchester to Cedar Creek to lead a counterattack against Jubal Early. Following Sheridan's victory, poets rushed their laudatory verses to the public. Read's caught on instantly.

Mr. Sothern, a transplanted British actor, stepped to the footlights and declaimed, " 'Hurrah, hurrah for Sheridan! Hurrah, hurrah, for horse and man!' " Lon's eye kept straying to Margaret.

The second interval came before act five, advertised as THE SPECTACULAR FINALE! INFERNO IN THE SLUMS! Lon doubted a stage effect could duplicate what he'd experienced. He stepped into the passage again and there she was, a strange, pensive expression on her face.

"Hello, Lon. I nearly fainted when I saw you."

"I could say the same. You look beautiful, Margaret." And she did, wearing emerald green silk, a black shawl, her hair knotted high on the back of her head in a cadogan with ringlets and a decoration of little white roses.

The box door opened. Margaret caught her breath as Lincoln came out. He smiled with a warmth that relieved the ugliness of his mole-speckled face. "Hello there. Mr. Price, who's this charming visitor?"

"An old friend, sir. Mrs.—"

"McKee," she said. "Good evening, Mr. Lincoln."

"Good evening, my dear. We've not met before. Are you a Washingtonian?"

"Transplanted from Baltimore. To be candid, sir, I suppose you'd call me Maryland secesh."

"Well, Mrs. McKee, that can be forgiven. I'm in a devil of a lot of trouble with some of my friends because I don't believe we should flog Southerners unmercifully when we have peace again. I propose to hold out a hand to our brethren who strayed. Let 'em up easy."

"Who's that you're speaking to, Father?" Mrs. Lincoln exclaimed.

"Just a young friend of our bodyguard." Lincoln whispered, "I'm always in the soup if Mother catches me talking to another woman. Excuse me." He returned to the box. A gong rang to signal the last act. Margaret's beautiful green gown, cut low in the bodice, showed the soft, rounded body he'd held in his arms that night in Gramercy Park.

"Lon, why didn't you come for me?"

"I couldn't."

"Why?"

He took her hands in his. Her skin was warm, sweetly scented with a perfume reminiscent of rose petals. "I don't know that I can explain it without your hating me all over again."

"What do you mean? I threw my husband over for you. The least you can do is tell the truth. Will you be free after the play?"

"As soon as I escort them back to the mansion."

"Then come see me. I live—"

"I know where you live. Franklin Square. I ride by every few days. I've seen you moving past the windows."

"Then why haven't you—?"

"Because I couldn't face you, Margaret."

"—no business flirting with other women, Father."

"Mother, I wasn't, I was merely being courteous to a friend of Mr. Price."

"A *female* friend!"

"Mother, don't make a scene. People are staring."

The harsh colloquy went on, but Lon barely heard. Margaret's eyes shone with tears. The gas mantles dimmed. "Come to me, Lon. I'll wait all night."

"I'll come."

"You said it once before."

"I'll be there, I promise." He squeezed her hand and slipped from the passage into the box. Mrs. Lincoln's fury was evident in her face and posture. The President had moved his rocker away from her and sat staring at the stage in a vacant way. People said he had nightmares, and periods of depression. No wonder.

Lon leaned against the wall, churning. The curtain rose on the final scene, the interior of a tenement. Across the dress circle, Margaret's seat was empty. They would play their final scene before the night grew much older.

63

October–December 1864

"You don't know how you hurt me. You can't imagine."

In Franklin Square, wind blew dust clouds turned silver by the lightning. The thunder stayed far away in the Maryland mountains. Another storm would pass without rain.

Lon sat with a cigarette smoldering in his fingers. He'd thrown off his undertaker's coat and untied his cravat. Standing by a window, Margaret looked as neat and perfect as she had at Ford's. A hall clock chimed midnight.

"Lon, I have to know. Why didn't you come for me?"

"Because something terrible happened. I was responsible. Your brother, Cicero, was in New York—"

"I didn't keep it from you. I saw him in Gramercy Park, he came there." A flying branch hit a windowpane, loud as a shot. She hadn't lit a lamp because of the almost constant lightning. The wind made the upper stories creak and moan. Lon found a marble tray for crushing out his cigarette.

"I tracked him down. It was my duty. I knew he was a Confederate agent and I found him in a place known to be a secesh hangout. When I tried to arrest him, he ran. I chased him. He went into a building set on fire during the riots. He must have been frightened, not thinking. I cornered him and he tried to kill me. I barely escaped before the building burned completely. He didn't get out."

Margaret absorbed that. She reached behind her head, pulled out pins, and shook her hair so it fell rich and dark at her shoulders. Tiny white roses lay strewn around her skirt. "When you were imprisoned in Richmond, my brother tortured you, didn't he?"

"How do you know that? I never told you."

"He did."

"What?" Lon strode to her, trying to see her expression. She slipped around him, rattled a matchbox, lit a lamp. The cleavage at her bodice caused a reaction all wrong for this moment. He couldn't help it.

"Sit down, Lon. I'll tell you as much as I can."

He reached for her hand but she avoided him, choosing a settee across the parlor. She settled herself, clasped her hands in her lap.

"Cicero didn't die in that fire. Like you, he escaped. But he suffered horrible burns. He's scarred, here"—she touched her throat—"and on this hand. It's done something to him. Made him worse than he was, if that's possible. I have difficulty facing the truth about my brother. He's a terrible man. Full of— I don't know. Poisons."

"Where did you see him last?"

"Here. In this room."

"When?"

"July. Right after Jubal Early's raid."

"What was he doing in Washington? A spy mission?"

"I presume so. He was traveling under an assumed name, Hiram Seth. He carried on about saving the Confederacy single-handed. He talked about striking high. So high I'd be astonished. That was his word, astonished."

"Striking what? A person? A building? The Capitol? The Executive Mansion? We've had reports of reb agents in Canada plotting to start more fires in New York. Something like that?"

"Lon, I swear to you, he didn't say. He threatened me, and not very subtly."

"Threatened you how?"

"I understood him to mean there'd be reprisals if I repeated anything he said. I'm afraid Cicero is deranged. I can hardly think of him as my flesh and blood anymore. He's some sick, warped thing who delights in hurting people. He justifies it by saying they're enemies."

"I'm afraid you're not far wrong there." Lon gazed into Franklin Square, deserted in the blustery autumn night.

"You didn't come for me in New York because you thought you were responsible for his death?"

He walked to the settee. The scent of rose petals swirled around him.

"How could I face you? Live with you? I couldn't."

"God, this war breaks people like crockery. Look what it's done to us. Ruined us. Ruined me."

He sat beside her, not touching her, though he felt the palpable warmth of her body. "Margaret, you wanted a blood price for your father. You wanted to punish someone. It's understandable."

"I know, but it was wrong." She struck her fist on her knee. "Stupid. I never had the stomach for it. I'm not that sort of woman. I thought I was and I'm not."

"But you spied for them."

"It was a game. A lady's and gentleman's entertainment, with Rose leading it. Rose is gone. She drowned trying to reach Wilmington, did you know?"

"Yes, the papers wrote it up thoroughly."

"The war changed, didn't it? It isn't a game any longer. I found that out."

"So did I. So did every West Point general who said it wouldn't last ninety days. So did every reb dandy who put on a plumed hat and rode off on a noble crusade. The war changed and it changed everybody." He was so tense he felt pain in his arms and legs. He knotted his hands between his knees.

"I'm not unlike your brother anymore, Margaret. I've come to enjoy hurting enemies. It's partly from wanting to win, partly paying back for friends I lost. Most of all I think it's the work itself. The lies. The deceit. The thuggery. You get used to it. One of my dead friends, a detective named Greenglass, warned me. He said dirt rubs off. I didn't listen."

She clasped her arms across her breasts, bowing her head. He feared he'd anger her if he touched her, but he couldn't stay his hand. He laid it gently on hers. She looked up. Lightning showed tears streaming down.

They sat unmoving for a few seconds. Then, as if surrendering to some magnetic force, she lunged forward at the same moment he did. Their arms tangled, and their mouths met in hunger and longing.

* * *

Upstairs, in the warm and drowsy aftermath of lovemaking, he managed a wry smile when he said, "I believe I've overlooked a question that might have some bearing on this reunion. Where's your husband?"

"In some woman's bed, probably." She kissed the corner of his lips. "Who gives a damn?"

"You're still married, aren't you?"

"Not for long. Donal will sue for divorce. I've heard from his lawyers."

She turned on her back, nestled against his ribs. He drew up the starched sheet and rested his hand on her bare breast underneath.

"I have to go on with my work."

"I assumed you would."

"But I won't give you up. Not again. We'll have our own armistice, till it's over."

"Until the South surrenders?"

"Yes. Surrender's inevitable. The South can fight on for a while yet, but they don't have the men, nor the resources, to prevail."

"Were we wrong to secede and go to war?"

"Yes. All the rhetoric about states' rights and preserving a heritage, a way of life—a person can swallow some or all of that, maybe. But one hard lump won't go down. Slavery. It's evil. It must end."

"When do you think it will be over?"

"Next year, I hope. Sooner if we're lucky."

"Can we keep our truce that long?"

"By God I'll try."

"So will I."

He didn't dare tell her that he'd pursue Cicero to the end; use force to apprehend him if necessary, especially after the revelation about some great plan. A last flicker of lightning whitened the ceiling and died. They lay together in darkness as deep and impenetrable as the future.

* * *

Later that morning, Lon informed Lafayette Baker of Cicero's appearance in Washington. Before he left Margaret's bed he told her that he would. She was silent, neither granting permission nor withholding approval.

Baker copied Lon's description of Miller's injuries into a voluminous file of suspected agents of the Confederate Signal Service. "I'll advise Lamon that Miller was seen here. I can't imagine he stayed, but we'll be watchful. Whatever scheme he's hatching will probably require local accomplices."

"I agree," Lon said. "But who are they? How do we find them?"

Neither man could answer the questions.

* * *

Lon examined the locks on the front and rear doors of the town house and declared they weren't adequate. He bought new ones at a hardware, descended to the dank cellar for tools, came up empty-handed, and returned to the store. One morning when he wasn't on White House duty, he removed the old locks and replaced them with the new, which had heavy dead bolts. Margaret repaid him with a sumptuous breakfast of eggs with ham, grits, and biscuits she'd baked herself.

For Christmas he bought her a gift that puzzled her when she opened the lacquered presentation box.

"It's a Colt .31-caliber. Excellent weapon, I owned one for

a while. It'll fit nicely in your handbag. We'll go down to the flats behind the Executive Mansion and I'll teach you how to fire it."

"I have a derringer. Why on earth do I need another gun?"

"Because a derringer's only good for one shot. Because you live by yourself and I can't be here all the time. Because Grant's easing the ban on prisoner exchanges and the streets are full of Union boys who haven't seen a woman for months. Because there are nearly as many Confederate deserters in town. Because I love you."

Margaret kissed him. The discussion ended there.

64

January 1865

Washington celebrated the New Year with an optimism that sickened Booth. The damned tyrant in the White House had won reelection handily. Richmond still believed Lincoln could be used to bargain for peace terms, though not to free Confederate prisoners; Grant was allowing exchanges again.

By telegraph, the despicable General Sherman gave the President a Christmas gift—the seaport city of Savannah. Sherman's army, and a second army of bummers following it, had laid waste to Georgia. Now "Cump" Sherman was ready to carry his vicious program of total war to the Carolinas. The damned nigger-loving Congress was ramming through a constitutional amendment to abolish slavery. The whole world was being turned upside down, but the second American Revolution was failing. Booth's beloved South was careening toward defeat, surrender, humiliation. As this became ever more certain, his hatred of the chief culprit grew and grew.

On a gray January morning, dejected and battling a headache, he dressed for the street with the military touches he'd begun to affect: brass cavalry spurs, gauntlets, a Jeff Davis hat of dark gray felt with a black plume and the left brim looped up.

His career no longer interested him to the degree it once had. He'd done Romeo at Grover's recently, but he acted by rote, though somewhat more soberly than his late father, who liked to boast that he could play any role in the repertory of Shakespearean leading men dead drunk. Which he often did.

Let the others in the family take the glory: his older brother Edwin, who possessed the discipline he lacked, or his brother June—Junius Booth Jr.—who showed a strong interest in theater management. As the runt of the litter, Booth had always cared more for the fame, and the women, than for the hard work demanded by his craft. Now, at twenty-six, he was obsessed with his great mission.

To carry it out, he'd assembled a small group of conspirators, the best he could find. Samuel Arnold and Michael O'Laughlin were boyhood friends from Maryland. O'Laughlin was flamboyant and darkly handsome, Arnold quiet and plain. Arnold clerked in his brother's feedstore, O'Laughlin worked as a common farmhand. Both were ex-soldiers.

Booth had recruited buck-toothed Davy Herold with his simple mind and silly grin because Herold knew the back roads and byways of southern Maryland from hunting trips. Atzerodt, the little German from Port Tobacco, knew the Potomac currents. He worked as a carriage maker but soldiered for the cause as a secret ferryman.

And there was Johnny Surratt, whose mother ran the boardinghouse where they met, though never more than two or three of them at a time. None had met all the others, nor would they unless it became necessary. Booth deemed that a good way to protect the operation.

They were adequate men, but not ideal. Atzerodt and Herold were brainless, Arnold occasionally headstrong and argumentative. The group lacked a good soldier whom Booth could send out to kill someone, knowing he'd carry out the assignment. This lack was one of many things about the scheme that sent Booth to the liquor supply as early as eight or nine every morning.

"Johnny?" Ella whined from the bedroom. "Are you going out?"

He flung a cloak over his shoulders. Lord, how the sitting room stank. Soiled shirts and undergarments were draped on chairs or discarded in the corner. A half dozen whiskey bottles decorated the desk. He refused to have the chambermaid prying in his quarters and relied on Ella to clean up once or twice a week. The slut did a poor job of it.

"I'm going to Ford's," he called. His colleague Forrest was playing *Jack Cade* tonight. Booth wanted to book the presidential box one more time, to study it further.

"We haven't ate breakfast."

"Go to the dining room. Sign the bill."

Ella wrapped her pudgy body around the doorframe and pouted. Her gaudy dressing gown fell open. He saw the aroused state of her nipples and wrinkled his nose.

"I want you again, Johnny. Don't go."

"For Christ's sake, Ella, we fucked half the night. I'm tired. I have other things on my mind."

She lifted her wrapper to show her privates. "Johnny, please, don't go away. You've gotten very strange lately, hanging out with all those shiftless men."

"Shut up, shut up!" Booth lunged to the desk, lobbed a nearly empty bottle at her. Ella shrieked and ducked. The bottle broke on the wall, scattering shards of glass. The liquor stained the wallpaper as it ran down.

"Oh, you've got a terrible temper, Johnny, terrible." Ella peeped around the doorframe, ready to dart back if he threw something else. Booth smoothed his mustache with a trembling hand, pointed to the broken glass.

"Have that cleaned up when I come back."

* * *

That afternoon, in a coffeehouse at the edge of the Northern Liberties, he met Sam Arnold. They chose a corner table, away from other patrons.

"We will execute our plan two days from now, Wednesday, the eighteenth," Booth said. "Forrest is acting Jack Cade again. It's a play Lincoln likes."

"Why?"

"How the hell do I know? I'm not his confidant. Jack Cade leads a revolt of bondsmen. Maybe the ape sees slaves turning on their masters."

Arnold frowned at his crockery mug, the coffee untasted. "I have the same objection as always. How do we know he'll attend? Sometimes the papers don't announce it till late afternoon. Sometimes they don't announce it at all."

"It's a chance we must take. Ford's is the ideal place."

"Johnny, I keep telling you, it is *not* the ideal place. Abducting him from a theater, especially Ford's, is not smart. The box at Ford's has no separate stairway. The only way out's through the dress circle."

"We'll truss him and lower him from the box to the stage. It's a drop of only twelve feet. I can jump it easily."

"We'll do that with a grown man?"

Ashen, Booth whispered, "Will you keep your damned voice down?"

"Sorry, sorry. But it's a fair question. What if he struggles? He's big."

"He's a weakling. Half sick most of the time."

"There's always a bodyguard."

"You'll take care of him with a gun. We'll station Michael at the controls of the gas, next to the prompter's table. He'll black out the theater as soon as Linc—our man reaches the stage. Davy will hold the horses at the back door. I suppose he's not too stupid to do that," Booth added with a disdainful toss of his head.

Sam Arnold pushed his mug away. "I don't like it. I won't do it. That's my answer, Johnny. I won't do it unless we take him out of doors, where we have a better chance."

"God damn it—God *damn* it, Sam"—two grandmotherly ladies seated by the front window turned to stare—"this is *my* plan, to carry out as I see fit."

"Is that right, Johnny? I thought it was Richmond's plan."

Booth's hand flew sideways, knocking both coffee mugs to the floor. The mop-haired old man who owned the place lumbered from the kitchen. "What's this? Who's tearing up my—? Oh, Booth, it's you. Might have known."

The actor dug greenbacks from his pocket, threw them at the old man. "If you don't want my patronage, plenty of others welcome it." He snatched his plumed hat from the next table, glared at Sam Arnold, and marched to the door, brass spurs jingling.

The old man got down on his knees with a rag. "Those Booths, they're all crazy. Your friend's the worst."

Arnold said, "They don't call them the mad Booths of Maryland for nothing."

*   *   *

On Wednesday night, January 18, Lincoln did not attend the performance at Ford's. Not that it would have made any difference. Sam Arnold's objection prevented Booth from implementing the kidnaping.

He sent Arnold a note saying they would go at it differently, try to abduct Lincoln from his carriage, at the first opportunity. Booth could barely bring himself to surrender that way, but pragmatically, he had no choice. He needed Arnold. He needed all of them, even though not one of them was adequate to the task.

*   *   *

Muffled to the eyes against the blowing rain, Booth failed to see the man huddled by the National's front door. "Cap'n? Cap'n Booth?" The man stepped out. They collided.

"You damned cretin, you nearly knocked me down."

"Cap'n, I'm mighty sorry. I been waitin' half the day, hopin' you'd come by." Huge dark eyes sunken in pale flesh peered at him with childlike entreaty. The young man's broad, flat nose and overhanging brow gave his face a moronic cast. "Don't you recognize me?"

"No, and I'm thankful. Stand aside or—"

"Cap'n," the other interrupted, "we met down South. You was playin' a theater in Montgomery, Alabama."

A faint recollection stirred. "What's your name?"

"Paine, sir. Lewis Paine." A swift look along the rainy sidewalk; no one was paying attention, not even to the famous Mr. Booth. Paine crowded close in a way Booth found offensive.

"When I met you after the show and we had a real nice drink in your dressing room, the name was Lewis Powell. Powell, he was a soldier. Lately he was in Mosby's command, but he got sick of it. And don't you know, one day last week at Fairfax Court House, Powell just up and disappeared. Lost his uniform an' all. The Union soldiers takin' care of refugees said, 'What's your name, boy?' and I said, Lewis Paine."

A deserter, then. "Well, I do remember you, Mr. Paine, but you'll have to excuse me, I have business."

"Oh. I was just hopin' we could have another drink, so's I could ask how you been. I know you're more famous than ever. I always been proud to say I'm a friend of the great Mr. John W. Booth. But I understand about business, Captain." Looking sad, Paine held out his hand to conclude the conversation.

Suddenly Booth forgot the chilly rain, the dampness soaking him to the skin. The young man was splendidly built, obviously strong. Booth guessed he was also utterly stupid, but taken with Booth's celebrity.

And he needed an obedient soldier.

He smiled his most radiant and winning smile. "Mr. Paine, I apologize for being rude to an old friend. My business can wait an hour. We certainly must have a drink in memory of that pleasant meeting in Montgomery."

"We can go to the saloon bar, I'll pay," Paine exclaimed.

"Oh, no, Mr. Paine, no." Booth, the shorter, had to strain to throw an arm across Paine's broad back. "We'll drink some of the fine whiskey I keep in my suite. It's my pleasure. Come along, sir. I can't tell you how happy I am to see you again."

65

February 1865

The Richmond ring still operated successfully behind Miss Van Lew's facade of craziness. Her operatives sent word of unusual activity within the Army and the government, surmising that Lee was preparing to shift the bulk of his forces to North Carolina, there to fight on until the last man fell.

Meanwhile, Baker's detectives investigated every death threat against Lincoln, every rumor of a bomb plot, every fanciful tip from an informer. To deal with the reports, Baker ran his men days at a time without sleep. He dispatched teams to Montreal, New York, Philadelphia, Chicago, Columbus. Other teams searched the sordid corners of Washington and patrolled rural roads of Maryland. "When desperate men face defeat, they turn from victory to vengeance," Baker said. "We can take no chances."

On the thirteenth of February, a Monday, Lon and Sandstrom rode the cars up to Baltimore. Someone had boasted to a Negro servant girl that he would help kidnap Lincoln. The Baltimore police telegraphed the War Department.

Bundled in fur-collared coats, the detectives sat near an iron stove at the head of the car. Lon had started his beard again; it was coming out with white patches. He watched forlorn trees and fields pass by. The sky was spitting snow. "God, Eugene, I hate this part of the country."

Sandstrom said, "Why?"

"Bad memories. New York down to Richmond, nothing but bad memories. With one exception."

"That lady."

Lon nodded.

"I read a guidebook about California last year. Didn't sound bad."

"Isn't the gold all gone?"

"Plenty of sunshine, though. All year long."

"I didn't hate winter when I was growing up in Ohio," Lon said. "I loved to sled and skate. But I hate it now. I hate the cold, and the gloom, and the snow that's dirty five minutes after it falls."

"I'll bet it's the war getting you down, not the weather."

"The war, and this work," Lon said with his eye on the bleak horizon.

"I'll loan you the guidebook."

"Thanks. I'll read it." Though he wouldn't have to worry about changing anything in his life until the Confederacy threw down its arms and all the undefeated good old rebels, the would-be assassins and bomb throwers, were caught, jailed, or hung.

* * *

"He beat her," said the large lady who operated Mrs. Branson's Boarding House near the Baltimore harbor. "Poor Sabina resisted his advances and he turned on her like a wild dog. I'm not surprised. I smelled liquor on him every day he was here."

Lon asked, "When did he rent the room?"

"One week ago today. I had a bad feeling but—you know. Money's money."

Snow slanted past the windows of the cluttered parlor. Lon opened a notebook on his knee. "What was his name?"

"He signed the card Lou Smith, L-o-u. I could barely read his handwriting. He obviously wasn't educated."

"Describe him for me?"

"Tall, much taller than either of you gentlemen." Sandstrom examined his nails with an annoyed expression. "Six feet, perhaps an inch or two more. His forehead sloped out from his hairline, like this. Almost a shelf above his eyes. He looked like a mental deficient. But physically—oh, a Greek god." She fanned herself with her handkerchief.

Sandstrom said, "We want to talk to the girl."

Mrs. Branson led them to a cold garret lit by a barnyard lantern hung from a rafter. Sabina Lee was a well-fleshed young black woman. Her pretty features were bruised and discolored by a beating. Half a dozen stitches marked her forehead like a worry line.

"Sabina, these gentlemen are detectives, from Washington. Can you tell them what happened?"

"So we can catch the man," Lon said.

Sabina hitched herself up on her cot. She crossed her arms over the bosom of her flannel nightdress, as if she thought it too revealing, which it wasn't. "Saturday night, I was cleanin' the kitchen 'bout half pas' eleven. He come in, drunk as a polecat. We talked a little, then he put his hand on me. I axed him to stop. He laughed and kep' on. I told him again, stop it. I was real scared. I grabbed a cleaver. That made him real mad with me. He knocked the cleaver out of my hand an' punched me in the stomach. Called me nigger and a lot of other names. He punched me again and I threw up. He tore a leg off a kitchen chair an' whipped me with it."

"You see, gentlemen, my cousin Veronica's ill," Mrs. Branson explained. "I stayed with her until her husband's train finished its run Saturday night, he's a B-and-O brakeman. When I returned at half past twelve, I found Sabina unconscious and bleeding on the floor."

Sandstrom said, "That's a touching story, but what about threats to the President? That's why we're here. Tell us what Smith said about the President." Lon gave him a look which Sandstrom ignored.

"Oh, he talk a lot 'bout the Pres'dent before he started his dirty stuff. He was real drunk, so I didn't put no stock in it. He said him and some friends, they was going to kidnap Mr. Linkum. He called the Pres'dent awful names, makes me blush just to remember."

Lon said, "Sabina, this is important. Did Smith mention any day or date for the kidnaping?"

"Yes, sir, he did. Day after tomorrow. Wednesday."

"He was definite?"

"Yes, sir. Said he had to be back in Washington for the party—he called it the party—Tuesday noon."

"And where was this criminal act supposed to take place?" Sandstrom said.

"He said when Mr. Linkum went to see a play."

"Ford's Theater? Grover's? Which?"

"The play's at some hospital. Not at night, in the daytime. Mr. Linkum and his wife, they'd both go see this play and that's when it would happen."

Lon patted her hand. "Thank you, Sabina, you've been a lot of help. You also, Mrs. Branson."

"Don't let nothin' happen to Mr. Linkum, sirs. He a great man. He set the colored people free, and when the war's done, he'll bring the jubilee."

"But there are plenty who'd like to stop him," Lon said.

*   *   *

Tuesday morning, Lafayette Baker brought the White House schedule down from Stanton's office. Lon and Sandstrom jumped from their chairs.

"Gentlemen, that darky deserves a reward and a guaranteed ticket to heaven. Look here." Baker pointed to an entry on the closely written sheet. "Tomorrow afternoon, three o'clock, Campbell Hospital out by the Soldier's Home. E. L. Davenport and others from Daly's traveling troupe will present *Still Waters Run Deep* for the convalescents. The President and Mrs. Lincoln are to attend, then visit with the boys. The papers printed the story last week."

"They can't go," Lon said.

"That's what I told the secretary. He will inform the White House and send the President somewhere else. The President won't like it, but he'll go along. Stanton's got the wind up about this."

Baker laid his boot heel on the corner of his desk. "The presidential carriage will go to Campbell Hospital as scheduled. With its regular driver, but no cavalry escort. You gentlemen will ride inside. Armed," he said, almost as an afterthought.

*   *   *

Bitter air stung Booth's cheeks. His little one-eyed mare pranced. He'd bought her in Baltimore for eighty dollars and got his money's worth. He laid a gauntlet on the mare's neck to calm her. Everything was in place, nothing overlooked.

Behind him, partially hidden in a thicket of bare trees, Johnny Surratt fidgeted on the seat of an old Dearborn wagon, a plain gray vehicle with its middle and rear side curtains lowered. Lincoln would be removed from his carriage and trussed in the wagon. At a rendezvous in the District, Arnold and O'Laughlin would join them and escort the wagon across the East Branch bridge into Maryland. At Port Tobacco, George Atzerodt would supervise the night crossing of the Potomac. A detachment from the Virginia Ninth Cavalry would escort the captive to Ashland, a resort fifteen miles north of Richmond. Johnny Surratt had spent almost two weeks down there in January, arranging everything. Last week Booth had sent a signal to Miller by courier, naming the day. He wrote the message using the Vigenère tableau and a new key phrase, *come victory.*

In a hurried trip to New York, he'd said good-bye to Edwin at his Gramercy Park town house. Edwin of course had no idea why his younger brother seemed so passionate about the farewell. Next Booth called on their beloved sister, Asia, in Philadelphia. She sensed something amiss when he gave her a sealed pouch for her husband's safe. He wouldn't tell her what it contained: his will, leaving his meager assets to her, June, and Edwin, and a letter. *To whom it may concern.* The letter described Booth's lifelong loyalty to the South and justified the abduction of the Yankee tyrant.

This far past the city limits, traffic on the Seventh Street road was sparse, especially on a dark winter afternoon. Two ambulances had rolled by thirty minutes ago carrying wounded to the hospital. Three nurses shivering in an open buggy passed southbound a little later. In either direction, Booth saw a dreary vista of woodlands, farmhouses, livestock pens, and barns. Not a single person moved anywhere in the gray landscape. Atzerodt and Paine were hidden behind a dilapidated chicken coop across the road. Each carried a pistol and a double-barrel shotgun from a supply stored at the rural tavern still called Surratt's.

Booth heard the approaching carriage before he saw it. A half mile south, the road curved and dipped. "Johnny, get ready. I think he's coming."

Surratt picked up the reins. Two horses appeared from the sunken road, then the big vehicle, a somber black landau with its top raised against the winter cold. On each corner of the low rail in front of the driver, a small Stars and Stripes streamed out. Booth's stomach hurt. Into his head leaped Richmond's speech at Bosworth Field in the fifth act of *Richard III. O thou, whose captain I account myself—* He pulled his cloak away from his face, unconsciously mouthing the words.

" '—look on my forces with a gracious eye.' "

The carriage horses pounded the frozen road.

" 'Put in their hands thy bruising irons of wrath—' "

He raised one gloved hand, drew a little circle in the air. Paine rode from behind the chicken coop. He wore a greatcoat and a greasy plug hat. He acknowledged Booth's signal by thrusting his shotgun over his head.

" 'Make us thy ministers of chastisement!' "

Booth backed the mare to a position nearer Surratt's wagon. The landau was nearly abreast of them. A square isinglass window reflected dull daylight. The landau hid Paine when he fired both shotgun barrels. The reports reverberated.

The driver lashed the team. The isinglass window flew up. A man leaned out, aiming a pistol. Booth's smug smile vanished. Someone else in the landau fired shots on the other side. Booth's skittish mare snorted and sidestepped. "It isn't Lincoln!" Surratt exclaimed. "Who the hell is it?"

With a rattle of chains and a grind of wheels, the landau passed. Booth saw Paine and Atzerodt astride their horses, baffled and frightened. The driver kicked the brake and dragged on the reins; the landau rocked to a stop. Two men jumped out and ran back toward the site of the attack. "Get away, scatter," Booth yelled to his cohorts across the road. "Leave the wagon, Johnny. Climb up behind me."

"But there's pistols and ammunition left in—"

"God damn it, climb up unless you want to be caught and hung."

Johnny Surratt flung himself onto the mare's back and clasped Booth's waist. The men on foot fired a fusillade at Paine and Atzerodt galloping away. Booth spurred the mare into the thicket of bare trees. *They were ready for us. How did they know?*

Low branches whipped his face. Soon he had bleeding cuts on both cheeks. He could easily outdistance the pursuers, who had to be government detectives. That was no consolation. The tyrant in the White House was safe and unhurt. Booth roared every filthy oath he knew as the mare carried them away.

*   *   *

Lon slammed a fist on Baker's desk. "We shouldn't have lost them. We should have ridden horses."

"I agree. The fault's mine." Baker's words made Lon feel no better. "I should have sent six or eight men, not two."

"I recognized the man Sabina Lee described."

"We'll put out a dodger on Smith if that's really his name. Circulate it to our men, the provost guards, and the metropolitans, with orders to arrest and detain anyone who resembles him even slightly."

Sandstrom grimaced. "Good luck. There are a thousand

holes for hiding in this town. Couldn't it be that we've seen the last of them, Colonel? Maybe we frightened them off."

"And perhaps angels will dance on the Avenue at high noon. Don't congratulate yourself. They'll try again in some fashion. The war's ending. Richmond will fall or be abandoned. Jeff Davis faces the hangman or a lifetime as a fugitive. Remember what I said. These are desperate men."

66

March 1865

Four companies of Mosby's partisans wintered in King George County, on the Northern Neck between the Potomac and the Rappahannock. Their old territory, Loudoun and Fauquier Counties, couldn't support the entire regiment. Food and fodder could no longer be found in the burned hamlets and farmlands of Mosby's Confederacy. In bivouac on the Neck, they ate stale crackers soaked in muddy water and fried in old grease using half a canteen for a skillet. What little meat they had was strong with age, but roasting it over an open fire usually cured the smell. Fred's eight-man mess had only one knife, his; they ate with sticks, splinters of wood, or their hands.

Captain Smith had promoted him to second lieutenant. It wasn't a great honor; he was replacing a clap-ridden officer who had succumbed to pneumonia. His fine black horse, Baron, suffered foot rot from standing on wet earth. The steed's ribs showed as distinctly as bars of a cage. Weeping sores covered his body. Baron was dying for lack of feed. Fred intended to put him down before the inevitable happened.

He wrote long letters to Hanna, in his head; there was no paper. Sickly, spindly, tired beyond belief, he was sustained only by memories of their days together, and Hanna's promise to be waiting in Washington when this accursed war ended.

The loneliness and deprivation, the constant rain and sleet, revived his thirst for spirits but he resisted.

Late in December they had almost lost their commanding officer. Scouting a rumored advance of Union Cavalry in Fauquier County, Mosby stopped for an evening meal at the home of a friendly civilian in Rectortown. Horsemen from the Sixteenth New York spied military mounts tied outside. In the ensuing melee, Mosby took a bullet in the stomach. Even as he fell, he had the presence of mind to rip the insignia from his clothes. Lying in a puddle of blood, he gave the Union officers a false name. They left him, assuming he'd die. Mosby later told the Richmond papers he'd thought the same thing as he passed out. Phil Sheridan announced Mosby's death to his troops. Mosby fooled them all by recovering. He was given a hero's welcome in the capital, where Lee received him warmly, and the Confederate Congress honored him with a special seat during one of its sessions.

On a foul night early in March, Mosby rode into the camp on the Northern Neck with a small escort and a covered buggy. An orderly summoned Fred to the colonel's tent.

"How are you, Lieutenant?"

"Tolerable, sir. How are you?"

"Tolerable. Still feel it here." Mosby poked his belly. His wan smile suited his pallor. Rain sluiced off the tent. The desk lantern afforded no warmth, and only a patch of light. "I brought visitors from Richmond. They're drying out. I need a reliable man to lead a special detachment."

"Yes, sir?" Fred said, bouncing up on his toes. No one had used the word *reliable* to describe Fred for a long time.

"I'll explain further when they arrive. Rest yourself, and please excuse me while I finish this letter to Pauline."

Fred sat gingerly on a three-legged stool. He stank of dirt and wet wool. He scratched his hairy cheek, picked out a wiggling mite. He killed it between his cracked fingernails, flicked it away. Mosby concentrated on the letter to his wife.

Over the rush of rain, Fred heard men approaching. He stood up as an officer and two civilians entered. The officer, rail-thin with deep-set eyes and a yellow dragoon mustache, looked a shade fanatical. Both civilians wore cloaks and sodden felt hats. One removed his hat with a hand scaly with scar tissue. He was bald. The other, surprisingly plump in the midst of the Confederacy's collapse, had little round spectacles and queer tawny eyes that made Fred's flesh creep.

"Gentlemen, pull up those crates, be as comfortable as you can," Mosby said. "Introductions first. Lieutenant Colonel Rowland Harney, Second Lieutenant Frederick Dasher."

"Sir," Fred said with a quick salute.

"West Point man," Mosby said.

"Very good. I attended the Citadel." In Harney's eyes Fred thought he saw the fires of zealotry.

"Our visitors from Richmond. Mr. Miller, attached to the Signal Service—"

"How are you?" the bald man said, as if an answer didn't matter. He gave Fred his unscarred hand. The flesh was chilly and moist. "My colleague, Humboldt Cridge." The plump man nodded. Fred liked him even less than he liked Miller.

Mosby said, "Colonel Harney is here on a special mission authorized by President Davis. Attempts have been made to abduct Abraham Lincoln and detain him as a hostage during negotiations."

Stunned, Fred said, "Negotiations for what, sir? A truce?"

Miller said, "That's a matter for the President and his cabinet. Not necessary for you to know."

"In any event," Mosby continued, "the attempts have come to nothing. Richmond has decided on another course."

"We suggested it," Miller said with a preening smile.

"Colonel Harney's specialty is explosives," Mosby said. "He will be inserted into Washington, and when it's ascertained that Lincoln and members of his cabinet are meeting at the presidential mansion, Colonel Harney will place charges in or around the building and blow it up."

Cridge spoke for the first time. " 'For the great day of his wrath is come, and who shall be able to stand?' Revelation six."

"Mr. Cridge quotes Scripture as readily as the devil does," Miller said with a smile. It pleased the other man.

In the stillness that followed, Fred almost laughed. Could they be serious? Could they truly be contemplating such a dishonorable act? Then he remembered certain things: the mounting butcher's bill in the Confederate Army; the white-haired and downy-faced replacements being sent to the front to die; the desperate shortages; the mobs of deserters on the roads, jeering and cursing anyone who tried to order them back. Richmond must be striking out not for any military purpose, but to exact a last pound of bloody flesh, compensation for the coming defeat.

Miller scowled at Fred. "Something wrong, sir?"

"No, no, this is—surprising, that's all."

"No more surprising than it will be to the ape and his nigger-loving cronies. However, before Colonel Harney can carry out his mission, he requires drawings, plans of the presidential mansion and grounds. I am happy to say we've arranged to secure them from an agent who can gain access to most Washington offices, including that of the government architects. Just as soon as practicable, our agent will copy the plans, cross the Potomac at a site to be determined, and deliver the material to Colonel Harney."

"I want you to lead the detachment that escorts the colonel," Mosby told Fred. "You'll take orders from him."

"Yes, sir. Is that all?"

Miller licked his yellowing teeth. "Not quite. We don't want our agent talking to anyone after he's performed his, ah, patriotic service. When Colonel Harney is satisfied with the authenticity of the material, he will hand the agent his not insubstantial fee in cash, to lull him. At that point, Lieutenant, you're to kill the man."

"Sir?"

"Don't gawk, I said it clearly. Major Siegel makes a one-way crossing of the Potomac and we save the substantial sum we promised him."

Something crawled in Fred's underwear, but he didn't dare move. "The agent's name is . . . ?"

"Siegel. He works in the War Department. His rank has no connection with the Union Army. He served in Austria."

Hanna's father involved with these people? She'd told him more than once that the man he'd met briefly at their home near the Navy Yard was forever discontented with his low station and low pay. Fred kept his face immobile, to hide his consternation. *I won't be party to murdering her father. Not to murdering anyone in cold blood.*

Mosby rose. "If there are no questions . . . ? Very well. I must leave you in the morning, gentlemen. I'm afraid we have only one tent for you and your companion, Mr. Miller. We have gathered every spare waterproof cloth and blanket we can find. I hope you'll be comfortable."

"I hope so too." Miller scowled at Mosby this time. "Come along, Cridge, I need a dram of something strong."

The civilians went out. Mosby dismissed Harney. Fred lingered. "Something else, Lieutenant?"

Mosby stared him down. His nerve broke. "No, Colonel."

"I'm afraid I don't believe you. Is it shooting the spy that bothers you? Let that piggy fellow do it. I have an impression he might like it."

"Yes, sir. Thank you, sir." Then Fred blurted, "But good God, what have we come down to, sir?"

"I try not to ask myself that question, Lieutenant. Good night."

Fred stepped into the dark. Flecks of ice struck his bearded face. Sleet now.

Mosby had reprieved him from a direct act of murder, but left him a party to it. He couldn't be. Not when he'd finally reached across the dark chasm of his life and found someone to care for . . .

Almost unconsciously, he walked to a small lighted tent where a man named Peebles had set up as sutler. Fred coughed to announce himself. Peebles called, "Come," and Fred stepped into the malodorous tent. Peebles put down a yellow-backed pamphlet, open to a blurry photograph of a naked man mounting a woman. Peebles had the face of an aging cherub and the soul of a scavenger bird.

"Well, sir, look who's here. The cold-water soldier."

"Not tonight." Fred dug for wrinkled scrip in his pants. "What have you got to drink?"

Twenty minutes later, huddled under the burned beams of a ruined barn, Fred tilted his canteen and swallowed some of the sutler's busthead.

He gagged, spat, wiped his mouth. "Jesus." What the hell was in it? Pepper? Vitriol? It could poison him. But he needed it. For the first time in months, he needed it.

67

March 1865

Night fog hid the river and muffled the sounds of the horses. Fred rode a bog-spavined piebald ready for the glue works. Day before yesterday, after an hour of agonizing hesitation, he'd put a bullet into Baron.

Colonel Harney came next in the file, then Cridge, and finally three soldiers Fred had chosen. He felt huge as a bear in his patched greatcoat. He'd been unable to swallow a morsel of food all day. It wasn't sickness, just a soul-wrenching lack of hunger. Occasional slugs of Mr. Peebles's concoction blurred the reality of what was coming. Blurred it, but couldn't banish it.

A stake capped with a cow's skull marked the spot on the bank where the courier was to land. Here the Potomac ran northeast, just before turning again, to widen and flow southeast into Chesapeake Bay. Opposite them, concealed by the murk, was Pope's Creek in Maryland.

Fred pulled the wire loop of the tin lantern off his belt. He gave the lantern to the youngest soldier. "Light it but make sure you keep the shutter closed until we see their signal."

They sat six abreast at the river's edge. The air smelled dank. The water lapped quietly, the only other sound a night bird's call. After several attempts the soldier lit the candle in the lantern. Before he closed the shutter, the flame danced on Cridge's round glasses. The Richmond spy was smiling.

"You understand you're to bring it to a conclusion," Fred said to him. "I won't do it."

"Lieutenant, we discussed the matter and I agreed. I will handle it as Mr. Miller wants. I told you precisely how and when."

"I'll be damned if I know how you can be so happy about it."

"Because what I'm doing is right, sir. The Lord is on our side. Saint Paul counseled the Ephesians to put on the whole armor of God. The breastplate of righteousness, the shield of faith—"

"Spare me," Fred growled, but Cridge went right on.

"—the helmet of salvation, the sword of the Spirit. Thus armored, I can smite the wicked with a pure heart."

"Where does that bullshit come from? How can you possibly think that killing another human being is noble and righteous, for Christ's sake?"

"I object to your uttering the Savior's name profanely. I am a religious man. I have nine children I am bringing up in the ways of the Lord. I don't appreciate your scorning my beliefs, or Holy Scripture."

Fucking madman, Fred thought. *Or have we all gotten our brains boiled by the war?*

His men began talking among themselves. He shushed them, hearing a sound from the river; a whisper of water disturbed. An owl hooted. Fred signaled a soldier, who responded with the same call.

He stood in his stirrups; flexed his right hand to warm it up as he reached under his coat for his holstered pistol. Cridge tapped his arm excitedly.

"There's the light." Faint at first, then brighter. "Martin, signal them."

The soldier raised the lantern, opened and closed the shutter three times. The light on the water went out, then reappeared, three blinks, a pause, a fourth blink. Private Martin opened and closed the shutter once more.

Fred thumbed back the hammer of his pistol. The bow of a ten-foot dinghy came at them out of the fog. Fred called, "Identify yourself."

"Siegel." His accent made it *Ziegel.* The voice didn't belong to the man rowing the dinghy; he was elderly, and black. He wore a tattered military shirt but no coat. A lantern rested on a thwart behind him. Fred wondered how Negroes could ally themselves with people who wanted to keep them chained up, but many did. Some even fought wearing Confederate gray, so he'd heard.

The dinghy teetered as the passenger stood up. Fred had an

impression of stoutness, but it was hard to see clearly with the fog curling and drifting. The boatman jumped into the shallow water, shoes and all. He held the bow line while the passenger walked forward and stepped to solid ground. Cridge said, "Victory."

The passenger said, "Retribution."

"Major, we're overjoyed to see you." Cridge heaved himself out of his saddle; his weary horse seemed to groan with relief. Fred ordered Martin to open the lamp shutter, give them light. They had to risk it until the wretched business was concluded.

Siegel wore a dark brown wool coat with fancy buttons and braided loop closures. His brown felt hat had a high crown, a rakishly curled brim. He resembled a diplomat more than a spy, standing confidently, almost smugly, as he pulled the strap of a leather dispatch case off his shoulder. He'd replaced his monocle with eyeglasses. The lenses enlarged his eyes to the size of bird's eggs. His gaze skipped from face to face, Fred's last.

"I know you."

"That's right, we've met. No names, if you please." Fred dismounted, indicating Harney. "This is the gentleman who will inspect your package. Give the colonel the lantern," Fred said to Martin.

"Step over this way," Harney said. He eyed Siegel with distaste. Evidently it was perfectly fine to do business with traitors, but nothing said you had to respect them.

Siegel followed Harney, smirking as though to show he had full command of the situation. Little he knew. Cridge beamed as cheerfully as a man about to enjoy Christmas dinner.

A short way up the bank, Harney exchanged the lantern for Siegel's dispatch case. He crouched, unfastened the bright brass clasp, slid papers out. "Hold the lantern lower." Siegel obeyed, stamping his feet and blowing his breath in little clouds.

Using his knee as a table, Harney went through the half dozen sheets, unfolding each and studying them. Time ticked by. Fred's mouth felt parched. The moment this was over, he'd unhook his canteen from the saddle and gulp down all the remaining busthead.

Harney folded the last sheet, replaced the papers in the case, fastened it shut. "Pay him," he said to Cridge. The old boatman spoke to Fred:

"Glad it's quick business. We got to go back against the ebb tide. Take longer." *It'll be a lonely ride, old man.*

Cridge moistened his lips. "Major, I shall reach under my coat for the money." With his right hand he slowly drew out a fat brown envelope. "Count it, won't you? It's the price we agreed on."

Fred's nerves tightened. This was the planned moment— Siegel greedily distracted by real money, ignoring Cridge and all the rest of them.

Siegel's finger tore the envelope. Gleeful, he pulled out a banded, quarter-inch stack of Yankee banknotes. He'd refused to accept Confederate. As he licked his thumb and counted, Cridge slid his left hand into his overcoat pocket. Gunmetal gleamed; an imported five-shot Kerr.

The three soldiers threw looks of alarm at Fred. He pumped his hand downward in the air, signaling them to keep quiet. Siegel finished counting. He glanced up, saw Cridge with the pistol. "What's this? What the hell's this?"

"I'm afraid we can't let you go, sir. You might boast about this transaction. It will be easier if you hand me the money and take what's coming."

Siegel's eyes enlarged behind his glasses. "You fucking sons of bitches. You're selling me out."

Cridge held out his hand. "The money, sir." Siegel bowed his head, seeming to surrender. Suddenly he threw the envelope in Cridge's face. He dove to the ground, rolling with surprising agility for someone his age.

Colonel Harney had ridden from camp without a side arm, against Fred's advice. The young soldiers didn't know what to do. Siegel's fist filled with a stubby four-barrel hideout gun. Prone, he threw his hand forward to shoot Cridge, who was standing at Fred's left. Cridge grabbed Fred's arm, yanked him sideways, as a shield. He fired past Fred and missed. Siegel replied with two shots. Fred reeled from a heavy blow in the chest.

He sprawled in the mud, more surprised and angry than terrified. Then pain welled up.

The rest of it happened rapidly. Cridge didn't return fire but instead went pelting away from the shore, one hand clapped to his hat. Mouthing what sounded like Teutonic obscenities, Siegel shot at Harney and missed. "Get in the boat, nigger!" Siegel kicked the wild-eyed boatman, who managed to clamber in the dinghy and unship the oars. The pain beat higher in Fred's breast. He touched the front of his greatcoat and lifted his fingers near his eyes. In the poor light the blood looked like tar.

Splashing, Siegel regained the boat. "Push off, push off!" He fired his last round. The soldiers' mounts neighed and bucked.

From the darkness, Cridge exclaimed, "He took the money. He's getting away with the money."

Fred seemed to fly along the vividly colored road of his life. He was a boy skylarking in a sunlit meadow at Front Royal. Sleek horses raced by with manes streaming. He marched on the Plain at West Point to the sound of bugles and drums and wind-snapped flags. He saw himself seated in the Senate chamber before he resigned. He looked down on Garlick's Landing at the moment he killed the girl. Mosby by lamplight called him a reliable soldier. He held Siegel's daughter in his arms in the empty house . . .

Voices grew fainter. The candle flame in the tin lantern dimmed and dwindled. He had a sense of the end and silently cried out against it. He'd come out of the darkness, and now, with a chance shot, he'd go back. He didn't want to go back. Oh, God, no . . .

"Hanna," he whispered the instant before he died.

Part Six

ASSASSINS

68

March 1865

Hanna floated through the days and weeks in a haze of delicious anticipation. Grant hammered at Petersburg and threatened Richmond and everyone said the war would end by summer. Fred Dasher would take off his uniform and come riding up the Seventh Street road, and they'd sit on the porch, holding hands, and plan their lives.

Their few weeks together, their stolen moments at the house in the northern suburbs, had consumed her with physical pleasure and brought a womanly satisfaction she'd never experienced. Then one day he dropped from sight as abruptly and mysteriously as he'd appeared, though he sent a boy with a note saying he'd be with her soon after hostilities ended. He signed it, *Love always, Frederick.* She read the note so often, with such happiness, that whole lines had been blotted by tears.

On Saturday, March 4, she watched the inaugural parade under threatening skies. Crushed in the crowd below the steps of the Capitol, she saw the sun burst through like an omen as the thin and haggard President stepped to the iron table on the platform. The crowd buzzed with rumors that the new Vice President was drunk during the Senate swearing-in earlier. Florid and coarse as a peasant, Andrew Johnson sat blinking at the sky while the President spoke movingly of malice toward none, charity for all; of binding up the nation's wounds, and cherishing a just and lasting peace.

She spied Johnny Booth in the balcony above the President. She hadn't paid much attention to the guests and was startled to see him there. His eyes were feverishly dark in his pallid face. How had he gotten his ticket? Through the senator father of his inamorata, Bessie Hale? And why? The whole theatrical community knew he would be secesh to the end.

Hanna's father had paid an exorbitant ten dollars for a ticket to the inaugural ball at the Patent Office. She didn't ask whom he was escorting; some chippy, she assumed. He came home at eight the next morning, baggy-eyed and walking unsteadily, which he attributed to dancing too many polkas and schottisches and lancers.

Two weeks after the inaugural, Booth played a one-night benefit at Ford's for a fellow actor. Hanna attended. The theater was half full, probably because the papers had announced that the President and Mrs. Lincoln would be seeing *Faust* at Grover's.

Booth appeared in one of his famous roles, the villainous Pescara in *The Apostate*. Hanna found his performance flawed by fumbled lines, as though he lacked concentration or had imbibed. In the duel in the last act he misstepped. Booth's opponent raked the back of his hand with a stage dirk. He fell. The audience gasped.

Booth rose from his knee, threw a smile into the dark auditorium, and resumed the play with a bleeding hand. At the curtain the audience gave him an ovation. His smile seemed locked in place. Twice she saw his eye linger on the empty presidential box. She tried to get near him backstage to congratulate him, but the crush was so heavy, she soon gave up.

Washington's mood matched hers; the city felt a springtime exuberance. The major continued in unusually good spirits. He spent money freely on new clothes, frequented the city's gambling establishments, and once more promised Hanna better times to come, without explaining why. Then, with no warning, he failed to come home one night. She feared he'd been assaulted or killed in some deadfall.

Next morning she rushed to the War Department. A clerk said Major Siegel had sent a note yesterday, reporting that he was ill and would return to work when he recovered. She thanked the clerk and left. On her way out she passed a swaggering gentleman she recognized as Colonel Baker, the odious man whose secret police force terrorized anyone thought guilty of disloyalty.

That evening she ate alone. As she munched cornbread and absently ran her finger through crumbs on the plate, she struggled with the mystery of her father's absence. She washed the dishes in a tin tub using well water heated on the stove. As she finished and extinguished the lamp, she decided she'd report his disappearance to the Metropolitan Police tomorrow.

A spring wind out of the west battered the house as she prepared for bed. She was pulling her flannel gown over her head when a sound like a gunshot startled her. A door slammed by the wind? She'd latched the front and back doors. Her heart beat fast as she crept to the hall.

A lamp burned in the kitchen. A robber had broken in . . .

Ridiculous; robbers didn't announce themselves by lighting lamps. Barefoot, she stole to the kitchen door.

"Papa!"

"Hallo, Hanna." He sat at the table, pulling off boots caked with mud. His felt hat and brown wool coat were thrown on the floor.

"Where have you been? I was so worried."

"Took a little trip to Virginia." He unfastened the clasp of a leather dispatch case. From it he took a brown envelope, which he opened. He riffled a stack of banknotes. "Fifteen hundred dollars. It was a quick sale."

"Sale? A sale of what?"

"Plans. Plans of the White House."

"You sold—? Papa, I don't understand."

"What's to understand? I want to make money. The rebs have money to spend for information. I ain't got any idea why they wanted the plans, and I didn't ask." He tossed the notes on the table. "Go buy yourself a new dress. And don't say nothing about this."

Hanna slid into a chair opposite him. "Are you telling me that you betrayed the people you work for?"

"What do I owe them? They pay me dog's wages. This was business. Rougher than I expected, though. The rebs didn't want to pay me either, so they tricked me—tried to get rid of me. I had to fight my way out."

"Against how many?"

"Five soldiers and a man with glasses and a mean look." The wind overturned a porch chair with a crash. "That fellow you brought to the old house once, he was one of the soldiers."

"Frederick?"

"I don't remember his name but I recognized him. Bad luck for him, he got in the way of a bullet. Casualty of war," Siegel said with a shrug. "Any food left?"

Hanna dug her nails in her palms so she wouldn't become hysterical. "Papa, what happened to Frederick?"

"I shot him. What's it to you? Wasn't he just an acquaintance?" Siegel rummaged in a cupboard. "Goddam. All we got's soda crackers?"

"He was not just an acquaintance. He was my lover."

Siegel dropped a cracker on the counter. "Since when?"

"Since last fall. I saw him nearly every day for a month. I never brought him home when you were here because he was spying for the other side. I don't know exactly what he was doing, just that he was in Washington secretly. We're going to be married when the war's over."

The major seemed momentarily nonplussed. "Well, you got to change your plans."

"Is he dead?" She ran to him, unable to keep her voice from rising. "Is Frederick dead?"

"I didn't stop to feel his pulse, but I think so. Hanna, *Liebchen*—"

She wrenched away. "Don't you touch me! Don't you lay a hand on me. You betrayed people who trust you and you killed the only man I ever cared about!"

He shouted at her, "Another damned reb! I shot him by accident. I didn't have no choice, I was saving myself. It's war, that's all. An act of war."

"You're a murderer. A traitor and a murderer."

Siegel grabbed her wrist, bent it. "I had about enough of this. I make money for us and all I get is a daughter screaming at me like a harpy."

"Let go of me. You're going to pay for what you did. I'll report you to the authorities."

His eyes bulged. He released her wrist. She almost fell but caught herself on the back of a chair.

"Don't talk like a crazy woman. You wouldn't report your own father."

"You'll see."

The major's expression seemed to shift rapidly from worry

to anger and back to worry, as if he couldn't gauge her determination. Finally he made his judgment.

"Nah, Hanna, you won't. I'm sorry if you liked that reb, but I didn't know it. There's plenty other fish in the ocean. Go to bed. Cry yourself to sleep. You'll feel better tomorrow. We're fifteen hundred dollars richer. I got to find something to eat."

*   *   *

Hanna locked the door to her room. She dressed, tied her cape over her shoulders, raised the window against the gale, and climbed out.

She lit a lantern and hitched up the buggy mare. The horse was fretful over turning out in the middle of a dark, windy night. Inevitably the major heard the mare whinny. He stomped to the porch as she took the reins to drive away.

The major had stripped to his breeches. A schnapps bottle dangled from his hand. "Where you going? Hanna, come back here. We'll talk."

She whipped the mare cruelly and left her father standing in the wind, a pathetic, half-naked man with whom she no longer felt the slightest connection.

Because of constant telegraphic communication with the army in Virginia, the War Department kept its lamps burning all night. The sentry on duty refused her admission, saying Colonel Baker wouldn't arrive until six-thirty or seven. She pleaded. He relented and let her step into the reception hall, warning her not to move from there. She sat on one of the benches, staring into space. Upstairs, the telegraph receivers clicked like rattling bones.

*   *   *

Baker assigned two detectives to accompany her back to the house. One was named Sandstrom, the other Price. They had the look of men with a lot of hard experience and few scruples.

"He may have left by now," Hanna said as they drove up Seventh Street. "I don't know whether he'd try to bluff it out at work. He has pretty strong nerve sometimes. He thinks I don't."

Price said, "We'll take care of it."

On the porch, Hanna stood aside as Price drew a gun from

a holster under his coat. He eased the door open. "Stay here, miss." He signaled the other detective to follow.

Three minutes later Price walked out shaking his head. "Not in there. Bed's unmade. Coffeepot's still warm on the stove." His eyes shifted past her. "The barn."

"And the privy," Sandstrom said.

They stole toward the barn as a neighbor's hen ran through the yard, pecking at the ground. Price was reaching for the barn door to roll it back when Sandstrom said, "There he is." The major came out of the privy with his galluses on his hips and a newspaper in hand.

"Siegel, you're under arrest," Price called. The major spied Hanna in the blue shadow on the porch. She expected rage and was surprised by his unemotional stare. He dropped the paper and bolted for the rutted street.

Sandstrom caught him in three strides. The detective swung a fat leather bag on the end of a cord, smashed it against the back of the major's head. The major dropped to his knees, his scalp bleeding. Sandstrom hit him again, unnecessarily. Price held his arm.

"That's enough. Put the manacles on him."

Lying on his side, the major whimpered, "I got to get dressed."

Sandstrom sneered, "Right, you need to look your best for Old Capitol. Get up."

The major staggered past Hanna without looking at her. She sat in a porch rocker where Frederick had rocked on sunny afternoons. She stared at her hands until the detectives came out of the house with her father. He looked clear-eyed and spruce in his best brown suit and checked waistcoat. An improvised bandage wrapped around his head lent him a piratical air. A short chain dangled between iron cuffs on his wrists.

Price said, "I think it's best that you don't go with us, Miss Siegel."

"All right."

Sandstrom pushed the major. "Wait, I got to say something." Sandstrom started to object. Price's look silenced him. The major faced his daughter, shoulders back, eyes prideful despite his predicament.

"I never thought you'd do it. Not for a minute. I wronged you. For a lot of years I thought, 'She's just a girl. Soft, weak like all the rest of them.' A mistake on my part. A grave mistake." An odd, almost melancholy smile appeared.

"I raised a soldier after all."

Sandstrom said, "March."

Hanna heard the buggy leave but didn't watch. The noise faded behind the chatter of neighbor children bound down the road to school. The hen returned to peck at dirt. Hanna swept her hands up to her face and cried out, one long, shattered wail of pain and defeat.

69

April 1865

THE UNION TRIUMPHANT!

* * *

**Thanks to God, the Giver
of Victory!**

* * *

Hang Out Your Banners!

* * *

**Rebel Arms, Artillery and
Property Surrendered.
Officers and Men Paroled
and Allowed to Return Home.**

**War Department, Washington
April 9, 1865—9 o'clock P.M.**

This department has received the official report of the SURRENDER, THIS DAY, OF GEN. LEE AND HIS ARMY TO LIEUT. GEN. GRANT, at

Appomattox Court House, on the terms proposed by Gen. Grant. Details will be given as speedily as possible.

Edwin M. Stanton,
Secretary of War

*   *   *

Margaret learned of the Palm Sunday surrender the next morning, April 10. An artillery battery near President's Park fired off salutes at daybreak. The noise woke her. She sat up and brushed hair off her forehead. Her eyes focused on the two large windows opposite the end of her bed. Both were cracked.

So it was over. On her last night with Lon, late March, he said it wouldn't be long. He'd been assigned to guard the President, who was traveling down to City Point on the steamer *River Queen* to confer with Grant in the war zone. Lincoln took his wife along, and his boy Tad.

She stared at the damaged windows with mingled disappointment and relief. She'd come to believe that the South's cause had probably been foredoomed even when the Carolina fire-eaters were celebrating the fall of Fort Sumter. Over the past months, introspection had destroyed her old, unthinking loyalty to the South and its peculiar institution that had brought on secession, and all the bloodletting that followed.

Booming guns proclaimed the victory throughout the day. Church bells tolled. Newsboys shouted that the government would again celebrate with great illuminations on public buildings.

Only last week, a similar orgy of patriotism had lit up the city when Petersburg and Richmond had fallen and Jeff Davis fled. Then, freedmen had danced on the lawn of the old Lee mansion in Alexandria. Republicans held a rally on the steps of the Patent Office. Speakers reviled the Confederate leaders, and the Military Academy where many of them had trained. A District supreme court judge demanded that "those fed and clothed and taught at public expense be the first to stretch rope." Vice President Johnson, choleric but relatively sober, reviled the fugitive Davis until the mob screamed, "Hang him, hang him!" Margaret had read of it in the *Star* with a feeling of foreboding. Lincoln, who continued to promote a spirit of forgiveness, now had almost as many enemies in the radical wing of his party as he had once had in Richmond.

The Confederates had torched Richmond before they abandoned it. Margaret didn't know whether Cicero had survived the capital's apocalyptic end. She hoped he was safe and would come to his senses. Perhaps with the help of a pastor or a doctor he could drag himself out of his slough of hate. She harbored the hope even though she didn't think it likely to be realized.

Throughout Monday and Tuesday, carriages draped with flags and patriotic bunting rolled past the town house, the celebrants hollooing and waving wine and champagne bottles. Negroes congregated outside Secretary Seward's residence on the other side of the square. They serenaded the house with spirituals and "The Battle Cry of Freedom." A carriage accident had broken Seward's arm and fractured his jaw; he was still convalescing.

Lincoln had returned from City Point and Richmond on Sunday, but there was no word from Lon. She assumed he was weighed down with duties. Before he left, he'd said he'd be with her the moment he could, but if he was in the city and she needed him, she was to leave a message with a man named Mapes who tended bar at the National. "Send it, or if it's urgent, take it yourself. You won't mind that respectable women are never seen in the place," he said with a sardonic smile. For his sake too, she wanted the war over. Lon had a strange, almost dead look in his eyes of late. He walked and spoke like a man exhausted in body and spirit. His clothes bagged on him; he ate little.

In the wake of the surrender, Union soldiers streamed from the piers and across the bridges and were immediately offered liquor, handed laurel wreaths and flowers, hugged and kissed by grateful ladies of the town. Margaret went out on Wednesday and pushed through mobs of returning veterans. Oddly, many Confederate soldiers wandered the streets too, unmolested. On the Avenue, a band composed of four walking cadavers in rebel gray drummed and tootled "Dixie." Listeners whistled and clapped and, when the band finished, pleaded with them to play it again.

Wednesday's *Star* said General Grant would arrive on Thursday to confer with the President. Thursday afternoon, after an excursion to buy some groceries, Margaret returned to Franklin Square on foot. From a half block away, she saw a stout Union soldier reading a book on the stoop of the town house. The man's blue blouse and trousers were filthy with mud. She hurried toward him, ready to send him packing.

He heard her coming, glanced up from the small leather-bound book stamped in gold. A New Testament. He held it in his left hand; the angry red line of a healed knife wound showed between his thumb and ragged cuff.

He scrambled up, whipped off his kepi in an obsequious way. His face was pale as rice paper, his eyes a curious yellow-brown behind small round spectacles. He could have been a church sexton or a country lawyer except for those eyes.

"Mrs. McKee? We've been waiting for you."

"Excuse me?"

After swift looks up and down the street he whispered, "The name's Cridge, Humboldt Cridge. A gentleman you'll want to see is waiting inside. He posted me on lookout."

Bewildered and alarmed, she climbed the stoop ahead of him. "Hold this, please." She gave him the grocer's sack containing turnips, snap beans, and a small roast wrapped in brown paper.

"Happy to oblige." He ran his eye over her figure in a way that made her flesh crawl. "Needn't use the key, madam, it's open."

The downstairs hall smelled of closed rooms, dust, and a strong cigar. The cigar smoke came from the parlor. Before she stepped through the arch she knew who would be waiting.

"Cicero."

He sat on her best sofa in a dirty blue uniform. Somehow he'd forced a boot onto his crippled left foot, a boot with a loose sole and a run-down heel he rested on an embroidered footstool. Bits of dried mud littered the delicate needlework. He looked thoroughly comfortable with a long cigar tilted up between his teeth. "Sister dear. Greetings."

She tried to smile. "You certainly make free use of my houses."

"But you installed new locks here. However, I came well equipped, as usual." He jingled his ring of keys.

"Hardly a visit I expected," she said, trying to cover her uneasiness.

He gestured with his cigar, leaving a smoke tracery in the air. "You've met my lieutenant, Mr. Cridge. Cridge, this is my sister, Margaret."

"Yes, sir, we had a pleasant exchange outside."

"We need a safe haven to conduct some business, Margaret. Ordinarily we wouldn't trouble you, but our regular meeting place, a boardinghouse on H Street, isn't available to us. The poor landlady is so devastated by the surrender, she's turned her boarders out and locked herself away to mourn."

"How did you manage to get into the city?"

"There was absolutely no difficulty. The Signal Service, alas no longer operating in Richmond, maintained a warehouse of Yankee uniforms taken from dead prisoners. Cridge and I were welcomed here like conquering heroes. We won't trouble you for long, though we may need the premises again later tonight."

"How can I deny my own brother?" she said, though she very much wanted to do just that. "Would either of you like to wash? Are you hungry?"

Cridge perked up but Cicero answered for both of them. "No. Make yourself comfortable, Cridge. I'll speak to my sister privately a moment." Cicero gripped Margaret's elbow harder than was necessary, all but shoving her into the long, musty hall leading to the kitchen.

Angered, she wrenched away. "I don't understand why you're in Washington again, but I hope it has nothing to do with the work you did in Richmond. The war's over."

"Not for me."

"What are you—?"

"Kindly don't ask questions. Don't implicate yourself." She remembered his unsubtle threats of before. *Anyone* could be sacrificed.

"We'll use your house while we must, then we'll disappear. If anyone inquires afterward, we were never here. You saw nothing, heard nothing." He ran the index finger of his scarred hand over her wrist, a caress that made her shudder. "I have one last mission to complete."

"For Davis?"

"The cowardly Mr. Davis packed his bag and ran while Richmond burned. This mission is mine." He waited a moment. "The tyrant will be punished."

"Tyrant?" she repeated, afraid that she understood him too well.

"I believe I would like to wash my hands. If you'd be kind enough to brew some tea for us, that would be excellent. We've had a long walk, and frankly I'm quite worn out from all the adulation I received from the populace." His mouth twitched in a ghastly attempt at a smile.

"I'll brew the tea. I must say I don't care for your companion."

"Cridge? He's a fine soldier. A Christian gentleman. I'm not sure which of us hates Lincoln the more."

He patted her, as though she were a wayward child. "Bring the tea, then we'll sequester ourselves. One more visitor should arrive within the hour. I'll admit him. I think it's best if you remain upstairs. In fact I insist."

She turned and walked stiffly to the kitchen.

Ten minutes later she carried a tray to the parlor. Cridge looked up from his Testament and smiled in a smarmy way. She thought of Lon, wished he'd walk in suddenly, then realized it would be catastrophic. He might fall on Cicero and tear him apart.

"Thank you kindly," Cicero said from the window where he watched the square. "I'll pay you a more leisurely visit when the campaign's over." *Campaign. Lieutenant. Mission.* My God, did he fancy himself some kind of soldier, fighting on like General Joe Johnston off in North Carolina?

Upstairs, in the lowering twilight, she sat with a book Lon had given her, *The New Eldorado of Wealth and Health* by T. Fowler Haines. The pages extolling California might as well have been printed in Russian. Her eyes blurred. Her palms sweated. She heard every tick of her bedroom clock.

Lamps burned all around the square when noises in the lower hall announced the visitor's arrival. She tiptoed to the stairs and craned around the newel post.

Cicero had limped to the hall to receive the caller. He clasped the hand of a well-dressed gentleman, then gestured him to the parlor. The visitor swept off his wide-brimmed hat. Margaret recognized the dark hair and profile of the actor, Booth. Both men disappeared. The parlor doors rolled shut.

She gazed through the cracked windowpane at blue and red fountains of fireworks splashing the sky. The explosions thudded; the colored lights flickered on her drawn face. After an hour, she saw three men in the street below. Two of them, wearing blue uniforms, shook hands with Booth before they went opposite ways. She counted to twenty and hurried downstairs.

The silver teapot was empty. Mud speckled the fine carpet. The reek of cigars lingered. *Cicero, don't do this. The war's over.*

She saw his shiny bald head, his queer, sad eyes, his ruined body. Heard him say, *Not for me.*

She knew what she had to do. She prayed that God would forgive her afterward.

70

April 1865

Lon said, "Unbelievable, there's no other word." He hunched at the National bar, lost among men whose rowdy jollity he couldn't share.

His fourth whiskey sat in front of him, between his hands. In the amber depth he saw whole blocks reduced to a few windowless walls; scavengers, white and colored, picking through rubble piles or simply wandering, stunned and disbelieving.

"Richmond," Sandstrom said.

"The damned rebs burned down their own house. The city provost ordered it, to destroy government records. They'll be years rebuilding the burnt district. A hundred years healing the scars."

"But the war's over, that's something."

On the Avenue, the blaring brass and ruffling drums of another parade testified to it. So did all the shouting and joking and backslapping in the smoky taproom. But Lon saw and smelled the Virginia countryside. Miles of artillery-blasted roads, hills, and fields. A miasma rising from the earth where decaying men and horses lay in a few inches of soil. Burned trees reaching into the spring air like blackened hands.

"I don't know how it can ever be over for anyone who lived through it, Eugene. It'll never be over for me." Lon drank the whiskey at a gulp.

"What are you doing the rest of the evening?"

Lon stared at his hollow-eyed image in the back-bar mirror. He hadn't seen a barber in months. He needed a change of linen. Wrinkles in his black suit were so deep, he wondered if an iron would touch them. The shoulder rig bulged his coat on the left side. Gentleman Lon was dead.

"One more drink, then I'll decide."

"We've had four. I'm about to fall down."

"Hold onto the bar." Lon snapped his fingers at his friend Mapes, signed to his empty glass.

"What's the time?" Sandstrom said.

Lon pulled a fat, gold-plated watch from his vest pocket. He exposed the dial with a flick of his thumbnail. "Ten past nine."

"Watch's chain's long enough to choke an ox. New?"

Lon held the watch so Sandstrom could read the delicate script engraved inside the cover.

With gratitude
for your service
A.L.
1865

"The President gave one to me and another to Bill Crook for guarding him on the City Point trip. He said it was his wife's idea, but I doubt it. These days she stares through people like they're made of glass. I think she's ready for a nervous collapse." Lon shut the lid and tucked watch and chain back in his pocket.

"I should go see Margaret. I haven't called on her since I came back. Baker's kept us too busy."

The saloon's noise level dropped suddenly. Silence ran down the bar like a wave rolling in. "Don't think you'll have to go looking for her," Sandstrom said.

With the shot glass at his lips, Lon glanced in the mirror. Margaret's face appeared behind him. The only woman in the room, she was clearly nervous.

"You said I could leave a message if it was urgent. I didn't expect you'd be here."

"Baker released us tonight. I intended to knock on your door as soon as I finished my drink."

She could count the empty glasses in front of him. "Please come outside with me."

A stridency in her voice cleared some of the fog from his head. He slid greenbacks over to Sandstrom, grasped her arm, and steered her to the street, passing between slyly smiling men at the bar and others at tables. Lon's truculent expression forestalled comments.

A dusty wind buffeted them on the Avenue. "What is it, Margaret? You look upset."

"I am. My brother and a man named Cridge came to the house earlier. Lon, they're planning some kind of violence. I think it's directed at Lincoln."

He was awake, as surely as if Mapes had served him cold water. "Now? The Confederacy surrendered."

"Cicero said Davis had no part in this. He claims it's his scheme. You know he's never been the steadiest of men."

"And I know Cridge from Richmond. He's a thug. How did he and your brother get into the city?"

"Dressed as Union soldiers. They met with another man—"

"Who?"

"John Wilkes Booth, the actor."

"Where?"

"Franklin Square. They were there until half an hour ago. Cicero said they'd reconvene later tonight. Some boarding-house where they usually gather is closed because the land-lady's mourning the surrender."

"Then we go to Franklin Square."

"I have the buggy. A boy's holding it around the corner." Two minutes later, with Lon driving, the little piano-box buggy clipped toward the town house.

In Franklin Square, black folk were serenading Seward's residence again. Margaret dug her fingers in Lon's arm. "Drive past, don't stop. I left the house dark." Lamplight shone in the fanlight above the entrance. He shook the reins and they sped on.

"Drive around to the alley. I left the back door unbolted."

"I don't want you to go in there with me."

"Oh, I'm going," she said with a queer catch in her voice. "I may be able to keep Cicero calm enough for you to arrest him."

The buggy turned into the alley. "You're sure you can let me do that?"

"Yes. He's doing wrong, but he's a sick man."

They came abreast of a board fence. She said, "Here." He jumped down, wrapped the reins around the whip socket, and stretched his hands out to help her alight. She fell against him, clinging a moment. He stroked her hair.

"Be calm. It will come out all right." He said it with no certainty that he was correct.

They crept through the small garden where an ornamental fountain reflected the hazy moon. Lon loosened the buttons on his coat, pulled the shoulder sling forward. He eased the revolver from the leather. The back steps creaked. He hoped no windows were open.

"Going in," he said with his hand on the knob. He turned it, pushed. The oiled door swung silently.

He could see the kitchen worktable and chopping block against a spill of light from the far end of a hallway. He heard conversation. "They're in the parlor again," she whispered. He cocked the revolver.

"Stay behind me."

"Yes, all right."

He left the kitchen, treading softly, testing every floorboard. It seemed an age before he flattened his back against the wall beside the parlor entrance. He recognized voices and fought back the rage they induced.

"Sniveling yellow bellies lost their nerve," Cicero Miller was saying. "We're down to three, plus Johnny. But they're good men. Paine and Herold will dispose of Seward."

"In his house."

"Yes, just across the way. It should be easy, he's still bedridden. Atzerodt breaks into Johnson's hotel room and kills him. Booth has the honor and pleasure of dispatching the tyrant and General Grant."

"It's definite that the Grants will attend Ford's tomorrow night?"

"The papers announced it. Lincoln has a taste for cheap comedies, as you might expect. I'll see that Booth gets out of the city afterward. Paine and Davy Herold will ride to Surrattsville, meet Atzerodt, and go on to Port Tobacco. I really have no fear about the escape. A War Department telegrapher will be slow to issue warnings. Certain soldiers guarding the city bridges will look the other way. Certain patrols will take the wrong roads. It pays to have friends in Washington."

"It's really true there are Yankees who want him dead?"

"I wouldn't care to sign an affidavit, Hummy, but we've been told so, through a long and complex chain of informants. We may not have complicity, but we're supposed to have a measure of silent cooperation."

Stiff from standing in one position, Lon shifted weight to his left foot. The board under his heel squeaked. In the parlor something overturned noisily. "What the hell's that?"

Lon stepped into the doorway. "Gentlemen, you're under arrest."

Miller blinked. "Well, our old friend Price the spy," he said with surprising aplomb. "Or is it Rogers? How many other names do you have?" Lon yearned to put a bullet in him, and another into the mealy-faced Cridge, who sat with his hands clawed on the arms of his chair. Cridge sneered.

" 'His mouth is full of cursing and deceit and fraud. Under his tongue is mischief.' "

"Shut up, you blaspheming son of a bitch. Remember the next verse? 'He sitteth in the lurking places of the villages. In the secret places doth he murder the innocent.' I'd say that describes you two jackals."

Margaret's skirts rustled behind Lon. Cicero saw her, said

to Lon, "I wondered how you knew. I should have seen the weakness in her." Cicero screamed at Margaret, "Are you in bed with him? Is that why you sold us out, you whore?"

"Oh, Cicero, what's happened to you?" She slipped past Lon, reaching out with an unsteady hand. "Let us help."

Lon's shouted warning came too late. Miller darted at her, one lurching step. He caught her wrist, swung her in front of him. His other arm hooked around her waist. "Go on, shoot her," he crowed with a demented exuberance.

Lon sensed movement to his right, started to pivot. Cridge threw a stool at his head. When he dodged, his foot slid a small rug sideways and unbalanced him. Cridge laid hands on the revolver. Lon's finger jerked; the bullet tore through a framed chromo of a mountain lake and buried itself in the wall. Cridge wrenched the gun away, flung his arm back, and pistol-whipped Lon, two slashing blows of the barrel. Margaret cried out.

Lon staggered and fell. He broke the impact with his hands, flopped onto his back, started to rise. Cridge's spectacles flashed as he brought his foot back, kicked Lon's jaw. Lon's head struck the wooden floor. Sparkling lights danced in a darkness that quickly closed and obliterated everything.

* * *

A flame shone, dimly at first. He smelled the kind of moldy dampness that pervaded rooms below ground. His cheek rested on a dirt floor.

His eyesight cleared. He could see Margaret standing to his right. The flame danced in the chimney of a lamp held by Cridge. In his other hand he had a long blue Colt. Miller stood on the lowest stair riser, grinning like a goblin.

"Good evening again, Price, or Rogers, or whoever the hell you are. Mr. Cridge conveyed you to your new quarters while you were drowsing. The cellar has no windows, and no exit except this stair, which Mr. Cridge will faithfully guard until we finish our business tomorrow night. Johnson dies. Seward dies. Butcher Grant and his tyrant Caesar, they die with their women. I'll be waiting behind Ford's with horses to carry us away safely. You'll be left to spend the rest of your life remembering you did nothing about it."

"Miller, if you kill anyone, there won't be a safe place on earth. You can climb the mountains of Tibet and it won't do any good. You'll be hunted and hounded till you're caught."

Cicero tapped fingers on his other palm, applause with a touch of effeteness. "Very pretty speech. Fruitless, though. The Union may have won the battles, but I'll win the war. Think of that between now and tomorrow, you piece of egalitarian shit."

He spit; it landed in Lon's eye. Cridge laughed. Lon struggled to sit up. Margaret restrained him.

Cridge left the lamp on a small nail keg. He stood aside so Miller could precede him up the stairs, dragging his foot and whistling "The Bonnie Blue Flag." The heavy door closed; the bolt shot home. Lon reached across to find Margaret's hand, cold as marble to his touch.

71

April 1865

The wick of the lamp burned blue and sputtered. Lon's watch showed ten past two in the morning. He pounded the door at the head of the stairs.

"Cridge!"

It took five minutes to rouse their guard. Finally, plodding steps brought him down the hall.

"We need oil for the lamp."

"I'm not opening the door."

Lon swore and descended to the hard-packed dirt floor of the cellar. Margaret sat forlornly on an old trunk. Whatever powder and paint had graced her face was gone, leaving it white and stark.

"What are we going to do, Lon?"

"I don't know." He'd been asking it of himself for hours. Together they watched the wick sputtering toward darkness.

*   *   *

When the light went, his time sense distorted. He sat against a bank of shelves, Margaret beside him, nestling in the curve of his arm. Silently he concocted schemes. He rejected every one. Cridge was a brute, but he wasn't stupid.

He guessed it must be morning. He heard a scurrying noise. Margaret flung herself against him. "There are rats in here. I felt one on my leg."

He scrambled up, stamped like a Spanish dancer until he caught something under his heel that squealed. He listened.

"I think I killed it."

The darkness filled with the sound of Margaret's strident breathing.

*   *   *

Later, he climbed the stairs again. Pounded the door again. Yelled until Cridge came back.

"What is it?"

"The lady's uncomfortable. We don't have a sink down here."

"Use a bucket. Use the floor. She has no claim to modesty. 'I saw a woman sit upon a scarlet-colored beast, and the woman was arrayed in purple and scarlet color—' "

"Cridge—"

" '—having a golden cup in her hand full of abominations and filthiness of her fornication.' "

"Damn you, have the decency to—"

"She's a whore. Let her piss in the dirt."

"Fucking *bastard*!" Lon bashed the door so it shook.

*   *   *

They fought the terror of isolation, the knowledge that madmen were readying the assault on Andrew Johnson at the Kirkwood House, William Seward in his residence, the Lincolns and Grants at the evening performance of *Our American Cousin* at Ford's.

"Your brother may have help from people in our government," Lon said. "Help with getting away, at least."

"How can that be? How could anyone turn traitor after the war ends?"

"Hate runs deep, Margaret. I've heard rumors about Stanton for a long time. I have a hard time believing in a conspiracy, but why would your brother invent it?"

Silence. Faint chittering came from the direction of the stair. On his feet, he waited, tense.

The rat never approached. After ten minutes Lon sat down, incredibly sleepy. In his head a clock ticked.

God Almighty. They *had* to get out.

* * *

Margaret was first to fall asleep. Her head tilted to his shoulder, resting there while he sat motionless so he wouldn't wake her. He kept concocting plans, all of them flawed. He had no weapon. Well, possibly one, but no match for a pistol. Worse, he had no means of inducing Cridge to open the door.

His head ached from hunger and the blows he'd absorbed. One foot was numb. He tried not to yawn; he felt himself drifting. He imagined an hourglass with the sand running out. Bright red sand, the color of blood from a wound.

The image possessed him. He slept.

* * *

He woke in panic. An hour might have passed, or a whole day. Blinking in the dark, he struggled to throw off his sleepiness.

He eased himself away from Margaret; she was snoring softly. On the other side of the cellar, he unbuttoned his trousers and relieved the fullness that had come while he slept.

Standing that way, seething with frustration, he thought of Cridge shouting the words from Revelation 17. The woman on the scarlet beast. Babylon the great mother of harlots . . .

He caught his breath.

Back at Margaret's side, he touched her shoulder. "Wake up."

Muttering, she came out of sleep. She found his stubbled face, caressed it. "What is it?"

"I want you to be an actress. I saw the way Cridge looked at you upstairs. You heard him call you a bad name. All right, you'll pretend to be what he thinks you are. I imagine he'll like that, fine hypocritical gentleman that he is."

He crouched down beside her. "This is what we'll do."

*   *   *

"Mr. Cridge?"

"What do you want, woman?" Cridge's voice had a heaviness now; a weariness. It might slow him. Lon lay curled on his side near the foot of the stairs.

"I want to wash and clean myself. The detective's asleep. You have a pistol. I can't hurt you. Open the door. Give me five minutes in the water closet, I beg you."

Her voice dropped, husky and insinuating; Lon almost smiled at the performance. "I saw you watching me last night. You're right, I know tricks that please men. But I'm starving. A basin of water, a little something to eat—there's a loaf of bread in the painted box in the kitchen. Give me five minutes and then I'll be good to you, Mr. Cridge."

Lon hardly dared breathe.

"If I do it, and find you've deceived me, I'll put a bullet in you."

"You won't have to do that, I promise."

Another silence. "All right. Wait."

Cridge plodded away, returned moments later. "Stand away from the door." Lon's upper teeth cut into his lower lip until he tasted blood. He'd told Margaret to step down three steps, no more.

The bolt rattled. The darkness against his eyelids lightened. Margaret said, "See, there he is. Asleep, just as I told you."

"Come up a step at a time."

"Oh, thank you, I'm so grateful." Lon slitted one eye, watched her lift her skirts. Cridge carried the same lamp and revolver that he had had last night. As Margaret stepped on the top riser, within reach of him, she said, "Can you tell me the time?"

"Almost ten-thirty."

"At night?" Her anxiety almost gave them away.

"I didn't let you out so I could answer questions. Clean yourself, then we'll go to the bedroom. Move out here so I can shut the door."

Margaret stepped into the hall. Cridge reached for the doorknob. Her hands flew to the lapels of his coat. With an enormous sideways tug she pitched him onto the stairs.

His pistol went off. The lamp sailed out of his hand, arcing into the basement as he rolled and bounced down the steps. The lamp's reservoir broke, threw a stream of oil over the packed earth. The wick ignited the oil, which burst into a streak of fire.

Cridge sprawled on his back, gasping. Lon stamped on Cridge's arm, snatched the gun, his own five-shot. Cridge struggled upright, slid a case knife from a sheath under his coat. His clenched teeth shone with bubbling saliva. He stabbed at Lon, who sidestepped and fired a shot into Cridge's wrist. The knife spun away in a shower of blood.

Lon dropped on Cridge with both knees. Hair hung in his eyes. Cridge clawed at him. Lon knocked him back with a blow of the pistol. He threw the pistol away and pulled the watch and chain out of his vest. He wrapped the long chain around Cridge's neck.

Cridge's eyes bulged. His pudgy fingers flew up to the metal links tearing his skin. After that, Lon's memory blanked.

* * *

When the rage passed, he looked up to see Margaret pressing her hands to her mouth. Drops of sweat fell from Lon's chin. His breathing slowed. The watch chain had dug so deeply, it had all but disappeared, leaving a thin necklace of blood on Cridge's throat. Dizzy and nauseous, Lon pulled the watch chain loose. Cridge was dead.

He wiped the bloody chain on his torn trousers. The oily fire was burning itself out in the dirt. He opened the watch case with his fingernail. The crystal showed a spiderweb of cracks. The hands had stopped at thirty-five minutes past ten.

Margaret dropped to her knees, threw her arms around him. "We're all right, we're safe," she said, soothing and rocking him like a child.

* * *

Minutes later, when he recovered himself, they ran upstairs to Franklin Square.

Fire bells rang in the distance. Soldiers and Metropolitan Police with torches surrounded the entrance to Seward's town house. Lon and Margaret hurried across the trampled grass to the cordon of armed men. He showed his badge to a police officer. "What happened here?"

"A man said he was delivering medicine from Mr. Seward's doctor. He got into Seward's bedroom with a knife. He stabbed a male nurse and a State Department messenger. The man beat young Fred Seward so bad, he's in a coma."

"What about the secretary?"

"Had the sense to roll out of bed. Fell smack on his broken arm, but he wasn't attacked."

"Was the culprit caught?"

"No, he escaped. That's not the worst. An assassin shot the President at Ford's a few minutes ago. Grant wasn't there, he and his wife changed their plans. Took the train to New Jersey."

"Is the President . . . ?"

"Wounded. They carried him to a house across from the theater. That actor, Booth, shot him, then jumped from the box to the stage and ran out the back way."

Lon took Margaret's hand. They moved east from Franklin Square, through dark streets where crowds gathered and cavalry galloped. In Tenth Street, police with locust sticks formed a human barricade in front of Ford's. People pushed and shoved, shouting, "Burn it down."

The house across the street belonged to a family named Petersen. Those outside were quieter than the theater mob, though as Lon and Margaret moved among them, they heard wild and contradictory rumors asserted as fact. The entire cabinet had been assassinated. The Grants had been murdered on the train to New Jersey. The President was already dead. So far as anyone knew, no attack had been made on the Vice President. Perhaps the man assigned to kill Andrew Johnson had lost his nerve.

Lon ran into a journalist he knew and questioned him. Yes, many in the audience and in the cast had identified Booth. "He dropped his pistol on the floor of the box. He shouted something in Latin when he jumped to the stage. He caught a spur on some bunting on the box and landed hard. Might have broken his leg. Better if he'd broken his neck."

Carriages rushed physicians and general staff officers to the Petersen house throughout the night. The mob frenzy to burn

Ford's wore itself out. Hundreds gathered in the chilly darkness but few spoke, and then only in hushed voices. Lon and Margaret sat on the curbstone in front of the theater. After daybreak, rain began. Lon took off his coat and draped it over her head.

Soaked and cold, they kept the vigil. At seven-thirty, a colonel opened the door of the Petersen house. All conversations stopped. The rain fell with a cold, rushing sound.

"Ladies and gentlemen, I regret to inform you that at twenty-two minutes after the hour, the President expired."

Margaret began to cry. She wasn't alone. Lon said, "I'll take you home. Then I have to report. I have to help catch the men who did this."

A carriage arrived for Mrs. Lincoln. She tottered down the steps, wailing as she clung to two Army officers. Somewhere in the city a church bell tolled. Others rang and clanged and resounded until the pealing filled the sky.

"What day is this? I've lost track," Lon said as they pushed through the silent crowd. Margaret leaned against his shoulder, the rain and her tears mingling.

"Saturday, the fifteenth. Tomorrow is Easter."

He listened to the bells and remembered Easter sermons preached by Mathias Price. "Then Lincoln was martyred on Good Friday too." This time there would be no resurrection.

72

April 1865

Ever afterward, Lon remembered it as the black Easter. Huge swags of crepe appeared on government buildings and office blocks, theaters and music halls, residences rich and humble. Women donned mourning weeds. Men wore black armbands or lapel ribbons.

Sunday brought glorious sunshine ill suited to the capital's mood. Baker called his men together at the War Department. Secretary Stanton spoke to them in a meeting room thick with smoke and speculation. Every man wore a bit of black.

Stanton's pug-dog face had a strange lividity. He marched back and forth in front of the detectives like Napoleon before his troops. "I take a large measure of responsibility for the tragedy which has occurred. I opposed the President's attendance at the theater, but not forcefully enough. I did not prevail. Now I will not rest, and you will not rest, till the arch-conspirators who planned this outrage are brought to justice. We know the principal perpetrators. A boarder at the Surratt house, a school chum of John Surratt's named Louis Weichmann, came forward yesterday. He identified Surratt's gang and confirmed that Booth met with them frequently. I have authorized a reward of $25,000 each for the apprehension of David Herold and George Atzerodt, in addition to $50,000 for Booth. Baltimore police will locate and arrest men named Arnold and O'Laughlin. However, I call all of these persons mere pawns and hirelings. The murder of our beloved President was planned and approved at the highest level in Richmond. Booth and his cohorts were maneuvered by the cold-blooded gamesman who laid out the work. I refer to the unscrupulous Jefferson Davis. He will hang. So will they all."

Squeezed between Sandstrom and another detective, Everton Conger, recently released from the First D.C. Cavalry, Lon was plagued with doubt. Cicero Miller said the plan was entirely his. Did Stanton know that? If so, was he purposely shifting blame to the Confederate president?

"Colonel Baker will supervise pursuit and apprehension of the suspects. Arrests will begin immediately, with a presumption of guilt in all cases. Show them no mercy, gentlemen. They showed none to our slain leader."

* * *

Lon said, "Use the ax."

Sandstrom swung it into the door of the Ohio Street sporting house. The result was predictable: feminine squeals and shrieks, an odd counterpoint to the church bells calling the faithful to worship.

Lon led the charge into the downstairs hall. "Secure the

back door. Throw the women in the wagon. Ella Turner?" he shouted. "Where's Ella Turner?"

That night, locked in Old Capitol with the other whores, Booth's mistress somehow obtained chloroform and attempted suicide. When they heard about it next morning, Sandstrom said, "Too bad she failed."

*   *   *

With the suspect roundup under way, Baker's men were far removed from preparations for the state funeral. On Monday, the moronic Lewis Paine returned to Mrs. Surratt's boarding-house. Waiting detectives arrested him along with Mary Surratt and her daughter Anna. Lon at the time was busy on Tenth Street.

"Keep moving, all the way to the front of the wagon." He jabbed the suspect, John Ford, with his gun barrel.

"This is outrageous," the theater manager said. Members of Ford's cast, including Mr. Hawk, Mr. Emerson, and Miss Keene, loudly seconded the protest.

"You're lucky we don't torch the place," Lon said. "Eugene, once they're all out, padlock it."

The cowed actors, stagehands, and box-office cashiers squeezed and pushed until they packed the police wagon like tinned herring. One old fellow pleaded with Lon.

"Sir, I'm Buckingham, the doorkeeper. I only work here part-time. Been a carpenter at the Navy Yard for years. I'm loyal. Ask my bosses."

"In the wagon," Lon said.

*   *   *

On Tuesday, Abraham Lincoln lay in state on a black catafalque in the East Room. The commander of the Military Department of Washington posted an additional $10,000 reward for Booth. The city council added $20,000. Cavalry, mounted Washington police, and independent searchers charged off to Maryland in pursuit of the conspirators still at large. That evening, after two days spent hauling suspects to the Old Capitol, Lon went to Baker's office.

"Sir, I ask to be relieved from duty here in the District. I want to join the chase."

"All those rewards enticing you, Mr. Price?"

"Colonel, I don't give a damn for the money. I have an account to settle with Davis and his crowd." Especially one of them. Lon hadn't breathed Cicero Miller's name to anyone. Whenever he was tempted, he pulled back because of Miller's statements that persons high up in Washington were implicated. Lafayette Baker was only one step removed from Edwin Stanton.

"Do you have any special knowledge of where the suspects might be?"

Lon remembered Miller mentioning Surrattsville and Port Tobacco. He hated to lie, but he did. "No, sir."

"Well, in consideration of what you suffered in Richmond, I'll let you go."

"Thank you, Colonel."

"Like everyone else under my command who has ridden off to Maryland, you'll keep me informed. That isn't a request, it's an order."

For which Baker might have a private and urgent reason. Miller could hold the answer.

* * *

Wednesday, April 19, church bells and cannon fire announced the noon funeral in the White House, to be followed by a procession on the Avenue. Lon heard the tolling and cannonading as he cantered over the East Branch bridge into Prince Georges County. An hour before, as he had left headquarters, Baker told him that the German conspirator, Atzerodt, had been caught near the hamlet of Surrattsville.

Riding there, Lon passed large parties of mounted soldiers, and other, smaller groups of armed civilians. Lon neither stopped nor spoke to them. He reached Surrattsville in mid-afternoon. There he found Army pickets guarding the Surratt tavern, and a crudely lettered notice nailed to the door.

CLOSED
Order U.S. Govt

He rested his lathered horse in the shade of a huge oak just beginning to leaf out. People imagined police work to be romantic, but as he'd learned long ago from Pinkerton, results were mostly gotten by plodding. He fed his horse from a nosebag, watered him at a trough, and set out southward in search of Miller.

He rode into lanes leading to farmhouses and cabins, showing his badge each time. "I'd like to describe a man and ask if you've seen him."

"One of Lincoln's killers?" the farmer or householder usually asked.

"Yes, and if you've seen him, you'll remember."

But no one had.

Dusty and saddle-sore, he made camp in the woods that night. Fighting off gnats, he dined on a hard biscuit from his saddlebag, washing it down with creek water. Throughout Thursday and Friday he continued the search, getting mud and manure on his boots, getting chased by roosters and pigs, but getting no clue to Miller's whereabouts. Perhaps Margaret's brother had already slipped across the Potomac to Virginia, with or without Booth.

Friday night, bedeviled by a mounting sense of failure, he settled down with his head resting on his saddle and his horse tethered nearby. Lincoln's funeral train would have left Washington by now, bearing the President's casket along with that of his son Willie, exhumed for the sad journey home to Springfield. Lon wished he'd been at the depot to pay last respects.

On Saturday morning he rode into Port Tobacco. The place smelled of the leaf it was named for. He found a tavern and drank a pint of beer with his hard-cooked eggs and hominy grits. When he paid his bill, he asked about Miller. The publican, a wisp of a man, brightened noticeably.

"Oh, I seen him. His horse went lame. He bought a new one at Fuller's stable. Fuller couldn't get over what a queer sort he was. Bad limp. Awful scars on his neck and hand. Myself, I didn't like his looks much. Struck me as kind of crazed. He ate supper here before he bedded down at Fuller's."

Fuller, the stable owner, said, "I sold him an old bay. His clothes was all-over dirt, like he'd slept out a lot."

"Where was he headed?"

"He asked the best way down to Riverside. That's on the west shore of the inlet."

"Close to Virginia?"

"Pretty close, yes."

"Boatmen work out of there? Ferrying people over to secesh territory?"

Guarded all at once, Fuller said, "Don't know nothing about that."

Lon was already in the saddle, turning his horse's head out of the stable yard.

* * *

Saturday night at dusk, he rode into Riverside, little more than a way station on the water. A streak of sulfurous yellow daylight lay above the trees. He passed Negro shanties and heard the pleasing sound of a mouth organ playing "Aura Lee." His back ached. The insides of his thighs burned from hours of riding.

He jogged past ramshackle piers where dinghies and rowboats and a shrimping skiff were moored. An elderly black man sat on one pier repairing a crab trap. Lon repeated his description.

"No, I don't believe I seen anybody like that, sir." The man's nervous eyes gave him away.

Instead of threats, Lon offered a gold dollar. "The man is one of the rebs who conspired to kill Mr. Lincoln."

The old man bit the dollar, then pocketed it. "I'll take the money 'cause I got nine head of children to feed, but I'll tell you the truth because of what Mr. Lincoln done for my people. Go 'bout a half mile along the south shore. Turn off on a sandy track marked by a round stone, big as this." With upraised arms, he described a two-foot arc.

"Travel down to the river 'bout a quarter mile. You'll find a cabin belonging to my cousin Wilf. Wilf's a high yella who knows the Potomac like he knows his own hand. I sent the white man to Wilf this morning. Seemed a pale and sickly sort. Said he felt poorly. You say he's a bad man?"

"He's a killer," Lon said, mounting up. "Much obliged." He tossed the man another gold dollar; his last. "Take care of those children."

* * *

He missed the stone and the sandy road in the dark. When he realized he'd gone too far, he turned back. He waited until moonrise, munching his one remaining biscuit. As soon as white moonlight flooded the woodland, he found the sandy track with no trouble.

He tied his horse, checked the Deane & Adams to make sure it had shells in all five chambers, hooked his flat-crowned hat over the saddle horn, and walked toward the murmuring river. He smelled chimney smoke.

The cabin appeared when he rounded a bend in the track. Lamplight glowed in a window with no glass. Creeping closer, he failed to see a horse tied in the darkness. The horse whinnied. Someone in the cabin threw down a metal utensil. "What's that?" Miller's voice.

"Don' know, suh. Don't get many callers out this way."

"Damn it, we should have crossed an hour ago."

"You said you wanted to eat, suh."

"Not this slop."

Crouched below the windowsill, Lon silently counted three, jumped up, and pointed the revolver into the room. There sat Margaret's brother, feverishly sweaty in the light of a kerosene lantern. A spindly young man, yellow as a butternut squash, stood with his arm around his ebony wife.

"Miller, sit still or you're dead."

A confusion of emotions sped over Miller's face, ending with a curiously smug smile. He raised his scarred left hand. "Guess you've caught me."

Lon's eyes were blurring from tiredness. "Both hands," he said, just as Miller's right hand crossed over his left with a revolver. The barrel spouted flame. The bullet whispered by Lon's ear.

Miller overturned the table. The wife screamed. Miller wheeled and shot her in the stomach. He snatched the lantern and threw it down. Rushes on the floor ignited instantly into a carpet of flame. Miller ran out the door on the river side.

"Oh, Dee, oh, Dee, he done killed you," Wilf moaned as he tried to lift his inert wife away from the spreading fire. Lon ran around the corner of the cabin, saw a shadow shape moving down the moonlit bank to a rowboat. Miller heard him coming. He fired twice. Both shots missed.

Miller struggled into the rowboat and untied the painter from an iron stake. Lon dropped his gun and waded in. He threw himself over the gunwale, dragging Miller by the shoulders. Both of them tumbled backward, into the river.

Miller was no weakling. He kicked Lon savagely as they floundered, then slashed his cheek with fingernails. Lon seized Miller's throat; the two submerged. Lon held his prey tightly, choking him, wanting to stop his breathing, end his life . . .

He remembered Margaret. He remembered that Miller had secrets. Panting and spitting, he dragged Miller up from the shallows, spun him around, and bashed his jaw. Miller fell on the bank.

"Kill me, get it over."

Lon picked a bit of river weed off his forehead. He spotted his revolver on the ground. Miller spied it too, rolled toward it. Lon ran up the bank and stepped on Miller's groping hand.

"Oh, no. You have questions to answer. Where's Booth?"

"Who?"

Lon jerked Miller up by his lapels. "Don't try that. Where is he?" He pushed, slamming Miller's head into the dirt. "Where?"

"You can just go to hell."

"Trying to make it harder on yourself?"

"Harder?" Miller laughed; he showed a strange mixture of fear and defiance. "You don't know the meaning. If I told you what I know, my life wouldn't be worth a gob of Yankee spit. You can drive nails through my hands and feet, you'll get nothing out of me. Go find Booth yourself."

73

April 1865

Lon rode the whole way to Washington with his revolver drawn and ready. Miller preceded him, sagging in the saddle with his hands roped behind his back. The two-man procession drew farmers and their families to the roadside, but no one interfered. Lon's gun deterred questions. They reached the city before midnight on Sunday.

With his stomach growling and his clothes stinking and his skin feeling filthy, Lon delivered Miller to the steps of the Old Capitol. He said to the guard on duty, "Lock him up by himself. No outsider is to see or speak to him unless authorized by Colonel Baker." The jailer signaled another guard, who cut Miller's wrist ropes. Miller swung his leg over the saddle and tumbled to the ground, limp.

The soldier with the knife said, "Should we call a surgeon?"

Lon looked at the pathetic heap lying at his feet. Miller's eyelids fluttered.

"No. He's faking."

Lon turned his horse away before anyone could argue.

*　　*　　*

He slept two hours, woke, and filled a basin with tepid water. He washed his body and watched the water turn from clear to dark gray. He shaved by candlelight in front of a small mirror, then wrapped a skimpy towel around his waist and sat down to write a report, which he delivered to Baker's office at seven o'clock.

"Miller says that he, not Davis, planned the assassination. He claims that persons high up in our own government cooperated and helped the conspirators escape."

Baker laid his boot heel on the desk, a perennial sign of skepticism.

"What persons? You don't name them here."

"He never told me. If he knows, he won't say. He's afraid of retribution."

"We'll keep him isolated. That may break him down." Baker tossed the report aside in a dismissive way that disturbed Lon. Or maybe everything disturbed him. He still ached from hours in the saddle. He wanted to see Margaret.

It wasn't to be. A few minutes after nine, an uproar in Baker's office brought Lon out of a little cell the detectives used for desk work. Choleric with excitement, Baker stood in the hall conferring with an Army lieutenant. As Lon ran up, Baker exclaimed, "Major O'Beirne's search party is at Belle Plain, on the Virginia side of the Potomac. O'Beirne found witnesses who saw Booth and Herold riding south, toward the Rappahannock. Booth's leg is splinted. He must have broken it jumping to the stage at Ford's. He can't be traveling fast. I will lead this expedition personally. Are you fit to ride with us, Price?"

Ready to drop from exhaustion, Lon said, "Yes, sir."

"Find Conger, Sandstrom, and three or four others. Be ready in one hour."

*   *   *

They boated across the Potomac in midnight darkness. Fresh horses waited on the Virginia side. They pushed south through the war-blasted countryside at a killing pace, greeted every hour or so by a military courier who came pounding up the road. About ten-thirty in the morning, after dismissing the newest courier, Baker wheeled his horse around and addressed his sweating and disheveled detectives.

"Booth and Herold have gone to ground on a farm near Port Royal. A detachment of the Sixteenth New York Cavalry discovered them. Apparently they've been there some time. The trap is sprung shut, gentlemen."

Baker galloped away on the sunlit road. Lon dug his heels into the sag-bellied gray he was riding. He and Sandstrom and Everton Conger and the others ate Baker's dust trying to keep up with him.

About two in the afternoon, guided by an Army corporal, they reached a gate at the head of a tree-covered lane. At the lane's far end Lon saw a white-painted farmhouse, a hen-house, a corncrib, and a large tobacco barn.

Near the gate, a cavalry officer and a corporal held a pris-oner at gunpoint. The prisoner was a young man of twenty with terrified eyes and tattered butternut clothing. The officer saluted Baker. "Lieutenant Jethro Murdock, sir."

"Colonel Lafayette Baker. I'm taking charge. Who is this man?"

"Name's Willie Jett, sir. He brought Booth and Herold to the farm last night. He knows the Garrett brothers, who own the place. He suggested the fugitives rest here until a boatman could be hired to ferry them over the Rappahannock. He broke down the moment we caught him."

A yellow butterfly circled Lon curiously. A mockingbird warbled in a bush nearby. Baker drew his Army Colt, leaned down, and pressed the muzzle against Jett's forehead.

"Where are they hiding?"

"In—in"—Willie Jett could barely sputter it out—"the to-bacco barn. Leastways I think so."

"Murdock, where are your men?"

"Just up the lane, sir. Out of sight behind that hedgerow."

"We'll dismount and walk in. No talking. Divide right and left once we reach the property, but wait for my signal before advancing further." Lon slid his Deane & Adams out of the shoulder rig.

Puffs of dust rose from the sun-dappled lane as they took their curiously pleasant walk in the spring air. The humming and buzzing and rustling of the new season contrasted with the tense faces and wary eyes of the soldiers who melted out of the hedgerow behind them. Baker's eyes shone under his hat brim.

The lane widened into a dooryard. A civilian, middle-aged, dressed in plow shoes and overalls, eyed them from the porch of the well-kept farmhouse. Baker walked directly to him.

"I am Colonel Lafayette Baker of the Washington detec-tive police. Who are you?"

"R—R—" The farmer shook his head, angry at his stam-mer. "Richard Garrett. M—m—my brothers an' me own this farm."

"We understand you're sheltering two visitors."

"N—n—no, sir, ain't no visitors hereabouts. We—" He got no further because a long-eared hound ran from behind the tobacco barn and barked. Other dogs, unseen, joined in. Another civilian, younger, peeked out of the corncrib. One of the cavalrymen aimed his carbine. The younger man flung his hands over his head and came toward them, cowering.

"I'm John Garrett. Please don't shoot me."

Baker said, "Not if you cooperate, Mr. Garrett. Where are Booth and Herold?"

One of the hounds kept yapping. John Garrett glanced at his brother, who scowled to silence him. John Garrett bobbed his head, apologetically, Lon thought. "Richard, they'll arrest us if we don't tell." Before his older brother could react, John Garrett rolled his eyes toward the tobacco barn and whispered, "There."

Baker smiled. He hitched up his wide belt and strode toward the barn, signaling men to follow. Lon fell in behind him, Sandstrom and Conger on either side. Outside the barn, Baker called, "Booth? Herold? We have you surrounded. Throw down your arms and surrender."

The ensuing silence was so protracted, Lon wondered whether the Garretts had gulled them and the conspirators had slipped away. Finally someone answered. Lon recognized the voice, rich but weakened.

"I will not play the coward. I demand a fair fight."

Baker gave a scornful snort. "Well, Mr. Booth, you won't get that, and you have no right to ask. Will you come out?"

"No."

Someone else in the barn yelled, "I will."

Baker waved Conger forward to the barn door. Lon and the rest heard Booth arguing and swearing at his cohort. The door rolled open. A stocky young man stumbled into the sunshine, hands over his head. Baker shouted, "Booth?"

A pistol shot from the dark interior scattered the detectives and the soldiers. Baker dropped to the ground. Conger rolled the door shut as two of Murdock's men seized Herold and hauled him off to the corncrib. Baker jumped up.

"You men gather up some of that loose hay. Pile it around two sides of the barn. We'll burn him out."

In five minutes, they were ready. Baker called, "Your last chance, Mr. Booth."

Silence. Baker slapped his hat against his leg.

"Mr. Conger, set the fire."

The old, unpainted barn burned like fatwood once the flames reached it. The fire licked through cracks in the siding and spread rapidly inside. "Price, go up there. Look in. Tell me what's happening."

Lon trotted to the side of the barn where no hay had been piled. He pressed his eye to a crack and saw Booth on his back holding a carbine, his splinted leg stuck out in front of him. Hay bales in the barn had caught fire. Booth's red-tinted face had a mad, wasted look.

"I see him, sir. He's obviously in pain."

"Shoot, then." Hair on Lon's neck stood up. "Kill him before he gets away."

Lon spun around, unable to believe he'd heard correctly.

"Sir, he can't run. He's injured."

"Do as I say, Mr. Price. Shoot him."

And then Lon saw it all slipping away, the answers to questions about who had really planned the heinous murder in Washington. Baker's face had a sweaty, expectant look. The men around him, civilian detectives and soldiers alike, stared at Lon.

"I said shoot him, Mr. Price."

This has been a long time coming, Lon thought.

"Sir, I won't do it. Booth must stand trial, along with Cicero Miller."

"I gave you an order."

Smoke blew past Lon, stinging his eyes. In the midst of a sunny spring afternoon, everything was crumbling away, all reason, all logic, all humanity . . .

A peculiar calm descended on Lon suddenly. His pulse slowed. He felt as if a cool breeze bathed him, though in the fire's heat that was impossible.

"Colonel, I refuse. The country deserves to see Booth tried and punished."

Baker raised his Colt; sighted along the barrel at Lon's head. "Obey the order, Mr. Price. You work for me."

Lon fished in the sweated pocket of his black suit; found the badge.

"No, sir. Not as of this minute I don't." He threw the badge in the dirt, took his revolver off cock, and shoved it under his coat. He stepped away from the burning barn.

Baker held his Colt at arm's length for ten long seconds. Lon waited, not breathing.

The gun barrel dropped to Baker's side. Flushing, he shouted, "Conger! Roll the door back. Someone—anyone—shoot Booth. I order it!"

A sergeant of the Sixteenth New York Cavalry ran up to the open barn door and fired once. The man capered and waved his weapon. "He's down. Got him through the neck."

"Bring him out, bring him out," Baker yelled. Sandstrom trotted forward, giving Lon a pitying look. Lon walked toward half a dozen men in the center of the dooryard, a human barricade. Other soldiers and detectives brought Booth's limp body out through the firelit smoke.

Lon kept walking toward those standing between him and the lane. Every man except Lafayette Baker fell back. Lon's heart pounded. He walked straight up to Baker and stopped.

Baker raised his Colt. He tucked the muzzle under Lon's chin.

"Mr. Price, you're finished."

Lon touched the gun barrel; pushed it aside.

"And none too soon."

He sidestepped, strode past Baker, and walked down the lane to his horse.

*   *   *

He learned later that the bullet fired by Sergeant Boston Corbett effectively paralyzed John Wilkes Booth. The actor lay on the Garrett porch until seven that evening, rousing twice to speak. "Tell my mother I died for my country," he said. And then, when he caught sight of Willie Jett, "Did that man betray me?" He died a few minutes past seven, taking his secrets with him to whatever hell awaited assassins.

*   *   *

Lon's solitary ride brought him to the city at first light. A tarnished silver sky spread overhead. Swags of funeral crepe lay in gutters, befouled by dirt and dung. A few crippled veterans were already out, wearing their ragged uniforms and begging with their caps. One sleepy drab, fat as a house, screeched an invitation with her rouged mouth. Lon rode on.

As his horse plodded up the Avenue, a drizzle began. By the time he handed the reins to a black boy in front of Willard's, heavy rain pelted the crown of his hat and dripped off the brim. He dodged inside while the boy remained on the curb, hatless and miserable.

Half a dozen early diners occupied tables in the saloon bar. Another of the many barkeeps Lon knew, an Irishman with flowing auburn mustaches and his left sleeve pinned up, greeted him. Michael had lost an arm serving with McClellan on the Peninsula.

"Bourbon, Michael."

"This early?"

"Just pour, if you please. The good bottle."

Michael filled the glass. "Supposed to rain like the devil today and tomorrow. Maybe longer." He slid the brimming glass to his customer. "I see one of your birds flew away Monday night."

With the glass near his lips, Lon said, "What do you mean?"

"The reb at Old Capitol. You didn't know? Wait."

Michael rummaged in a pile of newspapers on the back bar. He found the one he wanted, a *Star*. "Second page."

CONFEDERATE SPY
A SUICIDE.

*   *   *

OLD CAPITOL INMATE
FOUND HANGED IN CELL.

*   *   *

Government Promises Investigation
to Rule Out Foul Play.

Lon found Miller's name in the first paragraph. Margaret's brother had died sometime during the second night of his incarceration, when Lon was on the chase in Maryland.

He remembered Miller's statement that his life would be worthless if he revealed what he knew. Had he foreseen his own weakness, then a confession, and the consequences? Had he insured against retribution with a noose made of bedsheets? Was it the act of a deranged man, or had others with access to the prison silenced him? Like Booth, Cicero Miller had taken the answers with him. Did they include some that Lafayette Baker and the Honorable Edwin Stanton might want concealed in the silence of eternity?

Michael cleared his throat. "Care to order breakfast?"

"I don't think I'm hungry." Lon paid for the drink and left it unfinished on the bar when he walked out.

74

May 1865

Persistent rain hammered the depot shed. The funnel stack of the B&O 4-4-0 woodburner trickled a thin line of smoke toward the shed roof. The dampness created a haze, giving the hurrying passengers and porters an insubstantial, wraithlike quality. Lon stood with luggage by the rear steps of a passenger car, perfectly attuned to the morning's melancholy darkness. It felt more of March than May.

He smoked a little cigar while he waited. Margaret had gone back inside to look for her friend. The noise of small wooden wheels on the platform caught his attention. A boy of twenty, or what was left of him, sat on a square dolly. He propelled himself toward the head of the train with leather pads tied over his knuckles. Leather protected the stumps where his legs had been sawed away.

The boy's sullen eyes touched something in Lon. He tipped his broad-brimmed hat. "Morning, soldier."

"Morning."

"Which side were you on?"

The boy braked himself with his knuckle pads. "Does it matter?" He pushed off and disappeared in clouds of steam.

Searching in the other direction, Lon saw Margaret coming out the depot doors with her friend Hanna Siegel. Hanna's father languished in Old Capitol, accused of treason. The young woman, an actress, hardly fit the part with her blonde hair crudely chopped short and her clothes all gray and black, like a nun's. Margaret said she'd lost a lover in the war.

"I'm sorry I'm late to see you off," Hanna said as she shook Lon's hand. Her face was pale, without a single touch of color. "Margaret described your journey. It's fearfully long."

"It should be pleasant and interesting," Lon answered, precisely because he suspected it might be otherwise. In his carpetbag he carried ship tickets from New York to the Isthmus of Panama, which they would cross in two days, using a second set of tickets for the voyage up the coast to California.

"It's exciting that you're going," Hanna said. "And very courageous."

Margaret said, "We've both had our fill of the East."

"Do you have any plans for San Francisco, Mr. Price?"

"No plans. But we'll be fine. California's rich with opportunity." So said the rapturous prose of T. Fowler Haines, anyway. Mention of the future reminded him of the letter folded in his inner pocket.

Negro porters hurried the last luggage into the cars. A conductor bellowed the all-aboard. "I'll write," Hanna promised, embracing her friend.

"Write me of your father, too."

"Even if they hang him? It's the likely outcome."

"Oh, Hanna." Margaret drew her in, the embrace this time almost motherly. Hanna struggled to smile. Lon tipped his hat and helped Margaret up the steps.

"Poor dear thing," Margaret sighed as they settled on the plush seats. "She's utterly lost."

Lon tossed his hat on the overhead rack. "She has a lot of company."

The car was infernally hot. Flames flickered behind the slotted door of a stove at the forward end. Margaret waved at Hanna Siegel as the train began to move. When they passed out of the shed into the rain, she and Lon settled back in a moment of silent communion. They held hands. Lon's index finger gently caressed the plain gold band on her ring finger.

"I have something to show you."

"What?"

"A letter. It was at the desk when I settled our hotel bill." He took it from his pocket and unfolded it on his knee. Inscribed in an elegant hand, the paragraphs brimmed with complimentary phrases. *Outstanding ability. Sterling character.* And promises. *Glowing future. A firm with plans for rapid national and international expansion.* Margaret fixed on the signature.

"Your old employer."

"Yes, the boss. In Chicago. Mr. Pinkerton wants to hire me again."

"Is it something you want to do? We can cancel our tickets."

"It's the only thing I know how to do," Lon said as the cars clicked and rattled through the northern suburbs where dead trees stood, never to grow green again. Shell holes cratered the fields and road. He thought of all the killing and brutality; of how for a time he'd become a machine fit only for that.

"I want no part of it, Margaret. I just had to show you."

"It's your decision."

"Thank you."

He tore the letter in half. He walked to the head of the car, spit on his fingers to protect them, pulled the hot handle of the stove door. He tossed the pieces in the fire and walked back up the aisle while they burned. It would be a long, hard recovery. People such as Margaret's friend, with ruined lives, might never recover. At least the clandestine war was over for him, though he'd be haunted forever by Sledge's words. *Dirt rubs off.*

He'd covered himself with it. Would he ever be clean? Only the night before, readying for bed, he'd lost his temper when Margaret had made an innocent joke about the number of times he dipped his hands in a washbasin every day.

Her war was over too. She felt she'd failed her father; it would haunt her. She admitted she'd grieve for her brother, Cicero, because that was necessary and proper, but the love she had felt for him had been withered by what he had become.

No matter how any of them tried to forget, the great struggle would be the single most important event of their lives. They would never be free of it. As they passed through Baltimore, Lon held Margaret in his arms while she stared at familiar sights and wept.

Afterword

The history of spying in the American Civil War is a subject that intrigued me the moment I discovered it years ago. I promised myself that someday, when I had an opportunity and a publisher who shared my excitement, I'd write a novel about it.

What I found remarkable is the arc of Civil War espionage throughout a relatively few years. At the beginning, the effort on both sides was founded on enthusiasm, not experience. The spying was laughably amateurish during the first months, when martial ardor overruled common sense and everyone predicted a quick end to the war. Soon enough, Pinkerton operative Tim Webster was caught and hanged in Richmond, and spying was no longer a game for genteel men and women, but a savage battle without rules.

The literature on the subject is not large. Some of the primary sources, written by real players in the drama, are unreliable. I refer particularly to Allan Pinkerton's *Spy of the Rebellion* and Lafayette Baker's *History of the United States Secret Service*. Scholars long ago dismissed both as self-serving and far off the mark historically. Both books are interesting to read, but not for useful information.

To this day, Lincoln's assassination by John Wilkes Booth and his fellow conspirators remains mysterious and in some respects controversial. Among the questions:

Did the Richmond government and its secret service create an "action team" led by Booth? A recent work called *Come Retribution* makes that case.

Did radical Republicans, enraged by Lincoln's moderate approach to Reconstruction, encourage or collaborate with the plotters? In 1937, Otto Eisenschiml, a lay historian, published a book called *Why Was Lincoln Murdered?* Eisenschiml advanced the theory that Edwin M. Stanton, hiding behind a mask of loyalty, conspired to murder the President and then facilitated the escape of Booth and his cohorts. The book was popular for a decade or so, until its "evidence" was finally proved wrong and its thesis dismissed except by those who see conspiracies everywhere.

Of course, both theories are grist for novelists, and I've taken advantage of that, just as I did in *Love and War*, the second volume of the *North and South Trilogy*. In that book, building on the "what if?" premise, I invented what I felt was a plausible plot to assassinate Jefferson Davis. Davis was hated by many of his peers, and his life, like Lincoln's, was threatened many times.

The Booth conspiracy to kidnap Lincoln, then kill him along with Seward and Johnson, literally fills huge books with details of the movements of the those involved: who met whom when; who checked in or out of which hotel; so forth. I have simplified much of this and shifted dates slightly in a couple of instances. The essential details have not been altered, though I must caution again that Richmond's involvement in the scheme remains a theory, not a fact.

The comic-opera surveillance of Rose Greenhow's residence on a rainy night in August 1861 happened as described, though of course the fictional characters weren't present.

The flight of the balloon *Liberty* is fictitious, though representative of the scouting done by Professor Lowe's aerial unit.

Hanna's capture at Catlett's Station is based on fact. An unidentified young woman disguised as a soldier was apprehended and hauled before J. E. B. Stuart, who ordered her sent to Richmond for very much the same reasons that he states in the novel. The young woman's fate is unknown. She had no gallant officer to countermand Stuart's order.

For purposes of the story I moved the residence of Secretary of State William Seward to Franklin Square in Washington. Actually he resided in Lafayette Square.

The lives of historical figures didn't end when the war ended. Here is what happened to a few of them:

Lafayette Baker's harsh methods tarnished his image and brought denunciations from the press. He retired from the War Department in 1866 with the rank of brigadier general.

The following year he published his highly suspect memoir mentioned earlier. He died in 1868.

Federal troops captured Jefferson Davis in Georgia a month after the surrender. Two years of imprisonment ruined his health. Though indicted for treason, he was never tried. After Johnson's amnesty proclamation of 1868, Davis returned to his Mississippi plantation. He spent his last days writing a two-volume history of the Confederacy. He died in 1889.

John Singleton Mosby resumed his law practice in Virginia after the war. He became a Republican, endorsed Grant for president, and was appointed U.S. consul at Hong Kong by another Civil War foe, President Hayes. One of the more interesting and enigmatic leaders of the rebellion, Mosby died in 1916, at the age of eighty-three.

George McClellan carried only three states as the presidential candidate of the Democrats in 1864. His reputation never quite recovered from his hesitant Peninsula campaign. He served one term as governor of New Jersey and died in 1885. A son, George McClellan Jr., was both a member of Congress and mayor of New York City.

Allan Pinkerton's brief career in military intelligence is generally considered undistinguished, if not inept. This is usually attributed to his blind loyalty to McClellan—the desire to please and support his patron at the expense of truth and good judgment. Following his return to Chicago, Pinkerton continued to head what became, and remains, an international private-detective and security agency. Pinkerton operatives fought crime all over the country. They pursued Western outlaws, including the famous Butch Cassidy gang. But as the years passed, the original focus changed. The agency, a Civil War bastion of liberal abolitionism, marred its image by hiring on for thuggish strikebreaking against the Molly Maguires in the Pennsylvania coalfields, workers in the Homestead steel mill strike, and the like. Even so, Allan Pinkerton is regarded as a pioneer and innovator in crime fighting. After his death in 1884, his sons Robert and William carried on the business he founded.

Edwin M. Stanton lived only four years after the war ended, and they were stormy ones. He feuded with Andrew

Johnson, who removed him from office. When the Senate refused to confirm the removal, Johnson dismissed Stanton a second time. Stanton barricaded himself in his office where he remained for several weeks. He left government service after the failed impeachment of Johnson and lived only one more year, his health broken.

The remarkable Elizabeth Van Lew continued her secret work for the Union until the end of the war. Though constantly under suspicion, she survived unscathed thanks to a combination of influence and her carefully cultivated image of craziness. While most of Richmond mourned when the Yankees marched in, Miss Van Lew exulted. "What a moment! . . . Civilization advanced a century!" As a reward for her services, President Grant appointed her postmaster of Richmond, a position she held for eight years. She died in 1900. Her gravestone in Shockoe Hill Cemetery was later defaced in retribution for her spy work.

The fates of the Lincoln conspirators were varied. Edwin Stanton ordered Booth's body rushed to Washington by steamer, his identity concealed by an anonymous canvas bag. A similar secrecy attended Booth's burial in a hole dug in the dirt floor of the old capital penitentiary. Only Stanton and a few trusted associates knew the whereabouts of the corpse.

Under Stanton's guidance, Lafayette Baker assembled the evidence against Booth's co-conspirators, eight in number: Herold, Paine, Atzerodt, O'Laughlin, Arnold, and Mrs. Surratt, plus Edward Spangler, a sometime carpenter and stagehand at Ford's who tended Booth's horses in the small stable behind the theater, and Dr. Samuel Mudd of Maryland, who treated the actor's broken leg. The outcome of the trial—eight verdicts of guilty—was never in doubt. Herold, Paine, Atzerodt, and Mrs. Surratt were hung. The other four were shipped to the Federal prison on the Dry Tortugas off the coast of south Florida.

As it has in the past, the University of South Carolina at Columbia served as my research base. I thank the staff of Thomas Cooper Library, under the direction of my friend Dr. George Terry. Thanks also to librarian Jan Longest of the University of South Carolina, Beaufort branch at Hilton Head.

Helpful people and institutions cleared up many a difficult

point or question for me. I thank especially Denny Hattler, and the research staff of the Virginia Historical Society in Richmond. I am particularly indebted to Pat Falci, past president of the Civil War Roundtable of New York. Mr. Falci vetted the manuscript, and caught a number of small but meaningful errors, now corrected. He understands my passion for trying to get it right in every instance. As always, I must state for the record that no person or institution providing help is in any way responsible for the story I have crafted with a mixture of fact and invention.

I owe a debt to several individuals at the Dutton and NAL divisions of Penguin Putnam for their enthusiastic support of the project. I warmly thank Clare Ferraro, president of Viking Penguin, Plume; Louise Burke, who heads Signet/NAL; Carolyn Nichols, the Signet/NAL editorial director; and of course Phyllis Grann, who presides over all.

On this book, my editor, Doug Grad, and I worked together for the first time. I happily add Doug's name to the list of fine editors who have spotted flaws and smoothed out wrinkles in my novels over the years.

This afterword is being finished in the late summer of 1999. By the time it sees print, I will have passed a big milestone:

On April 12, 1950, *The Magazine of Fantasy and Science Fiction* cut a check for $25, payment for the first piece of fiction that I sold after several years of trying. I was all of eighteen at the time. The fifteen-hundred-word story, "Machine," still occasionally surfaces in sf anthologies. April of 2000 will mark my fiftieth year as a professional writer.

Publishers, editors, and the public have made it possible. Readers have been extraordinarily good to me over the years. I hope I've returned the favor somewhat. Far more important than earnings or bestseller status—neither of which I ever expected—has been the Niagara of written and electronic mail telling me that my books have done more than merely pass the time, they have brought forth entertainingly some of the history of the United States and its involvement in world events.

To work for fifty years as a writer takes not only a lot of sweat and angst, it takes a lot of help and support from others. Notably, I must acknowledge my debt to my attorney and good counselor of the past twenty-five years, Frank R. Curtis, Esq. He is always there, and always right.

I thank my four children, who grew up splendidly in spite of having their father disappear into his smoke-choked cellar office several nights a week. Most of all, I owe everlasting thanks to my wife, Rachel, who for almost fifty years of marriage has put up with, but still encouraged, a sometimes-temperamental author. Her love and understanding are boundless.

—John Jakes

Greenwich, Connecticut
August 15, 1999

www.johnjakes.com

Classic John Jakes...

The New York Times *bestselling*
Crown Family Saga

❑ Homeland   0-451-19842-5/$7.99

"A powerful tour de force, a rich, sweeping story of America as only Jakes can tell it. *Homeland*...is a marvelous blend of fact and fiction, the stuff of great historical novels."

—Nelson DeMille

❑ American Dreams   0-451-19701-1/$7.99

"Exhilarating...*American Dreams* allows readers to vicariously experience a time and place far removed from their own... Top-notch."

—*Chattanooga Times*